"Have you ever felt lust?"

Aaron's words seemed to boom through his empty room.

"Oh yes," Isabelle answered in a throaty whisper, her dark eyes twinkling up at him. "Rather frequently as of late."

"Really?" he nearly stammered.

"Yes. Very much so." And, wonder of wonders, she drew closer, nearly pressing herself against him, a mischievous smile spreading over her face. "I'm just not sure what to do about it." Except she clearly was, tilting up her chin as she rose just enough on her toes so her lips were a breath away from his, tempting him.

A thousand nefarious reasons for her behavior—from experimentation to securing his loyalty to extortion—flickered through his mind. But at the moment, none of them mattered. The recklessness that had been born of frustrations at his position, at *their* positions, combusted against his own attraction and desire in pure need.

"Well, madam, then I suggest we put our heads together and find a solution." He lowered his head, locking eyes with her. Willing her to say yes, even if this was a terrible idea.

That delightful dimple deepened. "Like what?"

"Like kiss."

FALL IN LOVE WITH
FELICIA GROSSMAN!

"Felicia Grossman gives me everything I'm looking for in a historical romance—her books are powerful and passionate and swoon-inducing!"
—Eva Leigh, *USA Today* bestselling author of
A Rogue's Rules for Seduction

MARRY ME BY MIDNIGHT

"What a wonderfully fresh voice! Felicia Grossman's MARRY ME BY MIDNIGHT has it all—a clever heroine, a dreamy hero, and a gorgeous fairy tale romance that had me enthralled well past my bedtime. Historical romance readers will delight in discovering Grossman's impeccably researched Jewish London society. Brava!"
—Elizabeth Hoyt, *New York Times*
bestselling author

"MARRY ME BY MIDNIGHT charmed me! Very swoony and rich with historical detail, it is sure to delight fans of historical romance everywhere."
—Evie Dunmore, *USA Today* bestselling
author of *Portrait of a Scotsman*

"I adored this rich and unflinchingly feminist historical romance. Isabelle is my favorite kind of heroine—passionate, tenacious, and complicated, and who never wavers in going after what is her due—who finds her perfect match in steadfast and deeply swoony Aaron. This star-crossed-lovers romance shines with its fairy tale whimsy and beautifully rendered glimpse of the Jewish community in the nineteenth century. I cannot wait for more tales from Grossman's corner of the East End."

—Adriana Herrera, *USA Today* bestselling author of *A Caribbean Heiress in Paris*

"Romantic, clever, and irresistibly charming. Fall in love with this fiercely feminist heroine and her sweet cinnamon roll of a hero as they navigate family, community, loyalty, and love."

—Amalie Howard, *USA Today* bestselling author of *Always Be My Duchess*

"MARRY ME BY MIDNIGHT is a scorching and swoon-worthy reimagining of Cinderella set in the 1830s London Jewish community. Felicia Grossman writes with passion and sensitivity, imbuing her characters with humor, heart, and strength. An excellent start to the series, and a much-needed addition to the historical romance genre!"

—Mimi Matthews, *USA Today* bestselling author of *The Belle of Belgrave Square*

"Felicia Grossman is a shining star in historical romance! No one writes love stories with more heart, more swoons, and more sizzle. I adored MARRY ME BY MIDNIGHT!"

—Joanna Shupe, *USA Today* bestselling author of *The Duke Gets Even*

"With a fascinating glimpse of Jewish life in nineteenth century England, a complex, ambitious heroine, and a hero with a heart of gold, MARRY ME BY MIDNIGHT is a bewitching Cinderella retelling that's pure magic!"

—Liana de la Rosa, author of
Ana María and the Fox

MARRY ME BY MIDNIGHT

FELICIA GROSSMAN

A Once Upon the East End Novel

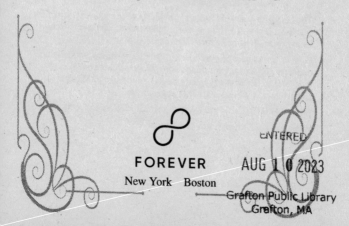

FOREVER

New York   Boston

Forever
Hachette Book Group
1290 Avenue of the Americas, New York, NY 10104
read-forever.com
twitter.com/readforeverpub

First Edition: August 2023

Forever is an imprint of Grand Central Publishing. The Forever name and logo are trademarks of Hachette Book Group, Inc.

The publisher is not responsible for websites (or their content) that are not owned by the publisher.

The Hachette Speakers Bureau provides a wide range of authors for speaking events. To find out more, go to hachettespeakersbureau .com or email HachetteSpeakers@hbgusa.com.

Forever books may be purchased in bulk for business, educational, or promotional use. For information, please contact your local bookseller or the Hachette Book Group Special Markets Department at special.markets@hbgusa.com.

ISBNs: 9781538722541 (mass market), 9781538722558 (ebook)

Printed in the United States of America

OPM

10 9 8 7 6 5 4 3 2 1

Content Guidance

This book contains grief, familial death (death of a parent), limited violence, and discussions of antisemitism.

For my dad: the self-anointed best-dressed man in Wilmington. The ride was far too short, but not one did it like you. You are and will always be loved and missed.

MARRY
ME BY
MIDNIGHT

Chapter One

April 1832
Aldgate, London, England

If one wanted to hide, the front row of the women's balcony in the Great Synagogue at Duke's Place was not where to do so. But hiding wasn't part of the plan, no matter how tempting. Staying at the top of London's Jewish community required a particular type of husband. And to land him, public perfection was required. Or at the very least, expertly feigned perfection.

Luckily, projecting an ideal image was—like for her father before her—Isabelle Lira's specialty.

With deliberate angling, Isabelle raised her neatly bound, personally commissioned, English-transliterated prayer book. She held the volume high enough that the small metal sequins dotting her sleeves, which sparkled against the light streaming from the giant arched windows, drew every eye to her position.

"Performance time," she whispered to herself as the murmurs echoed over the cantor's voice.

Framed between the proud Ionic columns, she adjusted the velvet ribbon holding her bonnet in place, the dark blue chosen to make the black of her hair gleam, highlighting her best features.

Most who attended the Great Synagogue were not in the Liras' social circle. Except for holidays—when her family made an appearance at Bevis Marks, the congregation long favored by the Sephardi side of the Jewish community—they mainly used the private synagogue in their Mayfair townhome.

But with leadership from the Sephardi and Ashkenazi sides now united, she'd be foolish not to at least give the appearance of considering their men for the husband she currently required. After all, thanks to several Ashkenazi's rising fortunes, some gentiles were even willing to enter business relations with them now—despite their "newer" presence on English shores.

"Tip your chin a little," her grandmother hissed against her ear. "Everyone is dying for a glimpse of your face, so let's show it off to its best effect."

"A good thing we maximized my physical charms, then." Such was the purpose of the artfully applied soot and powder, as well as the beeswax she'd donned. Not that she needed to remind her grandmother—they'd already had a row over the enhancements earlier that morning. But given the approving murmurs from below, Isabelle had clearly been in the right.

Isabelle adjusted her ankles behind the metal crosshatched barrier further dividing the women from the men. "Everyone received the invitations for the festivals yesterday, guaranteeing we are at the forefront of their minds. It's only polite to give people the gossip they crave." Squaring her shoulders, she gazed over the covered, swaying heads of the men below. "And the gown is flawless." She smoothed the navy and powder-blue silk stripes.

"We'll have to work on your modesty." Her grandmother gave her a pointed nudge.

Oof. Isabelle rubbed her side. How the woman's sharp elbows always slipped between the whalebone was a miracle. "You taught me to be clever and charming, *not* modest or sincere."

"We can still call this off. Work privately—with a matchmaker." The older woman patted the evenly styled row of gray curls peeking from beneath her lace-and rosette-lined bonnet.

"We're making a statement, blending gentile culture with our own traditions. The matchmaker you hired already scouted and gave us her thoughts. Our family, and whoever we decide is most suitable, will still come to an agreement, but we will have the façade of modernity."

At least that was the story they'd woven for the London Commission of Delegates. The organization not only acted as a liaison to the Crown on the Jewish community's behalf but also decided upon—and carried out—the community's political objectives, all while assuring its safety, security, and continued legal presence within England.

Not to mention the tight control they exerted over the image the community presented to the outside world.

The Commission's approval of the Liras' public endeavors was, while not required, important. Especially considering her father's seat on the Commission had remained vacant since his death. Given her family's influence—and coffers—the tacit understanding among the delegates was that her husband would fill the role.

Provided he was suitable for such an appointment. All she needed was a man worthy of it.

Isabelle twisted the enormous square diamond buckle on her waist. "Besides, if we cancel now, everyone will be disappointed."

Or worse, realize how desperate she and her grandmother truly were. How fragile their individual power was without her father. And how easily they could be dethroned, moneyed or not.

"I don't care about them. I care about you." With discreet fingers, her grandmother adjusted her own crisp pleated skirts. "You don't need to rush. Your father's first yahrzeit isn't for another three weeks."

And his death still felt like it had happened yesterday. But time had passed. Enough for the vultures to circle. Or to plot a coup d'état, as the French said.

The threat made by David Berab, the eldest of her father's business partners, still echoed in Isabelle's ears, as did his deadline—the day after Shavuot—which loomed now less than six weeks away.

"It's time that I marry." Isabelle squeezed the brass railing in front of her, the metal chilling her palm despite her gloves.

And she would. To a man who could force David Berab to accept her as her father's successor in their company. A man who would assume her father's communal role in a manner fitting her family's reputation. A man who would see that none of them fell from their place of admiration and power. A man who'd be unwaveringly loyal to her and her family.

And, best of all, a man she would choose—and in such a way designed to entertain key prominent gentiles.

The community's permitted existence depended upon those people's favor. Not to mention their interest was the best way to justify holding celebrations between Passover and Lag BaOmer, a period of semi-mourning with a myriad of restrictions.

"Three festivals in three weeks." Her grandmother scoffed. "The timeline is understandable given the holidays. But inviting every eligible Jewish man in the city to parade before you and vie for your hand? At least the gentiles are more subtle with their Season and balls. One might call *this* presumptuous—or dare I say greedy?" The older woman's eyebrows rose almost to her hairline.

"The merits of subtlety are greatly exaggerated. Besides, reviewing all my options isn't greedy, it's intelligent. The men on the matchmaker's list are only suggestions. Good suggestions, but it would be foolish of me not to confirm that no one is being overlooked." After all, why meet only six rather predictable men, when you could meet six hundred surprises? She turned back to her grandmother. "Who I choose must benefit the family, the business, and the community. His power, his contacts, and his loyalty to us must be superlative in every respect."

"I would hope you'd prioritize his willingness to love and care for you," her grandmother said with disapproval, as if her own marriage nearly fifty years prior hadn't been calculated to raise her family's communal status in exchange for a decent dowry and an uncommonly pretty face. Her fondness of Isabelle's grandfather had been a happy accident. Until he succumbed to age, leaving sorrow and a deep longing that her grandmother thought Isabelle didn't notice.

The older woman smoothed the edges of her own yellowed prayer book with her long, slender fingers.

Isabelle gave her best emulation of her grandmother's vague, noncommittal tut to stave off the brewing argument. She would have a traditional marriage—two strong families pooling their resources and influence, with a common vision for the best future. A union that would enhance her abilities to achieve her goals, instead of subjecting herself and her family to the unnecessary risk of ephemeral emotion.

The ridge of her thick bracelet dug into Isabelle's fingers as she clasped her wrist, trying to calm herself. She would succeed. Her future husband and his family would be in agreement, and her grandmother would acquiesce, despite her recent uncharacteristic sentimentality.

All too soon, the prayers concluded—unfortunately for her, with the Ashkenazi-favored "Yigdal" and not the rousing "Adon Olam" to which she was accustomed—so when she faced the crowd, she forced the most dazzling expression she could muster as she followed her grandmother through the throng of women, murmuring polite greetings. They spiraled downward, a heavy cloud of perfumes, florals and fruits and powders mixing and latching onto every pore in a nauseating crush. Isabelle clutched the rail in an effort not to swoon and crash into the hundreds of well-dressed ladies.

At the bottom, just outside the main sanctuary, her grandmother placed a hand on her puffed sleeve. "Are you all right?" she whispered.

"Why wouldn't I be?" Isabelle asked to avoid a lie. Her skin itched beneath her collar as nerves swirled.

Why was it so hard to breathe in such close quarters? "It's just, I want to leave a little mystery for the festivals, build the anticipation."

Always the worrier, her grandmother examined her face, searching for any sign she was upset and not merely tired.

"You're just like your father, always so dramatic," she said, seemingly satisfied. She pointed over Isabelle's shoulder. "Stay over there until the majority leaves. I'll do the greetings and hint at what's to come—add some 'anticipation,' as you call it."

Isabelle backed away to the outer wall, leaning beneath yet another set of impossibly high arched windows. As the sun trickled in through the glass, the crowd thinned until quite suddenly—she was alone in the stone corridor.

Well, almost alone.

A small wooden door to the side of the sanctuary creaked open. Out stumbled a dark-haired man wearing no coat or vest, merely a dusty shirt and trousers, with a group of small children following in his wake. They hurried past, near enough that the flannel beneath her skirt rustled but oblivious to her position between the massive columns.

The man paused in a nearby alcove, reaching into his pockets. Out came—she twisted to get a better view—lemon drops, deposited into tiny outstretched hands. Mercy, she could use something to settle her stomach. Pity she was no longer a child.

With his head bent, she could view only the stranger's profile—soft, thick wavy hair; full lips; a firm, sculpted jaw; and a coarse stubble of hair dotting his cheeks and chin that somehow made him more, not less, attractive. He was young too. Most likely around her own age.

Though clearly without her heavy responsibilities.

"Tell us more of the story," the smallest of the boys demanded in a soft but insistent voice, the early-afternoon sun setting his face aglow.

"I have work." The man ruffled the child's hair around his yarmulke. "And you have parents to mind, who will not take kindly to finding you here."

Why not? Isabelle wondered. They were in a synagogue, for goodness' sake. Isabelle craned her neck to get a better view.

"Please." Another child tugged on his rumpled trouser leg. "Just a bit."

The man glanced at a tatty broom leaning against the stone wall, as well as a large stack of books set haphazardly atop a cart, begging to be reshelved by—*ah*. A custodian. That was who he must be. This was the best entertainment the Great Synagogue could muster for its children?

"Please," the tiny chorus resounded.

The stranger brushed a hand through his thick hair and held up a single finger. "Just a bissel more, but then you need to run along. You have real meals to eat."

Isabelle's lips twitched as a cheer rose and, in an instant, the small bodies made a circle around the taller figure.

"Where were we?" He crossed his legs and settled on the bare, probably freezing—not to mention dirty—stone floor without hesitation.

"The prince had come upon the tower with no windows and no doors," a boy with curls so voluminous they nearly swallowed his yarmulke shouted out.

"A good place to start." The man gave a serious nod, and Isabelle edged closer, despite her low expectations of the man's tale-telling prowess. After all, who didn't enjoy a good fairy story?

He beckoned his little group closer. "Just as the prince was about to search for an entrance, he heard footsteps approaching. And"—he scrambled back, crouching down to the level of his audience and lowering his voice—"Quick as a wink, he hid behind a tree. From that position, who did he see but—"

"The witch!" all the boys cried at once before devolving into hoots as the man threw the tail of his shirt over his head like a cloak.

"Rapunzel, Rapunzel, let down your hair," he called in a warbled, cawing voice that had the boys doubling over. Even Isabelle had difficulty not giggling out loud. The custodian was actually entertaining—magnetic, even. Who'd have thought?

A pity he was performing menial tasks instead of performing on stage. He'd probably be enthralling.

"Morris," a woman's voice boomed over their merriment.

"Oh, no." One of the children shot to his feet, dusting off his garments. "That's my mother."

The man gave a gentle nod and raked his fingers through his own hair once more. "Which means it's time for you all to leave, lest you be found with me."

The custodian smoothed and retucked his smock into his trousers. "Until next time."

With the spell broken, the children, including the one called Morris, were off in different directions. Sighing, the storyteller adjusted his garments one last time before facing the broom and books, staring between them, until he hauled a stack of tomes into his arms, readying himself to descend into the cellar or wherever he was supposed to be working.

Which was for the best. She had more important things to do than trifle with a custodian. Besides, her grandmother had probably finished. But dust rose as she shifted forward to exit, tickling her nose until she cried out.

The sneeze reverberated through the domed corridor. The young man whirled, dark eyes falling right on her. Isabelle's cheeks burned with embarrassment.

Ridiculous. It wasn't her fault she'd sneezed. *Someone* should sweep better if he wanted to prevent that.

Besides, it wasn't as if she was spying. She just happened to be in his vicinity.

"Good Shabbas," she called, straightening her shoulders, the Germanic pronunciation slightly awkward on her tongue. "How do you do?" she added in her most appropriate tone—polite and friendly but still a touch aloof—to set suitable, modest boundaries. After all, even if he didn't suit her particular marital needs, who knew whose ear he had?

The custodian took a step forward, his boot catching on a crack in the old stone floor. In an instant, he and his load were airborne, books and tangled limbs all coming straight at her. With a small shriek she threw her arms over her head and ducked as two bound volumes bounced off her back and shoulders, only to teeter off her feet, right into the somehow-still-standing man's rather firm chest.

Strong arms encircled her waist, keeping her upright, as her heart beat against her stays. Isabelle glanced up to find herself staring at, upon closer inspection, a not merely attractive but extremely beautiful man. Even his unruly hair added an enticing fierceness to his features. Her breath stuck in her throat for a moment as desire stirred throughout her body.

Which was not what she needed. At least not now.

"I'm so very sorry." Stepping back from him, she lowered herself onto the floor in the most graceful manner possible, kissing each fallen book and cradling them in her lap. "I would put these away for you, but unfortunately, you'll have to direct me. And perhaps take half?" She gestured to the rising stack that was threatening to render her legs immobile.

"No, it's all right." Grunting, he bent and grabbed the entire load from her arms, not even bothering to brush his now filthy clothes. "You've done enough. Just tell me what needs to be cleaned or fixed and I'll get to it right away. Go have your meal."

"There's nothing that needs to be done." With as much dignity as she could muster, Isabelle glided back to her feet, careful not to stumble, her fashionably short hem swishing against her ankles. "Or at least not anything I know about." She beat her skirts, and a cloud of dust rose off the silk. "Though I have to say, while I'm sure your cleaning abilities are unparalleled, I couldn't help but notice you were so skilled with the boys, so compelling..."

"I don't know what you think you saw, but there wasn't anyone else here, only me." His dark eyes bore into hers from beneath his thick brows, and she shivered, the temperature dropping.

"What?" Isabelle took a step back, shaking her head.

"No. I know what I saw." She gazed around the empty alcove, the scene still fresh in her mind. "There was an entire group of—"

"I don't have time for this." He waved a dismissive hand, moving to leave. No—to flee.

Isabelle froze.

Clever, making her question her senses, but Mr. Storyteller-Custodian was an amateur. She saw what she saw. He just didn't want her to have seen it. He was hiding something.

And suddenly, returning to her plans was not quite as important as satisfying her curiosity. And besting this unexpectedly clever stranger.

At least for the moment.

"Perhaps, but I have a feeling you're going to make some time." Isabelle snatched back half the siddurim from his arms, clutching them to her chest. "Now show me where these belong, so we can get better acquainted." She inhaled, her nerves finally calm at the thought of matching wits with this handsome, rather surprising man. "Unfortunately, I find ladies in towers boring. Witches are far more interesting."

He gawked at her.

She tapped a finger to her chin as if she were considering the matter and not just delighting in keeping him off balance. "Though you storytellers lack imagination. Why are witches always old and ugly? Even if everyone ages, no one comes out of the womb a crone. I can't imagine anyone with magical powers not using them for aesthetic purposes. I certainly would."

The man opened his mouth and closed it before making a low, grumbling sound in his throat, his grip tight. She bit her cheek so as not to giggle.

"Yes, I'm sure there are plenty of powerful, young, attractive women running around fairy-tale forests, making all sorts of trouble." She snapped her fingers. "Come along—you can tell me what you think while we work."

She smiled to herself, already feeling a great deal more like the ruler she intended to be—like she would be, once she won.

After all, practice made perfect.

Chapter Two

Rebalancing his load against his hip, Aaron Ellenberg narrowed his eyes at the stunningly beautiful woman in shimmering blue silk. What was she about? She might talk of witches, but for now, she just seemed meshuggenah.

Did she really not know who he was? Impossible. He glanced around for the gaggle of friends hiding behind a pillar and waiting to witness whatever prank she was about to play—the only reason her set ever bothered with the likes of him. They'd get him all tongue tied and flustered, proving their superior intellect—well, that, or they'd point out a spill that needed his attention.

And yet they were still alone, and she'd not commanded him to clean any additional messes.

"Are you going to tell me why children shouldn't accept candies and stories from you, or am I going to have to guess?" As she lifted her wrist to adjust her stack, rings and bracelets covered in twinkling stones glinted in the sunlight. A perfect complement to her impossibly white gloves. "I'm good at guessing."

She stuck out her rather determined chin, her deep red, shiny lips parting. Oy. What was she playing at?

She knew his position. No one who attended the Great Synagogue escaped the gossip, told in hushed tones he somehow always managed to overhear: how sad it was, the orphan with neither a head for knowledge nor talent for a trade, with no prospects, and completely dependent on the community's largesse.

The least valuable among them. Who parents strove to prevent their children from becoming.

Only one step above those who'd left the community altogether. He shuddered at the memories of the brief time he, tired of the whispers and tuts, had attempted that life, rendering himself vulnerable to the far less forgiving gentile streets.

But that was neither here nor there. She was.

And no matter how she flashed her rather charming dimple or how mesmerizing he found her thick, dark lashes, she was not going to force him to say all his failings out loud. He had some dignity.

"And here I believed witches were above menial labor. I'll have to note that for future stories." He kicked at the ground, and a new cloud of dust spotted his already filthy boots. A sharp contrast to her shimmery, polished ones. Foolish rain. He'd be sweeping for hours after the sun set. Aaron cracked his already sore knuckles. "Though I didn't know witches took the form of aspiring toffs."

"Aspiring?" She cocked her head. "I thought I managed the full effect. I'll have to go back to my spell book." She twirled from side to side, skirts lifting even higher to reveal not only her ankles but bits of stockinged legs.

Not that he was staring.

"All the magic in the world couldn't make you a real

toff in the goyim's eyes." Even he knew that, despite his lack of brains. The children probably did too.

With her free hand, she loosened her bonnet's tie, sliding it back. "It's getting hot." Shiny sable hair, parted in the center, glistened in the sunlight, begging to be touched. Not that he could. For a hundred different reasons, not including the fact that they were practically in the middle of shul.

"Though you've made me curious," she continued. "Why don't you think it's possible to be accepted by them? After all, the Duke of Sussex intends to introduce a new bill in the next session of Parliament, one which would allow us real rights."

"If it passes, you truly believe they will make you one of them? That when they need you, they won't secretly hate you? That when you become expendable or when there's trouble—when their own power wanes, they won't strip everything away again? Either by their own hand or by feeding you to the mob in their place? After all, nothing unites disparate goyim more than a quest to be 'saved' from us." A familiar occurrence in their history. It was why his parents had fled Trier after Prussia took the city from the French, along with their people's newly bestowed rights and access to trades.

Her lips twisted in a wry sort of smile. "What if I intend never to become expendable? What if I intend to amass enough power, inside *and* outside the community, that no one will ever challenge me, out of fear and respect?" Her clear, high voice echoed against the arched ceiling of the empty vestibule. "Well, out of fear—I have no illusions regarding respect."

He leaned against the wall as stories from his pilfered collection of books—ones for which he'd always been mocked, for their frivolousness, for their uselessness in both study and business—flitted through his mind. Never mind they were the only type he was ever able to understand—or enjoy.

"You solely addressed the easiest scenario, where only the rich goyim turn on you. But even then, you have no guarantees. You can't always conform to their definition of a 'good Jew,' when it changes on a whim. Your power will slip and fade. And then won't people rise up and slay you?" He grimaced. "So to speak. Obviously they would be more likely to—"

"Exclude and bankrupt me? I'm sure many of them aimed to do just that to my father and my grandfather before him." She gave an imperious wave of her bejeweled hand, adjusting the stack of siddurim on her hip with her other. "Though with us, 'expelling' and killing is never off the table." Raising a pristine gloved finger, she tapped her chin, drawing attention to her glossy red lips once more. "As it is with witches when they falter—a group of men always bands together and vanquishes them. I'll have to take that under advisement," she said, her tone serious but her eyes sparkling.

Was she putting him on? She had to be. Because this was the most ludicrous conversation he'd ever had. Aaron grunted as he lifted the books higher against his chest.

"Bah" was all he managed to say as he turned to the cellar, away from her and whatever trouble came with her type.

"Oh no, you're not leaving." A pattering of feet followed him through the dark, squat passages as he began shelving the siddurim. Why would someone like her traipse about where she'd not been asked, demanding his time and energy, if not for some nefarious purpose? Panting, she tore down the last few steps, clutching the siddurim to her chest. "I'm coming with you. I haven't discovered what you're hiding yet. Who are you?"

"Someone marriageable girls shouldn't talk to," he said, giving his best impression of gruff annoyance, but his tone, instead of frightening her off, only elicited a giggle. Why did she have to see him with the children? It was much easier to play the big bad wolf when one hadn't been caught giving out candies. Not that he'd ever pulled such a performance off, but there was something about her that made him itch to appear more substantial than he was.

A foolish notion, no doubt. Probably brought on by a flying siddur to the head. He rubbed a tender spot on his brow, opening his mouth to continue, but she was already speaking again.

"It's a little late for that. We've both done quite a bit of talking. A rarity, as my grandmother likes to tell me. I'm often too enamored with the sound of my own voice to let anyone else get a word in, so you should take my pursuit as a compliment." Her eyes crinkled. "First, I'm three and twenty, hardly a girl. And second, my 'marriageable' days will come to a close in mere weeks." She twisted a loose lock around her finger, almost nervously. "Provided I find the right match."

A twinge of disappointment wormed through him. Witch, eh? Since when did they blush and stammer at the prospect of some undoubtedly pompous, rich husband? And wasn't landing one a rather ordinary goal for a witch? Besides, she didn't seem like the type who'd need much maneuvering for that. He swallowed, looking back down at the siddurim. After all, who wouldn't want someone so arresting?

"How big is your dowry?" he asked, working to keep his tone aloof.

The question was fair. The money was what actually counted, wasn't it? The wealthy and beautiful had every option open to them. Goodness or kindness mattered only in stories.

"Large." She glanced downward, flicking the plethora of jewels on her wrist. One stone could feed a family of eight for a year.

Well, there was his answer.

A bitter lump settled in his gut. "Don't worry. The matchmakers like their commissions. They'll find someone appropriate for you and your money, to feed your ambitions." Someone whom, unlike him, the matchmakers would not laugh at before giving sympathetic tuts and telling him to come back when he'd found a more valuable position and lodging.

"A pity I'm not relying on one, then." She pulled a book from the top of the stack she'd somehow managed not to drop and slipped it into a spot. Aaron blinked. Not in all his years—at the synagogue or the Jewish Orphans' Home or at any of his five failed apprenticeships—had anyone provided him assistance.

With a grunt, Aaron returned to his work before pausing. "Did you say you weren't using a matchmaker?" He couldn't name anyone—especially among those with money and status to protect and defend—who didn't use some form of a marriage broker.

After all, matchmakers didn't only suggest prospective brides and grooms—they used their intimate knowledge of the community to ensure that harmonious and successful new families could be built. Ones with valuable partners from both parties.

"We consulted one to create a short list—but instead of merely meeting with their families, my grandmother and I are choosing publicly. In a rather spectacular way, to benefit both us and the community." She selected another book.

Perhaps she wasn't so ordinary after all.

He reached into his pocket and fingered the parchment that a moving carriage had tossed at him the prior day. Well, near him. The flyer had hit him in the head, actually.

He slid out the invitation and pointed at the words he'd read too many times already.

> *Miss Isabelle Lira is ready to marry.*
> *To celebrate this momentous decision, in*
> *concert with our gentile friends, three festivals*
> *shall be held in her honor. Every eligible man*
> *in the Jewish community is invited to attend and*
> *seek her favor. At midnight, on the night of the last*
> *festival, she will announce her betrothed.*
>
> *Proper attire required.*

"You're this girl?" he asked.

The woman poised to present the greatest entertainment anyone in the East End could imagine, permitted during the Omer and open to everyone. Well, almost everyone—everyone who wasn't him. Even if he had the means to travel from the old Jewish quarter to Mayfair, he certainly didn't have the proper attire.

Not that he hadn't pictured attending. No, like a schmuck, he'd spent last night imagining himself entering a grand room to trumpets, with all eyes on him, people smiling and nodding in approval. As if he were someone to be proud of. Someone deserving of a proper, happy family.

Someone important. Someone *special*.

But he wasn't. He was just Aaron. He needed to accept that truth and be grateful that he was still fed and sheltered despite all he lacked. That he had been permitted a place at all. He pointed once more. "This is you?"

"Yes." She bent her knees and bobbed a little curtsy at him, like the goyim did. "Isabelle Lira, at your service," she said with a cool dignity.

"I doubt you serve anyone, Miss Lira." Not with her fortune. He squinted through the dim light at one of the wealthiest heiresses, if not the wealthiest, not just in England but likely in all of Europe. A woman who not only wielded enormous power in the community but also had a fighting chance of having influence outside it.

This was the closest he would probably ever be to a real princess. Another twist in his gut. Witch, his foot. She didn't need magic to get what she wanted.

She palmed another siddur. "I suppose not. Though I am willing to provide help—if given a chance. To anyone in the community. Including..." She looked at him expectantly.

As if he was going to confirm his name, break the spell completely. Especially if she truly didn't know who he was, which was beginning to seem more and more likely.

"I don't need your help," he said instead. He nudged another book with his elbow. Trouble wasn't the half of what she was. Isabelle Lira had power. Lots of it. On a whim, she could crush him like an ant. "This doesn't happen that often, does it? You not getting exactly what you want?"

"No. And I intend to keep it that way." She winked at him, which shouldn't have made his stomach tighten—but did.

He shoved the invitation back in his pocket, and before he could think better of it, the words were out of his mouth. "Then I wouldn't get married."

Her lips parted. "Why not? I know I'd cede some control to my husband, and I ought to compromise at times." She wrinkled her nose as if she'd tasted something sour, and he couldn't help but laugh. "But our purposes would be joint. If he hurts the business or our standing in the community or, say, becomes a spendthrift, he would suffer too," she continued. "And if he misbehaves or wants what I'm not willing to offer, we end the marriage. I intend to have very specific terms from the outset."

Oy. That was optimistic. Especially as "misbehave" was such an inadequate word for the danger of a bad husband. In his two years of fading into the background at the synagogue, he'd witnessed quite a few quiet, limited, and often less than adequate attempts by the Jewish leadership to fix such dangerous situations for members of the community. The results were mixed, at best—even for the women who, like Miss Lira, had their family names etched on countless plaques around the synagogues and community buildings, denoting their generous donations.

This was what happened when a person wasn't exposed to their limits—they believed themselves invincible. A get might be billed as the right of any woman, but in his experience, obligations were not always practiced, and men were unlikely to resist the power and leverage withholding gave them.

Aaron clucked his tongue. "Being married to you is more profitable than not. He'd have no incentive to give you a divorce willingly, and the community's reach is only so long. Your family might still care, but there are plenty of others who, with enough coin, are perfectly happy attempting to walk with the gentiles. So if you two couldn't compromise—couldn't become family— it would be in his interest to siphon away as much money as possible and abscond."

"He could do that?" She knit her brow as if the idea had never occurred to her.

Poor princess was in for a rude awakening.

"Don't worry—I'm sure there will be funds left over for you. Your family's fortune is legendary." He returned to the books, lest she see his embarrassment at how far apart their stations were. "But yes, many a man would do that to many a woman. Especially one who is a proper villain." He threw her his best glare.

"Is that what you're supposed to be? A villain?" She cocked her head, her expression curious—and not the least bit intimidated. "Is that why children aren't to come near you?"

If only. Such a reputation would probably garner him quite a bit more respect, if nothing else.

"Perhaps." He cracked his knuckles in an attempt at malevolence. But she didn't even flinch.

He sighed. Time for more honesty, no matter how

humiliating. "No. I'm not a villain in your story. Think of me more as a bit player. And I'm no get refuser," he added, "never mind the kind of man women like you look for. I don't have the pedigree."

"Well, you certainly aren't on the matchmaker's list," she said thoughtfully. "Those, I presume, are the men you believe could conquer me, instead of the other way around." Brows knitting, she sank back against the bookshelf, her posture bent. As if his words were actually making sense to her. As if she was listening. To *him*.

That would be a first.

Except, as his gaze traced over her face, her jaw tightened, and her nose tipped into the air. And when her eyes met his, they twinkled, well, deviously. As if she was plotting something. Never a good sign. He'd heard enough gossip to know that schemers, especially the charming ones, wreaked havoc.

Which meant he should keep his mouth shut, but at the thought of the vibrant woman before him trapped or brought low, the useless words poured out.

"I know you don't want my advice, but I would search for a partner who cares for you. Be the princess, not the witch. In the end, they're the ones who get to be happy forever, after all." He brushed the hair off his forehead as she simply stared back at him.

Oy. He was making a fool of himself. More than usual. He sucked in a breath. "And you should leave. Someone is probably looking for you, and I have work to do."

"You aren't supposed to work on Shabbat." She narrowed her eyes. "Why are you? Shouldn't you be off until sundown?"

"I'm not working, really, just arranging." He rubbed the back of his neck. Perhaps he was working a touch. However, Old Will, the goy they'd hired for Shabbas, was getting, well, old. The man had another head cold but needed the money and the work. And what the rest of the congregation didn't know couldn't hurt them. Not that he could explain that to her.

"Alone and out of sight." She raised a single finger to those plump red lips. "Why? I mean, you're awfully young for this sort of job, aren't you? Shouldn't you have a trade?"

Aaron stared at her. Wasn't she full of surprises? *Clever, clever girl—woman—witch—whatever.*

"Shouldn't you?" she repeated, pushing herself off the shelf, hands on her hips.

"This is a trade, in a way. It's better done by someone young, as it's rather physical. I'm good at it. I earn my keep." And he enjoyed it. At times. It was better than stewing and living on the community's charity alone. Well—on only its direct charity.

"Your keep? That's a peculiar way of talking about your salary, especially as you're too old to be an apprentice. Who 'keeps' you? And from what?" She frowned.

Was she truly so naïve? Did she not understand what happened to those who were neither "learners" nor "earners" within the community's bounds? Who didn't have families to prop them up financially?

There was a shrinking number of menial and serving jobs to be had among their own kind. While some of their people had managed to both remain Jewish and financially thrive in spite of the myriad of legal, political, and social obstacles, their number was not large enough to independently support the entire community.

After that, you were at the mercy of the gentiles and whatever treatment they deemed fit.

He was quite lucky, he reminded himself. Not only had the London Commission of Delegates saved him the moment he'd encountered real trouble on the gentile streets, but they'd pathed the way for his return, with a position even he could manage.

Aaron's lip twitched. It truly was funny she hadn't heard his story. Her own father had headed the Commission then. Though the Sephardis, who claimed to be more civilized, like their gentile counterparts, usually acknowledged his ilk only if they had a certain amount of money and power.

Or were causing problems.

He leaned against the shelf, letting the hard wood dig into his back. "That's not important. But think about what I said—look for a love match. That's the best way to protect yourself."

She sucked in a harsh breath. "Love is for children and innocents. I'm neither."

"Then marry one." He crossed his ankles.

"I can't marry a child." She gasped in obvious horror. "That's disgusting."

"No, marry an innocent, a man who believes in love and marriage and family. Who will want to give all that to you." All the dreams to which he'd once secretly clung, even if they'd never be available to the likes of him, even if he could imagine such a future only in stories. Dreams that she—unlike him—could obtain. He drew in a breath through his nose, willing down the stab of jealousy in his gut. It wasn't her fault that he was merely who he was and no more. "You've all the makings of a princess: you're rich, from a prominent family, and pretty—with a sharp tongue and a wicked sense of humor. It should be fairly easy."

She gave him a wink. "Unfortunately, I require a husband befitting my family and its status, one who is properly clever, ambitious, and charming." As if he didn't know that. "One who believes himself a prince." She flashed a lopsided smile. "One who would believe that a biddable, sweet wife would serve him best. And as I'm neither, I'm going to need to stick to the arrangement I have planned. But thank you for the compliments. It's good to know—"

"Aaron!" The call from above, sharp and loud, cut her off. "Aaron," the voice repeated. "There's a spill."

Aaron glanced upward and sighed. Just like she was no witch, he was no storybook prince. Not even an ogre. Just a character in the background, with no hope of changing his circumstances.

"I'm being summoned," he said. As if she didn't know. Foolish. He shook his head before coughing a little, willing the right words to leave his mouth. "Good luck to you, Miss Lira. I'm sure you will find someone right for your purposes."

Her gaze, bold and bewitching, searched his for what felt like a stretch of time, and his breath hitched in anticipation.

But the spell had broken.

She stepped back from him, giving another formal curtsy. "Thank you. I apologize for taking so much of your time." The words were stiff and her bearing straight as she walked past him with a dignity worthy of a princess. Worthy of more.

He would regret this later, but he couldn't stop himself from trying one last time. "Miss Lira?"

"Yes?" She paused, her back still to him, her hand on the iron banister.

"You have the opportunity to ask for more than most people can even imagine. Please don't squander it. Especially as us minor characters can never expect anything close." And before she could respond, before she could force more truths from him, he turned on his heel and stalked deeper into the cellar.

Back where he belonged.

Chapter Three

Shabbat came and went, as did most of Sunday morning. Isabelle's eyes swam as she read the same scrawled note in her father's file for the fourth time. A reminder to verify that cargo was limited to spices before approving a potential client. Their company worked not to support certain trades. Admirable, provided she didn't think too hard about the interconnected webs of business. How profit wasn't always direct.

And how none came without a hefty price, paid mostly by those who never reaped its rewards.

"Miss Lira?" A male voice echoed from the door, and she nearly jumped from her seat. Tipping her chin to collect herself, she blinked back up at the well-dressed man standing there with slight crinkles at the corners of his eyes, hands folded in front of him.

She held back a gasp. "Mr. Berab. I didn't know you would be visiting." Isabelle rose to acknowledge Roger, the youngest of her father's business partners. One of the two seeking her hand.

"We were on our way to a meeting and thought we'd attempt a brief word." Before she could question his word choice, he stepped through the threshold to reveal the bane of her existence: his oldest brother, David.

The man who had betrayed his friendship with her father when he'd given her an ultimatum over their shared business: marry a man *he* approved to act in her father's stead—preferably one of his brothers—or watch as he divided the company, taking her father's clients with him. *Good luck if you choose that route,* she remembered him scoffing. *How many gentiles do you think will deal directly with a Jewish woman?*

This day was just becoming better and better.

"Hello there, Miss Lira." David gave a small bow. "Always a pleasure," he added, the words tight. He strode in front of his younger brother, thankfully followed by another taller, slightly older man, with sharp eyes and gray hair.

Isabelle's chest relaxed at the sight of Pena, her father's former valet and companion. The once jovial man used to perform puppet shows and sneak her sweets, but since her father's death, he had taken to growling at anyone who dared to cross her.

Not that she minded his behavior where the Berabs were concerned. Though, she grumbled to herself, she'd eventually need to make peace with them if business was to survive.

Even if they'd been nothing but condescending and hostile toward her from the moment she'd announced her intention to personally assume her father's place.

"A very brief word." Pena coughed into his hand, his eyes flashing. "As I said, Miss Lira is quite busy."

"As am I." David glared, then turned toward her. "Which is why I am here. Do you have the Agha file?" he demanded. As if her possession of the material were a crime.

With as much calm as she could muster, she pulled

the soft leather-bound volume from the desk. "Naturally. My father negotiated the relationship."

"And the contract it yielded includes a clause I drafted—and now need to reference for a new and potentially much more important arrangement," David snapped, swiping the file from her hand, oblivious to the rather dangerous step forward Pena took toward the two. She shook her head at him because his defense, while appreciated, was very much not needed and would only add fuel to this fire.

"This should have been at the office," David continued, still oblivious, and blood raged through her veins at his ungratefulness.

"I needed to review it," she snapped back, rising to her feet. "And I work better here."

"At the expense of the company," David retorted.

How dare he? She balled her hands into fists. "I would never do anything to hurt the company my father built. Never."

"You have al—" David started but was cut off by his younger brother.

"I was quite fond of your father, Miss Lira." Roger tugged at his cravat. "And of your late mother, actually. She and my older sister were friendly."

Mercy, she wanted to smack David in the face. Or "accidentally" spill hot tea in his lap. Again. But despite that fact, she reined in her temper and frowned in consideration at Roger's words. Beside her, Pena finally drew back and positioned himself by the fireplace.

Not that Roger's prior relationship with her mother was a surprise, per se. They had common cousins in Amsterdam, and even in a growing community, like attracted like. It was just she'd died so young, Isabelle had no memories to judge what, if anything, that connection meant.

"We all grew up together. I was just the runt who tagged along after them." He shook his head, and a shadow flitted over his light eyes despite his next words. "It's funny."

"What is?" she asked.

"When she passed, I wasn't yet thirteen. At the time, I shrugged when my own mother and sister worried over your father—how much he had lost and how hard it must be." He crossed farther into the room, creasing the red floral rug. Isabelle's fingers clenched together as David took the opportunity to drag one of her father's neatly positioned chairs to her desk before hunching down, file still in hand.

"I couldn't see his struggles," Roger said. "He was so young and strong, after all." He inhaled sharply as he reached the mantel. "I'm more than a decade older than he was, and I find the weight of the responsibility crushing. There's not just the business and community, but my duties to my children." He ran a thumb along the smooth black marble. "They're practically infants, and yet I am both father and mother, alone...like your father was."

Only that wasn't quite true, was it?

Isabelle's heart squeezed at the memories his words sparked. Late in the evening—or really, in the night—she and Pena would sneak into her father's study, creaking open the door, to see him sitting there, bent over the books, hand in his thick, shiny black hair. He'd raise his head, and when he saw them, the widest smile would come over his face. She'd run and leap into his lap to tell him of whatever adventure Pena had created for her.

And then both men would take her by the hand and lead her into the nursery, letting her ramble. By the time she was in bed, her eyes would already be drooping. Side by side, they'd take turns reading her bits of history or philosophy as she drifted off.

"He had help." She glanced back and met Pena's eye.

"Your family. Yes." Roger cleared his throat. "We have that in common." He craned his neck to David, who was still flipping through the file.

She pursed her lips.

Roger gave a nervous cough. "I merely want you to know that I understand you and your position—how much pressure there is, how much weight you have on your shoulders right now. Your many duties and expectations." Tugging at his collar, he took a deep breath. "I know if you consider our solutions fairly, you will come to see…my family only wants what's best for the company and the community." He turned to his brother, but David only grunted from his chair. "This really is quite awkward," Roger finished quite morosely.

She folded her arms and glowered. "You and your brothers have already said that, so perhaps—"

"Why can you not just accept this is the right course for everyone?" David snapped the file shut and rose. "Do what is needed and act like a properly raised adult for once in your life. Or are you still so much a child?"

Why did he always have to needle?

"My actions always meet the moment and the company," she retorted, moving toward him, her hand itching for the knife she kept in her sleeve. Not to hurt him, just to scare him a little, like he deserved. Like *both* brothers deserved.

Glaring himself now, Roger stepped between them.

"My brother might not be stating things in the most delicate manner, but he is not wrong. You need to grow up, Miss Lira. For the company you claim to care so much about and for your family. And for the community and our place in it. Uniting as one true force is best for everyone." His voice strained. "I cannot promise you love. But I would maintain your status, give you protection, and shoulder some of your responsibilities. With the signing of our ketubah, you'd gain a house of your own, with children to raise and a position in any women-led charitable organization you'd like. Would that truly be so terrible?"

Not for him, perhaps, but for her...

Uniting would be more like being subsumed. However right he was—in *some* ways.

Isabelle swallowed. If she married Roger or his brother, she could ensure social protection for her grandmother and Pena. Their statuses would never falter. Their lifestyles would never have to change.

But as for her father's legacy, well, what would become of that? Not to mention her own future.

Perhaps what she was attempting was selfish as well as dangerous, but could she truly sacrifice everything that should rightfully be hers in exchange for a modicum of safety? All because David Berab was unpleasant and odious and sought to thwart any independent success she had at every turn?

And more, why did *she* have to be the one to compromise?

"You would be one of us," Roger added, moving so close that Pena pushed off the wall and crossed to her side in three steps, placing himself between the two. David scowled but said nothing.

"And no longer my father's daughter," she whispered. No longer a Lira.

Roger gave Pena a nervous glance before returning his focus to her. "You'd always be that."

"Would I?" Her throat tightened. "Would I really?"

David released an exasperated huff. "Consider what you are doing. Your father was bold and talented, but the company needs to find a way to move forward without him."

As do you was implied. A slight growl from Pena confirmed that she wasn't the only one who'd heard it.

"The other members of the Commission are already anxious to fill his seat. My brother is the one holding them back," Roger added.

"And yet you continue to be difficult," David continued, even as his brother touched his arm.

Roger smoothed the front of his coat, giving her a pointed stare. "The Commission trusts and respects our commitment to them and to the business." As if she couldn't read between the lines.

"And my husband can be part of this future, but not me—is that it?" Her chest heaved.

"First, a woman could never be a delegate and I doubt you would even want to be. And second, you know that the gentile clients will also not negotiate business matters with a woman, especially not a single woman. *Especially* not a single Jewish woman. You know their customs." David's exaggerated patience made her skin itch.

Isabelle gritted her teeth. "And you will do nothing to change that." No, instead, the brothers elevated themselves by conforming to the aspects of gentile culture from which they benefited the most and women like her—their own kind—the least. And yet, provided they gave the community enough financial support, they were declared heroes.

"You know we don't have that power," he responded in the same irritating tone.

True. But they could make room for her in the company, willingly and graciously. As had always been the plan—her father's plan.

David—and Roger and Louis, who were clearly content to fall in line, based on Roger's appearance—just didn't want to. Because even if the company split, no matter how good her work, the Berabs would have no issue stealing all their gentile clients—and with their standing and experience, probably a great deal of Jewish ones—burying her and the Lira name for good. Leaving her with no choice but to find a man with whom to ally that she could trust to push her agenda.

But as the handsome custodian had warned, it was hard to resist power once one had it in hand.

She knit her fingers so they'd not shake. With rage, she told herself, not fear. Because she was not afraid of any of them.

"Don't you have a meeting, Mr. Berab?" she asked in her coolest, most regal tone.

"I do." David nodded and tucked the Agha file beneath his arm. "I ask you to consider what we said."

"It isn't too late to change your mind," Roger added from his brother's side. "If you find no one fitting after your festivals conclude, my offer will still be on the table. As will my brother's."

As would be the threat marriage to any of them posed.

"Noted." She stuck up her chin as she marched past

him to the door. "Thank you so much for stopping by, Mr. Berab, Mr. Berab. It's always a pleasure to see you both."

"Likewise." Roger gave a small bow, and they both trudged out, Pena following behind them, leaving her alone.

Surrounded, in her father's former study, by books and notes and contracts that still smelled like him.

Isabelle sank into her chair once more and rubbed her temples. A lump welled in her throat. But she swallowed again and again until it was gone, because the time for tears and mourning was over. She would be fine. She'd find the perfect husband to give her what she wanted. Certainly neither of the Berabs, and…it had become clear that it could not be anyone within their sphere of influence.

She pulled out the matchmaker's list from the desk drawer and stared at the names. All schooled, monied, and from her part of the community. The Berabs' part of the community.

Isabelle frowned, again recalling the custodian's warnings from the day prior.

No. None of them would do. She crumpled the sheet in her hand.

She needed someone else. Someone free of their influence, or whose influence was at least up for grabs. Someone from the other side of the community. Still scholarly and monied, and clever—though not too clever—and socially adaptable for the clientele.

And most importantly, someone she could ensure was loyal to her and only her. Which meant she needed to put together a new list. Using new sources of information.

Her lips twisted into a smile as a plan, a rather clever—no, *brilliant*—one, if she said so herself, came into her head. And she had just the man to help her make it a reality. Provided she found the right leverage to get him on her side. Which shouldn't be too much trouble.

After all, she was still her father's daughter.

Chapter Four

She might not be a maiden locked in a tower, but she risked a similar fate if her grandmother discovered her sneaking about. However, her research excursion this morning had proven fruitful, and this next step was necessary. After having the hack drop her off at Bevis Marks so she'd not arouse suspicion, Isabelle strolled southeast toward Aldgate, past sloped wood-roofed houses and storefronts. Jewish tenants lived here now, but this neighborhood had been built at least two centuries ago, generations before her family had come.

Before the likes of her could live legally in England.

The bright midday sun didn't chase the grayness from the sky, nor the last bit of bluster from the wind as it flitted over her least conspicuous gown, a dull green with tiny lavender flowers that did nothing to flatter her hair or complexion. To complete her disguise, she'd borrowed a maid's apron in an attempt to downplay its limited charms even more.

Winding down streets she'd never needed to travel on foot, Isabelle squeezed between chatting women carrying baskets from the market and past shopkeepers sweeping the steps of their open doors. The thudding of a cart's wheels filled the air, along with the cries from merchants and the calls from the docks.

Quickening her strides, as she didn't have time to gawk and dawdle, she worked to match the frenetic pace of the thoroughfare named for its locale, alive with commerce. Not like Bond Street, where well-heeled gentiles lingered and socialized while gazing at pretty trinkets, avoiding her and her grandmother's eye. No, Aldgate was different. Even the breeze was filled with alacrity, with aim, with purpose.

She stepped through the throng, crossing toward the Great Synagogue with its plethora of arches when—*whoosh*—the clatter of horse hooves heralded a wagon from seemingly nowhere, sailing over the cobblestones as onlookers scrambled to get out of its path. Isabelle scurried back, only for the heel of her slipper to catch on the curb. She flailed and fell backward, curling her arms to her chest even as she braced for impact.

And then... nothing.

Well, not nothing. Large hands gripped her elbows, crushing her against a firm chest. Panting, she spun around and stared into the face of the man she'd come looking for, still clasped in his arms. No need to scour the synagogue now. His dark waves flopped over his brow.

"What are you doing here?" The custodian stared at her, his lips a thin, rather disapproving line.

Not that she'd expected a warm reception, but still, after the way they'd left things, one would've thought he'd give her at least a smile. Apparently not. Isabelle straightened her skirt. She'd sought his attention, so it was time to make the best of it, despite her less than graceful entrance. "I came to see you."

"I told you the other day, I'm not the kind of man you should seek out." Releasing her, he turned and started back to the synagogue, muttering curses.

Not an invitation, but not exactly a send-off—good enough for her. Lifting her skirts, Isabelle picked her way through the street, avoiding the muck and mud, as he rounded the side of the building. Unlatching a door, he ducked through.

"We are steps away from two synagogues and a church. No one would hurt me here." Fast as she could, she caught the door and maneuvered inside before he could shut her out. "At least not intentionally." She swallowed as the hinges creaked and a bolt clicked, plunging them both into darkness.

"You have a lot more faith in strangers than you should." She heard his garments rustling, then the snick of flint. The light of the candle bobbed as she took in the scant furnishings of the room—a table, a chair, and a narrow desk with a basin on it. Not even a mirror or a window. In the far corner a stack of discarded papers and books sat beside dingy linens draping a narrow wooden frame that could be called a bed, if one was charitable.

Well, she needn't worry about her future anymore. It was going to be rather short, as her grandmother would surely murder her if her presence here was discovered.

Ignoring the horror on her face, he continued, "Or you have too much faith in your own power." He landed on the bed with a rather graceful flop for someone his height. Reclining against the wall, he folded his hands behind his head. "Did it ever occur to you that wealth is a magnet for thieves as well as obsequiousness?"

Isabelle blinked at him. Apparently the alleged "bit

player" was taking a stab at villainy. A little late for
believability, though considering her intended purpose
for him, practicing his acting skills would serve him
well.

Besides, he wasn't half bad. Not exactly intimidat-
ing, but more confident. Dashing, even. All right, not
quite dashing, but at least slightly naughty. She ignored
the thrill that sent through her, working to focus on her
new plan and its accomplishment.

"It's the middle of the day." She turned up her nose
in her most imperious manner before pulling out her
dagger from the sheath buried in her skirts. It was the
first weapon her father and Pena—well, mostly Pena—
had trained her on and the weapon with which she was
most comfortable. "I was perfectly safe."

He gave it a rather unimpressed glance before she
tucked it away.

"Were you?" He stretched further, cocking his head,
a smirk forming on his full lips. "A half-decent cut-
purse doesn't need darkness and knows how to avoid
knives."

"Good thing I don't carry a purse." She plucked a
pouch of coins from the hidden pocket inside her sleeve
and held it aloft, reveling in the surprise that spread
over his features. *Take that, Mr. Villain.* Or in his case,
Mr. Harmless. Sneaking into a few gentile businesses
for warmth did not exactly make one a true wolf lurk-
ing in the night, or whatever he was playing at now. At
least according to her research.

She had visited the community midwife Dorothea
Adler and her daughter Rebecca that morning to great
success. They were her sole connections to the Ashkenazi side of the community: Mrs. Adler had helped care

for Isabelle as an infant after her mother's death, and Rebecca had grown from childhood companion to her closest female confidant. Though Rebecca's opinion of Mr. Aaron Ellenberg had been less than flattering. *He's a complete draikopt*, she'd scoffed before asking what in the world Isabelle could want with him.

When Isabelle had asked her to explain, stumbling only slightly over the Yiddish descriptor, Rebecca had chronicled Aaron as neither an earner nor a learner, nor clever enough to survive without the community's largesse. And then proceeded to tell her quite the tale of the man's background.

The man who still, apparently, thought he could fool her, of all people.

"A good confidence man doesn't require darkness either." He slid off the bed with a catlike ease and brushed past her. "A good con can sweet-talk you into an alley or cellar with just a few words, make you drop your guard. After which, he'll take everything you have." Rooting around the basin, he leaned over, his shirt straining over the defined muscles of his back. Did he ever wear a jacket?

Isabelle almost suggested he wear a touch more garments—she was his guest, invited or not—but he wasn't finished.

"And you'll give it to him. More, you'll thank him, and he'll be long gone before you even realize what occurred." He turned back around and tossed a small bag—*her* bag—in her direction, causing her to scramble lest it hit the floor.

"That seems very unlikely." She tucked the small sack back inside her sleeve as she straightened once more, flushing a little when he dipped his head in approval. "I can't imagine giving all my coin to a stranger." She sniffed. She was sheltered but not naïve.

"No?" He folded his long arms, biceps flexing. How laborious was a custodian's job? "How about if they were injured?"

"Injured?"

He lowered his voice to a whisper. "Bleeding after being punched in the nose, saving a beggar from a ruffian, but instead of thanking the rotter, the woman disappears to leave him in the street." He sidestepped her so he could come from behind and lean right against her ear.

Likely yet another attempt to make her believe him a villain. Though...perhaps he was more adept an actor than she'd previously thought. Her skin prickled at his nearness, his warmth sending tingles up and down her body and making her want to do a million ridiculous things, like arch her back and rub against him.

"What would you do? Would you go and see if he was all right?" he asked teasingly, clearly oblivious to her rapidly increased breathing.

She swallowed as she worked to regain her focus, concentrating on his words instead of how closely he stood. "Naturally. I wouldn't leave someone lying there to suffer or die." She skittered back, using the distance as a shield from his theatrics.

"Oh, I know you wouldn't." He gave a dark chuckle. "You'd probably tend to him and bandage him and wait until he could stand, and when you go to your purse to buy him just a little bread and ale to get his head on straight, you'd find it gone. Again."

She opened her mouth to argue, but he'd caught her in his story now.

"So you'd help him still, give up one of your fancy rings or bracelets. Gladly. And he'd be kind and charming and properly guilty, which would make you want to give him more." With a deft movement, he grabbed her wrist and pulled her front against his long, narrow torso, his voice soft as he bent his lips toward her neck, grazing the lace of her collar.

She might need to reassess the actual danger he possessed.

"And he'd have a full belly when he celebrates with his partners." He turned her round to wrap his arms around her, holding her firmly.

The room spun. Closing her eyes, she struggled not to moan as she leaned back against him, melting into the firm warmth of his body. She was tempted to stay there forever, reveling in this delicious tension...

He exhaled sharply.

And thankfully, before she could make more of a fool of herself, he released his hold on her, dipping back in the shadows, leaving her alone in the center of the cold room. When she raised her head, she found him lying on the bed, the bag of coins dangling from his finger and her jewelry held aloft in his hand.

Bastard.

Now only one emotion reigned supreme—annoyance. She was Isabelle Lira, and no one got the better of her. Not the Berabs with their self-serving ultimatums, not the gentiles with their constant scrutiny and suspicion, and certainly not this man. So he wanted to play the wolf?

Well, she could do some biting and scratching of her own.

"Who were you—the injured lad or the daring

rescuer?" Or, given Rebecca's assessment, the "helpless" victim? Was that how the fight that almost ended his life had started? She placed her hands on her hips, daring him to lie.

"It depended on the neighborhood and the mark." He dipped his fingers into her purse and shrugged, not meeting her eye. "I played quite a few roles when I left Aldgate. Despite what you think, despite what you saw the other day, I'm not a good man, Miss Lira." He glared at her. "You shouldn't seek me out."

Isabelle smiled to herself. She had him. And while his performance had been better than she'd expected, he was no Edmund Kean. But he would do. After she negotiated the proper deal.

Isabelle raised her chin, making sure she emphasized every word. "But you don't even know why I'm here. Though I can assure you, it isn't to steal everything you have—including your garments—then stab you twice in the chest and leave you for dead."

His eyes grew wide and she could barely hold back her grin. Oh yes, like her father before her, she was thorough when it was important. He should remember that.

"I want something else from you, Mr. Ellenberg," she told him. "And, in turn, I'll make sure you're rewarded." She pulled out her knife again, petting the steel with her gloved finger. After all, one good villain deserved another. "Don't worry. I'm harmless."

Mostly.

Chapter Five

So much for scaring her off for her own good.

Not that he hadn't had a steep hill to climb, given all she'd seen the prior day. As for harmless, that was a laugh. This woman was trouble of the highest order: clever, attractive, and powerful. In short, everything he wasn't. What could she possibly want with him? Nothing good, that was for certain.

"I see you've done your research." Or more likely, pumped her remaining powerful relatives for information. Fighting back the familiar shame, he focused on a large crack in the plaster above her head. "What did your grandmother tell you about me?"

And how many humiliating details of his life did she now know?

"Do you really think I'd be here if I'd asked her?" She smoothed down her voluminous skirts, hiding her dagger once more within the hidden pocket. Perhaps high fashion wasn't so silly after all.

His lip twitched. "No, I suppose not." No well-dressed matron would allow her precious granddaughter to traipse within a hundred yards of him. "You might be proving yourself a nuisance, but you're no fool."

"Don't sing my mind's praises yet. I can't guarantee her suspicions aren't aroused. I asked four maids and two footmen about you before learning that I would need to ask elsewhere." She coughed a little. "A rather grave oversight, considering my own contacts would end up sufficing." She didn't elaborate, instead picking at a loose string on her sleeve, avoiding his gaze as if *she* was the one who should be embarrassed by her past.

But not embarrassed enough to stop her from continuing.

"I know you and your parents came from Trier when Prussia captured it from the French and made the lives of its Jews much less…comfortable. They passed away less than a year after you arrived." She glanced up at him through impossibly thick lashes. "Something we have in common. Both my parents are also gone— though I don't remember my mother. She died shortly after I was born and…"

She coughed again, shaking her head a little. "I apologize—that information isn't necessary. We were talking about you, not me—or more, my knowledge of you." Her voice became firm and formal. "You were then raised in the Jewish Orphans' Home. After not being sent for further education or landing in one of the trades the community usually funnels orphans into, you briefly left for one of the shabbier gentile neighborhoods," she recited, as if indeed she were reading from notes, thankfully no longer looking at him.

Not that his cheeks weren't already burning. Lifting himself off the bed, he strolled close enough to use all of his height to his advantage, folding his arms over his chest. "You know, this would take far less time and words if you just came out and said, 'you're a schlemiel, Aaron.'"

And better for them both if she stopped bringing all of this up, stopped making him relive it.

Miss Lira ignored him. "There, you were robbed and came rather close to meeting an untimely end. Though rumor has it, you broke two noses and a jaw on your way down. And managed to shove an attacker so hard, he fell on his own knife."

"I'd have been hanged if he'd died," he said, his stomach turning from the horrible memories. "See? Schlemiel."

She finally glanced up at him again, her lips spreading into that glorious dimpled smile. "'Schlemiel' means all that? This side truly does have the best words. I really should've made more forays here earlier."

He opened his mouth to speak, but she held up a finger to shush him, nearly grazing his lips.

Oy.

In his own home. Well, a home leased to him by the synagogue and maintained by the generosity of the community. Including, almost certainly, her family.

"I wasn't finished." She folded her hands once more. "The Commission brought you back to Aldgate, ensured you recovered, and found for you what they considered suitable employment, so you're now—"

"Their pup?" He couldn't help interrupting again. Because that's how everyone thought of him—something to feed and house, even use and protect, but never a true adult in the community. At least not one who mattered. Not one who could study the Talmud and contribute to their understanding of the world, or who could amass the funds to keep their people safe and fed in a tumultuous, often hostile city and country. Not one who could make anyone's lives better.

And certainly not one who could be a husband and father, with a wife and children of his own, for whom he could make kiddush on Friday nights. For whom he could bring home candies or toys or funny anecdotes to make them smile and to whom he could tell the stories of their people before bed. The fun tales, with the monsters and ghosts and demons and talking fish. The ones people like the Liras probably found "provincial" or what have you.

But none of that was possible for him. No, he was just no one, to no one.

Of no value to anyone.

"And here I was always led to believe that we Jews were natural cat people. But that's neither here nor there." She curled and uncurled her fingers. "What matters is that the community is misusing you."

"They treat me fine." He thrust his hands in his pockets. Because it was true. He had a good life. A far better one than someone who contributed as little as he did deserved.

"I didn't say mistreating. I said misusing." She swayed closer, her clean, pressed gown rustling like pages in a new novel. "You've been relegated to menial labor, but you have other skills that can be far more useful in the right hands."

"And those hands would be yours?" His muscles tensed, the air between him and her heating. Why had he even tried to play the villain against this woman?

But before he could make a fool of himself, she stepped back to pace the small space as if she were getting ready to present a heroic monologue. Though princess or not, she was certainly a lead.

"You were right the other day. I can't expect to find a proper husband, with the attributes I need, who will not, someday, seek to overpower me—no matter how clear I am regarding our arrangement from the outset. Once he has full access to the business and money, my good graces may become unnecessary for success, and any and all control disappears."

Aaron swallowed. She was not looking to him for a love potion, was she? Even in the low light, her dark eyes shone with a terrifying determination.

"Which is why I need a husband with an additional quality." She leaned against his table, most likely dirtying her skirt. Not that she seemed to care. Though, he supposed, she'd not be the one to clean it. She pointed a finger at him. "Well, two qualities. But regardless, you are going to help me find him."

Had she been hit too hard in the head by a falling siddur the prior day? How in the world could he help her?

"I highly doubt that." He widened his legs, taking up more space in a last attempt to intimidate her.

But she didn't even flinch, just shimmied a little, as if she was enjoying herself and her power. Which she probably was. "You're going to find me information, the sort that suitable suitors won't willingly share, and in return, you'll be rewarded."

Huh. She really was full of surprises. And in need of a spy. *Not* a profession he'd tried. Though one that certainly held more respect than "custodian." His body hummed with temptation. *Foolish* temptation, as it was almost certain he'd muck up whatever she asked as well. And probably get into a heap of trouble. He sighed. Time to talk her out of this. "You want me to make sure your husband-to-be is aboveboard, has no secrets?"

"No." Her voice edged on exasperated. As if she was being the rational one. "I want to know their secrets and pick the man with the best one—something he'll desperately want to keep concealed but that will not jeopardize me in any way—to act as a surety."

Aaron squinted at her. "Come again?"

"That's how I'll protect myself. I won't set out to use the information, but if he breaks our agreement, I want to ensure I'll still come out on top." She nodded, her expression guileless, as if this was something perfectly sensible and agreeable to do.

"With extortion? How romantic." He coughed. Someone should wake Shakespeare from his grave, because Isabelle Lira made Lady Macbeth look downright apathetic.

"Insurance, not extortion. And none of this is romantic." She sniffed and slapped a hand on the table. "I don't want romance. How many times do I have to say it for people to believe me?"

"It's rather fashionable these days. Isn't that the aim of your set?" Aaron eyed her as his mind spun, working to process the concept of someone with all of Isabelle Lira's power and privilege not wanting all its spoils. Especially when so many were digging for scraps.

She returned his gaze with a glare. "Perhaps I'm not interested in fashion."

Not interested, his tuchus. He ducked his head to hide his smile. Even dressed down, or in whatever she called her costuming, the woman's garments screamed "style" from the full skirt, which fell only to her ankles, to her winglike sleeves.

"Ephemeral emotions are more trouble than they are worth." Her jaw tightened. "I need sureties."

Aaron blinked. What had made her so cynical? After all, it wasn't as if she'd reached for the stars only to be kicked down into the mud again and again. She had everything she could possibly want. She had all the community's adoration and respect. She was literally the best of them.

"Which is why I need you." She raised a gloved palm as if to stop whatever interruption he might make. "And in turn, I can give you what you want." Her throaty whisper echoed in the small chamber, tempting him.

As if she really was the enchantress from a storybook.

"And what's that?" he managed to ask, knowing he should be clever enough to run from such situations. However, once a schlemiel, always a schlemiel.

"Independence. A life that is only yours, where you are free to do as you please. That's what you were looking for when you left the community, wasn't it?"

Was it? He chewed his lip. Perhaps. In a way. He'd merely wanted to no longer be a burden. Or to not feel like one. To be respected, with a family of his own to share his life with. Things out of his grasp until now. Unless...

"What I want would cost a great deal of funds." His voice was scratchy, an unfamiliar whisper over the impossible image rising in his mind—himself, well dressed and clean, welcome and sought after by matchmakers and families alike who desired him as a spouse and father.

Impossible. It had to be impossible, surely?

"If you get me what I want..." She trembled a little

but puffed out her chest—which he was *not* improperly staring at. "My grandmother and I are my father's only living relatives. In addition to my dowry, there are trusts—ones that protect the property for us and pay expenses. From those additional funds, I could take, say, two hundred pounds without anyone's notice or concern."

Two hundred pounds.

With that he really could—well, he could rent a place of his own. More than rent. And perhaps—with the right advice, perhaps from someone like Moritz Seltzer, a minyan regular with a head for investing, who always looked him in the eye instead of pretending he didn't exist—he could find a way to turn the funds into a living, one that would make him desirable as a partner.

So he could be the desired one. So he could have a family of his own—with a wife and children, for whom he could love and care and whom he could escort proudly to events like the Lira festivals, as a valued member of the community.

Hope danced in his belly. It was almost too good to be true—or more likely, very much too good to be true. He narrowed his eyes.

"And if they notice? What will you say? Will you confess or call a constable? Can you guarantee you won't betray me?" He turned to spit on the dusty floor.

"As if I'd trust a constable. I may do business with gentiles, but I'm not one of them." She gave a derisive sniff. "My family's made a fortune buying and selling sureties, so I can say with confidence, there are no true guarantees." The shadow of that tempting dimple dipped in her left cheek. "Nevertheless, if you are somehow injured due to your involvement with me, it will not be by my hand. I might be a witch, but I'm a fair one. And I protect my own."

There was such a stern resoluteness to her tone that he could almost believe her. But before he could decide, she smiled at him once more, her deep brown eyes twinkling through the darkness. "Besides, I suspect that my offer is the best you've heard in a long while. Any additional protection is for you to build on your own. However, be warned: I do the extorting, not the other way around."

Miss Lira had impressive guts—he had to give her that. Well, she had more than guts, but it was almost certainly hazardous to his health for his mind to wander in that direction. He folded his arms over his chest.

"Furthermore, none of this really requires much risk or effort on your part, only reward." She threw him a charming smile. "You're too recognizable to a significant part of the community to play a potential suitor or servant. However, each of the festivals will involve performers. Not much of a stretch for you, at least from what I've observed." She tipped her chin. "I'm very resourceful, so I can outfit you appropriately. All you have to do is play the part, interact with a few guests, and we each get what we want."

His heart thrummed. Not because her plan guaranteed success, but because she was offering him, well, everything. And while so much could go wrong, especially given their positions, he knew opportunity wasn't a particularly lengthy visitor.

"You're playing with fire." He gave her a hard look and held his breath, half expecting her to think better of the whole thing and snatch away the gift she'd offered.

"I have a high tolerance for heat." Her voice was calm and strong, but she still fiddled with her fingers. "No husband will take all my power. Not if I have any say." She stuck out her hand. "Will you join me?"

"You shake hands?" He eyed her gloved palm.

"My family does for business." She didn't remove her offering.

Aaron drummed his fingers on his thigh. Oy, he wanted this. Too badly. And in his experience, desire led to tsuris. And trouble was the last thing he needed.

"I'll consider it." Taking her elbow, he guided her out the door. "You should too. You might enjoy flames, but those who taunt wolves still get bit."

"You're a wolf now?" Her eyes twinkled in the low light. "I'll believe that when I see it. Besides, I bite back."

He blinked as she shimmied a little again before saying, "You don't have to decide right away. Take some time to think." She raised a single long finger. "If you agree to my plan, come find me in two days. Third floor, second window from the back, midnight. We're in Mayfair, not quite on Berkeley Square, but close. I'd use a small rock and work not to break anything."

Before he could tell her that her wand was worse than her bite—and probably more useful—she'd slipped out, shutting the door behind her.

Chapter Six

The bells of St. Botolph's rang twice as Aaron stretched, cramped after pondering in his room for far too long after Isabelle Lira's exit. Cracking his tense back, he readied himself for more scrubbing. All the banisters required his attention, not to mention the railings in the ladies' section. And the rabbi and his students had probably finished their crumb-filled meal, leaving the remnants for him to sweep. He pushed open the door to his home, ready to enter the main part of the building from the alley.

Sunlight streamed in so bright he had to shield his brow. Yes, this was just the type of day he wanted to spend inside cleaning. Scowling a little, he stepped down from his raised doorway to the street, almost tripping on the cloaked figure kneeling in his path. A soft voice made chirping noises as a bony hand pushed bits of bread through the wooden slats of the small crate he'd secured to the backside of the building's waste-water trough.

A home for his neighbors, to keep the mice free from prying eyes.

Well, from most eyes. But old Miriam wasn't most. No, the mysterious widow was the Commission of

Delegates' most unlikely henchman, offering information only someone who haunted the night could provide. More than a touch odd, the woman had no past to speak of, a face always hidden beneath her cloak, and the uncanny ability to be about only when the community wanted something from him. He sighed before clearing his throat.

"You shouldn't feed them," he called down to her.

She didn't turn around. "And you don't?"

"Only when it's cold." He bypassed her and moved toward the back entrance. "And just a little, to make sure they stay in their home and out of mine." Which was why he'd built their house. And occasionally engaged in one-sided conversation with them. Showed them a bit of kindness and respect to entice them to do the same.

Aaron's lip twisted. If only people were more like mice.

"Hmm." She continued feeding them, this time imitating their squeaks.

Aaron rolled his eyes. "They carry disease, you know?" He pursed his lips. "At your age—"

"Do you truly care to finish that sentence, Mr. Ellenberg?" The woman finished and stood, assisted by her gnarled wooden cane.

"Not really." He grimaced. Oy. What was wrong with him today? Yes, he was often a dunce with small talk, but he usually didn't insult his betters. Especially not Miriam, who had been the one to suggest his job at the synagogue as a way to reintegrate him into the community.

What was it about Isabelle Lira that got under his

skin so easily? It wasn't Miriam's fault that he was likely going to get kicked on his schlemiel tuchus yet again after involving himself in her dangerous nonsense.

"I didn't think so." She turned to face him, her hood drawn so low it cast even her mouth in shadow. With a careful glide, she centered herself.

"I know what side my bread is buttered on," he replied with probably more glumness than necessary. He toed a chipped stone with his boot, drawing a groove in the graying mud.

"Do you?" Her head tilted beneath the voluminous brown fabric.

A shiver ran down his spine, bringing with it a wave of tension that undid any and all benefits he'd received from his stretching and back cracking.

"I'm very grateful to the community for all they've done." He threaded his fingers together and squeezed. "And I like my job." Which was true. He did like it. He just wished for more. Especially when talking to someone like Isabelle Lira. He closed his eyes. Oy, he truly was the worst sort of schlemiel, wasn't he?

The woman barked out a laugh so hard she wobbled. Aaron dashed out to catch her arm, but she pushed him away as she righted herself. "Never attempt the stage, Mr. Ellenberg. You would be better off becoming a shochet first."

"I was an apprentice shochet. For three months," he reminded her. "It almost cost me an arm." And he'd cost his former employer enough money—especially from bleeding all over the meat—that he'd been out on his ear that night, injury or not.

"Exactly my point." She tutted a little. "Spying,

however, can be more easily accomplished with neither a silver tongue nor good aim with a cleaver. Depending on the strategy. As I've told you before, there are advantages to being old, invisibility being chief among them."

Aaron bit back a gasp. How had she—

"What did you hear?" he asked, his throat dry. Or more importantly, what mistake had he made with Isabelle Lira, and how much would it cost him?

"Enough to know that you might have a new employer soon." Though her face remained hidden, the wryness in her tone was unmistakable. "A young but rather formidable one."

Soon? Did that mean that Miriam's employers, the fourteen—well, thirteen, as Isabelle's father's seat was still vacant—most prominent and trusted men in the community, actually wanted him to do Miss Lira's ridiculous bidding? And better, take her money?

"If she knew what she was doing, she'd hire you. You're the much better spy," he managed to reply.

"True, but her offer was for you and you alone." Miriam hobbled closer.

"An offer I haven't accepted." Yet. He rubbed his temple. "Aren't the delegates nervous I'll muck it all up? This woman and the man she'll marry and the children they'll produce are the community's hope for a successful future, and I'm the community's shande."

"I'm not sure it's that stark." Her cloak bobbed as she nodded.

"Isn't it?" He knelt as the nut-brown mouse he'd named Lady Dashby tiptoed to his boot. Sighing, he reached into his pocket and proffered the half crust of bread he'd been saving.

With a gleeful nod of her pink snout, she accepted the gift before hurrying off back to her family. Because she, like Miss Lira, had one. Whom she could care for and love and who loved her back.

A family who depended on her. He couldn't even depend on himself. Couldn't do anything without charity. He closed his eyes. Five different businesses had been cajoled into taking him on as an apprentice when his lack of facility with Talmud—or numbers or sciences or languages—had proven his mind would be no asset, to either himself or the furthering of the community.

With a tailor, a cobbler, a candlemaker, a baker, and the shochet, he had failed at everything from making product to serving customers.

All had turned him out, closing the door on any small chance of him being able to support a family of his own. To make it so he'd not go alone from the Jewish Orphans' Home to the Jewish Home for the Aged to the grave. Now it was his inevitable future unless something changed. Something like two hundred pounds.

"Mr. Ellenberg?" Miriam's voice, laced with concern, broke him from his woolgathering.

He bit his lip. "Sorry, I was—"

"Not listening, but I don't blame you. You have a great deal on your mind." She lifted her cane, indicating his head with its tip. "What I was saying is that you're being offered—"

"An opportunity. Something that doesn't come along very often for the likes of me. Especially considering how many I've previously squandered." He rubbed the back of his neck. "And it's not as if she's suggesting I do something illegal or hurt the community."

Miriam made an odd noise. "As of now, no. Though I wouldn't underestimate the demands of a powerful, determined woman."

At that, he rolled his eyes. "I'll not permit Isabelle Lira to charm me into trouble." An image of her flashing him that wide, irresistible, beautiful smile winked behind his eyes.

Or at least he'd do his best.

Miriam snorted. "How about you take care instead and promise you'll come to me at the first *sign* of trouble?" the woman said with a firm, demanding note in her voice.

Aaron frowned. That was an interesting request. "And the Commission of Delegates wants this?"

"You were invited to the festivals already." She shrugged beneath her faded cloak. "As you said, what she's asking isn't illegal or designed to cause mischief. Provided you take care not to embarrass or jeopardize the community, what objection would there be?"

"I don't know." He shoved his hands into the pockets of his trousers, turning the information over and over in his brain. "It just feels... Why would they approve?"

"Why wouldn't they?" Miriam ground her cane into the dirt. "They have an interest in keeping Isabelle Lira both happy and safe. Couldn't that be more easily accomplished if someone like you is doing her bidding?"

So that was it. The Commission wanted to protect Miss Lira by preventing her plans from having any effect. And they'd decided the best course of action was to make sure she had a toothless henchman.

Insulting. To both her and him. It irked him that they

assumed he'd be useless, no matter how likely that was to be true. As for her, while blackmailing one's husband was wrong, it wasn't as if she didn't have a right to be nervous. He didn't see the Commission finding any actual solutions to Isabelle's problems beyond the usual pressure—legal and less than—that they applied to get refusers.

"It's quite the sum. Money that could change your life," the older woman added quickly, interrupting his thoughts. "Money which is hers to freely give."

"Something doesn't seem quite right." He pursed his lips.

"I am confident that while Miss Lira may be flummoxed that she's not as subtle as she thinks, she would merely shrug at the Commission's opinions and focus her efforts on proving them wrong." With a grunt, Miriam turned her back on him and headed toward the mouth of the alley, putting an end to the conversation.

"Where are you going?" he called after her. Not that she would necessarily answer. That was Miriam's way. One moment she was there and the next she was gone, often fast enough that it seemed like magic.

"I have work to do." Miriam continued toward the street, her cane scratching over the ground. "As do you. Because regardless of whether the Commission approves of your employment with Miss Lira, they would still be rather unhappy to receive complaints from the synagogue about you neglecting your duties." Then, before he could respond, she scrambled around the corner, out of sight.

Aaron stared, a thousand questions on the tip of his tongue. No, instead he heard the faint but distinct sound of his name being called from inside the building, along with a request to bring his broom.

Time to get to work. No matter what he decided, Miriam was right on that account. He'd not be going to any festivals if he didn't start cleaning, fast.

Chapter Seven

It had been a long time since he'd scaled a wall. And certainly never one with such a fancy address. Aaron muttered a few choice words as he vaulted over the ivy-covered stone two nights later. Climbing had never been chief among his physical skills. Part of the reason he'd never attempted burglary.

Not that his other skills were so useful in the criminal trades. Good thing he'd never become desperate enough to engage in illegality more complicated than pilfering from a cart or two. With his mazel, he'd be dead or transported. Or both.

At least there was no chance of that now. Though Miss Lira might make a fearsome crime lord if she put her mind to it. He smiled to himself before cursing once more as he scraped his knee hard enough to tear his trousers. Repairing them would be another chore for later, along with mending the edge of the Torah cover he'd noticed was frayed. Even with Miriam's encouragement, he never should've come. There was no way this would end well, despite Miss Lira's promises of making his dreams come true.

And yet there he was, gazing up at the massive town house, counting the windows until he found the right one. He crouched behind a budded hedge and patted around for an item to throw. A rock was too heavy, and even pebbles a bit dubious. He could not afford a new window nor repair one himself—scrub one, yes; fix one, no. But a twig wouldn't have the right impact.

So a pebble it had to be. He rolled one in his palm as he stood, then cranked back his shoulder and took aim.

Thump.

Nothing happened.

She was home, right?

A single, soft candle glowed in the assigned window. He might not have been the most diligent student, but he could read and write and do maths well enough to count to the correct room.

All right. Again. He grabbed a second pebble and repeated the action, followed by a third try. He was winding up for a fourth when the yipping started. And yapping, which quickly became full barks as a black ball of hair threw itself at the glass windowpane.

A dog. She had a *dog*. And him throwing rocks at her window was her plan? She was going to wake the entire house and get them caught.

Correction. Get him caught and in trouble and—

The window flew open with a thud.

"Baron." A loud whisper echoed in the night as a white figure entered his view, just inside the room. "Hush."

But the creature continued its barking. Only muffled now, as if she was snuggling it, not muzzling it like she should. Gauzy fabric billowed, obscuring his view.

"Now, Baron…" He heard the pout in her voice and rolled his eyes. Not quite the commanding master, was she? Perhaps he should rethink her potential as a crime lord. "Baron, stop. Come. Let's—"

The yipping only increased.

"Darling, come. Shh." She was near begging as the curtains parted and the light grew brighter. "What do you want? What can I give you to make you quiet?"

Oy. She really believed she could make a wealthy, spoiled husband bow to her will?

"How about a little liver? Hmm…" Her voice had taken on a rather nauseating high pitch for the creature. "There we go, darling. Lick that."

Aaron wrinkled his nose. Good thing they hadn't actually shaken hands. Though she'd probably think the same of him if she knew of his friendship with the mice. And the birds. And the few cats he'd enticed with bits of his own food to stay away from both.

"Yes. Perfect," she continued cooing as the thing finally stopped its noise. After a few more rustles and a creak, she pushed the shutters farther apart and stuck half her body out into the night air. Her hair had been tied back into a long braid. She brushed it over one shoulder before cupping her hands over her mouth.

"Hello!" she half yelled, half whispered.

It really was a wonder all manner of people hadn't arisen from the house, brandishing weapons at him. Perhaps her grandmother was a sound sleeper. Or hard of hearing.

He stepped forward into the beam of light emanating from her window. "Since your hair is too short to climb, do you want me to stand here and holler at you?"

"If you'd like," she returned, resting her elbows on the sill. "Or you can use your stomach muscles to project your natural voice better and save your throat. One or the other."

His lip twitched. "Aren't you concerned I'm going to wake the household and all your schemes will be foiled?"

She leaned a bit farther over the edge, so the wind billowed at her garments. "My grandmother is visiting a friend, and the staff is used to Baron yapping at everything from tree branches to mice to too-loud clock chimes." She dropped her voice to that half yell, half whisper. "Oh, and I also might have persuaded our cook to slip the tiniest bit of laudanum into the stew. Not enough to hurt anyone, just enough to assure everyone has a full sleep."

Which explained quite a bit. So she still was no fool—but definitely a touch evil. "Your dog is called Baron?" he asked instead of pressing her on the rest of his questions.

"My father named him. Said one of us should have a title and we aren't the type to wait for the crown to bestow one." Her lip twisted into a cross between a smile and a grimace as the creature's head popped up. She scratched his ears, and he nuzzled against her side.

Apparently, her late father had a rather realistic view of his own position in society as well. Not a surprise, as this woman was quite keen on—what was the word she used?—"insuring" herself against her husband's vulnerabilities.

"And here I thought your family's promotion was all but guaranteed, provided the bill passes," he teased.

"My family adores the Duke of Sussex. He's coming to the festivals." She twirled a lock of hair around her finger. "And we welcome advancement. After all, we've been very keen on expanding our business's reach to more gentiles."

Quite the articulate nonanswer. Very appropriate for the daughter—and soon-to-be wife—of a delegate who was angling for an even more elevated status. Aaron rocked back on his heels, his boots sinking a bit into the damp, sticky, pitch-like ground.

"Anyway, wait right there. I'll come down." She heaved a small sigh. "Without Baron," she added before slamming the window shut.

Several minutes later, a blur of white dashed around the corner and into the garden. "I can't believe you actually came." She stepped into the moonlight, and Aaron bit back a gasp.

Fuck. She was naked.

Well, not naked. She was wearing a night rail. A flimsy white night rail trimmed with silky blue ribbons and delicate lace, to be sure, but still merely a night rail. A very thin, clingy one. He swallowed. Good Lord, even her feet were bare. And her ankles. And a good bit of calf. And now he was imagining parts of her that he really shouldn't be seeing.

Not that it was easy to redirect his thoughts, given that it was cold and the gown was so snug and—

Oy. No. This woman was a potential employer, and he needed to focus on that, as she'd never—

"What's the matter?" she asked, her nose wrinkling, as if she didn't suspect.

"You're not wearing any clothing." He pinched the bridge of his nose as he finally averted his gaze. They would be in so much trouble if they were discovered— well, *he* would be.

"That's a bit priggish. Though I suppose you do work

in a synagogue." She glanced down at herself, shimmying her hips from side to side as if she was judging the veracity of his good-sense observation. Apparently completely oblivious to the effect that the action and the fabric gliding over her hips had on him. "Still, it isn't as if anything of consequence is showing," she added, solidifying how very different their two realities were.

Aaron gaped at her. "I can see your ankles." He waved a hand at the delicately bared skin and only that, nothing else. "And elbows. Your bare ankles and elbows."

"What is the obsession with those?" She strolled over to a stone bench, spreading her skirts and crossing her legs as she sat with practiced, graceful poise, as if she were wearing a real gown.

Except she wasn't. She was hardly wearing anything at all.

Oy. He should never have come.

"Are you even listening to me?" Isabelle snapped her fingers at him, demanding his focus. "What's the preoccupation with them about?"

"Preoccupation?" he repeated, his mind still sticking as it worked to sort through the multiple warring—and mostly inappropriate—emotions in his brain and body.

"With ankles and elbows?" She huffed impatiently. "I'd never do any staring if our situations were reversed."

Truly? He could flash all sorts of inappropriate flesh, and the woman who had definitely run her fingers over his chest on two separate occasions wouldn't even look at him?

Emboldened, Aaron drew closer, leaning against an ornamental arch covered in tiny-leafed branches and buds. "How many men's ankles and elbows have you seen?"

"I see more of an outline than you usually get." She folded her arms, her lower lip pursing in a pout.

"So, none?" His lips twitched as he resisted full-on laughter. "So you have no idea how you'd react."

He cocked his head, waiting for her to flounce back into the house, but instead she rose, halting mere inches from him, close enough that the lacy edge of her gown brushed his knees. The thought rose in his mind that he could encircle his arms around her waist once again with no effort.

Not that he'd do that again, unless she was falling or needed help. But the possibility . . .

She widened her stance, like a fighter, her hands on her hips.

"Are you going to test me?" she asked, a defiant tilt in her chin, as if she was actually issuing a challenge.

He opened his mouth to say no, but instead he popped out, "Not now."

Damn it. He should've said "never." Aaron stepped back, digging the heels of his boots into the soft ground. "We have business," he reminded her. Which was all this was, no matter how disarming he found her when she became piqued like a normal human instead of acting the lofty princess or power-obsessed witch.

"Right," she said, her tone more serious, as she took a step backward. "I apologize. That was inappropriate. We have a precise arrangement, and we should keep to those boundaries." She bent down and lifted a parcel that had somehow escaped his notice, as well as a scrap of paper. "Take these."

"What is this?" He placed the package on the ground and unfolded the note.

"Your costume for the first festival and a list of men for you to study," she replied as he stared at the scrawled handwriting. He squinted at the six names. Six very prominent, very wealthy, very proper names. Six men who'd suit her very well.

Though six names from his, not her, side of the community. And suddenly, his presence in her scheme made a touch of sense.

"These are the men with whom you need to engage at the festivals, and if possible, leading up to them, given your proximity to them and their families." She tapped the edge of the page. "You need to find out any possible weaknesses—or better, secrets—especially ones that suit my purposes."

"I recognize that your family doesn't have the strongest personal connections to my side of the community, but you are clearly overestimating my relationship with these men. Cleaning the mud from their boots when they come to synagogue does not constitute 'proximity.'" His lip twitched despite the stone growing in his stomach, telling him this task was as impossible and foolish as separating seeds from lentils. And it would get neither of them what they wanted. He poked at the bundle of fabric. "And what is..."

"A juggler's costume. That way you'll be wearing enough powders and paint, so you won't be recognized. And don't worry—you don't actually need to perform. You can pretend to tend to your equipment or what have you. Your only real job is to get me what I need." She waved a hand. "Talk to them or find a magic wand, but get me information that I can use and balance against all the rest."

"The rest?" He blinked at her. Did she mean all the qualities that would actually bring her happiness? The qualities she should actually be investigating, like a man looking for love, instead of the nonsense she'd hired him for? One could only hope. Not because it would necessarily benefit him, as taking her money served him better.

But even if they were strangers, he could not help but dread the day when she would wake up bound to someone who didn't care for her or appreciate her—when that was exactly what she needed, more than all the money and power she was fighting to hold on to.

"You know, their personal qualities—their social status and familial connections, as well as their manners and appearance." She waved another dismissive hand.

"Appearance?" He couldn't help but raise an eyebrow. Perhaps Miss Lira was not so dispassionate about her marriage as she'd claimed.

"Naturally. How he carries himself and the image he projects are critical to our future success as a family," she said with a slight roll of her eyes. "Obviously, I can tutor him in those areas if necessary. Though doing that with the right balance of tact is never easy, so having those set beforehand would be quite strategic." She blinked at him. "What?"

Aaron closed his gaping mouth. Because what could he say to that? He glanced at his boot, staring at the frayed leather. He certainly did not have a suitable "appearance"—that was for certain.

"Oh." And this time her eye roll was followed by a raised brow. "You thought I meant 'handsome.'"

"I mean...one would presume that you...Don't you..." He coughed a little, unable to find suitable words. *Schlemiel, schlemiel, schlemiel.*

"Well..." She tugged at the ends of her hair. "As you suggested, I suppose that I would like to enjoy living with my husband, like every wife would." Her swallow was visible. Most certainly she was blushing, and for the first time she didn't meet his eye. "And if we are to engage in certain...acts...I'd like to be attracted to him. At least a little. So those acts would be...pleasing and—you understand what I mean." She licked her lips, and his foolish body reacted with dizzying speed.

That hadn't quite been what he'd meant when he'd advised her to find a husband she could love. But he did understand. Very much so. And because he remained a schlemiel, he was most certainly now picturing her on a bed, wearing exactly what she wore now, a sly smile on her gorgeous mouth as she crooked a finger and—

"However," she said, raising her actual finger pertly and interrupting his thoughts. "I do not want to consider that part of the equation unless or until I know if he's suitable."

"Ah. So you can guarantee you aren't attracted to the wrong person." *Someone like me.* The reminder was like a dash of cold water on his senses. This was no story, after all. Here, paupers were never princes.

And yet there in the moonlight, the ground between them still felt different—charged, even. Aaron threaded his fingers through the lattice in the arch, stroking the soft new leaves. "So knowing if someone lacks the status and power to give you what you want—as well as if he has the right vulnerabilities for you to exploit—will prevent that?" he asked, unable to let the topic lie just yet.

She rubbed her elbows, closing off her body. "Yes."

"Even if he's very handsome?" He gripped the wood and lifted himself up, swinging his legs, before jumping back down at her feet. "Even if he's in love with you?"

"I can control myself, Mr. Ellenberg," she snapped, jutting out her chin, which, before he could consider his actions, before his mind and body remembered who he was and what he was permitted, he caught in his palm.

"I'm sure you can. You seem very in control, Miss Lira." He stroked her cheek as she stared up at him.

"I—" She shivered in his grip—or perhaps that was him. But regardless, she didn't pull loose, only gazed back, as if she was challenging him once more.

Which was not what was supposed to be happening. He released her, shoving himself back into the darkness.

"All right, I will do your bidding," he said, his body still shaking. "Though I can't promise you success." He infused the words with as much formality as he could muster, forcing himself into the role of accomplice—no, henchman.

"And I will give you what you want in return," she called as he turned his back, sprinting away.

"I'll believe you when the coins are in my hands," he returned as he slipped over the wall and onto the empty street. Because making his dreams come true, *that* was what this was about, he told himself as he broke into a run, not stopping until he reached Aldgate and his own bed.

Everything else was none of his business.

Chapter Eight

There was nothing quite so relaxing as lying in a large tub filled with hot water, perfumed with oils from her favorite shop on Jermyn Street. Isabelle closed her eyes and inhaled, orange and ginger and amber enveloping her. The first festival was to begin in a mere three hours, and her nerves wouldn't calm. Especially not after the note she'd received from David Berab demanding figures for various accounts her father had led, with the distinct implication that failure would further prove how unfit she was to work in the company.

Culling the information from her father's files ate the entire morning. The man had been fanatical about keeping a tight rein on the business, which unfortunately meant he'd kept so much of its vital information to himself.

Not even Pena knew his organizational system. And while she'd spent most of her childhood at his side—first playing on the floor in his office, then listening to him expound on the ins and outs of contracts and formulas and charts, as he ensured she understood how best to serve their clients—he'd kept the more mundane tasks locked in his mind. For her to decipher now.

Without him.

She glanced at her chemise draped on the nearest piece of furniture. Grabbing the chair's leg, she yanked it flush against the tub so she could rub the lace-edged fabric, her palm immediately settling upon her sheath hidden underneath, her dagger always ready. The one *he* had given her—the one Pena had taught her to use. As she stroked the hilt, the knots in her back loosened a smidge. She could do this—rally and fight—defend what was rightfully hers.

With a partner. A loyal, dutiful, and fine—handsome, even—partner. She set down the dagger once more and leaned back in the tub, her fingers now traveling right between her breasts as another memory rose in her mind. One involving the other night when she'd met Aaron in the garden and, for a moment, believed that he would take her in his arms and...

Closing her eyes, she moaned a little as her fingers dipped lower. Even if the fantasy was ridiculous. Aaron, while handsome, was not husband material and was a good, if not rather prudish, person, who would most certainly never consider touching her like this— not that she even wanted him to outside of her imagination. However, if she could find, among the suitable men, someone who would—

A knock on the door interrupted her cycling thoughts. Splashing a bit, she dipped lower in the water. "You may enter."

Her maid Judith stuck her head through the door. "Your grandmother is looking for you, Miss Isabelle. And Miss Adler has arrived."

Isabelle huffed. So much for her soak. "Tell my grandmother I'm just about to finish and will attend to whatever business she has shortly. And tell Rebecca that we will talk after—"

Judith darted forward as the door swung open behind her, the knob banging against the wall, rattling the large portrait of Isabelle and her grandmother that hung above the granite-covered fireplace. A blur of elegantly set gray curls stormed into the room, followed by a tall woman with neatly tied-back auburn hair.

"We have a problem," her grandmother stated.

"You have a problem," Rebecca clarified before sitting on the chair nearest to Isabelle's remaining morning refreshments. "I'm just here for an early run at the food." As if to demonstrate her point, she plucked a bun between her fingers and took a large bite.

Judith coughed into her hand. "I'll excuse myself. Ring if you need assistance."

"Did neither of you hear the part about me bathing?" Isabelle indicated the water and sudsy bubbles around her, her cheeks pinking from embarrassment. Normally, she didn't mind their lack of boundaries—after all, hers were rather limited as well—but she had just been, well…And while Rebecca's profession and knowledge of anatomy made her friend well suited for certain types of discussions, this was not one she wanted to have when she was nude.

"This is more urgent, given how soon this festival is going to begin." Her grandmother nudged the copper edge of the tub with her satin-slippered foot. "Unless you'd like to call it off?" There was an inquisitive note to her words, as if her grandmother expected an answer different from before.

Even Rebecca looked up from her eating to stare at her curiously.

Traitor.

Resisting the urge to stick her tongue out at her friend, Isabelle rose and stepped out, suds sloshing onto the thick rug. "You know that's not possible," she replied over her shoulder as she wrapped herself in a thick cloth. "The Berabs' ultimatum is not going away, and matchmakers take time. Besides, even if we *had* time, canceling the festivals would be a social disaster. The community would be understanding, but the gentiles would not. The vote on the bill is coming."

"If the bill fails over a canceled festival, it would never have succeeded in the first place." Her grandmother wrung her lace handkerchief. "I just wonder if you might want to slow down. Is there really a need for a husband right away? Perhaps with proper assistance, a staff to do our share of the governance, you could argue—"

"You mean hire managers? Make myself a passive investor? I'd be giving over control to people with even more motive to undermine me and align with the Berabs." Isabelle worked to keep her tone level and respectful, but given Rebecca's expression, she was not quite succeeding. Calm—she needed to be calm. She tossed her waterlogged hair over her shoulder and squeezed, droplets rolling down her arms. "They will steal what my father built."

"He was my son as well." Her grandmother drew in a sharp breath. "Though I cannot say he did either one of us a great service in this regard."

Isabelle fought to not snap at her. "He did his best. He provided for Pena and you and me, and there's enough money that none of us will ever starve." Only *she* would become irrelevant and obsolete. A means to an end in someone else's story.

Dropping her towel, she plucked her chemise and slid it over her head. "So long as half the company is still in our hands and the Lira name on the door, it's my responsibility to fight for his legacy, to prove that I should lead—by my works, not merely my birth." Isabelle grabbed her dagger and sheath, hooking it around her waist, before combing her fingers through her hair so it wouldn't tangle too badly before Judith could brush it out.

A derisive snort sounded from behind her.

"What?" She glanced over her shoulder at both women. Each stared back at her with identical bemused expressions.

"I'm surprised that you managed to listen to this week's sermon while catching your reflection in others' jewelry. Though you clearly missed the rabbi's reminder of how much help Moses had—from his family and friends," Rebecca said.

"And that we, as humans, were not made 'good' or 'bad.' Our state is never static. We are merely charged with trying to continually do better." Her grandmother smoothed her pale green silk skirts as she settled into the high-back chair near the window. "So do remember I'm seventy, not dead. And while I might not have helped with the business, I still have quite a few skills that I can contribute."

But her skills were political ones, the kind that had helped their family muscle into plum roles in the community and make headway with the gentiles from the moment they'd set foot in England. Important skills, but only half of what was required to maintain the place they'd created for themselves. And far less potent without a male ally to act as their figurehead—an advantage that was growing more and more necessary in order to access the gentiles' upper echelons.

Isabelle sighed. If only the Berab brothers weren't so keen to leverage her father's death for their benefit. To forget that they had all once been not just friends, but nearly family.

If only her father were alive, and life were as it had been a year ago.

"We've discussed this before," she reminded her grandmother. "I need to marry. Who and how are the only questions. This spectacle is the best way to control those choices and maximize the benefits my husband will bring, while protecting all of us—you, me, and Pena." She indicated for Rebecca to lean forward so she could ring the bell to recall Judith. Her friend grudgingly acquiesced between bites.

She turned back to her grandmother. "What I am doing is reasonable and rational and the best way to solidify Father's legacy."

"*You* are his legacy." Her grandmother frowned as Judith reappeared in the doorway, ushering Isabelle to her rather messy dressing table, the marble top covered with pots of creams and powders. "You and your happiness, and I fear that this will bring you no happiness."

"I'll just have to prove you wrong as well, then." She sank onto the tufted cushion in front of the heavy framed mirror and straightened her spine, readying herself for the brush whose coarse bristles always nettled her scalp. Rebecca, who had come to sit beside her, winced and touched a hand to her own tight curls.

"I suppose so." Her grandmother rose and strolled toward the window. "Though I'm rarely ever wrong," she added, with a resolution Isabelle could only envy.

"There's a first for everything. Besides, how is this truly different than if father was alive? We'd search for a man who'd suit both me and the entire family and its needs. People have done so for centuries." She winced as Judith struggled through a particularly tight tangle. "More than centuries—since biblical times." She turned back to the stern-faced woman. "We can just pin it simply. I don't need a full Apollo knot. Though make sure my face is properly framed."

Her grandmother traced a finger over the window glass. "Odd how no one in the Torah had a series of festivals where they forced potential mates to strut around for them."

Isabelle bit her tongue, her mind flitting over the entire Tanach and their other writings, searching for a counterargument until—*aha*—

"Ahasuerus did." She motioned to Judith, who set about assisting with her undergarments.

Rebecca released a snort before coughing. "I'm sorry," she said as she tapped her chest. "I just swallowed..." She shook her head. "I apologize—did you really just compare yourself to Ahasuerus? Is there something more to these festivals I should know?"

Isabelle rolled her eyes. "I'm not hosting orgies."

"It would be a touch awkward with your grandmother and Pena in attendance," Rebecca conceded.

"Ahasuerus wasn't a Jew or in the Torah." Her grandmother sat herself on the window seat, placing a cushion on her lap before smoothing the fabric, purposefully ignoring her friend's comments.

"He was a king," Isabelle pointed out. Which was even better than a princess and whatever titles the bill promised. Isabelle held still as Judith slid the busk into the front of her corset.

"A foolish king who was constantly duped by advisors." Her grandmother rubbed a tassel. "And his wife."

"Who was most certainly not who she seemed to be," Rebecca The Traitor chimed in.

"Which was a good thing for us and our continued survival." Isabelle's stomach rumbled. "It's only a few hours until guests arrive, and I need something to eat." Another pot of tea was certainly in order. With more cakes. She whispered the request to her maid as she thanked her. Judith nodded before stepping out of the room to do her bidding.

"I'm just asking you to be careful, Isabelle." Her grandmother heaved another sigh. "I want you to consider all the angles, lest you do something that you'll regret."

"You know I will. And you know I'll put in place every possible barrier against any potential consequences." Isabelle dipped her hand beneath her skirts to where her dagger lay, fingering the design of a carved shell on the hilt. "That's what we Liras do, after all. If you'd like, I can look for a man with qualities I enjoy *besides* business acumen, political shrewdness, and power to use against the Berab brothers." She bit her lip. "Perhaps one who is not a chore to look at."

Rebecca slapped a hand over her mouth, suppressing sounds suspiciously similar to giggles.

"How magnanimous of you." Her grandmother flatted the cushion with her palm. "Meanwhile, we're already running into issues. Which is what I came to inform you of. A guest has appeared inappropriately early, despite the explicit instructions on his invitation."

A million curses echoed in Isabelle's ears as she froze in front of her wardrobe. "A man?" she asked, pitching her voice as innocently as possible as her fingers flitted over the silks.

"Yes. His name is Aaron Ellenberg." The older woman stood, clutching the bench for support, as her legs didn't bend quite like they used to. She was supposed to use the gilded animal head walking sticks that Isabelle and Pena had commissioned for her as gifts, but her grandmother often "forgot" when they failed to properly complement her attire.

"I've never heard of him." Isabelle ducked her head so she'd avoid Rebecca's now-curious eyes. "Is he someone else to add to the list?"

"Not unless you've decided penniless orphans with neither pedigree, trade, nor connections is what would best suit your purposes," her friend said loudly, redeeming herself with the show of loyalty in a clear, if clumsy, attempt to fortify her lie.

"I would prefer you both to be more tactful when discussing people not as fortunate as us, but no, I suppose he is not being added to any matchmaker's list," her grandmother said with an exacerbated sigh. "Pena's instructing him on proper attire before sending him on his way with the directive only to return at the proper time."

"Good to know." Isabelle's heart thumped faster. Poor Aaron. Apparently, he was in need of a rescue. First, though, she'd have to finish mollifying her grandmother. "Is that all that's wrong?"

"If he does attend, please do not toy with him or, for

that matter, any other people of his status." Her grandmother moved to her side and offered her arm. "Let them have their fun, but respect their feelings and dignity. Offer no false hope nor cruel send-offs. Behave like the leader you supposedly want to be."

Isabelle threaded her arm through the other woman's before motioning for Rebecca to follow. "I'll be the picture of perfection all evening—with the gentiles, with the suitors, and with everyone in between."

"I'm sure you will, dear." Her grandmother patted her hand. "And I, in turn, will try to behave the same. With the least amount of meddling possible."

Isabelle resisted a snort. "I have no doubt." She gave her grandmother a broad smile before glancing back at the crumpled missive she'd fought so hard all morning to answer. All would be fine. This was her festival, her plot, and her responsibility, and she'd not fail.

Chapter Nine

Two long hours.

That was how long Aaron had been forced to listen to a man named Pena lecture him on decorum and proper attire—which he very much understood included a jacket, he'd just given his to a beggar who needed it more on his way over—in a small, dark, windowless room behind a servants' staircase. Because God forbid they admit him to a parlor or study or anywhere private and leave him alone so he could change. It wasn't as if he could travel in full grease paint.

Not that he'd had the opportunity to explain. No, this stranger had trapped him, despite giving no indication of his own authority or title beyond that of Scowling Man Who Thinks Very Highly of Himself. Not a profession of which Aaron was aware.

Perhaps he should inquire if this Pena was in search of an apprentice.

A rap on the door finally put his words to a stop, giving Aaron the chance to slump against the wall for a damned minute. And better yet, think.

The obnoxious man swung the door open, revealing his rescuer—or his doom, for he'd be damned if Isabelle Lira didn't look like a queen. The shimmering silver silk of her gown made her skin glow and her black hair gleam. Even her eyes sparkled.

He'd known she was a beauty, but despite how much pressure she had to be under, she radiated confidence and what could only be described as "presence." And when she smiled at him with that deep dimple, well, for one glorious moment anything seemed possible. Even magical.

Except magic didn't exist.

This was no princess looking for a diamond peasant in the rough—she was a mercenary witch trying to force a rich brat into an alliance he couldn't later abuse. And while her ambition was admirable, extortion was still extortion. Not an attractive trait. No matter what his shmendrick body wanted.

The man cleared his throat, startling him out of his gawking. "Isabelle, don't you look lovely?" He waved a hand in Aaron's direction. "This is Mr. Aaron Ellenberg."

"Thank you, Pena. I was hoping for 'passable,' but 'lovely' will suffice." Isabelle Lira beamed at the man, her smile glowing even more brightly than her dress, before turning to Aaron and dipping into a low curtsy, as if he was someone important. "And it's a pleasure to meet you, Mr. Ellenberg." She stepped aside to reveal another woman—less well dressed, in a simple dark wool gown, but her well-made garments were still miles above his station.

"This is my friend and chaperone, Miss Rebecca Adler." She squeezed her friend's hand. "There will be quite a few gentiles in attendance, and we aim to make sure they're, ah, comfortable."

Aaron nodded. As to be expected. After all, the

Commission of Delegates relied on families such as the Liras to master keeping the balance between being mindful of the gentile gaze and maintaining their own laws—to assure the entire community's safety and survival. Such as by not permitting an unmarried daughter to wander without a companion when guests were about—to guarantee her "purity" or whatever they called it. Isabelle had probably been taught those skills from birth. He turned to the other woman.

"We've met." Unfortunately. Aaron rubbed the back of his neck. This must be whom Isabelle had been referring to when she said her own contacts had given her the information on his past.

The daughter of the community's midwife had been called the night of his attack and subsequent rescue from the West End, thanks to skills she possessed that were beyond her mother's specialty. She'd stitched the knife wound in his side, but the entire time she'd worked, she'd subjected him to a quite self-righteous, however accurate, lecture on how he'd risked the community's safety.

An interesting choice in companion, especially considering she was certainly not a social favorite across all of the community, despite her capabilities elevating her standing. Though given the loftiness of Miss Lira's stature, he supposed she could afford associations based on qualities other than mutual status.

Within reason.

The woman in question adjusted her spectacles with a slight sniff. "Always good to see you." The words were drier than the desert Moses had crossed.

"Mr. Ellenberg was on his way out, to change into his proper attire," Pena said before grabbing his shoulder and marching him toward the door.

"All the way back to Aldgate? That's quite a long way for him to travel."

The general—because that seemed like the most apt description of Pena, he decided—paused at Isabelle's voice.

Odd. Why was she hiding her scheme—or his part, at least—from a mere employee? It was his job to please her, not the other way around. Though perhaps she was afraid of loose lips around her grandmother?

Not that he could imagine Isabelle truly fearing the elegant but elderly woman who'd snored softly from the ladies' balcony during the rabbi's sermon last Shabbas. More likely she didn't want her to fret and worry—or meddle. A common practice among their kind. Especially where family was concerned.

Not that he had experience in such matters. Though hopefully, that would be rectified with the two hundred pounds.

He bit his lip as an image rose in his mind, of two little children running to greet him after shul, a woman behind them, wrapping her arms around his waist, eager to inquire about his day and give him a long list of tasks they could do together to assist in their offspring's happiness.

"You must have a million things to check upon, besides dressing yourself. How about we escort him to the gentlemen's smoking room, where he can change and wait for the festivities to begin?" Isabelle continued, interrupting his thoughts. Rebecca Adler's eyes darted to her, narrowing.

Pena released him with a shove. "I think more, you two want to sneak around places you aren't permitted." He folded his arms, looking back and forth between the two women.

"Us?" Isabelle batted her eyelashes as she dipped her head coyly, hands behind her back. "Come on, Pena. Please? We won't go in. We'll just glance around a little."

"At what? There will be no one in there." Pena closed his eyes for a long moment before sighing. "Fine, but do not linger and do not cause any trouble and do—"

"Not tell my grandmother?" And there was that smile again, though sadly not directed at him. "You have my word. We'll be positively angelic."

"The four-headed type, no doubt." The man stuck a thumb in Aaron's direction. "See that he behaves as if your grandmother was in the room."

Isabelle pursed her lips. "If he doesn't, I can take care of him." However, her eyes still twinkled as she tried—and failed—to hold back giggles.

"That's what I'm afraid of," Pena muttered. He angled his body between Aaron and the women, and Aaron wondered whom exactly he was protecting.

"I'll see that Isabelle doesn't draw too much blood." Rebecca sidled up to Isabelle's shoulder. "After all, it's such a bother to remove from tapestries."

"You're no fun." Isabelle pouted at her friend until Pena exited with an exaggerated grumble, closing the door behind him.

There was a beat of silence.

He stared at Isabelle, waiting for her to elaborate, or more importantly, assure him he'd not actually lose a limb around her. However, the woman neither faltered nor blushed, her expression slightly piqued.

"This way," she instructed as she led him and the midwife's daughter out of the room, up a staircase, down a long corridor, and through an impressive double-doored entryway.

Once inside the high-ceilinged but somehow intimate chamber, she turned back to him. "This is quite the start." She had the nerve to sound annoyed as she folded her hands in front of her skirts, revealing a line of what had to be at least two dozen tiny jeweled buttons on each of her gloves. "Rebecca knows everything, so you can speak freely," she added, waving her hand as her friend took up a seat on the far fainting couch.

"I couldn't very well walk through the streets dressed as a juggler." He coughed into his hand before strolling to the rather welcoming fire and leaning against the black marble. "But you should know, I ran into one of the men on your list this morning and we had a chat. It's amazing what people will say while you're shining their boots."

His chest puffed with more pride in the ruse than he should possess at such a small success. However, in his life even victories like that one were large. He swallowed. Unlike for Isabelle, or any of the men whom she was considering.

"Who? And what did you learn?" Isabelle's voice brought him back to the present.

"Jacob Shultz, despite having a degree from Rotterdam, a successful coral import business with his family, and a scholarly lineage he's taken to claiming includes Moses Kohn of Narol, owes quite the number of gambling debts. To several gentile clubs. Here and in Paris." Aaron straightened, tugging on the ill-fitting, dull waistcoat that Miriam had helped him negotiate from a rag dealer—a far cry from Isabelle's silver and metal sparkles. "As does his father."

"That gives me no leverage and could damage our respectability." She stuck out her lower lip, huffing in clear vexation. Oy, was she going to stamp her delicately shod foot too? "I suppose that means he's one to avoid at all costs."

"That's a pity." Rebecca tutted from the leather couch in the far corner.

"Why?" Both he and Her Highness asked in unison.

"You've not seen him, have you?" Rebecca smirked with such glee that he couldn't help rolling his eyes. Shultz was decent to look at, for sure, but not smirk level.

"No. What does he look like?" Isabelle moved to her friend, sinking down on the seat next to her. Which was not at all irksome.

"Tall. Broad. Robust. With thick lashes and sculpted cheeks and a rather nice jawline with and without the beard he's been growing between Fridays during the Omer." Rebecca ticked off each quality. "The best on the list by far. At least to view."

Aaron glanced at Isabelle to gauge her reaction. When she appeared unfazed, he released an odd breath he hadn't known he was holding. So those were *not* physical qualities she admired? Not that it mattered to him, per se...

"The type of jaw one might want to kiss along," the midwife's daughter added.

"Do men like that?" A lock of hair slid across her forehead as she addressed him, her dark eyes sharp. "Being kissed along their jaw?" Her gaze was direct, almost serious. As if his answer mattered.

Aaron blinked. That wasn't possible, so what did she really want?

"I can picture enjoying kissing with Shultz, certainly. You really should see him." Rebecca rose—her expression, to Aaron's chagrin, almost dreamy.

Aaron ground his jaw. Did they really have to keep on about the man? And Rebecca was supposed to be Isabelle's friend, so she should be reminding her that there was more to life than a handsome jaw-line. Though, given Isabelle's criteria for a husband included someone she could control at work and enjoy in bed...

He rocked on his heels, his worn boots chafing his ankles. This was none of his business. None of his business nor part of his job and—

Isabelle placed a finger to her lips. "Is this Shultz really that good looking?" But she squinted at him, not her friend, making his breath hitch once more.

He tugged at his collar. Mercy, it was getting warm. Someone should open a window. "I wouldn't know— I focused mostly on his shoes." He mumbled the lie. "And listened to his answers to my questions."

"Naturally." Isabelle's lip quirked. "Then back to my first question—kissing along the jaw—is that enjoyable? It's an important question if I'm to consider your advice about...compatibility with a husband. Your advice on attraction and physical capabilities specifically." The last she added sharply, a reminder of her stance on the more "ephemeral emotions," as she'd called them.

"And I ask because you're the only person in this room with actual experience. Unless I've missed events in Rebecca's life?" She glanced at her friend, who only rolled her eyes behind her spectacles before shaking her head.

But before she could continue, a sharp bark broke the air and the same creature from the prior night rushed into the room, jumping at his mistress's legs. Isabelle bent down and scooped the black ball of fur into her arms, allowing him to lick her neck as he squirmed.

"I'll take him, while no one's about," Rebecca interrupted, easing the dog from her friend. She hurried from the room before either of them could object—but not before sending Isabelle a sly nod.

The air still charged, Isabelle continued, so unperturbed by the quick entrance and exit he almost had to wonder if it had been planned. "As I was saying, you're the authority. So again, do you enjoy being kissed on your jaw?" She tapped her lips with a single finger.

"Or maybe your neck?" This time she swiped one of those graceful hands up her bodice, fingering her necklace and bringing to mind improper images. Ones *he* certainly shouldn't be picturing. Her eyes widened a little. "I think I'd like that, definitely." Her tone was a bit breathless, and he nearly needed to fan himself.

Calm. He needed to be calm. And appropriate.

He cleared his throat. "Well, um, as you've demonstrated, everyone is different." Digging his fingers into his thighs, he fought for composure. "So theoretically, yes, either of those would be enjoyable—with the right woman, naturally." He gave her a withering once-over, despite the wrestling match in his head between his more lurid imagination and common sense. "Though I can think of better places to kiss."

"Where?" Isabelle asked, arching both dark eyebrows. With a graceful sweep, she settled into a chair inches away.

Flexing her potential power, no doubt. For why else would she continue to talk to him, of all people, about this? He was her employee, not her friend.

Which should annoy him, as she was wasting their

time—time he needed to properly costume himself for her benefit—but irritation was not the emotion stirring in his gut.

Before he could think better of it, Aaron chose his own chair and leaned back indolently to show that she was not in full control. "I'm not sure. Can you repeat the question?" He gave his best imitation of her sly smile. "Please."

But without a flinch, she asked, "Where else would you like to be kissed by women?"

"If it's the right woman, anywhere she wants." He shrugged, giving her the truth. "Her desire makes it all the better." Better, a hundred times over.

She hummed and ran a finger over her collarbone, almost absently.

"Does that not ring true?" He shifted in his boots, working not to picture his own lips in its place. Because that would never happen. Though the image was a lot better than picturing her and Shultz. He squeezed his hands into fists at the thought of that pompous, spoiled schnorrer daring to even breathe the same air as her.

"I wouldn't know." She gave a prim sniff.

"Think of it in the reverse." And before he could think better of it, he took her gloved hand, running his thumb over her knuckles. "Think of all the places a man could kiss you and how it might feel. How it might set you alight, with how beautiful and desirable you'd feel." He gazed at her, his own set of mental images starting again, in which her fingers were bare. As well as her legs. And her shoulders. And a few other parts. "Then imagine you doing so with that same man, but this time, his eyes are alight, and he's murmuring uncontrollably how beautiful and desirable you are."

His voice had grown thick and—damn it all. He should not be engaging this way with her.

She gave him a dark glare. "He'd have to be a very good actor."

Aaron started. She had to be joking. She owned mirrors, didn't she? And no doubt had been told how beautiful she was every day, her entire life.

"I'm not going to dignify that with a response." He shook his head in disbelief. "And if you really need one, I'm sure you have a dozen people you could command."

"That's why I like you. I may be paying you, but you aren't a sycophant." She wagged a finger at him.

His gut warmed with pleasure, despite himself. "You like me?"

"And now we're even, as you aren't getting a response either." Isabelle rolled her eyes. "As for the rest, I recognize that I'm not unattractive. I'm rather pretty, even. Though I have a great deal of assistance there." She stroked her lace-edged sleeves. "It's just that I think the rest of my...accoutrements outshine, well, any other aspect of me." She swept a hand over her entire body, as if to demonstrate her point, but she failed miserably, as her considerable beauty certainly had his attention.

"Even if I didn't intend to marry for business, I have no delusions any man wedding me would be doing so for physical desire alone," she continued. "I come with too much money, too much influence, so any attraction would always be tangled with that. I'm an entity more than a person."

Something within him twisted painfully. Even if he was only an employee to her. But despite the sad, almost too-old look in her eye, he said, "I'm not going to feel sorry for you." Which would be ridiculous given her pampered life.

"I'm not asking you to." She straightened, looking impossibly regal once more. "Besides, it's better this way. I like to know what to expect, so I can better protect myself. As I told you, I was raised to run a surety company, so guarding against disaster is in my blood."

Still, not a particularly pleasurable way to live. What was the purpose of all her money and power if she spent her entire life avoiding risks instead of enjoying it?

"Fair enough." He rose, offering her both hands. "So are you ready to begin?" She accepted and he pulled her to her feet. When she stumbled, he steadied her, until they stood face to face.

"After your transformation." She slid her arm into his, fitting easily at his side, giving him a slight, playful squeeze, before exiting the room, leaving him more confused than ever.

Chapter Ten

Straightening her gloves for the fiftieth time as she readied herself to greet her guests, Isabelle worked not to flush at the memory of Aaron's supportive warmth. Such a contrast to the nervous chills that she'd been struggling to hold at bay. The effect of his presence ought to be immaterial. He was practically a stranger. And the wrong sort, as he could offer her nothing of use beyond the task for which he'd been hired.

Yet she'd found comfort in the way he guided her, the way her skirts brushed against his legs. The way everything seemed to melt away when they were together.

Which was ridiculous.

She didn't need comfort; she needed control. She straightened her spine—like her father and grandmother had taught her—as she forced herself toward the front of the house, the roar of the already crowded ballroom ebbing out to meet her. Her guests demanded perfection.

And she needed to perform.

The chatter grew louder as she paused just outside the two-story paneled doors her father had specially commissioned, the crest he'd designed etched into the ebony-stained wood. He'd wanted something that would be permanent, proof that they'd been there, whether or not they were permitted to remain.

And now he was the one who was gone.

It contrasted with the floor-to-ceiling gilding inside the room, the architecture bigger and bolder than anything she'd seen before its installation when she was a girl or since. A signal from her father that not only did they belong, but it would take quite the feat to push them out.

Plastering her largest smile on her face, Isabelle stepped over the threshold as the doors opened at the sound of her name, her grandmother and Pena closing ranks around her. The arched ceiling with its frescoes and dotted windows exposed the starry night sky above as the golden chandeliers bathed her in light. No matter what happened, at least her family would put on a show.

Even the Duke of Sussex would be impressed.

Oh, how her father would've loved this: the lights, the food, the people, the promise of fun in the air.

But he couldn't. And now she'd have to enjoy it all without him.

Swallowing a hard lump in her throat, she lowered herself in her most proper, practiced curtsy to the mass of guests lining the silk-tapestried walls. Each one returned the gesture, offering applause as well. "My grandmother and I are so honored to welcome you to our home to help us celebrate our continued good relations with our neighbors as we prepare ourselves to welcome a new member into our family," she said. "I know we will be pleased with our decision, though it will be quite difficult, as we hold you all in high esteem."

Her grandmother said a few additional words of

welcome before introducing the troupe of acrobats and jugglers who'd serve as their entertainment for the evening. Isabelle squinted, working to find Aaron as a raucous cheer rang from the crowd—loud enough that the other woman began stealing glances at the gentile set to make sure they weren't offended. But none of the assembled group were frowning, and the Duke of Sussex himself—Prince Augustus Frederick, the king's younger brother and the most critical of their guests— appeared relaxed. A relief for sure. After all, there was only so much worry one could manage at once.

With another set of bows and curtsies, she and her grandmother retreated to their seats at the far end to watch the performances. They were joined by Sussex, the rabbis of the major synagogues, and a few select business acquaintances, including, unfortunately, all three of the Berab brothers.

Her breath hitched as she spotted Aaron weaving through the crowd, tossing three clubs—one at a time to give the illusion of skill—amusing and distracting guests with smiles and presumably a few jokes.

However, despite the talent of the main performers at the center of the room, she could not seem to stop staring at him. Because he might have already gathered more information, she reasoned. She twisted her favorite opal ring over her glove.

Patience. She needed to be patient. There would be time for her to decide. She had her own job now.

Turning to Rebecca, who had taken the seat to her left, still playing with Baron—who was *her* dog—she lowered her voice. "You're useless, you know?"

"The job you've assigned me is keeping up appearances for the gentiles and enjoying the spectacle. I'm

quite adept at both aspects," Rebecca whispered back as
Baron scrapped and settled upon her skirts. "Besides,
you're practically invincible. Not only are you charming and attractive with more money than God, you have
your own henchman."

"He's only temporary. And doesn't come cheap," she
murmured. She'd have to forgo the pearl earbobs she'd
been eyeing for the past few months. At least until the
rest of her finances and her marriage were settled.

"You were the one who offered him all your easily accessible funds." Her friend sniffed. "And here I
thought you were supposed to be the master negotiator."

"I am, which is why there was no negotiation—
I made a proposal and he accepted it. I assessed him
correctly and offered him what he wanted." Isabelle
leaned in closer to the other woman, willing herself not
to glance at Aaron and study how his face was now lit
almost as brightly as it had been when he regaled the
children with stories and sweets. Or worse, stare at the
way his costume pulled tight against his body every
time he threw and, more, bent.

"Who wouldn't want two hundred pounds?" Rebecca
had her eyes on the other performers as she spoke, her
lips barely moving.

"It's not the money—it's what the money can offer
him." Isabelle clapped and smiled as a man in shock-
ing yellow did a backflip, landing perilously close to her
feet.

"That sort of money offers a great deal to many people." Her friend rubbed Baron's ears.

"True." Isabelle wrinkled her nose. "But he wants
more than mere material things."

"Does he?" Rebecca itched her ear. "And how might

you know that about a man you didn't know existed before last Shabbas?"

"Master negotiator, like I said." Isabelle glanced at the rabbis and their families, all enthralled with the jumps and leaps. Pleased with her and her family. No, the Liras couldn't boast an impressive scholarly lineage, but they were important, damn it. And would stay that way. She'd make sure of it. That was why she was doing all this, after all. Well, that and to assist with the community's advancement and protection and such.

And provided she obtained the perfect husband, she would succeed on both fronts. "I research and use the information I glean to make certain I get what I want, no surprises."

"Clearly." Her friend gave an enthusiastic clap as a man was tossed so high, he near touched the painted cherubs on the ceiling, grazing the largest of the dozen jeweled chandeliers. Her grandmother would not be pleased. Rebecca released a slow breath before turning to her again. "Which is why you definitely needed to know his opinion on kissing."

"Yes. He's a man and I'm going to marry one, and even if he doesn't come with the necessary stature and accoutrements—thus, who better to ask?" Isabelle squeezed her hands together, sneaking another view at Aaron, who was now teasing an elderly guest, appearing to attempt some sort of flip, but then flopping on the floor in an exaggerated fall as the man whooped great belly laughs. With a broad, warm grin, he pushed back onto his feet, giving a bow to happy applause. She wet her lips. He was certainly quite a bit more…limber…than she anticipated.

"No, I don't suppose you could ask Pena." The other

woman snorted, though Isabelle could not quite tear her eyes away to even glance at her friend.

"No, I could not." With all her will, she forced herself to gaze down at her gloves. One of the beaded buttons was loose. Twirling it, she worked to retie the thread. "And while I don't expect love, like I said before, I would like physical compatibility."

"And a synagogue custodian can assist you with that?" Rebecca's eyes were on a man walking on his hands, technically superior to Aaron but without his inexplicable flair—at least to her untrained eyes.

"He's smarter than people give him credit for. And if you ask me how I know, I'll stab you with a hat pin. I have good sense in such matters. That's all." Isabelle cheered as the performer bowed. "I certainly wasn't picturing kissing him." On his lips.

On his neck.

Her companion said nothing, just patted her hair and snuggled the dog once more, her eyes now on Isabelle alone. Judging.

"Don't look at me like that," she hissed at the other woman. "My head will not be turned by anyone inappropriate. I will pick a suitable, useful husband. I promise."

"Be careful," Rebecca hissed in return. "You're playing with...well..." She indicated a juggler—a real one—who was now holding a torch. "And I'm not sure you're trained on how not to get burned."

"You'd be surprised," Isabelle muttered under her breath before turning and raising both eyebrows at her companion. "And if not, I have access to a great deal of water."

"You did have plenty to amuse yourself with earlier."

Rebecca's knowing look made Isabelle blush. "You're determined—I'll give you that. And no fool." Her friend glanced to the side before dropping her voice. "It's just, I—"

"Pardon me." Her grandmother stepped between them and tapped Isabelle on the shoulder. "Prepare yourself. It's time that you meet some people—clients and their favorites."

Isabelle ground her back teeth to stop from grimacing. That was what she was there to do. Swiping her thumb one last time over the loose button, she nodded to her grandmother, readying herself.

Everything would turn out for the best. She'd choose wisely, and her life would be right again. She reached out to squeeze Rebecca's hand, but her grandmother had already nudged her friend to the side.

She followed the older woman toward a line of men, only to start at a light tap on her shoulder. Before she could pivot, Aaron's lips grazed her ear as he whispered, "You dropped this."

Glancing down, she found her fan pattering against her elbow. "Thank you," she murmured through the odd tingles that seemed to always rise when he was near. Robbing her of necessary focus. She snatched the object back from him.

"Good luck finding your charming prince," he replied, distinctly smug, as he moved back into the throng, approaching a group of young men—two of which were on the list—with a bow, leaving her alone once more.

Not that she could object.

It was her time to shine and seize control of the life and status that were rightfully hers.

Aaron worked not to injure himself as he pretended to throw a juggling club, torn between listening to the third man on the list converse with a companion, and working not to glare at the back of Solomon Weiss's head as Isabelle eyed him with interest.

A banker whose family had all but left the community, he was the boldest would-be suitor yet. The others had stayed within earshot of not only her grandmother but the rabbis. And they had kept a respectful distance.

But Weiss had somehow managed to maneuver the lady of the hour onto a gilded fainting couch beneath a large window and behind the dais. More importantly, out of her grandmother's direct line of vision.

Setting down the clubs, he held his breath and darted behind a potted plant next to the couple. Not that he was curious about their conversation—he just needed to regroup for a moment to decide whom to spy on next.

After all, that was what he had been hired to do.

Still, he couldn't help peeking through the leaves at his employer, who was sitting on blue velvet, her knee nearly touching her current suitor's. His hand was perilously close to her arm, above the bare, tempting skin between her sleeve and glove. Reminding him of the other night and of how soft he'd imagined it would feel.

"So, Mr. Weiss, what did you think about *William Tell*?" Isabelle flitted her fan away from her body, shielding her face and her actions from anyone but her guest.

Aaron froze. The opera had premiered at Drury Lane two springs prior, during his brief time on the West End streets. He'd sneaked into the wings for shelter during a downpour and been enthralled enough to return every night of the run. The story, along with his off-key humming, was now a favorite of the synagogue's children.

And to think, while he'd been in the back, peeking out between the slats of an abandoned crate, she'd been in the front, in a velvet-covered seat, with a full, unobstructed view of the stage and all its magic. Though that wasn't such a stretch. That was where she, unlike him, belonged. Where Weiss belonged too, probably.

"He was quite the historical figure." The oblivious dandy's eyes narrowed despite the practiced smoothness of his words.

Isabelle raised both eyebrows. "Yes. Quite an excellent choice for Mr. Rossini to use as an inspiration." Her lip twitched, hiding her amusement.

Weiss blinked, realization flashing on his features. Good—perhaps he'd slink away now, properly humiliated, as he clearly was not worthy of her time and attentions.

But no such luck.

Instead, the other man cleared his throat. "Yes, his operas are spectacular." Weiss reached out to stroke Isabelle's thumb. "I presume you caught that performance?"

Not appropriate at all for the edge of a ballroom. Though one had to admire his moxie.

"Yes." She nodded sharply but did not pull away. "The music was quite effective."

Moving back toward the center of the ballroom, lest he be spotted and accused of neglecting his entertainment duties, Aaron did a series of the clownish twirls the children at the synagogue liked so much and glanced toward Pena, but the man was focused on Mrs.

Lira, who was chatting with a few older couples and, naturally, the Duke of Sussex himself.

"I shall have to see it someday." Weiss leaned closer, not releasing her hand. No, now he was pulling her wrist onto his lap. "Or perhaps we could see it together?"

Oy. Aaron rolled his eyes as he retook his juggling clubs. He mimicked tossing and strolled back toward the couple—someone should be watching them, right?

"Maybe. I'll have to consult my schedule." She lifted her fan with her free hand, hiding her mouth, though there was a distinct sarcastic note in her voice.

"Perhaps it could be our schedule." The other man delivered the line smoothly before gracefully drawing even nearer to Isabelle. "Or perhaps it will be."

The man was skilled. And determined. *More* than determined. A bit like the lady herself, not willing to leave the negotiation table without a commitment. Aaron caught a pin behind his back and squeezed, his fingers itching to, well, grab the man by the necktie and shove him off the chaise.

The corners of Isabelle's eyes crinkled, though her back was rigid and her lips tight. "I believe I'm the sort of person who prefers their own schedule."

"That's important too." Weiss nodded with a quick vigor. "Claiming one's own time. I respect people who do that." He leaned in further, as if he was going to attempt a kiss—with the entire community watching.

Oy. He needed to stop this. Aaron bent to set his clubs on the ground.

After all, the princess would not be able to pay him if her grandmother actually locked her in a tower.

But before he could physically interrupt the couple, Isabelle was on her feet, nearly knocking into Weiss's nose as he scrambled back. "That's a very lovely notion," she said with an implacable, polite calm. She adjusted her gloves as she glanced down at him. "Will you excuse me for one moment? I have a loose button and should repair it before the next performance."

Weiss retook her hand. "Perhaps we can chat more later?" He arched an eyebrow, his playful tone at odds with the intense look in his eyes.

"Perhaps." She deftly extricated herself from his grasp and pressed a coy finger to her lips. "I *have* been meaning to sample the refreshments." Then she touched him, laying a hand on his shoulder. "I just adore berries." When she winked, Weiss near tripped over his own feet hurrying to do her bidding.

Aaron held his breath as Isabelle's shoulders finally relaxed, only for her to exhale harshly when she called over her shoulder. "You should step back, Mr. Ellenberg, lest you upturn the fig tree, and we couldn't have that. Especially since you've given such a robust performance so far." She threw him a wink of his own. "I knew you'd be a good hire."

And with a snap of her fan, she swept past the potted plant, leaving him to stare after her.

Chapter Eleven

Isabelle smoothed her petticoats and stepped away from the now vacant chaise, heart thumping against her ribs. That was—well, what exactly? Solomon Weiss had touched her. And touched her. And *touched* her.

And it hadn't been completely unpleasant.

He was charming and clever, but perhaps too clever? Or too slippery. Or too likely to trounce her in chess. An uncomfortable flush flooded her senses. The sensation akin to doubt—or worse, nerves. Which could not happen. Certainly not in public.

Sweat pricked her brow and she flipped her fan a few times, but the noxious heat did not cease. Mercy, she needed quiet, just a minute to collect herself and her thoughts and strategize. She scanned the throng for Rebecca, but her friend had wandered to one of the long refreshment tables and was sipping punch, deep in conversation with two older women. She could use something a touch stronger than whatever was in her friend's glass.

Isabelle went to her grandmother, her silver skirts contrasting with the woman's burgundy. The elder Lira squeezed Isabelle's hand as she nodded at whatever the Duke of Sussex was saying to the assembled

Jewish leaders. The only words Isabelle could make out over the murmurs were "emancipation" and "oath" and "lower house."

Not that she couldn't guess at the conversation. Even before this new potential bill had been introduced, the Duke of Sussex had been the biggest gentile champion of Jewish rights in England. A powerful ally, to be sure, but unfortunately a rather singular figure, both among the gentry and among the greater communities that inhabited the land.

On her toes, she pressed her lips right above the older woman's earbobs and whispered. "I'm going to adjust myself in the ladies' lounge."

"Return quickly," her grandmother commanded, eyes still on their guest. "You have quite a few people to meet— gentiles as well as Jews. See that you follow all their rules. Proper greetings, proper curtsies, while addressing every- one by their proper—albeit confusing—titles."

"I'll be sure to correctly place my hands and only ask questions—not expound—about only the most, by their definition, 'ladylike' of subject matters." Isabelle smoothed her skirts again. "They may lock the gates to their power tight, but no one learns and memorizes rules like Jews."

"Perform well, but not too well." Her grandmother whispered the familiar instructions, ones that had been repeated as long as Isabelle could remember. "Flatter them, not yourself."

"Noted." She bussed the woman's cheek. "I will do what is necessary. And be back quickly."

"And be careful." Her grandmother's sharp eyes scanned the crowd and paused. "There are eyes and ears everywhere, and not all are friendly."

Isabelle followed her grandmother's gaze to a group of well-heeled gentiles before another form distracted her.

Aaron.

She cocked her head as he made a handkerchief disappear with one palm while helping steady an elderly gentleman's drink with the other. A grateful flush spread over the other man's cheeks, but Aaron only gave a slight nod.

Clever, preserving the man's drink and dignity without the distracted crowd noticing, saving him quite a bit of embarrassment.

"Ahem." The tut from her grandmother brought her back to their purposes. Her gaze now having followed Isabelle's, the woman's lips tightened, and her eyes narrowed, almost as if she was studying his grease-paint-covered face, working to place him.

Not good. She needed to divert her grandmother's attention. Isabelle cleared her throat. "The main performances are going to begin again soon—will you check all is ready? I need to hurry. As you said, there are others you want me to meet before the evening is over. If I'm going to escape for a moment, it has to be now." She wove around the back of the group so as not to attract too much attention as she exited.

However, instead of retreating to the area designated for ladies to freshen up, Isabelle trotted up the back staircase toward the library, where her father had kept a decent bottle of gin behind a bust of Julius Caesar. It was still there when last she checked—the prior day.

Inhaling the far less stifling air, she moved past the comfortable fire. Crossing to the far side, she rooted around for a glass inside a hollowed globe and poured herself a drink.

At the sound of scraping behind her, she whirled around. But it was only Aaron sliding into the room, quietly shutting the door behind him. A pleasant humming stirred beneath her skin at his presence.

Though, why shouldn't she be happy to see him? His appearance undoubtedly meant that he had news and her plan was coming to fruition. Reaching back into the globe, she pulled out another empty glass and raised it to him. He shook his head, dimming her excitement a touch. Ah well, his loss. She replaced the empty glass and raised her own to him.

"It isn't kosher, and I know people can become carried away with it, but..." She took a long sip, savoring the burn, leaning against the two-story-high bookcase. "Sometimes one needs something a bit more pungent than champagne."

Aaron paced over the bright red-and-orange patterned rug, tracing a finger along a distant shelf. "You're a terrible liar," he called to her without turning around, his arms straining at his tight costuming.

Isabelle wrinkled her nose. What did he mean by that?

"Oh, I promise you, this gin is most certainly necessary and not something my family should have lying about. But no one ever said we got to where we are by asking permission—within the community and outside it." She took another gulp before straightening herself and crossing the room so she could read his face better in the firelight. "And if you were referring to my earlier performances, I believe I was rather adept. Especially with Mr. Weiss."

"Really?" He plucked a slim volume from the shelf and turned it over in his hand.

"And he handled his stumble well." She glanced at the spine. The Grimm Brothers. Fitting, given his performance in the synagogue. Not a book she'd picked up in years. Perhaps she should reread it if she was going to make up more stories in the future. Though she'd skip all the ones where the happy endings were predicated on Jews coming to an untimely demise, of course. Hard to do, as—like with most literature written by gentiles—their belief in her kind's superlative villainy was a popular trope, whether explicit or implied.

Her thoughts returned to the man before her. "I didn't leave him much room to not look foolish, yet he managed to keep his head above water." Weiss's deflections replayed in her head. He was smooth under pressure; she'd give him that.

"So he passed your test? Or at least one of them?" Aaron had turned around fully. His eyes gleamed with intensity beneath the white grease paint, which only served to make his thick black brows more prominent. But he was more house cat than wolf. No matter how fierce he appeared or what role he played at.

"I suppose." She stepped back to lean against the mahogany reading table—fine, not lean, but sit atop. Crossing her feet, she allowed them to swing a little. "He could've been honest and admitted his mistake. But the ability to adapt in social situations is an important skill, at least in our world."

"In your world," he corrected.

"In my world." She pursed her lips. "And yours too. You're my spy now, after all."

"I don't have any illusions. I'm a custodian playing

at henchman, nothing more. Whether I obtain information that's useful to you or not, tomorrow morning, I'll wake up, splash some water on my face, and scrub the floor. Before dusting. And sweeping." Aaron ran a finger over the ornamental bust of Virgil, stroking his laurel, his voice a tad thick. "You need to remember that before you make me into something I'm not."

What did one say to that? Isabelle glanced down at her gloves. The thread she'd wound before had come undone and now threatened the button anew. Placing her drink on the wood, she started on her other glove so she could reclaim the dexterity of bare skin.

"And he certainly seems to like you."

She near jumped as Aaron's voice seemed to boom from his new position, a plush armchair at her side. He tugged at the collar of his harlequin costume, pulling it taut. It was rather flimsy, wasn't it? Not that she was staring. She averted her eyes once more, returning to her task.

"I'm not sure about that," she muttered. Fiddlesticks. Why were these buttons so small and plentiful? Or more, why were her fingers so clumsy?

"He was practically ravishing you in public." Aaron leaned forward, frowning—at her incompetence or actions, it was rather hard to tell.

Ugh. If she'd wanted to be chided, she'd go be with her grandmother. Or Pena. She continued her slow, clumsy progress. "He was doing no such thing. He touched my hand."

When she was finally free, she raised the appendage as if Aaron needed a demonstration. "My *gloved* hand, and I didn't tell him to stop. I didn't take you for a prig regarding such things." With a bit of flourish, she bent and tied off the loose thread on her other glove.

"I'm not." Aaron rose and grabbed her glass, finishing it off.

"Good thing I didn't want any more," she grumbled.

He shook his head and glanced toward the window, a small sliver of the moon visible against the dark sky. "I thought you and your family cared about your reputation and all who rely on you to advance their standing. That's certainly a breach of goyishe etiquette." He laid the glass down with a thud and turned to her. "The rabbis are probably apoplectic."

"Ha. If they saw, they're pretending they didn't, as it helps the greater good, and at least he made an attempt not to flaunt his flirtations in front of the community. And I promise, there were no gentile witnesses. I've performed in front of them since I was a child, and I've yet to drop a cue." She slid her glove back on and worked the first button. "As I said before, while attraction is not the most important factor ideally, I'd like it to be present. After all, if I'm going to marry someone, shouldn't I—I don't know—not find his touch repulsive?" She sighed. Fifteen more to go.

"Do you find Weiss's touch repulsive?" He folded his arms tight across his chest, the fabric straining against his muscles.

"No." She shook her head to further affirm the answer. It was the truth. His touch was indeed not repulsive per se. Just not quite what she had envisioned, that was all. But really, few things in life were.

"But you didn't like it?" He rounded the table and leaped so he was sitting atop it behind her, his legs hanging down, close enough to breathe down her neck. "Wouldn't want him to do this?" His voice was soft, with a slight tremor, but he reached out and lightly stroked her neck with a single finger, in the exact same spot she'd touched back in the men's smoking room.

Almost as if she'd willed him to do it. Her breath caught in her throat for a moment as every part of her being rose to attention. Desire swelled in her.

Not good. Nor appropriate. Nor useful. She needed to save those feelings for her suitors. She turned back to her—what did he keeping calling himself?—henchman and gave her best impression of her grandmother at her most imperious.

"Are our chairs not good enough for you?" she asked.

He raised both shoulders but didn't rise.

"And I didn't say I didn't like Weiss's touch." She picked at a button with her blunted, gloved fingers, guiding the slippery silk through the hole. "It was fine." Something she could get used to, even. And maybe one day enjoy, which was frankly better than most of the scenarios she'd considered.

"So you have a well-heeled, well-connected liar whose touch is 'fine'? A stunning recommendation as a husband." Aaron's sardonic chuckle vibrated into her.

"I'm a liar at times. Everyone is. And his lies were clever and useful, which bodes well for his negotiation prowess." She poked at the next button. *There we go— just come right through.*

"But? I hear a 'but.'" He leaned forward, close enough that she could almost feel his legs wrapping themselves around her hips. She sighed and turned to face him, halting her progress with the buttons. "But I wonder if he will prove too useful. If he will seek to manipulate me, instead of manipulating *with* me to our joint, familial advantage."

"Ah." He gave a slow nod. "Because one good turn does not deserve another?" He gave her the closest thing to a smile he'd offered all evening, and it felt like a victory, even more than her performance with the banker.

"He doesn't need more power over me." She grimaced.

"Is Weiss off your list, then?" But before she could answer, he crooked a finger at her. "Give me your arm. Otherwise, we're going to be here all night. Someone will notice your absence, so that Pena will come looking, and if he finds us, well... I saw his fists."

"Don't you know there are more ways to assert control over a situation besides violence? And here I thought you had a good imagination." She snickered before shaking her arm in frustration. "This is why I should've gone to the ladies' salon. I'd have maids to assist with these sorts of things." But he did make a point. And she was certainly adult enough to control whatever misdirected attraction her overtired body was directing at him.

Ah well, her grandmother would not be pleased, but what she didn't know couldn't hurt her.

She laid her wrist in his hand. His finger brushed the inside, and she shivered despite the fire. Yet her face was hot, though she neither sweated nor felt those damn nerves like she had in the ballroom.

No, it was almost as if she was coming down with a fever but hadn't quite gone under its spell.

"I'll try to be up to their standards with my measly menial skills," he said before lowering her arm to his lap. Now her hand shook too. And there was definite dizziness fuzzing her brain, especially when she tilted her chin up to meet his gaze. "But you didn't answer my question—is Weiss out of contention?"

She swallowed, averting her gaze so she could ground herself, fight whatever illness this was. "Not in the slightest. Besides, I have to know his secrets before making a final decision."

"So if he has a good secret you can extort him with, you'll take him?" He tugged her closer to him as he moved up her arm, expertly fastening each button, his tone cool and even against the rising heat in the room.

"Perhaps." She breathed the word, forcing herself back into her head, back to her plan, back to picturing Weiss. "Honestly, he's a solid choice. He's not a fool, he's ambitious, he's reasonably agreeable to view, and he has enough charm and connections that he should be able to assist in not only maintaining but expanding the company, but hopefully allowing me to retain control since his family has a business of its own. Further, he'd make an excellent delegate and probably relish that opportunity enough to make that his focus, not controlling what is mine."

Aaron chuckled. "You really aren't romantic in any way, are you?" He gave her arm a pat as he finished, his hand lingering on her wrist. "Despite your quest for a handsome husband."

"Under Jewish law, I'm owed physical pleasure as a wife, so it would be...goyishe for me to deny myself that," she told him, stumbling only a touch over the Yiddish. "Romance is entirely different and unnecessary." And to her utter embarrassment, she made a small whimpering noise as he rubbed her wrist, making a circling pattern right on the most delicate spot—the joint that connected to her hand. Yet somehow, she couldn't quite pull away or stop staring, even as her cheeks burned. "Is that something you want?" she managed to ask.

"Yes." He released her wrist and sprang down from the table. "It's unfortunate."

"What is?" she asked as he dusted his trousers.

"Having all the money in the world and still limiting your possibilities." He straightened to his full height, as if to remind her that he was indeed quite a bit larger than she.

"Money is a tool. Even the sharpest knife can't cut butter that doesn't exist. Besides, if you know you can't have what you want, there's no profit in wishing for it." She gave him her most imperious nod. "As is arguing when it gains you nothing." She edged toward the door as she worked to regain all her composure.

But he gave her a surprisingly full smile in response. "I won't say it gains me nothing. I enjoy arguing. It makes the time go by. Besides, isn't that what we're known best for?"

"Indeed." She glanced toward the doorway, already bracing herself to rally for the crowd once more. "I should get back."

"Perhaps Weiss will have brought you more of these." He reached behind his back and thrust a plate filled with berries at her.

Had he always had that? Where had he been hiding it? His sleight of hand skills truly were impressive. No wonder children adored him so much. The Great Synagogue should really pay him double. Perhaps her family should make another donation after her marriage.

"Thank you," she murmured before popping one into her mouth—and another and another as he watched. She pushed the plate toward him, offering them to him, but he shook his head. Finally, she'd filled herself and they were left staring. At each other. Again.

She inhaled. "So."

"So," he replied, running his hand over the top of the table. "Out of curiosity, did you enjoy *William Tell*?"

She started. Of all the questions . . . She wrinkled her nose. "Very much so. Why?"

He stared at her for a long moment. "I saw it too. Well, some of it. I'd sneaked in and hid backstage . . ."

Excitement rose and she leaned forward. "I wish you could've seen the whole thing, from a seat. It was just . . ." She wobbled a little. "Foolish rug," she muttered as he raced over, threading his arm through hers, steadying her against his body. And the heat was back.

"Clearly." Amusement in his voice as those odd tingles shot through her entire being.

"Anyway." She righted herself against him before pushing off, onto her own two feet. "It was brilliant— the cast, the score, all of it. I saw it with my grandmother, Pena, and my father, but I—you would've been excellent company."

His eyes grew wide, and he stared at her for a long moment. "I see Weiss isn't the only charming liar about."

Only years of practice hid her flinch. What she'd said was true—while she adored her family, it would've been enjoyable to watch with someone closer to her age. Especially someone as handsome and easy to speak with as Aaron. Not that she could tell him that. Instead, she adjusted her bracelets and stuck her nose in the air, in her best, most haughty imitation of her grandmother. "Takes one to know one."

He blinked at her before a wide smile spread over his lips, and the blasted tingles were back.

"We'll have to see how many more you find." He winked at her, and damned if she didn't threaten to wobble once more. After this was over, she was going to bed. For a day and a half. At least. Someone could bring the contracts and books and information files to her.

Chapter Twelve

Ears still ringing from the conversation with Aaron, Isabelle reentered her festival with the poise and grace that had been drilled into her from birth. With her most practiced, solicitous smile, she greeted each guest carefully and personally as she pressed farther into the room.

"There you are." Her grandmother took her arm the moment she passed the refreshment table, preventing her from grabbing a glass of champagne for fortification. She pulled Isabelle along with a forceful yank. "I need you to make more time for a few people, starting with His Grace," she whispered in her ear before releasing her hold.

Isabelle rubbed her arm before tipping her chin to acknowledge the tall, regal man, of whom her father had always been so fond. She bobbed into her deepest, most formal curtsy, despite the fact she'd once rode the man's back as if he were a horse while he crawled on the floor of her father's office. In her defense, she had been five at the time.

"Miss Lira, how are you?" The Duke of Sussex brushed his now gray curls from his forehead, his smile as kind as she remembered.

"I'm well, Your Grace. A trifle nervous, but well." She pushed to match his warmth. Her grandmother gave her one of those famous nudges—*ow*. Isabelle rubbed her side. Now that was going to bruise. "Thank you so much for honoring us with your presence."

"It is I who am honored to be your guest. I was so fond of your late father." The duke inclined his head, lowering his voice to a conspiratorial whisper. "And I don't fault you for being nervous. It's a lot of attention at once, but I know you're more than worthy of it."

Isabelle flushed. If only. Though this was a man to emulate. His propensity for charm was unparalleled. If there was anyone who could succeed in pushing through emancipation, it was most certainly him. She fluttered her fan. "Oh, Your Grace, that's very kind of you to say."

"It's very true," the older man said. His voice lowered more. "Which is why I wanted to mention something to you." He glanced around before beckoning her a few steps farther away from the crowd. "I couldn't help but notice you spent quite a bit of time with Solomon Weiss."

Isabelle frowned. Was there an issue with Weiss? One Aaron hadn't identified? Or worse, hadn't told her? A small sting twisted in her gut, even as she schooled her features and searched for the proper response to the duke's query. "He was very attentive, Your Grace, though I do not know him well. Do you know his family?"

"Only a touch," the man said. "His older brother is friendly with the Viscount Penrose and his sister. Decent people." The duke pursed his lips. "And I'm sure not a bad choice. Though I know you have many excellent choices at your disposal. Choices who will no doubt benefit your standing in your community and ours."

Isabelle searched her mind for a proper response, to not offend their most important ally.

"I truly hope so," she said simply.

"The younger Weiss might do quite well," the duke continued. "He and his brother seem to learn fast. However, I have found even allies in my world hold onto prejudices, ridiculous as they may be. Especially against those who are more newly arrived in England," he added. "Not that your charm can't smooth those relationships. It's only...I have met so many excellent men at Bevis Marks through my friendship with Rabbi Raphael, whose council I value dearly. Though I am sure you too are acquainted with such men and are carefully considering them as well."

"I certainly am. It would be an honor to marry any of them," she said with her best nod, her throat burning at the lie. Well, not exactly a lie. Many would make excellent matches, as the matchmaker had pointed out. But could she ever truly trust them, in the end, to side with her and not the Berabs—their own true peers? Even *with* leverage.

Though she couldn't explain that to Sussex, not when his support of the community as a whole was so critical. After all, while their permitted existence should not depend on their perceived goodness, the gulf between *should* and *is* was far too wide. Best for all their health to keep their less-than-flattering intercommunal battles hidden.

"Well said, Your Grace," Isabelle replied instead. "Your wisdom and counsel is much appreciated."

"I'm very glad to be of service," the man said with a small bow. "Your father was such a good friend to me, and you are such a lovely girl. I do want the best for you and for your people."

"I will work very hard to make both of you proud." She gave the man another curtsy, her mind spinning with—not doubts. She never had doubts. She had thoughts—and a longing to share them with someone.

Two hours later, the crowd finally began to thin. Aaron stood back with the other performers for the entire long line of goodbyes from the multitude of people important enough or brave enough to approach the family.

The next festival might prove a challenge—musical performances. He was sure to be stuck in the shadows for that. However, the third—now that was his best chance of capturing just a bit of magic. It was to be a masked ball with no dancing, as even that could not be justified during the Omer, but a full theatrical production instead. Hopefully, Isabelle would costume him as a performer, maybe one playing a soldier or an influential townsperson. Just something more than what he was. Just to let him imagine for a few minutes.

Or, better yet, just to prelude his new reality, after he earned his fee and found a wife of his own.

What would Isabelle think of him dressed like a true gentleman? She'd never treated him with pity, but they were so far apart...What would it be like if they were equals? If he really was the one to accompany her to the opera like she'd suggested. Would she like him better or worse than Shultz or Weiss or whomever she was being pushed toward on her side of the community? Would he be enough? Even if he'd been born with more luck, would he have still failed to make, well, anything of himself? Or more, if he did earn the two hundred pounds, would it truly change his life?

"Mrs. Lira, this evening was just spectacular." A deep male voice boomed across the room, drawing Aaron's attention.

"Mr. Berab, it was so lovely for you and your brothers to honor us with your presence tonight." Isabelle's grandmother blocked the man who spoke, and presumably his brothers, from view.

"It was our honor to be invited," a different man responded in a strong tenor.

"As if there was any doubt? Your family has been our dear friends for so long," Isabelle's grandmother replied, her voice warm—almost as warm as when she had addressed the Duke of Sussex. But not quite enough to hide the clear note of insincerity underneath, piquing his curiosity.

Not that Isabelle's grandmother's social life and political rivalries were his business. However, it was odd. And there was something rather familiar about her, something he couldn't quite place, that drew him in.

Quick as he could, he slid away from the group and ducked behind a large fern, contorting to hide his limbs. Pivoting, he dipped farther into the shadows, angling himself so he could still watch the family—and these brothers, of whom he now had a clear view.

"And we feel the same way about you." The eldest of the three's tone was congenial, but his eyes narrowed beneath his large brows. "And we care about dear

Isabelle and making sure her future is successful and most beneficial and pleasant for all involved."

"Which is why my brother and I want to reiterate our offers of marriage. Either of us would make a superior choice." The second of the group clasped a hand on the shoulder of the youngest and, by far, the most handsome of the three, who glanced down at his polished boots, his cheeks coloring.

Oy. More suitors. Berab...Berab...Why did that name sound familiar? Aaron ran his tongue over his teeth. The eldest, the one not offering his hand, he was a delegate, right? Which should make either of the other two much more desirable, and yet the way Isabelle's grandmother spoke to them...He stared harder as his mind churned.

"We're so very flattered by your generous offer, Louis. And Roger's as well. They are much appreciated." Mrs. Lira practically batted her eyes at the men. "You both are being carefully considered."

"Excellent. I'm glad *you* at least are open to reason." The eldest's jaw tightened. "Perhaps you can convince your granddaughter that marrying one of my brothers would be best for not only her but for your family, for ours, and for the community. Both my brothers are far better matches than someone like Solomon Weiss, with better connections and established places in the community. Not to mention, the integration into the business would be a great deal smoother."

"Oh, but smooth waters make for a dull ride." It was Isabelle who spoke, drawing closer, her inflection and tone almost identical to her grandmother's.

Four heads turned. Even the youngest—Richard?

Roger?—was no longer studying the wood grain in the floor—instead staring shyly at her. Though who could blame him? She really did carry herself like a queen.

"I didn't take you for an adventurer." The middle brother—what was his name again? Levi? Lionel? Louis?—edged toward Isabelle, a genuine curiosity in his tone.

"I'm a Lira. I assess risk, but I don't shy away from it when there's a good reward," she told the middle brother, her bright smile now competing with the chandeliers.

"You sound like your late father," he murmured before moving so close to Isabelle that his sleeve brushed the gap between her gloves and her sleeve.

Aaron moved out from the shadows, to Pena's side, using the other man's body to shield him from view, though still keeping close enough to—well, he didn't know precisely what, but at least put some sort of end to anything inappropriate, he supposed.

What was with these men taking unrequested liberties with her person?

"Louis," the eldest snapped.

Isabelle, however, merely laughed. "I can't decide if that's a good thing or a bad thing, considering your plans for me." Whipping out her fan, she backed away, far enough that this Louis would have to reach out to touch her again.

The knot in Aaron's chest loosened. She truly was quite adept, wasn't she?

"It's a compliment. David thought of him as blood, and you could make it a reality." He stepped forward again but kept a more polite distance and thumbed the tassel hanging off her fan. A low growl erupted from

Aaron, loud enough for Pena to turn around and give him a quizzical glance. He inclined his head back to the group, trying to signal to the older man that he ought to do his damned job.

"I really hope we can all come to an understanding, no matter whom you choose." The eldest brother's voice was oddly rough, almost emotional, as he slipped next to Louis, blocking Aaron's view. "Even if my preference for your future husband is a touch biased."

"I hope that too, very much." Isabelle's voice, in turn, remained cool and detached. "And we do appreciate your support." Her dark hair gleamed onyx beneath the chandelier lights as she slid both hands behind her back. "No matter what happens, I also believe the festivals will benefit us all. We're reaffirming once again that both our families put the community first, even if we no longer live in Aldgate, court gentile clientele, and attend the synagogues less regularly. That we still care and can still lead."

"Yes, we certainly do and can. Better than most." Roger's voice was equally even as he leaned away from Isabelle and toward her grandmother. "I appreciate that we all still agree on that. Though I truly do believe we can agree on so much more."

Oh, I'm sure you do, Aaron thought silently—or so he had believed until Pena's elbow came in contact with his ribs. *Ow.* He rubbed the spot and glared at the man.

"Think carefully about how you want the future to look, and make your decisions accordingly—that's my advice. We are certainly operating under that strategy." The oldest brother's tone was grim. "And best of luck to you, Miss Isabelle."

"Thank you." She gave him a polite, formal curtsy.

"Thank you all. No matter what, I look forward to our continued partnership."

"Yes," her grandmother said, a bright smile on her face. "I am sure we can all come to an agreement soon, assuring that both families will live happily ever after."

"Oh yes, I'm sure." The man did not smile, but he gave her a small bow before strolling out, head held high, his brothers flanking him.

Aaron glanced at Isabelle, who was now nodding as her grandmother furiously whispered in her ear. Her face tightened as something unreadable flickered in her dark brown eyes, but she then lifted her chin defiantly, accepting the woman's arm and strolling back to a crowd of well-heeled young men, each with powerful families of their own.

What was that? And who were they? And why did her grandmother's statement sound suspiciously like a ketubah was already being negotiated?

Aaron frowned. If that was true, why would Isabelle have hired him? And have him look into Ashkenazi men? Was another game afoot? His chest tightened as he glanced back at the woman herself. Not that the situation was his business. He was merely a henchman there for a specific job, not her actual friend. Thus, what did it matter if she hadn't told him everything about the situation?

She was now speaking to a group of poorer families, tradesmen and their wives. Her smile, however, was just as broad and natural as it had been for the rabbis.

As they strode away, her grandmother again whispered in her ear. Isabelle turned and embraced her companion, her eyes shining with warmth. She said something he couldn't make out, but the clear love and admiration on both women's faces made Aaron's heart squeeze.

Despite being rather ruthless, Isabelle clearly loved her family and the community and would do right by both. Thus, whomever she actually married was none of his concern. She was paying him for information on six specific men, nothing more and nothing less. After that, well, there would be no reason for either of them to think of the other again. He needed to remember that.

Chapter Thirteen

After bidding the final guests farewell, Isabelle and Rebecca trudged upstairs to her private sitting room. And while her friend yawned and retired to the pink guest room after just a few sips of milk, Isabelle had remained wide awake. For a full half hour, she and Baron paced the stones before her fire, first going over old research files and her father's contract notes, then just walking. However, her mind refused to quiet. The dog, though, fell into a sleepy heap, leaving her completely alone.

With a sigh, Isabelle tied a dressing gown over her night rail and crept down the hall, past her grandmother's rooms, to the small bedchamber adjacent to the one that had belonged to her father.

With her usual three raps, she knocked on the door.

The hinges swung open to reveal Pena, his shirt hastily buttoned but still somehow uncreased, his boots already on his feet. He rubbed his eyes. "You should be asleep."

She bit her lip. He probably had been, despite now being fully dressed. She shouldn't disturb him. But she was selfish, and he was one of the few people who could understand. Had always understood.

"I find I can't." She pushed open the folds of fabric to reveal the sheathed stiletto she still wore. "Will you indulge me?"

"Have I ever not?" He dipped back into the room.

"Never." She followed him, sweeping through the doorway.

"So what you're saying is that the fact you're a spoiled beast is my fault alone?" He yawned, the crinkles beside his eyes deepening.

"Father helped a smidge." She squeezed her thumb and forefinger together. "Though I've always known who to ask if I wanted my way with no resistance."

"What shall it be tonight? Your dagger, or something a bit more challenging?" He moved to the space where he kept his own weapons, and opened the vast cabinet holding the collection.

Isabelle hesitated. The single two-handed sword, her weakest dueling option, would tire her earliest. However, she was not quite in the mood to lose. "Two swords," she replied instead.

He gave her a nod. "You want to actually work instead of playing with the cloak?"

"It comes with a dagger." Her special one. From him. She stroked the metal next to her skin. "And it requires as much skill as the others."

"It doesn't challenge you." Pena adjusted his collar as he glanced in the mirror. Did he see his face as it was now, or the way it'd been before they'd lost her father, when they were both still men in their prime, invincible and in love?

"I don't always need to be challenged." Especially not after performing all night.

He made a noncommittal noise before grabbing

what he needed so they could retreat to her parlor for a greater expanse.

As they entered, she moved to the case on the far side, selecting her weapons from the collection that had once belonged to her grandfather, and his father before him, and his before, and so on. Gifts from the Medici family when the first Liras had been appointed to the Jewish courts in Leghorn. An august body rendered near powerless by changing regimes.

Isabelle gripped the shorter twin swords, preparing herself to strike, just how Pena had taught her. Leaning to her left, she lunged, parrying with her right blade. Quick as ever, the older man met the thrust, as well as the angle from the left, steel crossing steel. He pivoted and turned, so she could circle and ready for her next strike.

"I noticed you managed not to stab any of the Berab brothers," Pena called as he planted his feet. "Your grandmother is pleased."

"Our image is paramount. I'd never stab someone in front of those who hold our future in their hands, let alone current and potential clients. Unless it was for their benefit." Isabelle raised her right blade and struck, just as he'd taught her. "Besides, I had other things on my mind."

"Or people." Steel clashed against steel and he spun from her hold, getting in his own knock to the middle of her left blade. "On your body."

"'Next to' and 'on' are very different, and I promise you, only the latter occurred. Besides, it wasn't as if he even touched bare flesh." She righted herself, bringing up both hands to defend, sweat marring her brow. Two quick strikes and Pena whirled back once more, leaving her dizzy. How the man knew all the older Italian techniques was a mystery. French fencing was all the rage now, so much so that wealthy gentile women indulged. However, what Pena had taught her was far from the genteel show matches held in fashionable drawing rooms or the pantomimes of courtly sparring that were featured onstage.

"The one I saw." The older man leaned an elbow against a wall, calm and collected as she retightened her grip.

Bastard.

Pivoting to hit low, she swung upward. "Roger Berab touched nothing." A clank rang out as he deflected her, though she was ready this time, thrusting with her left blade. "Nor Louis." She repressed a slight shudder. Not that she liked *any* of the brothers, but as for the middle one, there was something about the way his eyes lingered on her breasts. It didn't make her feel wanted and powerful like the few times she'd caught Aaron glancing there—no, Louis's expression was almost…she wrinkled her nose, searching for the word. Perhaps *possessive*? Which made absolutely no sense. With a half step, she caught Pena's second sword.

"You know I was not speaking of them." With a shove, he pressed her back and off him.

"The duke was in good spirits," she said, shifting the topic again, jabbing a little.

"He has no reason not to be." Pena parried back. "We presented him and his allies with quite the entertainment."

"Hopefully more than entertainment. Hopefully grounds for an investment in our inclusion when it comes time to vote." Isabelle quickly countered his blade, only a touch winded.

"You're quite on your game tonight. Impressive attempt at distracting me from the subject at hand. But we must return to it." Pena slammed his steel into hers, raising an eyebrow. "Though I'm not your father, my eyes are still focused where his would've been. Grease paint and a costume are *not* the 'proper attire' the invitation intended."

Isabelle swore under her breath but beat him back with a clang. "You'd still be the one doing the actual watching if he was alive. He'd be socializing. As for Mr. Ellenberg, yes, he's not the husband I need, but that doesn't mean I should be rude." She gave a sharp left thrust and disarmed his dominant side, raising her other arm for the final blow. "Besides, he never touched me."

"If you say so." Pena's back landed against the wall, and he held her gaze. "You were completely alone with him." He dropped his remaining blade to the floor in surrender.

"None of the gentiles saw. I was careful about that. And he's one of us." She released hers as well and paced to the opposite end of the room as she worked to catch her breath. "Besides, do you not trust me to tell the truth?" Isabelle glanced over her shoulder as Pena bent down to palm his fallen swords.

"I have nothing against those among us who cannot learn nor lead, especially those who do contribute what they can. They are valuable in their own way. And you are right not to be unkind to him—you just don't receive any benefit from developing any further acquaintance." He flipped the weapons in his hand and turned sad eyes on her. "And I trust you to tell the most convenient truth for you."

"Like father, like daughter," she muttered, rubbing

her lower back as memories returned, those of a man who never believed he could lose. Who bent all the rules, took all the risks, and reaped all the rewards. Until fate stepped in.

"Very much so." Pena sighed, no doubt drawing on memories of the same time. The narrow escapes he'd made as her father gained and traded on information to build the business—actions that skirted the law but led to his larger-than-life reputation, a legend that only enhanced his appeal, even outside the community. "Though I hope you're a bit cleverer."

"I'm trying to be." Isabelle laid her weapons on the reading table and stroked the twin jewels on the hilts of the swords.

Unlike her father, she was avoiding risks and seeking only to maintain, not build. Protecting the status he'd worked so hard to craft. The only life she knew how to live.

"By focusing on the business and the community's wants and needs instead of your own happiness." Pena moved around the table so they could be face to face.

"He focused plenty on his own happiness." She let go of her weapons and pressed two fingers to her temples. His health was another story, but that was neither here nor there.

"You're gambling with your own future because like him, you can't help yourself." Pena leaned forward, elbows on the table, worry etched into the ever-increasing lines on his face. "And worse, you've enlisted a stranger with his own agenda." He clenched his fists. "Instead of asking for help from those who love you."

"I still want your help, your advice." She laid her

palms flat. "But sometimes another perspective is needed, from one who isn't so close, who isn't so invested in the outcome."

"We want you to be loved and happy. We know there are dangers, that it's hard to trust someone, hard to let them in, but you don't need to worry." Pena took her hand in his, opening her fingers and squeezing, just like he'd done at her father's funeral, and every moment before when she'd felt scared or alone. "We will always protect you. *I* will always protect you. No matter what."

And he had. Like a second father. But now it was her turn. After all, it was her shoulders upon which the weight of the business—and her father's legacy—now lay. This wasn't about her physical safety; it was about the survival of everything she was. And she could not and would not falter.

"I know," she lied.

"I will always be a part of your household, as long as you'll have me." He stared into her eyes. "You know that, right?"

"I know," she repeated, her throat growing tight. Because he shouldn't have to. He shouldn't have to be chained to her forever, looking after her. She wasn't truly his stepdaughter, and that wasn't his job. And it certainly was not what her father would've wanted.

Pena gritted his teeth. "I promise, Isabelle. I failed him, but I will not fail you."

"You didn't fail him. He made his own choices, refused to listen to the doctors, worked when he should have rested." She shook her head, even as the older man scoffed. "But in these matters, I am in the best position to protect us all. I know what I am doing."

"Right. You and only you know best and have

everything under control. Just like him." He dropped her hand and stalked away, staring out the window as the first hints of sun rose over the horizon.

"I do." She laid a hand on her sheath. "And if you think that display was good, you know I'm better with a dagger."

"Naturally. But you chose swords, so you'll live with them, whether you prefer them or not." He strode over to his weapons, taking them up once more. "Now let's do this again, as I'm not changing your mind about anything and you won't stop until you collapse."

Isabelle's eyelids drooped as she settled on the paisley silk fainting couch next to Rebecca later that morning. She yawned as she took a long swig of coffee. Delicious. Her friend slurped her own and stuffed a raisin-filled bun into her mouth.

Her grandmother sat in a high-backed armchair, legs crossed, sipping tea, eyes as sharp as a falcon's—today's cane topper.

"So last night went very well." She held out a newspaper. "We made the gentile gossip pages—well, you did, Isabelle. Not by name, of course, but by description."

"My mother will be quite disappointed. I mean, that's what she always dreamed for me—being referred to as an 'elegant Jewess' in a goyishe scandal sheet—right after I give her grandchildren." Rebecca's lip twitched. "It's a very common goal. And not condescending or offensive in any way."

"Are you quite finished?" Her grandmother stirred her tea and continued without waiting for a response.

"While it might seem silly, these people do hold our futures in their hands, and staying in their good graces, taking what is meant as a compliment as such, benefits all of us. My late son and Sussex enjoyed each other's company, but there's a difference between having a Jewish friend and sincerely advocating for the entire community, seeing us all as people, and not just their special exceptions. So if we attract more gentiles to the next festival, it's important to be prepared."

"Better start stretching now so you can bend and grovel with even more ease." Her friend sniffed into her cup. Isabelle sucked in her lips so as not to giggle.

"We didn't design this world and its hierarchies." Her grandmother tucked a loose curl beneath her lace cap. "There's nothing wrong with acting accordingly if it will be to our long-term benefit, allowing us not only to be permitted to stay here—never a guarantee—but to thrive. Respectability has been the tool that's yielded us the most rights in this society." Her fingers gripped the handle of her porcelain teacup so tight it was a wonder it didn't crumble.

"And privileges." Rebecca near sneered the word.

"And privileges." Her grandmother set her saucer down with a loud clank. "Which we are entitled to as much as anyone else. My husband and I might not have been born here, but we contributed. As did my son. As do all of us. Leghorn's loss has been England's gain. We should not only be allowed to live here but to have a say." She wagged a finger at Rebecca. "We're better as part of their circle than living in an entirely parallel sphere, only to interact for business purposes."

"You mean our wealthy living among their wealthy, adopting their values and hierarchies until they figure out new ones so their top tier can exclude ours again? Or decide that wealth and titles are the root of all evil? Then their association with just a few of us will give them better justification to take everything away again. Or worse, regard it as proof we are the monsters their fairy stories and church sermons make us out to be." Rebecca took a large bite of toast. "But only after we abandon our own community, so we'll have nowhere to go back to. We'll be divergent and alone, more vulnerable than ever to their more violent whims."

"That's rather cynical. Besides, we'd never abandon our community—it's who we are." Isabelle took another sip of coffee. "As for the rest, I think they're too enamored with the idea of noble blood and titles to ever truly declare them evil. Yes, perhaps including us will cheapen certain privileges in their eyes, but maybe that's the first step to extending rights to more people. Like Catholics gaining rights can be the first step to our rights. When we succeed, we can build something new, where everyone is permitted to be who they are, but with full participation and equality."

"You'd be happy in this Eden, even not being on top of the heap?" Rebecca arched a light brown eyebrow. "With real equality, not just our leaders being equal? Well, almost, as even if we had the numbers, or more, especially if we did, they'd never truly grant us that much power—with theirs?"

"Even when everyone has equal opportunities, leaders are needed to ensure it," her grandmother retorted before Isabelle could respond. "And certain people were born to lead, no matter who they are or where they come from, provided they have equal access." She gave a pointed smile in Isabelle's direction.

Which she returned—as best as she could. Because more responsibility and pressure, that was exactly what she needed.

"Which brings us to your next steps, your future partner," her grandmother continued. "Speaking of which, it seems Solomon Weiss has captured your attention." She sniffed a little. "Be careful with that boy. His family all but left the community, so while their appearance was not unexpected, given the political pull of the gentiles present, his interest in you certainly is."

"Perhaps I am truly irresistible," Isabelle muttered. "Besides, I had the situation under control. And he's twenty-six, so hardly a boy. He's probably just spoiled and used to getting what he wants."

"Shall I direct you to a mirror?" Rebecca smirked and Isabelle rolled her eyes. Not that there wasn't truth in her statement. The question was who would be in charge of whom if two such people joined.

"I suppose he is rumored to be intelligent and certainly fine to view," her friend said. "Important since that's been added to your husband criteria."

"He might well be the correct choice. I'm just advising you to be mindful of what you are doing with him, so it is still a choice, not a compromise to save face," her grandmother said, stirring her tea once more. "Especially if you permit him to guide you over to fainting couches."

"I'm always careful with my face, but duly noted." Isabelle sighed.

"What is it?" Rebecca scooted forward in her chair, inspecting her as she struggled to articulate the odd, disquieted gnawing which had taken root in her ribs.

She bit her lip. "Do you think Weiss likes me?"

"Since when is that part of your criteria?" her friend asked. "I suppose you can't marry someone you despise and vice versa, no matter how handsome or good for the business and the community, but—"

"The question is, Do you like him? The idea that he or anyone else wouldn't like you is absolute nonsense." Her grandmother rolled her eyes. "You're attractive, you're charming, you're confident, and best, you know what you want and aren't afraid to demand it." She waved a hand in Isabelle's direction, jeweled bracelets glinting in the late-morning sun. "You speak well. You're friendly. People like you."

Did they? Or did people just like what she could do for them? And would she be satisfied with a husband who saw her accoutrements first and her second? Even if, in a way, she was looking for the same thing.

Because one good turn does not deserve another? Her conversation with Aaron echoed in her head. She twisted her ankle beneath her skirts. "I suppose."

Her grandmother reached out and tapped her knee. "Don't scrunch your nose like that, dear. It'll cause premature wrinkles."

Suddenly, she was no longer hungry. She laid her half-eaten sweet on the silver tray next to her.

"Sometimes it's better to have a smaller circle of trust. Especially when you are so valuable in your own right," her grandmother added. "I believe you will find the support you are seeking in the right husband."

Isabelle swallowed another sip of coffee so fast she burned her tongue. Which was somehow less painful than the gnawing in her gut. She should be excited and relieved. Solomon Weiss was still a solid choice, and if not, there were still two more festivals. Plenty of time to bring her goals to fruition without marrying anyone named Berab. And yet somehow, she was more confused and unsure than ever.

Before she could attempt a change in topic, Judith brought in the mail. And while several important families sent rather lovely compliments, another note took her breath away—one from David Berab. A request for another ream of unnecessary accounting to eat her time and keep her from the aspects of the business that mattered. Not that he would succeed. She'd do both, exactly as her father would have.

It would have been nice, though, if she'd slept more the prior night. However, once she was married, once she executed her plan, all would be right. She could sit in her father's chair and do the work to his standards, and everything would remain as it should. She just needed to finish what she had started. She closed her eyes for a moment, working to visualize her options once more, but the only face that came to mind was Aaron Ellenberg's.

She blinked them open once more to find both women still staring at her. "I'm just tired," she lied. "But I'll rally." After all, her family, the community, and the company all depended on her—something she could not forget.

Chapter Fourteen

Despite the fact his legs jiggled with fatigue, Aaron was awake and scrubbing the floors of the synagogue right as the men filed in for their morning prayers. There to help Mr. Baum find his missing button—the man had become forgetful since his wife passed last year. And to stitch together the knee of Rueben Loeb's trousers, lest the other boys tease him again.

Wiping his brow, Aaron lugged the bucket of now dirty water into the back alley, careful not to dump it too close to the sparrows' nests he'd fortified with bits of straw and scraps of cloth he'd found lying about. It was blustery between buildings, after all. Familiar with his presence, or more likely, the food he left for them, the mother bird popped her head out and chirped merrily at him.

If only people were as easy as animals. Or more, people his own age, as neither the very old nor the very young ever made him feel like a waste of resources. Not that he wasn't used to it. That had started the moment he entered the Jewish Orphans' Home and mixed up Rashi, Rambam, and Rema. The laughter and the jokes had lasted years. And hadn't stopped.

You can't expect him to do more than clean floors.

After all, he wouldn't know which direction is east if it wasn't spelled out for him.

Shutting out the smug stage-whispered comments from the prior week, he struggled to his feet.

Only to find Isabelle Lira, shiny hair secure beneath a bonnet, a lace shawl covering her shoulders, contemplating him from the mouth of the alley.

Aaron could only stare as she approached. Yellow flattered her. Set off her hair. And the climbing rose embroidery brought out a little pink in her lips. Not that her garments were his concern—she just looked...nice. All right, more than nice. And bright colors were a welcome sight on a dreary day in general. He leaned against the top of the broom and told himself it was those bold hues that held his focus, not the way the bodice outlined her curved body, nor the way the neckline fell wide, exposing her smooth, probably soft skin.

He swallowed as the memory of her quickening pulse beneath his thumb rocked through his body, his muscles tightening. Curses. He didn't need those sorts of thoughts. They had a business arrangement and that was it. One that would hopefully yield him the family and life in the community he longed for—one so full that he'd never think of her again.

"To what do I owe this pleasure?" he asked, attempting the role of reluctant servant instead of recalling how she smelled like oranges and flowers and everything fresh and nice and clean. "Are you here to noodge me?"

"Well, I am paying you for a certain amount of work." She traced a gloved finger along a stone groove in the wall. "And I have a limited amount of time. I meant to come earlier but was delayed. However, I still wanted to make sure we understood each other. And the, um, task."

He raised a brow, and she continued, "Based on our discussion in the library, my focus has narrowed." On a rich man who probably didn't deserve her and had his head too far up his tuchus to realize how lucky he would be if she picked him. Aaron's nostrils flared.

"To Solomon Weiss, first and foremost, yes, very much." Isabelle nodded, a lock of dark hair falling from its pins across her forehead. "My grandmother doesn't disapprove, so I need to not only verify he is an appropriate choice for my purposes, but that he can be induced into complete loyalty." She untied the velvet ribbon around her neck and slid back her bonnet to smooth the errant strand back into place.

He squeezed the handle of his room, beckoning her inside. "So, to confirm, you're completely focused on Weiss?" Not that it was any skin off his nose. "Or is there someone else I should know about?"

She paused, puffing out her lower lip before chewing on it. "There's no one else in particular, though the Duke of Sussex is keen on the men with which he is more familiar from my side of the community. However, I believe his mind could be persuaded by the right performer. Perhaps someone like Weiss. What are your thoughts regarding him?"

"Beg pardon?" Was the room rather sticky and warm?

"Your opinion of Weiss. As a husband. I know it's not quite what I've hired you for, but…I was just wondering, if given the choice, would…you marry him?" She twiddled the ribbon before swinging her hat at her side.

"I don't think I'm what he's looking for." He smirked at his own joke.

"No. You lack a dowry." She rolled her eyes at him before ducking her head. "I mean, do you think, with the right leverage, he would suit my purposes, if you were to make the decision in my stead? Think as if you were my advisor." She traced her free hand over the shawl at her neckline.

"Why are you rushing this decision?" he asked instead. Not that it mattered for his purposes, but the way she was pushing, almost desperately...

"You're young," he continued, his foolish mind working to make sense of the situation. "And I haven't heard rumors that the business is in trouble. It isn't as if you'll be forced to marry an ogre if you don't marry one of these men."

Miss Lira, however, said nothing and instead lowered her eyes, tugging at the fingertips of her gloves, and Aaron's stomach twisted. But how was that possible?

He stepped forward, shaking his head. "But your grandmother loves you and..."

"It's not her. She'd never. Neither would my father if he were alive." She clasped her hands behind her back. "But if I want to keep the Lira name on the business, be an active part of it and keep my father's memory and legacy alive, this is my only choice."

Aaron blinked. Her only choice? What did she mean by that?

"That makes no sense. Is someone threatening you and your family?"

"That's none of your concern," she snapped, fire in her dark eyes.

"If it somehow endangers me and my part of the

community, it is," he retorted. "I may be disposable to you, but I'm still a person and I have a brain, and if there is trouble you aren't telling me about, trouble that could hurt me or this synagogue and the people who attend..."

"There's no danger to you or anyone else in the community." She inhaled before sighing. "Though I suppose I owe you a bit more than I gave." She shook her head as she glanced at her perfect jeweled slippers. "And you're not just an automaton for me to use, even if I hired you for a particular job, which you did accept." She gave him a rueful tight-lipped smile that did not reach her eyes. "The business doesn't only belong to our family—well, belong to me and my future husband, as the Lira portion is the bulk of my dowry. Anyway, we have partners. Another family. Three brothers."

"The men you were speaking with at the festival. The Berabs," he whispered as the pieces of the puzzle began to fit together in a dreadful way.

"Yes." She nodded and sighed. "The middle brother, Louis, is a bachelor. And the youngest, Roger, was widowed a short time ago, and he's already in the market for a wife. If either marries me, David, the eldest, could control two-thirds, with his brothers controlling the rest, effectively making the company no longer Lira & Berab Sureties, but merely Berab. They could bar me from making any decisions, take our name off the letterhead, subsume us. Erase us."

"They would do that to you?" He stared at her. But...they were partners.

"I wouldn't have thought so before, but..." She frowned. "They've made it clear they care about themselves, not us—not when we are weak. And our lack of men of prominence and power is what makes us weak. David doesn't believe I should have any role in the company." She knotted her bonnet ribbon again. "Thus, his brothers are the last people I should marry, as they will do his bidding, not mine."

Which made sense. Except...Aaron paused for a moment, recalling the night prior. "Even though you and the younger one are—well, seem compatible."

"I wouldn't say we're compatible, but as a person—I don't dislike Roger. Actually, I'm reasonably fond of him. There was a time, before his wife died, that I minded his children." Her eyes softened, and a hollowness crept into his gut.

"And I don't hate his other brothers. Even David, despite the fact he's thwarted almost everything I've done regarding the business since my father died. That was actually an impetus for the festivals." A sly smile spread over her face. "I needed a way to advertise and ingratiate myself with the gentiles as an individual, without him undermining me. As he'd never do so in public. After all, he does care for the community, and he doesn't wish us ill, per se. He just cannot stand working with me. Which, again, means I cannot marry any of them."

Her inhale was audible as her smile vanished. "However, if I don't marry someone else with power, I will lose as well." She shook her head. "They can split the business—something they're threatening to do the day after Shavuot if I don't find a husband to fill my father's role. Many of the clients, especially the gentile ones, no matter how charming I am, will not negotiate directly with a woman—Jewish or not. Moreover, such a path would likely cause us to lose social and political power, hurting my grandmother and Pena. We won't starve, but..."

"But if you join with a prominent man who can negotiate where you cannot, combining his skills with your aptitude, that would make you a force that the Berabs could not ignore... giving you leverage to keep the business together, with your family name still on the door. Provided that the man you marry is loyal and cannot be persuaded to join the Berabs, which is why the names you gave me come from my part of the community. They are the most likely to not have any preexisting alliances." *Fuck.* Her plan made sense.

His heart squeezed at the unfairness of it all. She really did need him to succeed.

He ran a hand through his hair. "Weiss is... not a bad man, but he's hard to read."

"Isn't that what I hired you to do?" She moved closer to him, her voice sharp with intent.

Aaron rolled his eyes. No matter how badly he felt for her, she was not going to expand his job, at least not for free. "You wanted blackmail—"

"Leverage," she corrected, folding her arms with an adorable pout. "And I still do, but could you possibly find out if he has any additional motivations I need to know about?"

"Like what?" He knit his fingers, glancing at her from the corner of his eye.

"Like connections to the Berabs." She pursed her lips to the side, flashing her rather attractive dimple. Tempting him to neglect more of his duties at the synagogue in exchange for nothing.

"You can't ask him that yourself?" he countered. After all, this was really something that could be accomplished better by her. "You are considering making him a member of your family, so one would think you two could talk."

"My interactions with him are too brief to properly charm him." Another pout drew his gaze to those perfect, plump red lips and twinkling eyes, both of which were definitely chipping at his resolve to do what was right and sensible. "And while a full interrogation would be more efficient, I lack the leverage, especially if I want to get my way in marriage later on."

Oy. Was she serious? "I didn't suggest you browbeat the information out of the man. You do have other methods at your disposal for getting information besides brute force or manipulation. Ones to which Weiss would definitely be receptive, given how he behaved last night."

"Do you mean seduction?" She twisted her hair before placing hands on her hips as he gave her a half nod. His voice felt stuck in his throat. She paced closer, lines marring her brow. "Weiss would be very receptive, I suppose, but only if he thought that would guarantee a marriage, and I'm not ready. At least without the information, so we are at an impasse."

"I'd want to be seduced for mutual enjoyment, not as tit for tat in separate schemes to gain dominance in a marriage." A pang gripped his chest, and he shoved his fists in his pockets. "Though, what do I know?"

"Not much, one would presume, as you've never been married." She rubbed her elbows and peered at him. "Why haven't you? You said you want to, and you're only a touch older than I am. Your salary isn't large, true, but you aren't unattractive and clearly have a brain in your head."

His cheeks warmed. Had she just complimented him? He goggled at her. Not just complimented him, but said that he was handsome? Him? Covered with grime and dust thanks to his broom? She must have something wrong with her eyes.

"High praise indeed." But he suppressed any pleasure her faint praise stirred. Nothing good could come from dwelling on it. "'Not large' is an understatement. Most of my pay goes to my room and board, which, as you've seen, isn't a place most women would aspire to live."

Nor would it be right of him to even ask someone he loved to share such a life.

Her brow furrowed, a speculative look in her eyes. "With the right furniture, though...or if you married someone with a decent dowry or a family with extra space, that wouldn't matter. Besides, you're hardworking and considerate and can tell stories that enthrall. I think quite a few women would enjoy that." She ran a gloved hand over the banister, stroking the wood absently. "I mean, I presume one would..."

An image rose in his mind of her having exactly that reaction. Which was a ridiculous wish, for it would never happen.

"Good marriages require both parties to come as equals, and I...I would always be someone's charity project." Aaron ducked his head. Now. But with the money she'd promised...He opened his mouth to remind her of it, but she flashed him another one of her dazzling smiles, stopping him short.

"Not if you find the right leverage," she said with a wink before wagging a finger in a delightfully teasing manner.

He rolled his eyes. "I'm not sure I have your skills at manipulation."

"I'm manipulating for survival." She puffed her chest, the smile gone, her eyes glowing with firm determination. "For my own and my family's and our business and my father's legacy." She stared up at him, so close now his worn boots near grazed the toes of her silk-covered slippers.

"What would you do if you weren't?" The question popped from his mouth of its own accord, but the moment it burst through, the greedy desire for its answer enveloped his senses, despite how unnecessary it was to what either of them wanted or needed.

"What do you mean?" She stepped back and tipped her chin, appraising him.

"What would you want in a husband if you didn't need him to be your business-saving puppet?" he asked. "What would you choose? Besides being handsome, of course."

"Rebecca is the one who harps on handsomeness. I'm focused more on general attraction, which is necessary for any marriage," she told him. "But your question requires the impossible: for me to have somehow acquired all the access and opportunity afforded our men as well as the immediate trust of the community so I could truly fill my father's shoes all by myself." Her chest rose with each impassioned word.

"Well then, imagine you did have all that." He nodded, leaning into her, suddenly desperate to know her answer. "If you didn't have to worry about your future, what would you want in a partner?"

"I'd want to laugh," she said, with not a moment of hesitation.

"To laugh?" He repeated the word. That was what the graceful, mannered, intelligent, wealthy, cultured, beautiful Isabelle Lira wanted? A man who would make her laugh? That was it?

"I'd want someone kind as well. Not someone who's merely nice, but truly kind. Who cares about others whether they're of use or not and perhaps influences me to do the same, if I'm capable." Both her hands clenched her bonnet now, crushing the expensive thing. "And I'd want someone to tease me and tell me wonderful stories and make me forget to be serious and responsible and careful and obedient and mindful of all the rules."

"Many people would find those good qualities." Even if she made them seem like a horrible yoke. Aaron's fingers twitched to touch her once more, but he forced his hands to his sides.

"They're tiresome when you can't remove them, even in private." A bitterness choked through her voice.

"What else?" His brain felt heavy, a drumbeat resounding in his skull as he drew ever closer to her.

"I'd want someone to make me shiver and heat at the same time." She tilted her face toward his, her deep dark eyes hooded by her thick lashes.

"What do you—*oh*." Realization engulfed Aaron like a gust of wind. "You want lust."

A feeling with which he himself was now becoming quite acquainted. Even if he couldn't act upon it.

Still, his body prickled with the memories: of the prior evening, when he'd caressed her arm and almost forgotten himself. In her garden, when she'd been so near and he'd felt such temptation. In the men's smoking room, where he'd reached out and stroked her impossibly soft skin.

And now he was feeling her again. Except this time, his hands were around her waist, her breasts skimming his chest.

"Have you ever felt lust?" His words seemed to boom through his empty room.

"Oh yes," she said in a throaty whisper, her dark eyes twinkling up at him. "Rather frequently as of late."

"Really?" he nearly stammered.

"Yes. Very much so." And, wonder of wonders, she drew closer, pressing herself against him, a mischievous smile spreading over her face. "I'm just not sure what to do about it." Except she clearly was, tilting up her chin as she rose just enough on her toes so her lips were a breath away from his, tempting him.

A thousand nefarious reasons for her behavior—from experimentation to securing his loyalty to extortion—flickered through his mind. But at the moment, none of them mattered. The recklessness that had been born of frustrations at his position, at *their* positions, combusted against his own attraction and desire in pure need.

"Well, madam, then I suggest we put our heads together and find a solution." He lowered his head, locking eyes with her. Willing her to say yes, even if this was a terrible idea.

That delightful dimple deepened. "Like what?"

"Like kiss." His heart pounded against his ribs.

"Please." She breathed the word.

And finally, he obliged, bending to meet her, wrapping his arms around her soft, warm body as she molded to him, melting into him. Their lips met and hers opened, welcoming him, and he felt fire and ice and tasted spun sugar and oranges as lust lit his every nerve. In an instant, they were a mess of limbs and tongues and fireworks as she near climbed on top of his feet. And he didn't care. There was no pain, only pleasure. Pleasure and need.

Moaning, she rubbed against him as he clutched her tighter, reveling in each breathy murmur. She clung to him, and for one brief moment, he believed anything and everything was possible.

"Aaron." She whispered as she dipped to kiss his neck. "Aaron."

God, his body responded with dizzying speed to just his name, and all the promise it seemed to hold when spoken from her lips.

But it was a promise she could not deliver.

Cold emptiness ran through him as he remembered their roles—she was to be the hero, saving her family business. And for that, she needed a prince. Which was certainly not him, not even in his wildest dreams.

He disentangled himself from her, ignoring how her cheeks flushed, her eyes moving from glazed to focused. As he stepped back, she coughed and stared at the floor, her blush turned to ash. With shaking hands, she slipped her bonnet back on her head and tied the ribbon. Tight.

"That was—um, I should—" She coughed again and straightened her shawl. "I need to return. There's much to do." She caught his eye, and Aaron planted his feet, steeling himself for the inevitable. Only when he didn't answer, he thought he saw a quick flash of hurt before horror took over her expression.

But surely, he was wrong. Because that was the proper reaction, right? The only possible reaction.

Deep disgust. Which wasn't like a stab in the gut. Aaron scowled and moved near his desk.

"Both on my end and on yours." Isabelle sniffed, her eyes and voice now haughty. "Come to me before the week is out, as there is another festival you need to attend and lots of information to gather. And don't forget Weiss."

Before he could respond, she rushed out the door, her clacking feet echoing on the steps. Shaking his head, he stared after her. Oy. Just oy. This is what happened when a schlemiel made a bargain.

And now this schlemiel was going to need to find an excuse to see that arrogant putz Solomon Weiss. And be servile and fawning in his presence. Aaron ground his jaw. Time to practice his acting skills. And see which congregants had business with the Weiss brothers. Perhaps someone needed a letter delivered. Hopefully not in the rain.

But he wouldn't count on it—not with his luck.

Chapter Fifteen

Isabelle sprinted out of the synagogue to the waiting carriage. Tears threatened behind her eyes as she permitted her coachman to assist her inside. Once seated, she buried her head in the crook of her arms, exerting as much pressure as she could to stop any inconvenient and unflattering emotion that had no place in her life.

"What's wrong?" Rebecca's voice startled her, even though she was the one who'd asked her friend to stay and wait until after she'd finished. "Or more, what happened?" The other woman had taken off her bonnet, and a book lay in her lap.

"I kissed him." Her lips still tingled, and she could taste him on her tongue.

"Who?" Rebecca laid the book to the side, hands clasped in her lap.

"Aaron Ellenberg." She sniffed his name. It was wrong—wrong in every way possible. Not the least of which because he'd been completely horrified and probably found it, and thus her—she swallowed—lacking. And she had never supposed herself to be lacking in anything.

"The custodian?" her friend asked, surprise notably

absent in her voice as something like a smirk graced her lips.

"I wish you would stop referring to him that way. That is his job, but that's not all he is." She pinched the bridge of her nose as she shook her head.

"I thought you wanted to be known as the Surety Queen?" Her friend arched a brow. "For that to be your entire identity?"

"We decided on 'Empress,' and it's a joke—at least partially—and an entirely other matter that is not here nor there." Isabelle shook her head, her carefully shaped curls bouncing off the edges of her bonnet. "But yes, him. I kissed the man I'm paying to find information so I can extort the man I'm supposed to eventually kiss." She pressed her fingers to her temples.

How had this happened? How did she lose control? It just wasn't possible. She was too trained, too careful, too clever. And yet...

"You plan to kiss all your suitors?" Rebecca cocked her head, interrupting her thoughts. "I mean, it isn't advised and not something of which the community would approve. Though in reality, it isn't particularly uncommon, especially when it's done discreetly."

Isabelle's breath stopped as the horrifying possibility of having to kiss, well, anyone else flitted through her mind—not only due to potential further rejection, but because of the distinct possibility that kissing anyone else would not be nearly as good.

She shook her head. No. That was illogical. And ridiculous. Kissing her future husband would be perfectly fine. Enjoyable, even.

Clearing her throat, she reached for a proper, appropriate response.

"You know as well as I that it doesn't matter what other people do. I'm not other people. I'm supposed to be a symbol or what have you." She waved her hand, her gold bangles clanking together. "So no, I plan to only kiss the one I'm going to marry."

"So kissing is only for your husband and Aaron Ellenberg?" An obnoxious smile spread over her friend's freckled face.

"Has anyone ever socked you?" Isabelle grumbled, but the lump in her throat dissipated just a little.

"No." Rebecca gave a bemused sniff. "But except for you, most people don't tell me their nonmedical secrets." The carriage lurched forward, and her friend braced herself against the pink silk cushioned seats. "They find me haughty and say I stand in judgment too much." This time, her smile didn't quite meet her eyes.

Forgetting her own troubles for a moment, Isabelle reached out and squeezed Rebecca's palm. "We all judge. That's what we're supposed to do: study, learn, and use good judgment."

"You've been reading too much philosophy." Rebecca released Isabelle's hand to glance outside the carriage at the crowded streets bustling with afternoon business. "And probably got hit on the head one too many times as a babe."

"You would know." Isabelle giggled. "You were already six when I was born."

"I tried my best. I couldn't help it if you weren't always so skilled at walking. Or jumping. Or diving off tables." Her friend's smile became full again, and the two dissolved into even more raucous laughter, snorting until they were both out of breath.

And yet the pressure in her head remained. And the worry.

How could she have behaved so inappropriately? His rejection served her right. She should not and could not want Aaron. And she'd force herself not to want him if she had to.

Though why couldn't he have wanted her just a little? Not that it truly mattered, but... She pressed her fingers to her temples, shaking her head. "What am I going to do, Rebecca?"

"About what?" Her friend fingered the thick tufted fabric of the seat, clutching the cloth as they rolled over another bump. "Yes, you kissed him, but what does that matter in the grand scheme of things?"

"I don't know." Isabelle squeezed her thighs together.

"You didn't enjoy it, did you?"

"No." Isabelle shook her head. "Well. Maybe." She sighed. "I'm not sure." She lifted a hand to her still-tingling lips. "I mean, I thought I enjoyed it. A lot."

"But?" Rebecca asked. "Because there's most certainly a 'but.'"

"But he pulled away and looked horrified by the whole thing." All over again, the tears threatened, moisture pushing dangerously close to the surface. Which was... awful. She did not cry. Not even a little. "And it was more than a kiss."

"What do you mean 'more'?" Her friend squinted suspiciously.

Isabelle ran her tongue over her teeth. She should probably keep this to herself, but Rebecca was her dearest friend, and she had to tell someone. She squeezed her hands together. "Well, there was touching too. Lots of touching. His arms were around me, and I made—" She grimaced and stared at the tiny gilded beads dotting the leather seams of her shoes. "Noises." Her cheeks were on fire. "Embarrassing noises. And rubbed against him, and there were tingles, and I became all wanton-like and he was repulsed. Completely repulsed."

And the catch was back in her voice, even as she fought against it. She was supposed to be perfect and well mannered and contained with her emotions, and this was anything but.

"How do you know he was repulsed?" her friend asked, and Isabelle rolled her stinging eyes.

"He stopped," she told her friend. "One minute he was stroking me and kissing me and his body was pressed against mine, and everything was hot and wonderful and firm but also welcoming, and then he just...pulled back. Completely." Her vision blurred. "What's wrong with me?" She hiccuped as the shameful tears began to fall.

"Nothing. Nothing at all. Except that you kissed someone you shouldn't have, who was most likely not repulsed, but afraid." Her friend pursed her lips. "No matter what angle you approach it from, he has a lot more to lose if he upsets you than the other way around." Rebecca scooted next to her on the seat, her petticoats rustling against the soft cushioning, and pulled Isabelle into her arms. "Now, if I was giving advice, I'd tell you to forget about him in all ways, cut him out of your life so there's no muddle. But I suspect that isn't possible."

"No." Isabelle shook her head between sniffles. "I need the information."

"Right." Rebecca gave a skeptical huff. "And there's no other way to get it?"

"Not in time." Pulling out her handkerchief, Isabelle patted her eyes.

"Naturally." Her friend sighed once more. "Then I suggest instead that you make yourself more interested in one of the other men. Fast."

"Which one? Weiss?" Desperation edged into her voice. If only someone would point her in the right direction, tell her who was best, who she could trust to help her save her father's legacy. "Or do you have someone else in mind?"

"That's for you to decide." Her friend smoothed her thick woolen skirts. "In my opinion, it should be a man you think about when he's not around, the man you want to tell things to, want to ask questions of, want to be with at all times."

"What if none of the men at the festivals, none of my suitors do that?" She took a deep breath. "What if I haven't met that man yet? Or worse, what if I never do?" Even if she saved the business, saved her father's legacy, when the danger was gone, *would* she be able to be happy with the man she chose? It was a question she hadn't permitted herself to ask.

Would she always wonder?

Or worse, think of someone else?

"Are you sure you haven't?" Rebecca peered at her.

"Yes." She swallowed the doubt swirling in the back of her brain. She could control this. Control the situation. Control her life. She just needed to work harder. Be stronger. Cleverer.

Somehow.

"Then keep looking." Her friend patted her leg. "You still have plenty of time."

Isabelle nodded, forcing up the corners of her lips

in a half smile she told herself was not a lie as the two rode on in silence the rest of the way to their respective homes.

Why could she never sleep? Isabelle paced before the fire in her room even as Baron snored upon his striped cushion in the corner, worn out hours before from his daily ramble. Hands on her hips, she gazed at her damask bed-curtains again, usually so welcoming, but somehow, she could not settle as she should.

She glanced at the clock above the mantel. Midnight. Dinner had finished more than two hours ago, and her grandmother and Pena had retired to their chambers. Even the staff was slumbering. And yet here she was, awake, working not to think of *him*. Because the kiss didn't matter. The rejection didn't matter.

He didn't matter.

Thwack.

Isabelle near jumped out of her skin, and Baron raised his head, letting out a low growl. She spun around toward the window just as the second stone hit.

No. It couldn't be.

This pebble struck even louder. She rushed over, throwing open the shutters. Isabelle bent over the ledge, and yes, Aaron Ellenberg was standing right there in her garden, wearing the same clothing as earlier that day—the same jacket she'd clung to, the same trousers that had skimmed her skirts, the same thin shirt that she could almost view his chest through.

"What are you doing here?" she blurted, even as her brain warned her to remember their roles.

He grinned before cupping his hands over his mouth. "Getting your attention in the manner you previously specified."

"That was supposed to be after I summoned you." She leaned her elbows on the sill, sticking her head farther out into the cool air.

"So even though you wander into my place of business unannounced whenever you want, you require appointments for me to do the same?" He cocked his head in a manner that should be obnoxious—and somehow, she found it charming, because apparently she'd lost all sense.

"'Business' is the operative word. The synagogue belongs to the community. This is my home," she returned, straining to match his light tone, but with more haughtiness to act as a distinguisher. "Though I suppose this is better than you climbing a trellis."

"Your henchmen probably would've stabbed me the moment my foot touched the ground." He traced a circle with his boot.

"You're supposed to be my henchman." She reached over to her bedside table, grabbing her stiletto.

"True. And thus, as you demanded information, I've come to deliver it." He shoved his hands into the pockets of his faded frock coat and gazed up at her, his smirk a dare for her to come down, to spar with him once more. "Well, I will deliver, once I tell you what I learned after calling upon the Weiss household this afternoon." His lips tipped farther up in challenge.

Well, that could not stand unmet, no matter what had happened between them.

"All right. I'll be down in a moment." Isabelle dipped back into the room, hastily tying her sheath at her waist before throwing on her lace-edged dressing gown over her nightclothes. She really should put on shoes, but it was so much easier to creep through the house on her toes.

Quick as she could, she hurried down the servants' stairs and out the side of the house, into the garden. This time Aaron was inspecting a fountain just off the terrace. More the statue, actually. The very naked statue with the very prominent... well, everything. She bit her lip. She'd not flush. Not after everything that had happened earlier.

Straightening her shoulders in her most dignified and mature manner, she marched up to him, standing a respectful distance from his side, and inclined her head toward the piece.

"It's a copy of *David*. From Florence," she said. "I'm not sure if it's accurate, though I presume it is. My family spent a great deal of money having it commissioned."

"He's nude." Aaron didn't look at her, just kept his eyes on the man's body, hands on his hips.

"He's a statue. He doesn't get cold." She shrugged and moved a bit closer despite herself. Now he turned. Raising his brow, his lip curved.

"No, he clearly does not. Impressive." He sat himself on the stone edge surrounding the sculpture, legs apart, as he studied her face.

"Yes, I suppose he is," she said.

Aaron snickered and drummed his hands against the side of the fountain. "So."

"So." She folded her arms tight across her chest. "What do you need to tell me about Mr. Weiss?" Because that was the only reason he was here—for what she'd hired him to do—something she could not forget again, lest she humiliate herself even more.

"It's about Frederick, not Solomon. The older brother.

Well, half brother." Aaron gave a quick, sharp nod.
"Impressive man. Their father nearly killed their bank,
and through sheer will he pulled it back from the brink.
Until now, he was careful, almost conservative with
funds. However, as of late he's been spending. A lot."

"They're in debt?" She kicked a pebble with her
big toe.

"Not that I've heard. At least not yet." Aaron
adjusted his trousers. "But he can't keep this pace forever. And while no one has heard of a debt in itself,
something requiring funds is certainly afoot. Frederick
is pushing his brother towards you with a rather strong
arm. So strong that he was inquiring about Solomon's
efforts regarding your hand in front of staff." He added,
a sharp edge to his voice, "Including errand boys."

Not a surprise. Her dowry was chief among her
charms. It was, and would be, part of the bargain, so
suitors having designs on it shouldn't concern her—or,
well, shouldn't sting. Except…She frowned as a fact
tickled the back of her brain. "Where does it go? Into
the bank?"

"No. By all accounts, the business is quite robust."
He shrugged, his voice near bored, which was fine. *She*
was fine. He would be dismissed soon enough. "What
Frederick spends the money on, that's anyone's guess.
There are rumors both about a gentile woman he's
courting, as well as a hobby. He's allegedly a collec-
tor of some sort. Old-fashioned glass? Vases? Mirrors?
Figurines? Something like that."

"I suppose it doesn't matter." She fiddled with the
ribbon at her neckline. "Just…poor Weiss."

"Poor Weiss?" Aaron sniffed, planting his legs
together firmly on the ground. "You're joking, right?"

He raised a hand. "I'm telling you he is conspiring with his brother to drain your funds, and you call him 'poor.'" His voice was incredulous.

"First, it would be quite difficult to drain our funds. Second, he is pursuing it and me on behalf of someone other than himself." She twisted the end of her braid, tugging it over her shoulder. "He's being called upon to serve the whole instead of his own interests." And this was the sort of information she'd wanted, was it not? Something that could be used to negotiate a bargain between them, to get them each what they wanted from the marriage—bind them to each other and make their goals one.

"There are more ways to make money than marry, as you well know." Aaron gave her a long stare. "But I'll admit, from what I've seen, you're probably more than a dowry to him."

"Oh?" She drew closer. That was a nice thought—to be wanted for something more than money and power for once.

Aaron stood and cracked his back with his palms. "Yes. The two seem keen on making a return to the community, at least partially. They want to expand and need political power. Your connections would be perfect." His voice was still so distant.

Well, she deserved that. And there truly were worse things.

"Despite not being from my part, he could be good for the community as a whole. With his charm and tenacity and knowledge of the gentile world." Isabelle rubbed her side, so the sheathed steel pressed against her palm.

"He could." Aaron moved next to her, peering at

her through the moonlight. A light breeze played with his jacket, pulling it back, revealing his ever-half-unbuttoned shirt. And heat began to prickle at her skin again, despite the night air.

"And he clearly has no connection to the Berabs." She ducked her head, forcing herself to not contemplate this man who didn't want her and to think of the one who did. "At least not yet. His needs and desires do leave him vulnerable to a counteroffer from them, I suppose, but if I cut the first deal..." She wet her lips, turning the information over in her mind, working to make it more, well, appealing.

"Do you like him?" Aaron's voice interrupted her thoughts as he paced away from her, back toward the fountain.

"What?" She jumped a little before wrinkling her nose. "I don't know him."

"Then why are you defending him to me?" He scowled at her.

"Perhaps because I can understand his motivations. And I like people who understand that leaders aren't entitled to their positions, that they must continually earn them, by serving the whole." She gritted her teeth. "And perhaps because I like the fact he appeared to actually enjoy touching me. Unlike some people."

Aaron halted, his mouth agape. "What did you say?"

"Nothing." Flames shot through her cheeks. She hid her face, already moving back to the house, ready to flee. Or more, calmly retire, as Liras did not run.

"Not nothing." He scampered around to block her path, holding up a hand. "Wait—were you implying that I didn't enjoy touching you?"

God. He actually wanted to talk about it? Confirm

his disgust? Isabelle closed her eyes. If the ground could just open and swallow her whole.

She hugged her body for fortification. "I'm not a fool. I saw your face after the kiss. You were horrified." She choked on the word as all the stinging hurt, which shouldn't exist, rushed back.

"Yes, because your grandmother would pitch a fit and probably cost me my actual job. Not to mention you are searching for a husband who isn't me. Not because the kiss wasn't good." He drew closer to her again, so close this time that her gown billowed against his legs. He didn't touch her, though, just stared down at her, disbelief etched into his features.

"You thought it was good?" Her voice squeaked. She cleared her throat, fighting to regain her dignity. Even if the question was inappropriate and unnecessary and—

"You know it was good." A sly grin broke out on his face. "Very good." He rubbed the back of his neck. "But that's not the point." And the grin became a stiff line as he took a step back. "Because it shouldn't happen again."

"Why not?" She marched forward so they were toe to toe once more, hands on her hips. "I mean, I'm not sure one way or the other, but I'd like your opinion."

"You listen to opinions other than your own?" He sniffed, but at least he didn't run.

She straightened her spine. "A true leader understands that she's only as good as those with whom she surrounds herself, and even if she surrounds herself with the brightest of advisors, if she is too arrogant to take their advice, she'll surely fall." That was how many a budding empire died, after all. Mistakes she would not make.

"And you consider my advice sound?" He gave her another skeptical gaze.

"Well, my knowledge of kisses is most likely rather limited compared to yours, but what you've shown me so far was…" She bit her lip as a heat rose not only in her cheeks but throughout her body, her breath hitching. "Anyway, yes." She pursed her lips. "For goodness' sake, Aaron, you aren't a fool. You might not have a head for Talmud or trade, but I still trust your opinion."

"You shouldn't. I could have my own motivations." His voice went singsong, but he didn't move away. Instead, his fingers twitched, near, so very near.

"Your motivations are to have a more respectable career, a better living arrangement, and a chance at a wife of your own." *One who is not me.* She gritted her teeth as if the vehemence in her thoughts could convince her skin to stop tingling—or force this unneeded attraction to dissipate. "Which you will receive means to after the last festival."

"You shouldn't guarantee delivery of full payment when you haven't received all the goods and the job isn't done. As for the rest, you have no idea." His tongue darted across his lips and she shivered, anticipation moving down her body. "And that's why we shouldn't engage anymore." He shook his head. "You're looking for a husband, and I don't think he would take kindly to us kissing."

"There is no 'he.' I'm considering Weiss, but there are still plenty more options and I'm not yet betrothed to anyone, let alone married." She blew out a long, frustrated stream of air. Honestly. She knew her argument was nonsensical, but what else could she say when to agree was to stop this? He needed to stop flitting back and forth between flirting and pushing her away. So much hot and cold together was going to force her to combust.

"But you will be. Soon." Aaron frowned as he held up a single finger for one long moment, his eyes looking back at the statue, before he collapsed his hand into a fist, then opened his palm.

Her heart leaped into her throat, but she didn't move. Everything in her yearned and wished for what she couldn't have and shouldn't want. But she craved him. Or at least his kisses. Again. And again.

God, fighting this was harder than she'd anticipated. She searched for her control.

"And so, the issue is what? That you don't think I have the will to stop after I choose?" she finally managed to ask.

He gave an incredulous laugh. "Do you think I do?" Aaron stepped away from her, hands clasped firmly behind his back.

"Yes. Yes, Mr. Ellenberg, I do." A lump rose, almost cutting off her air, as she remembered Rebecca's words. "However, if you never want to engage again, I understand, completely. There are dynamics that are uncomfortable, given that I'm paying you for information, and we don't want to get things muddled and—" She stuck her chin in the air with as much dignity as possible, stepping back so she could rush into the house before her voice cracked, or worse. "Thank you for the news on Mr. Weiss. You went above and beyond. As for the next festival, there shall be garments outside the servants' entrance. You're going to play part of the musicians' staff. Wear a large hat or cloak. Not as much access to guests, but hopefully enough. In the meantime—"

And her words were lost as he took two swift steps forward, cupping her chin, bringing her lips to his once more. With a moan, she opened her mouth and was lost again, pressing her aching nipples against his torso, thin fabric against thin fabric, his tongue mingling with hers. Whiskey and rain, and everything rich and dark and secret and powerful.

And she wanted it. Wanted him. Wanted more. What did his skin taste like? What would it feel like if there were no barriers between them? What would it be like if she rubbed against him even more?

But all too soon he stepped back, his eyes wild in the moonlight, lips swollen, hair mussed from her fingers, gazing at her with something very different than horror, something wilder. Something that should scare her but instead excited her.

She blinked at him. "Oh my."

"Are you still sure either of us can stop?" He panted a little but held fast to her waist.

"We're intelligent adults." The words were a bit of a whine as her hips bucked toward him of their own accord.

"Are we now?" he whispered as he pressed one hand into the small of her back while he fiddled with the buttons at the collar of her nightdress with the other.

"We are," she insisted, clinging to him, because she was not going to miss this for the world. "Which is why you should most certainly continue." She couldn't help adding, "Please."

He grinned before bending forward to kiss her neck, exactly how she'd demonstrated, his teeth grazing along her skin, as she dug her nails into his shoulders, trying desperately not to moan, lest he stop. Her nipples tightened beneath her gown as a thousand delicious sensations coursed through her body.

More. She needed more. Of this and him. Even if it was temporary.

"How about now?" he asked, returning to the buttons, flicking them open, one, two, three, four, exposing a great swath of skin she desperately wanted him to touch. "Do you still have all your wits?"

She groaned. "Yes," she managed to gasp as his fingers trailed down her bare collarbone, so close but so far from where she needed them. "Please," she whispered once more. "Here." Before she could think better of it, she grabbed his wrist and moved his palm to her breast.

Isabelle sighed as his thumb stroked her nipple, teasing the already exquisitely tight flesh, exactly where she burned for him. "More," she whispered again. Because it was so, so good, but not nearly enough.

She'd played with herself before, but now, with him, was unlike anything she'd ever experienced. God. She needed him to not stop. To never stop. If ever there was a time that a woman needed a spell book...

Thankfully, he obeyed despite her lack of magic, bending forward and licking her as she squeezed his arms for purchase. She bit her lip to not cry out, but a small whimper escaped.

Aaron glanced up, and a soft smile came over his lips before he kissed her again, fully and truly, taking all her cries as he continued pleasuring her breast with his fingers.

"And now?" he whispered right against her ear, nipping the lobe. And with that single delicious sensation, she nearly lost all control.

"What was the..." Still clutching his arms, she searched her mind for any semblance of propriety and polish and, well, her powers of speech. "Oh right, yes," she managed to say. "I'm definitely in full control of my..." Isabelle pulled her braid over her shoulder again, smoothing it, even as she could not look away from him.

Aaron snorted.

"I am." She giggled a little despite herself, fumbling with her buttons, fastening them once more.

"We're playing a dangerous game. But...I believe we can separate this from my work. Or at least I can. Consider me less of an employee and more a vendor you are paying for a product. Though..." He reached out and pulled her hand into his, bringing it to his lips. She sighed and he caressed her cheek. "You would need to agree with my assessment. After all, I'm just giving you advice that you are free to take or not."

"I'm taking your opinions under advisement." She lifted her chin and smiled at him, closing her eyes as he ran his fingers over her jaw once more. "All of them."

"Fair enough," he whispered, releasing her. "Miss Lira?"

"Yes?" she asked, watching as he stepped toward the shadows. Away from her.

"I'm not the hero. I'm not even a main character in your story," he said as he turned, striding toward the wall. "Remember that," he called over his shoulder.

"I won't forget, Mr. Ellenberg," she returned, rubbing her arms as he vaulted over the stone and into the night, leaving her alone once more.

Chapter Sixteen

Aaron's feet pounded against the cobblestones as he jogged eastward, the night sky still black and the wind from the river whipping at his coat. He hugged it tighter to his body, though the chilly air was doing a decent job of tamping down his unspent desire. At least enough to get him home.

Spring, his tuchus.

Huffing, he picked up the pace. He needed to get back to his room and rest. Because then he could sort everything out. Her. His life. The future he was striving to build. The sinking feeling that the memories he was making now would one day cause pain instead of pleasure. The fear that he wouldn't let it—or worse, her—go.

Raising the collar of his worn coat over the back of his neck, Aaron sank down as he kept moving, the streets silent except for the scurrying night creatures and the occasional ne'er-do-wells plying their schemes. He skirted them, sticking to the sides of buildings and small streets, avoiding alleys and using the occasional roof when needed.

Weaving through the dangers of the night was his specialty—the time and place where invisibility was a skill, not a curse—which was probably one of the major reasons he'd not been killed during his foray outside the community. A place where he could succeed, where he felt alive—

Crunch.

Aaron's neck hairs prickled as he worked not to react—that would bring on the attack before he could plan a counter—and instead stilled his mind to analyze it.

Splat.

A boot. Hitting water—to his left. Hurrying now, he darted forward as his mind worked. There was an alley ahead, not so narrow to be used for other purposes, but enough for a diversion.

Quick as he could, the moment it came into view, he pivoted down it, breaking into a run. Heavy feet followed as he raced, faster and faster. He jumped a trough, weaving through smaller and smaller spaces across the road as drunk revelers shouted obscenities when he whipped close.

He glanced over his shoulder, and a figure raced after him, ducking and bobbing, despite its relatively larger frame.

Blast.

While the Jewish parts of East End were certainly not immune to crime, as the watch could not be everywhere, he'd managed to avoid the more dangerous predators since his return. Apparently, his luck had come to an end. Oy. And he didn't even have anything for this ruffian to steal. Aaron's lungs burned as he raced farther and farther south, toward the river, away from the synagogue, because nothing good could come of whoever was chasing him knowing where he lived. A million, albeit poor, strategies raced through his brain even as he forced his feet to keep moving, even as his pursuer gained ground.

How did a man that tall travel so fast? Aaron shook his head, nimbly dodging a barrel. He kicked a second in his pursuer's path. A cry rang out, and he took the opportunity to duck into yet another alley, this one unfamiliar. He pressed onward until the toe of his boot stuck in a crack, tripping him.

Quick as he could, he threw out his hands to catch himself as he slammed against the dirt. Blood trickled down his wrists, and the sharp pain kept him on the ground, even as danger rushed in. In desperation, he kicked the approaching figure's legs out from under him and rolled onto his back, just as the other man tumbled on top of him with a thud.

Aaron grappled with him in the dirt, punching and yanking and tearing fabric as they battled for supremacy in the night. Squinting, Aaron worked to gain any advantage that he could, though truth be told, the shadows were a bit of a hindrance to his aim.

As if on command, distant lightning flashed in the sky, illuminating the alley and the other man's face—his familiar face. Aaron gasped. Not whom he'd expected at all. Especially not in this neighborhood. "Berab?" he said more than asked as he rose and stumbled toward the fallen man. An equally well-dressed man—one of the brothers, what was his name again?—rushed and helped his fallen sibling up before Aaron could offer his assistance.

The man who'd attacked him wiped his mouth on his coat sleeve, a flash of red reflecting in the moonlight as Aaron winced. Oy. He was going to be in trouble for this, wasn't he?

He backed against the wall as his eyes focused on the other man. The youngest. What was his name again? Not David—that was the deputy, the one Isabelle had all the conflict with. This was just one of the suitors.

The younger man tried to smooth his brother's rumpled velvet coat, but he was brushed off as his brother kept his attention on Aaron, gazing in distain.

"Mr. Ellenberg," he said with a small bow. "Let me introduce myself. My name is Louis Berab. Behind me is my brother Roger. We are the great-great-grandsons of the community's founders. Chief benefactors of our oldest congregation."

Aaron resisted rolling his eyes at the introduction. Yes, Berab's ancestors were among the earliest Jews welcomed back with the House of Orange, and their Bevis Marks might have been started by those first families, but the Great Synagogue was actually dedicated first. Not that it mattered. Nor could he say anything. It was two against one, with their side holding far more communal power than he could ever imagine.

Besides, if they wanted to puff themselves with nonsense, let them. He had more important things to do.

Like find a way home without insulting any of them or harming Isabelle's cause. Though their behavior certainly supported Isabelle's theory that they didn't have a strong reach in the Ashkenazi part of the community. It was probably beneath them to socialize with the "rabble," beyond what was necessary to maintain their political and financial positions.

Not that someone like him could say that out loud either.

"No, it's quite all right," he said instead as he brushed at his own now wet and filthy garments before turning toward Roger, who had pulled out a handker-chief in an attempt to halt the blood dripping from his brother's already swelling nose. "I, um, apologize to your brother. I didn't mean to injure him. I was just..."

"Startled?" Roger Berab winced before folding his arms across his chest, having convinced Louis to take the cloth. Roger arched an eyebrow at Aaron, a slightly bemused expression on his unfortunately handsome face. "You have every right to be," he said with a touch of sympathy, which managed to sound both sincere and doubtful.

"And we should have anticipated you'd defend your-self," Louis added, stepping forward. "It's rumored that your punch is near deadly. Perhaps you should have attempted a career in the ring." His voice hardened. "The gentiles do like it when we entertain them there. Instead of causing problems in their streets."

A shiver flitted down Aaron's spine. He may have the stronger fists, but he was definitely the prey in this situation.

"I'm not sure I understand," Aaron lied. "Though that's frequent. I'm just a custodian over on Duke's Place, after all."

"Oh, I think you are a touch more than that," Louis said, the corners of his lips turning up in a half smile. He indicated behind him. "Won't you have a conversa-tion with us? In our carriage?"

Not exactly an offer one could refuse, was it? Which was how Aaron found himself sitting across from the two a few minutes later.

Roger cleared his throat.

"You may be wondering why we sought you out," he said, crossing his brightly polished boots against the silk-covered seat. "Especially given that you are not from our part of the community."

Not really. But given how little they clearly thought of him, it couldn't be for anything good.

"I—I thought we were one community now?" Aaron asked instead, hoping they believed him as foolish as everyone else did.

"We are, we are," Louis said, his voice barely warmer than before, an inscrutable smile on his lips. "The integration has been good for all involved. It strengthens us. Allows us to work together and advocate as one, as well as lend our better qualities and knowledge to those who are new to this land, so that our position will not be jeopardized."

"And you…believe I can help with that?" Aaron squirmed in his seat, like all those times he had been called on in his lessons back at the Orphans' Home, when any response he could proffer was far below adequate, let alone correct.

"Yes. In a way." Roger clasped his hands in front of him, leaning forward. "Look, Mr. Ellenberg, let me be frank—you have the ear of someone very important to us and our family."

Oy. Apparently, his employer wasn't such a secret. Though if the brothers thought he, of all people, could make Isabelle Lira marry one of them…

"Miss Lira, you mean. I'm not sure I have her ear." Aaron rubbed the back of his neck. "I just, um…do some odd jobs for her and her family."

Roger's smile broadened. "You're very modest, aren't you? I believe you have quite a bit more influence than you might think."

"She's a good per—employer." A bead of sweat

dripped from his brow despite the cool night air. "I just want her to be happy," he added.

Which was true. And she would not be happy with them. No matter how they argued it.

"And we do too." Roger nodded vigorously. "She's been through a lot as of late. Losing her father and all. She needs a good husband. One to lean on. One who will protect her family."

"She's not interested in you," he protested, despite himself.

"No. She is not," Roger said plainly, while his more foreboding but less loquacious brother nodded. "Partially the fault of my eldest brother. She and David are like oil and water, it seems." He shrugged before raising a finger. "Nevertheless, even he cares about her and wants what is best for the community and the business. Which is not Solomon Weiss."

Wait—what? This was about...Weiss? They were going to all this trouble just to prevent Isabelle from marrying Weiss? A man whom he didn't even particularly like. Though, given the circumstances, he had suddenly shot up in his esteem.

"Pardon?" he managed to ask.

Louis leaned forward now. "He and his brother bring nothing but trouble. They are too bold, too ruthless, too ill equipped for the subtleties that are required for maintaining our clientele."

Perhaps the Berabs should look in a mirror.

"They risk turning them away from our community for good, at least based on what we've seen." Roger shrugged, too tense to be casual. "Charm only gets one so far without proper training."

"Or lineage," his brother added, sniffing. "He might

have the money and the garments, but he lacks the true spark that has made *our* part of the community the most significant contributors to our people's advancement. Keeping us free from degradation and decay."

If the Berabs' idea of advancement was to make themselves feel superior to their fellow Jewish people by spouting goyishe nonsense—as if elevating people based on where their ancestors had lived and the alleged purity of their blood was a concept that had even been theirs in the first place—then he was perfectly fine being one of the degraded. Aaron opened his mouth to make a smart remark about such, but Roger chimed in first.

"And if he becomes a delegate—almost a guarantee for Miss Lira's husband—he will throw off the balance," the youngest Berab added. "Which is why it's necessary for her to choose one of us." He flinched and hastily straightened himself with a cool dignity.

"Miss Lira knows her own mind. Further, she's clever and educated and savvy. She is the best arbitrator of her own future," Aaron burst out before grimacing at his own conviction.

As the two men exchanged inscrutable looks, he added, "But I'm just her errand boy. We've barely spoken." He swallowed. "I only suppose she has those qualities." The brothers turned back to him, their presences somehow growing larger. Had the carriage gotten smaller?

"Lying does not become you, Mr. Ellenberg," Louis said. Aaron shivered at the dark warning in his eyes.

Roger's smooth voice was a cool salve against his brother's. "We want what's best for everyone, including Miss Lira." He turned a sympathetic gaze on Aaron.

"Even the Duke of Sussex has made clear his preference for a man from Bevis Marks." Louis frowned, but his tone was near mocking. "In fact, if she chooses Weiss, he and the gentiles might see it as an affront." Louis folded his arms before leaning forward, as if sharing a secret. "Perhaps enough to pull their support for the bill. And then where will the community be?"

"I—" Aaron opened, then closed his mouth, unable to find the right words.

"But if she chose one of us..." Roger cocked his head, and Aaron could only stare. "Our family was one of the first here in England, even before the Liras, something gentile culture values."

"It's rumored that Weiss's mother never learned English," Louis added, shaking his head. "He had a German accent until she died, and his brother corrected matters with tutors."

This was wrong. So wrong. And not just because he'd spent years losing his own accent.

Isabelle was a person. A manipulative one, to be sure, who played her own games and had far more money than anyone should have access to, but still a person. With feelings. And a sly sense of humor. Who kissed well and cared deeply about her family.

Shame on all of them for trying to decide her life without her.

Roger leaned forward, clasping his hands on his lap. "You have a chance to finally help the community. To protect it. You want to protect the community, don't you?"

Aaron swallowed. Of course he did. The community was paramount. However, Isabelle was also important. And deserved better.

Better than them. Better than him. Better than all of this.

"Can, I, um, sleep on it? Consider the best approach?" he asked. Not that he planned on doing what they'd asked. But he needed to leave. And think. "It's been a long night, and I have floors to clean tomorrow."

"Naturally." Louis tented his fingers, that sly half smile grazing his face once more. "You wouldn't want to lose the first job you've held on to for more than three months. After all, a man can't make a match when he's fallen out of favor with both the rabbis and the delegates."

Aaron blinked as the words—as the threat—washed over him. Chilling him once more.

"You know what you need to do," Roger added coolly. His calm dignity—and handsome face—would make him a good match for Isabelle and her family.

The thought made his stomach roil. Aaron's throat closed tight, his skin burning, and he had to leave. Now. Before he vomited or swooned or, worse, gave into the fire in his gut and did irrevocable harm. He tugged at his suddenly too tight cuffs and turned to bid the duo good night, hand already on the door.

"Good night, Mr. Ellenberg," Roger said before knocking on the wall behind him. "Have a long rest, and in the morning, think about your duties and what it is you owe to the community which has given you so much."

Before Aaron could say anything more, the coachman swung the door open and nearly threw him into the street before closing it again and taking off, wheels spinning, showering him with a fresh coat of murky rainwater.

Alone again, Aaron slumped against the bricks.

He rubbed his still-sore hands together in the now frigid night air before shoving them into his pockets and slinking back to the road. Ducking beneath an awning, he made his way through the quiet street, his boots sloshing in the puddles as he traveled north and east, not another person in sight.

A few blocks from the synagogue, a cat hissed at him from its perch on a gate and broke the silence. He placed a finger to his lips and shushed the beast, who promptly jumped down and scampered away, past a glass storefront.

Aaron strolled to the window to check what little of his reflection he could see in the panes. Oy, that was definitely a bruise coming on his cheek. And temple. Too bad his Omer beard wouldn't cover that one.

Plink, plank, plunk rang into the air, like droplets splashing on boots.

For a moment, the temperature dropped and the shadows grew larger. Aaron froze, fisting his sore hands, readying them, as he turned to find—nothing. No man. No shadow. Not even the cat. He shook his head. His mind must be playing tricks on him. Something that was definitely not helpful at the moment.

Probably because of the guilt welling in his chest. But that was a problem for him to consider later. When he could think straight. *If that's possible*, he smirked, considering his limited smarts.

Perhaps he should contact Miriam. He had promised her that he would at the first sign of trouble. And this certainly rose to that definition. Besides, if anyone could find a way out of this mess, it was her.

With a sigh, he started on his journey home again, marching forward.

Plink, plank, plunk.

The noise repeated. He glanced over his shoulder and stared once more at the empty street. As if a ghost had been there.

Except there was no such thing as ghosts. Only men. Who offered illusions dressed up as choices.

A gust of air whooshed around him, and he broke into a run, not stopping until he reached his rooms.

Chapter Seventeen

The second festival was halfway done. Muted music from the ballroom below trickled into the library as Aaron stuck his thumb in the Grimm brothers' volume, skimming the story about the little girl with the red cape—the one who was devoured by a wolf while trying to take care of her sick grandmother.

Weiss's grin flashed through his mind and he shivered. A touch too close for comfort, eh? He bit his lip. The banker wouldn't eat the Lira family. Or if he did, Isabelle didn't need a huntsman to get her out. She had her own knife.

No, the danger was from the Berabs. Something he needed to discuss with her. Threats or no threats.

A decision he'd made earlier that day, eased by the idea he'd had when delivering Rabbi Marcus the mail. The man had received a letter from his cousin in Boston, and he'd shared revelatory news about the Americas.

Lovely city, apparently. And they have even decided to allow our men to vote, he'd said, skimming the correspondence as Aaron cleared the remnants of the rabbi's midday meal from his desk. *With a growing community as well. A good place for young people to go and establish themselves.* He'd glanced up with a small smile. *Hopefully, they won't steal too many of ours.*

Aaron had given the man a thoughtful nod as he spoke more about his cousin before changing the subject and giving him another letter to deliver to the Weiss brothers. But as he'd left, his heart had pounded in his ears.

America. He'd never considered leaving London, but why not?

It wasn't as if he had roots here. Or had ever truly belonged in the first place. No matter how much he loved the synagogue and the people.

Leaving the community before the Berabs could make good on their threats would free him to help Isabelle get what she wanted.

Even if that was Weiss. His stomach twisted at the thought.

Ridiculous. No matter their conversations or kisses, he had never been in contention. Which he'd known before every word, every glance, every touch.

Which was really another argument in favor of America—there he could more easily excise himself from any reminders of Isabelle Lira, for his own good. Allowing him to truly get on with his life and the dreams that were in his reach. Like he had always wanted to.

The concept had also made going to Miriam for help a great deal easier—she was old and vulnerable and no match for the Berabs and their power. The less she knew, the safer she was.

She had been amused with his request, however, teasing him. *You, asking for something? Wonders never do cease.* And she'd clucked sympathetically when he'd shamefully lied, hinting that he was in need of a fresh start.

Nodding from beneath her cloak, she'd tutted. *The price of a close community. I understand. Gossip is thick and memories are long, and it is hard to change your status. I'll look into it, see what possibilities there are in America for you.*

And before he could thank her, she'd hobbled out of his alley with a flourish. Leaving him alone.

Waiting.

Like he was now.

The door creaked open.

"What new information do you have for me on Weiss?" Isabelle's breathy voice was demanding even before she fully entered, champagne glass in one hand, fan dangling off her wrist.

Weiss. Aaron wrinkled his nose at the man's name. Not that he wasn't developing a sort of soft spot for the dandy, between what he'd heard from his servants and the Berabs' opinion of him and, really, everyone from their part of the community, but... He grimaced again. Still, this discussion was part of his job too, and what he was being paid to do. He stifled a sigh.

"Not much more than I had the other night." He slipped the book back on the shelf, facing her fully, and his mouth went dry.

Oy, she really was beautiful, wasn't she? Yes, her gowns and jewels always fit her well, but there was a glow about her now. She shone. But not like a twinkling fairy or cosseted princess or clever enchantress—no, there was something bolder and more substantial about her. Something that made all the inappropriate thoughts he'd been having since their last kiss rise to the surface with a series of new fantasies.

"Nothing? Nothing at all?" She stepped forward and his damned heart quickened.

"Well." He tugged at his collar. "I've learned that Weiss's brother is…"

"Is?" She shut the door behind her, leaning against it as she cocked her head at him, her silky-to-the-touch black hair puffing up behind her as she crushed her elaborate style.

"A mamzer." Because that was really the only word to describe the elder of the two brothers.

"Literally?" She narrowed her dark eyes at him speculatively, a thousand thoughts running through them. As if she was analyzing what could be done with such information—her mind terrifying and impressive all at once. She was definitely crime lord material. The thought was almost fond now. No wonder the volume in the room with the most wear and tear was the one written by Mr. Machiavelli.

"No." He rubbed the back of his neck. "Well, his parentage isn't part of the gossip." He'd heard nary a word either way about the deceased father. "Figuratively. Towards his younger half brother in particular." Not that Weiss would admit it, from what had been shared with him. It was amazing what was shared below stairs—or with sympathetic outsiders. Weiss defended the other man to anyone and everyone, but servants talked. He almost felt sorry for him, despite the difference in status and opportunities.

"Oh." Isabelle's eyes softened. "That explains a few matters." She fingered the champagne glass before setting it on a shelf and moving back toward him. "What does he do? The brother?"

"Tasks him with all the unsavory jobs to help the business succeed and raise his social standing outside the community. Makes his brother take all the risks while he keeps his own hands clean and his tuchus protected. Treats him more like a henchman than a brother." Aaron ran his fingers over the edge of the reading table before leaning against it, swallowing a little as he recalled the tone he'd overheard Weiss use when addressing his brother. It had set Aaron's teeth on edge.

Her chin shot up as she appraised him. "So effectively, you and Weiss have the same job."

He barked a harsh laugh. "Hardly. Though even if we did, I can assure you, whatever he endeavors, I can do better. At least for you."

"Can you?" She matched his posture. "So you're the superior hired muscle?" Her gaze drifted down as her fingers inched forward, nearly touching his. His breath hitched.

And despite everything—the Berabs' threats, his duties to her, his growing sympathy toward the still-obnoxious Weiss, and his lack of ability to figure out which way was up in this situation—the slightest bit of mischief stirred in his gut. He leaned forward on his elbows, gazing up at her. "I'm superior to him in every way that matters. Especially all the physical ones."

"I don't doubt it." Her lips twisted into a crooked smile, though her eyes still held a sadness, forcing him back to his task.

He cleared his throat. "Anyway, Weiss. A few years ago, he nearly died."

A gasp of horror. "Why?"

"The brother lost some money at a boxing match and thought he was cheated. Refused to pay and told Weiss to take care of it." Aaron winced despite himself. "Let's just say, while he talks pretty fast, some people punch a lot quicker. The worst part was, they had the money— the brother just wanted to demonstrate that they were not to be trifled with, and Solomon paid. However, I heard he found other ways to get the last laugh. Which is noteworthy as he is not the sort of man who should be underestimated in his own right."

Ways that involved a few well-placed rumors causing the men who took Frederick's money to turn on each other, resulting in a rather bloody battle among themselves. Effective revenge that allowed both brothers to avoid suspicion.

"You say that like it's a bad thing." Isabelle's lip twitched in amusement instead of proper fear.

"You were the one who said you wanted someone you could control, and Weiss..." Aaron couldn't help arguing.

"Yes, yes, I'm sure he's very clever and ruthless, as is the brother." Isabelle gave a dismissive wave. "But he *is* interesting if there was less risk. Or he at least employed some different maneuvers. Ones that could be beneficial to me as well, and align with my goals for the business and the community."

With a sigh, Aaron stood before pushing himself onto the table so he could perch as he finished his task. "So does that settle your decision?" He pressed his palms to the tabletop supporting him, rooting himself.

"Probably." She wound the strands of beads at her neck around a finger. "My grandmother is less convinced, and Pena doesn't like him. He thinks he's merely asking questions, but he should never play poker." There was a wry amusement in her tone, and a shadow of a dimple graced her cheek.

"Pena...your house manager?" he asked, hoping he'd guessed the correct title for the man.

"His official title was my father's valet, but in truth, he was my father's partner in everything, as my mother was before him. Which included raising me. And now he stands in his stead." She glanced at her lap, her voice achingly soft. "Just without the histrionics my father would've resorted to if he did not care for Weiss and was in danger of not getting his way. They were different people, which is why they were suited. A true love match."

Isabelle lifted her chin and frowned, the dimple disappearing. "Do you know what's odious?" Pushing herself up on the table, she sat next to him, her legs and skirts dangling over the edge. "People won't cease discussing things like happiness when it comes to all of this." She gestured toward the raucous sounds of the festival. "As if because I have funds, the most ephemeral concept of the emotion should be within my grasp. What no one seems to understand is that my happiness is linked to the duties and responsibilities they bring."

She pointed a finger at her chest. "Everything I want and need is here—the people I care about and will do anything to protect, who are plenty to worry over and hold on to as tightly as I can. The business my grandfather built and my father expanded—a business to be proud of, that I deserve to be a part of too." She clasped her hands together as she turned to him. "My father's legacy is here, and without me guarding it..."

"You fear no one will." Aaron closed his eyes as a large piece of the puzzle slid into place.

"Without me, what if no one remembers he existed? If I'm subsumed into another identity—another family— will he not die again?" She drew closer, so near he could see the rise and fall of her chest against her bodice. "This time at my hand."

"But you won't let that happen." He believed that. She would move mountains for her father's ghost.

"No." Her eyes shone. "I will fight for what he fought for, to honor him as best I can. Keep his memory preserved forever. No matter how foolish that seems."

"Not foolish. You love him." And she would protect that love above all else.

Even herself.

"I do." Isabelle rubbed her neck before giving him a rueful smile. "I want him back. I know I can't have him back, but this is the next best thing. I'll be wise and strong and clever and not permit myself to be distracted by anything. No wants, no treacly emotions to muddle one's decision-making. I need a husband who will support those goals, not a storybook prince. I will make the correct choice. I have to. And so..."

And so she needed something from him. The truth— what the Berabs had said. No matter the cost to him.

He tilted away from her, forcing himself back to his objective. "There's something I need to tell you."

Chapter Eighteen

Aaron held his breath, searching for the right words to convey the situation properly, to make sure she did what was right for her and for the community, without concern for him. Because she did not need the extra muddle.

Isabelle gave him a curt, queenly nod. He coughed.

Oy. Why was this so difficult? She needed to know. She specialized in risks and prided herself on analyzing them all. She wanted the information. All he needed to do was talk.

He rubbed the back of his neck. "Do you think marrying Weiss might undermine your broader objectives?"

She blinked. "Which ones?"

"Preserving your family's power and influence." He cleared his throat. "The gentiles could be insulted if you do not choose one of their favorites—a Jew who is not merely wealthy and learned, but who they find...more civilized." He swallowed uncomfortably.

Isabelle only frowned, raising an imperious eyebrow.

"From your part of the community," he added. "Which you have avoided."

"For good reason," she countered.

"I know the Duke of Sussex has indicated his

preference for Sephardi men." Aaron shook his head, cursing the man. "And few have comparable connections and standing—or longevity in England like—"

"The Berabs," she finished with a roll of her eyes. "Let me guess—David approached you with this argument?"

Aaron stared at her for a moment. Oy, she truly was sharp. "I, um . . . No, not him. The other two."

"Louis and Roger?" Her expression became thoughtful. "Interesting. I'd always assumed they hired others to do anything which would require exertion on their part."

"But you see the merit in their argument, do you not?" he said, knitting his hands a little. "Even if the bill doesn't fall apart, Weiss or someone like him isn't exactly what the gentiles are used to."

And to his great surprise, she laughed. Loudly. Beautifully. A full, enchanting laugh that lit her entire face, so much so he couldn't take his eyes off her.

"Are you all right?" he managed to ask, even as he could not stop staring.

"Very much," she said between giggles. "This is just delicious. And also inept."

"What do you mean?" Aaron shook a little, trying to make sense of her words and, more, her reactions to his.

"Yes, the gentiles favor certain Jews over others, especially ones with romantic notions about our ancestors, who they want to claim without having to abide real, living Jews, but I have found, at least from reading history, that as long as their pockets are lined and their rules are followed in their presence, in the end, for most, one of us is as good as the other. Or as bad, when they decide they want us gone. Or need a monster to slay." She gave a dismissive shrug. "Weiss is a fast learner. And the fact the Berabs dislike him so much is a point in his favor in my book." She wrinkled her nose. "Even though it won't bring about peace within the company easily."

He opened his mouth to respond, but she wasn't finished. She raised a single finger.

"Still, he's clever and ruthless, and they will not want a war with him, because he will fight to win." Her dimple appeared on her cheek. "David should understand that."

Oy.

Just. Oy.

So many plots. So many manipulations and machinations. How had these two families, who used to be so close, become like this?

It hurt to watch these clever people, who did care about the community, even if they all were not particularly... good, engage in a way that was sure to bring no one happiness. Least of all her.

But that wasn't for him to say. He was just the henchman.

"Though...," she said, frowning again as she interrupted his thoughts. "As I said before, I just wish my grandmother and Pena were more enthusiastic about the match." She pursed her lips.

"And there's no one else?" he asked. Not that it mattered to him. Not that it *could* matter to him.

"I don't know." She turned up her palms on her lap. "I'm running out of time, aren't I?" Her voice hitched.

"Do you even want to marry?" he blurted out before tugging at his hair. "I mean, if it wasn't for the business? If your father was still alive?"

"I don't have a choice now, so it doesn't matter." She pulled herself farther onto the table, moving toward him so her skirts blanketed his legs. "But I don't know. In theory, I suppose?"

"In theory?" He snorted. She either did or she didn't.

"I like the idea of it. The building of a family, the partnership, but..." She rubbed circles with her thumb on her wrist, like he had at the last festival, though much more frenetic.

"But...," he prompted, snapping his fingers and indicating her arm. With a small sigh, she offered it up to him.

"I just can't imagine having that level of trust with anyone. Even if my circumstances were different. Even if I could afford the consequences of not listening to my head. And without trust, there could never be real love, and in this dream world we're speaking of, a world in which my father was alive and I couldn't lose him or anyone else, I'd want—" Her eyes grew wide for a moment before she ducked her head.

A lump swelled in his throat. He never should've asked. Not after all she'd shared. She might be strong, but... Aaron bit his lip. What could he do to make it better—to help her put back on the armor she clung to so hard? That clearly made her feel safe and powerful in a world that wanted to strip her of both feelings?

He rubbed her gloved wrist with his thumb. "I'm not going to feel sorry for you."

And her chin was up faster than lightning, a proud, determined glint in her eye. "I didn't ask you to." She placed her free hand on her hip. "Anyway, that is neither here nor there, because we live in this world. A world where anything gained can easily be taken away. And you can only protect so much. Everything else needs to be useful but disposable. Meant to serve a purpose but its loss survivable."

He indicated the buttons holding her glove on, and she gave him a nod. "So speaking of uses you are keen on, are you attracted to Weiss?" Aaron popped open the first, exposing her skin as her breath quickened.

Or was that his? It was becoming hard to distinguish, they were so close.

"I—" She wet her lips with her tongue as he slid off the glove and deposited it on the table. "He's fine to look at, and I could willingly touch him. Same with probably a dozen or so men I've seen. Even Roger and Louis, ignoring their personalities, of course."

"Of course." He snorted to himself but cut off the biting remark on the tip of his tongue when she released a soft little sigh as the pad of his thumb hit flesh. He inhaled, the citrus already lighting his senses. "And yet with me..."

"You're different." She gave a soft moan as he stroked in lazy, easy, smooth circles.

"How?" he asked, his senses warring as he worked to keep up the conversation even as the heat of lust coursed through his body. "Because you already have control over me in one area?"

And this is meaningless. It feels good, like those stolen moments in the garden, yes, but it's meaningless. Because if it wasn't, if he let it form into something else, into a full dream, a wish, well, he'd be lost.

Perhaps America was really the best course of action. Because he couldn't stop and, worse, was already bending down to brush the same spot with his lips.

"You know it isn't about that." She closed her eyes

for a moment and shivered at his kiss. "As I said before, just because you listen to the elders at the synagogue and don't demand much more doesn't make you weak or malleable. I see you—you're your own man, who does what he thinks needs to be done for the community, just quietly." She shook her head. "No, I believe it's what you said the other day, 'lust.'"

And the word, from her lips, was like a stab. Was her wanting him for merely that any better than just needing him for a job?

Though what did he expect? And more, did it matter? He was the last person she needed to think of. In any way.

And yet...

He brushed his tongue against the back of his teeth as a hundred desires sparked in his mind. Not least of which was to make her cry his name and only his over and over, without concern for anything else.

"You're the only person who inspires it in me." She said the words so quietly, he almost thought he'd misheard her.

His breath hitched despite his lingering hurt. "Am I?" he whispered, her wrist still in his hand.

"Yes. I already said that." She pursed her lips, searching his face. "Why are you looking at me like that?"

"Like what?" A teasing tone edged into his voice. He shouldn't be doing this, shouldn't be engaging with her this way. She was danger of the highest order. And nothing about the situation could do anything for his future or health. Or hers, for that matter.

However...Aaron's lungs filled. They could be

extraordinary together. The fireworks in the garden would have nothing on them.

"Like you're proud of yourself?" She folded her arms, though her eyes danced with excitement. Oy, he truly was in over his head.

"Because I am." He chuckled to himself, already knowing he'd regret this later. "Because for some foolish reason, that makes me feel like a giant." He took her other hand in his.

"Oh." Her face broke into a full grin. "Well, I'm not sure that was my aim, precisely."

"What was it, then?" He paused, half willing her to tell him nothing, to make him walk away, to not engage in something that could only go badly for both of them.

"I wanted to make you kiss me again." She stared straight into his eyes. "I want you to more than kiss me again. To touch me again. Like in the garden. But more. I want you to make me feel something other than strain and worry."

"So you do want to use me?" And his innards were warring again, like they always did when she came at him with that combination of strength and guilelessness that near undid him—or more, made him feel things he did not wish to feel.

"No." She bit her lip before tracing a hand over his knee, her heavy lashes fluttering. "You made me feel lust and desire, so I only think it's fair that you help me quench it."

Mercy. That was not a princess line. Weiss might not be the only wolf in the tale. Not that he had a problem with that. His body tightened, or more his trousers did. Nope, no problem at all.

"And what will you give me in return?" he asked, waggling his eyebrows.

She giggled. "Always trying to be recast as a villain, aren't you?"

"I am, indeed." He gave her his best evil grin. "After all, heroes are often a bit boring."

"Yes, very much." Eyeing him, she reached out and grasped his wrist, tight. "Then I will leave the payment options up to you." She lifted his hand to her lips and kissed it, sending another course of need through his veins.

Oy, she gave as good as she got, didn't she?

Isabelle gave him a triumphant smirk. "Though I shall tell you, if you want my firstborn child, you should stick wax in your ears. I've been told I was a screamer."

"I noticed in the garden." He worked not to laugh himself. "Though I'd like to see if that holds true now as well." And with that, he pulled her fully onto his lap, where she belonged.

Chapter Nineteen

Her grandmother would murder her. But as she wrapped her arms around Aaron's neck, the necessity of living any longer than her current years suddenly wasn't so important. She pressed herself against his chest as her nipples throbbed beneath her now too tight bodice. His hand cupped her head, drawing her to his mouth once more. And it was as if stars shot through her body. Every sense was alive and dazzling.

She opened for him, welcoming him, drawing him in, moaning as his tongue mingled with hers, dark passion and whiskey and spice. With a groan, he held her tighter, moving his lips down the column of her neck as every muscle in her body grew taut. She tipped her head back, baring her entire throat to him, greedy for more.

"What exactly do you want?" he asked between nuzzles.

"Everything and anything that involves some part of you on me or, I suppose, in me." Isabelle clutched at the muscles of his upper arms, desperate for his flesh even through her remaining glove, his jacket, and his shirt. He was really wearing too much clothing. She tugged at the jacket, whimpering a little.

"That's a great deal of wants." Pulling back, he

shrugged off the jacket, grasping her again when he removed it fully. He ran the back of his palm over her cheek, eliciting a little shiver.

She worked double time on the buttons of her glove, yanking it off with her teeth and throwing it on the floor. "They're merely wants, merely ideas, not demands." And a pang slid through her ribs. Because even in this, even in this reckless, selfish, self-serving act, she couldn't have all she wanted. Not if she was to win the entire game.

He cocked his head at her. "Second thoughts?"

Isabelle slid back against him, her stays near bursting with unspent desire. "No, but it would be wise to discuss some boundaries." Her voice was a bit strained to her own ears.

"You know you can ask me to stop at any time and I'll obey." He traced her lips with his thumb, concern in his eyes.

"I shall do the same." Obviously. She bit her lip. How exactly did she explain without being crass or insulting? She threaded her fingers together, squeezing. "But this is more for expectations." Isabelle searched his face, willing him to be able to sense her meaning.

"You want to protect yourself." He squinted back at her, as if he was trying to read every thought, every gesture—as if he could come into her mind.

"I don't want to have a baby. At least not now." She bit her tongue. "I mean, I understand there are ways to prevent it, but I don't exactly have a, um—I haven't acquired a sponge or one of those sheaths, the ones made of animal parts, which isn't the most pleasant thought, but they're supposed to be effective and..." Her face grew hot, and Aaron's lips were pressed together as his face was turning a bit, well, purple. Oh, dash it all. She glared at him. "Are you laughing at me?"

"No, not in the slightest." He sniffed a little, but there was a distinct snicker behind it. "I'm just…" He coughed. "It's a bit dusty in here."

"You know, if you're going to laugh, we can just walk away and forget this ever happened." She folded her arms.

"How do you know I can? How do you know, now that you've tempted me with your very arousing discussion of—what did you call it? 'Animal parts'?" His chest vibrated and she rolled her eyes. It really wasn't that funny. He raised both brows in challenge. "How do you trust that I'd be able to just walk away?"

"Because it would violate your sense of morality." She ran a hand down his chest, reveling in the vibrations against her palm.

"I'm a custodian, not a tzaddik." The words held a bitter edge, and he grasped both her wrists, tugging them in front of him, as if demonstrating. He gave her a dark look, bringing each wrist to his lips and licking, not kissing, each of them. She squirmed against him.

"I don't know. You may scrub floors, but you seem rather wise to me, especially when you do what I say. Besides, everyone has a morality." She managed to speak between whimpers of desire as his tongue trailed the length of her arm where her glove had been. "Even you." She clenched her fingers on the table as she struggled to keep her head for this last little bit. "Especially you." She gasped as his mouth was at her throat once more. "You'd not go against my wishes, nor anyone's."

"Really?" He mumbled the word as he nipped a little at her earlobe and flames shot down to her toes.

"Really. You're a good man." She ran the back of her hand across his brow, pushing the flop of hair out of his eyes.

"You think more highly of me than I deserve." The words were flippant, but he planted a soft whisper of a kiss on her nose. His hand shook as he moved it up her back and rubbed a knot between her shoulder and neck. She near melted against him as he loosened the tension.

"And here I believed I was supposed to be the witch." She moaned his name as he pressed harder into the sore muscle. "That feels so good. How do you do that?"

"As if I'd tell you my secrets. I know what you do with secrets." He snickered a little but thankfully didn't stop.

"Are you mocking me and my plan?" She gasped as his fingers dipped down the back of her dress, beneath her corset. God, if only she could rip it off and give him everything, let him take away all the tension so her body was complete jelly.

"Not at all." He planted a kiss on her forehead. "I'm laughing because for some reason I find your willingness to manipulate men rather attractive, which is, well, continued proof that I'm a yutz."

"No, you just recognize and enjoy a true creature of the night." Isabelle rocked up so she could give him her own playful nip.

"You are no mere creature, madam." He cupped her head again, stroking her hair. "You were born to rule." And the way he gazed at her, as if it was true, as if he was actually impressed by her and not her money or her family...Tears swam beneath her eyes. As if she was really like her father. God, if only one of her potential husbands would look at her like that, would see her.

But they didn't. And wouldn't. They all had too much else to watch out for. So instead, she drew back from him and gave him her best bemused smile. "With an iron fist."

They stared at each other for a long moment, and a thousand words poured through her mind, a thousand things she wished she could tell someone—no, that she could tell him—tell Aaron. But that wasn't his role in her story. She would have to take what she could get while she still had him.

"So, no intercourse." He rubbed her thumb with his, circling once more.

"But everything else." She nodded, forcing herself into the moment, to take it as the gift it was.

"Have you done anything else? Besides what we did together?" he asked, with no mocking in his voice, still worrying and stroking with firm but gentle touches.

"No, though I've touched myself and I know what I like. At least a little." The honest words fell out with somehow no embarrassment and very little thought. Drawing up on her knees, she shifted so she could burrow herself against his chest once more.

"You're quite eager." He grinned at her as he matched her position, his hand coming around to grip her back.

"Well, we only have so much time, and I want you." More than anyone or anything. "Nothing else in my head makes sense right now but that."

"Then by your leave." He made a sweeping gesture, his eyes boring into her, as if he was waiting for her command.

Oh, if only there were more time and more privacy. What they could do . . .

She tapped her chin. "Well, we can't take off my gown. The hour is too late." A pity, such a pity. Though...she gazed at him, the buttons on his shirt already undone, revealing thick black hair covering his torso...Oh, to rub that against her...

"But I do have some loosening skills." He reached out and trailed his hand from her neck down the bodice of her gown and cupped her left breast through the thick fabric, but with a delicious firmness that made her gasp. "And I'm wondering..." He squeezed before tracing around her straining nipple with a single finger. "Are these a bit sore, Isabelle?"

Her moan was more of a whine as she closed her eyes and swore under her breath. "However did you guess?"

"I can be very, very, very, very clever in the right, limited circumstances." He fiddled with her buttons in the back and her stays and slid her gown down her shoulder. With a reverent growl, he bowed his head as he freed her breasts. Kneading one, he bent down and took the other in his mouth, his tongue swirling as his finger did.

"My God," she near shrieked before biting her lip.

"Shh," he admonished, drawing back. "Do we need to stop? Because if you're going to be that loud..."

"Oh, for goodness' sake, we're at the end of a hall, and there's music and a great crowd downstairs. No one will hear." She reached out and ran the palm of her hand over his chest.

"I don't know..." He was smiling, but his lips weren't on her anymore. He grasped her wrist, shaking his head as if he was actually considering stopping. "I'm not sure we should—"

"Bloody, blasted bastard." She pouted a little. He was mean when he teased.

"Now who sounds goyishe?" he asked.

"I pride myself on using accurate words, wherever their source." She slid her hands down his chest. "And I can give you more if you'll remove this for me."

"Fair enough." He shrugged his shirt off, leaving her to gape at his bare torso in the low light and wet her lips, desire mounting again.

Firm hands grasped her waist as he pulled her flush against him. "Let's see what other good ones I can get you to say."

She worked to keep her voice haughty as he started on her nipples again, the lazy circles building need all the way down to her toes. "I believe all my words are only carefully considered and by choice." She shrieked as his teeth grazed her, already grinding her body against his as the passion built.

"Is that a challenge?" He raised an eyebrow before lifting his head and kissing down her neck, all the while still thumbing and worrying and circling. Her hips made similar motions against him as her nails dug into his bare back.

"Perhaps," she gasped.

"Only perhaps?" he asked before swirling his tongue again, causing her to cry out. He was going to kill her. She was going to die on the library table and the Berabs would end her family line by default, but at the moment it didn't matter—nothing mattered except her body and his and all they could be together.

"Most certainly." She closed her eyes, allowing the glorious sensations to wash over her. And all too quickly, he pulled back from her. Isabelle straightened, opening her eyes wide. "What are you doing?" she asked as he stepped down, feet on the floor.

"Getting into a good spot." He planted his feet and positioned himself between her legs so if she extended them just a little more, she could wrap them around his waist.

A half moan erupted from her lips at the image alone and she scooted forward, doing just that. She buried her face in the crook of his neck, kissing down the same area he had, before taking his lips again.

"Are you sure about this?" he asked, breaking the kissing. Reaching back, he stroked her hair.

"About what?" She worked to summon all her courage as her heart pounded in her chest. "I mean, I was hoping you'd do the work of hitching these skirts—they're rather heavy—but allowing you to touch below them…" As if to demonstrate, she gathered up all the fabric and petticoats and even the hem of her chemise and threw them to the side, exposing her stockings and garters and drawers, working to keep eye contact and not flush. "I'm very certain." She tipped her chin. "Unless you don't think you're up to the task."

"Well, I'd prefer it without these." He fingered the lace edge of her drawers, traveling up and up toward the slit. "But at least there's some access."

He pulled apart the edges.

"I'm sorry? I suppose nex—" She gasped as his finger spread her curls and began those slow but firm circles right on her bud. "God." She almost choked on the word as the delicious tension spread through her body. "That's good." The word was a near whine.

"Just good?" he asked, pausing, a smugness in his voice.

"It would be better if you continued." She squeezed

her eyes shut for a moment, willing herself to say it out loud, what she had only heard whispers of in the back of drawing rooms, in conversations she was not permitted to be a part of. "With your tongue." She dug her nails into the wood, every inch of her yearning for him to not be horrified by the suggestion.

"Bossy." The smirk was audible, but with a whoosh he was on his knees, his hands on her hips, pulling her to the very edge of the table as she rested back on her elbows. "And impolite."

"Fine. With your tongue, please. You know, I'm a leader. I—" And her head rolled back as his tongue connected with her flesh, mimicking his finger. "Yes." The word was more of a half scream, half moan and near completely garbled. "Please." She swallowed as he obliged.

He pulled back and spread her a little with his finger. "Lovely," he whispered as he pressed the slick digit against her folds. She strained as her hips started to move almost of their own accord, causing her elbows to slip a little as she grasped for purchase.

Aaron planted a kiss on her thigh. "You know, this would be easier if you lay back."

"Then where would the challenge be?" She teased even as she analyzed the angles, or more the consequences, if she obliged and completely let go, completely trusted him, completely let herself take pleasure with no other concerns.

"Fair enough, though I'd like you to swoon with my prowess, not because you slip and hit your head." He kissed her again, this time right on her hip bone, laying his chin down to gaze at her.

For some inexplicable reason, something like tears marred her vision for a moment as an unbearable yearning welled in her chest.

"Well, I suppose that would get you in a bit of trouble," she managed to say as she swallowed down terrifying emotion. With as much grace as she could, shaking only a little, she lay herself back and closed her eyes, just as he gripped her hips to pull her closer.

Liquid desire stirred in every pore as he returned to her, keeping time with those slow circles as she moved her hips to the same rhythm. She ground against him, begging with her body as he slipped another finger inside her, the stretching, filling sensation sparking away any fears and doubts in a blaze of heat until there was only him.

She cried his name, reaching down to grip his hair.

"There you go," he whispered against her, his voice thick. "Just like that, love. Show me how much you want me."

Her breath caught in her throat for a moment at the word "love," even as she told herself it was a mere colloquial term of endearment and not to be taken literally. Mercy, she needed to get out of her own head and just feel. Just enjoy the pleasure she could have.

"I want you," she cried, pressing herself closer as his tongue stroked, firm and sure. "I want you, Aaron. Please."

"Please what?" he groaned the words, hot against her thigh.

"Please..." *Love me.* The words echoed in her head, and she had to bite her lip not to blurt them out. Because that was not going to happen. Not with him. Not with anyone. She had all the love she could handle in her life. She swallowed. "Please make me feel."

With a primal growl, he returned to her, taking her faster and higher all too quickly until she rolled over that impossible edge, crashing like the fireworks outside the window, her body shuddering and bucking even as he held firm, continuing through the shocks.

All too soon, they'd ended and he eased up between her legs, kissing each knee, before he pulled her up into a sitting position, rearranging her skirt so she was covered with an almost-sweet gentleness. A gentleness that near broke something inside her as the heaviness returned, filling all her cavities.

She forced a smile at him and nodded.

"Did I rise to the challenge?" he asked as he repinned a loose wave back into her chignon.

"Very much so." She made her voice bright before pausing and clasping her hands together. She bit her lip, but the truth somehow spilled out a little anyway. "Though if I had my way..."

"But you don't, do you?" He gazed at her, his deep brown eyes sad.

"No." She shook her head, the tears threatening once more, even as she forced them back again and again.

Aaron kissed the tip of her nose. "Then it's time for you to go. People will be looking for you."

She could only nod as he wrapped his arms around her waist, probably for the last time, and lifted her off the table, placing her firmly back on the ground.

Chapter Twenty

Aaron sneaked a fourth piece of cake into his mouth as he leaned against the curtain behind the ballroom dais. Neither the conquest in obtaining the food nor the act of eating assuaged any of the swirling mixture of guilt, joy, sadness, and more guilt in his gut.

What had he done? What had they done? *Schmuck, schmuck, schmuck.* The way she'd looked at him and screamed his name and told him things she'd allegedly told no one else and made him feel like he was, well, special. That he was enough just being himself with her, despite his lack of schooling and money and brains and—he was all muddled. Completely muddled. Which he could not be. Not now.

Which was why he needed to stay alert, finish his job, find a new community to which to flee when he was banished by the Berabs, and now, apparently, find a way to forget her and what they'd just shared.

Speaking of which—Aaron bit back a sigh as the younger Berabs strolled over to him, boxing him between a decorative shrub and a large gilded clock.

"We trust you've been doing what you are told." It was—what was his name again? Rupert? Roger?—who

spoke the words. The other one—Lyon? Lysander?—
stood beside him, arms folded across his chest.

"Especially as no suitable alternatives have stepped
forward," his brother said, with such an odd note in his
voice that Aaron wondered if that was their doing. Even
if that was impossible. The Berabs couldn't successfully
threaten every Sephardi man. There wasn't the time.

"Time is dwindling for Miss Lira," Roger continued,
breaking his thoughts, before sauntering away.

"And for you," the other brother—Louis! That was
it, right?—added arrogantly before scurrying after his
brother, nose in the air.

Ugh. They were truly awful, weren't they?

And he was a schlemiel. He should've never agreed
to Isabelle's offer, never started down this road, no
matter how much he wanted to see the festivals. He
should've kept his head down, stayed on his own path,
stayed in the shadows and—

"It's been quite the evening, hasn't it, Mr. Ellenberg?" Pena's voice boomed behind him. "I have to
hand it to you, acting as part of the entertainment is
quite a novel way to get around the attire requirements."

Oy, why was he so popular all of a sudden?

"I'm making sure I don't embarrass the family or
the community, just as the invitation required." Aaron
tugged at his now too tight collar. Blast it all, he'd
buttoned it wrong. Ducking farther into the shadows,
he adjusted it, his hands shaking only a little as the
older man's eyes narrowed. He settled into a lean next
to him and gave Aaron a slight sharp jab in the side.
"And the music has been lovely. I'm happy to help."

"Good food too?" the former valet asked with a
slight curl of his lip.

Aaron swore under his breath.

Pena released a low chuckle. "Oh, don't worry. No one has forbidden you from eating." Another sharp hit in the gut. The man had pointy bones. "You're still our guest, and the Lira family believes in honoring guests—even the ones of which I'm suspicious."

"How righteous of you." Aaron rubbed his probably already bruising side.

"We have to set a good example." The man shrugged before craning his neck around the crowd in front of them, indicating where Isabelle stood. "I see she's with Weiss."

Yes, she was indeed, chatting calmly, her manners perfect, her cheeks unflushed. As if she hadn't just screamed his name and clawed his back. He rubbed a spot on his shoulder, cursing the small thrill that tingled through his toes.

"She seems fond of him." Aaron gritted his teeth and toed the floor with the tip of his boot. "Likes him much better than any of the bores on the matchmaker's list."

"She told you about the list?" Pena gave him a sharp look. "Interesting." He drew out the word as he gazed at Aaron once more, his expression inscrutable.

"Why would it be interesting?" He shoved his hands in his pockets. "One would presume the family had people in mind even if the invitations indicated she might be casting a wide communal net."

"Fair enough," the older man murmured, returning his attention to the couple.

"Would you have preferred one of those men?" Aaron jabbed at the bottom of his pocket with his thumb as Isabelle laughed at something Weiss was telling her. A real laugh, not just a polite one. "The ones the matchmaker suggested?"

"I've not seen her with any of them. At least not the way I've seen her with Mr. Weiss. And certain others." Pena glared at him accusatorily, sighing. And all of a sudden, the man looked ten years older. "Though I have little say one way or the other."

"Really? I heard you practically raised her." Aaron leaned against the wall and ground his teeth as Weiss flicked the tassel on her fan. She bit her lip but smiled.

"From whom?" Pena turned fully toward him, both brows raised, his dark eyes intent, blocking Aaron's view of Isabelle.

Aaron shrugged. "Around." He wove a little, working to see her again.

Pena glanced over his shoulder and stepped to the side just as Weiss bent down to whisper something into Isabelle's ear. Aaron's jaw skittered as he folded his arms across his torso.

"Yes, well, while that's flattering, I'm uncertain that I have any sort of real influence." Pena gave him a firm clap on the shoulder. "You, on the other hand..."

"Me?" Aaron wrinkled his nose. This man was as meshuggenah as the Berabs.

"I have eyes, Mr. Ellenberg." The older man scoffed a little and resettled himself at his side. "You've developed some sort of...relationship with her. How and for what purpose, I'm not sure. Especially considering she's looking at men only as potential husbands, and while I'm sure you aren't the worst fellow, you aren't exactly suited for that. Nor are you her typical friend. And yet I've seen you two together."

"You have?" Aaron swallowed. Hopefully he'd not

seen more, because an elbow to the stomach was painful, but an elbow lower...

"Several times. Whispering. While I don't like it, I have no evidence of anything inappropriate. Moreover, it appears that she somehow trusts you." Pena's voice was soft but sincere.

"Isa—Miss Lira trusts no one outside her own family." He crossed his arms tighter.

"True. And even if she trusts us, she rarely listens." For the first time in the evening the man smiled, pride etched in the lines on his face. "But you appear to have some sway." He adjusted his cravat, giving Aaron a head-to-toe long gaze. "Though I'm still not sure why."

"Perhaps because I do more listening than instructing and advising." A strange tightness grew in his chest just as Weiss took her hand, lingering on her fingers. Aaron glanced around, but no one appeared to be watching the couple. Certainly no one who'd come and admonish the brazen touching. He clenched his fist. Someone should remind him that there were rabbis about. "Or perhaps it's because I merely want nothing from her."

"I'm not going to dignify that with a response, because I believe you want quite a few things from her—whether you've acted on those impulses or not." The man gave him a hard look that made Aaron's innards quake despite his annoyance at everyone and everything in the ballroom. "Though you're on the blunt side, so that helps." Pena lowered himself so he could speak directly into Aaron's ear. "She's not a person who requires delicacy, and prefers the opposite." The older man sighed. "She would've been better..."

"Born a man?" Aaron released a breath as Isabelle drew backward and clasped her hands behind her back, still nodding and talking but out of reach of the other man.

"No. Not at all." Pena grimaced before biting his lip. "Well, let me amend that. She'd have more opportunity that way, but I find her rather perfect as she is."

"I don't think she appreciates being called perfect." Aaron stepped forward, following Pena's gaze. She was lovely, though. Brilliantly so. And clever. And funny. And—

"Yes. Too many expectations with that as well," Pena cut in. He shook his head. "Though she's very skilled at meeting them all."

"But at what price?" Aaron murmured to himself.

"Indeed." The older man chuckled and gave Aaron a sharp kick in the calf. "Well, this is quite the development."

"What?" He rubbed his leg.

"You like her. Truly like her. And more, you care for her." Pena jabbed a finger into his chest. Sharp as well. Did the man not have a soft bone in his body?

"I do neither." Aaron picked the valet's hand from his sternum. "I neither like nor care about anyone or anything. I can't afford such things. I'm a mere custodian."

"Oh, Mr. Ellenberg, I know that isn't true." A sly smile broke out on his face, though his eyes remained narrow and judging. "I have some very good sources that tell me otherwise." The man clenched his fists. He took a step back. Those fists were probably pretty painful against flesh.

"Well, they're wrong." Aaron pursed his lips, glancing back at Isabelle and then at his feet.

"Hmm." More knowing humming. "Which brings us back to Mr. Weiss."

"You don't like him for her." Aaron nodded.

"Oh, I know how I feel." Pena sucked in his lips as if he was trying not to smile, his eyes glimmering a little in the chandelier light as he studied Aaron's face once more. "But I'm interested in knowing what you think."

"I think..." He stuck his hands back in his pockets and stared at the ground for a long while before he could force the appropriate words out. As it was one thing to give the information to Isabelle, but it was quite another to tell this man, whom he didn't know and didn't quite trust. "I think there are benefits to that pairing. Weiss's elevation might not assist with bolstering gentile support of the bill like someone prominent from your part of the community would—but if you look deeper, things might turn out better for her."

"Really?" The older man stroked his close-cropped beard.

"I believe he could be honest with her and the two could come to an understanding." Aaron sighed, though at least he'd spoken the truth and pushed what was probably the best, safest result for her. Even if it crushed him. "They're each ambitious, each clever, and each hungry. If you combine both of their qualities, they could do well together. For the business, the community, and themselves."

"Or they could encourage each other's worst inclinations." Pena cocked his head.

The two stood in silence for another long moment.

"Their motivations are different," Aaron blurted, instantly regretting the words. What was the matter with him?

"Are they?" The man's eyebrows were so high they almost disappeared beneath his graying hairline.

"She's protecting what she has, and he's searching for something of his own. Even if he won't admit it to himself." He shrugged. "Unfortunately, she's of much more use to him than he is to her. Though I suspect that's the way with most suitable potential husbands." Which was the rub and left her in more danger. "But I suppose if he's a good enough man, he could rise to the occasion, become better." He swallowed. "But she deserves someone..."

"Someone who what, Mr. Ellenberg?" Pena was at his ear again.

He stared out at the couple once more as they engaged. They did look so right together, so perfect. Neat, careful, clever, ambitious, and driven. Ready for the mantle of power despite their youth. And yet... Aaron turned back to the other man. "Someone who would want her even if she wasn't useful to them."

Blast. What was wrong with him tonight? He'd had only one glass of champagne. Perhaps he was getting soft, or his lips were becoming too loose from years of working alone.

"And she deserves to want someone the same way." Pena gave him a quick shove in the back before strolling away toward Isabelle's grandmother, leaving him to watch the couple progress, by himself once more.

Chapter Twenty-One

An hour later, Aaron was back at the synagogue, outside his own room. Pena had insisted he take one of the family carriages. And while part of his pride wanted to refuse, it was rather pleasant not to need to walk alone for hours.

Though...he leaned against the stone side of the building, twisting his fingers together, as the horses clopped off in the distance. His mind and body were still sizzling—with a thousand things, but mostly with her.

With Isabelle. And all the dangerous hope the glorious moments alone caused. He smoothed the front of his jacket before tucking the errant tails of his shirt into his trousers and pushing off the wall and into a trot. Puffing his chest, he sprinted past his own door and around the block.

Just three times. That would be enough to release the nervous energy and maybe knock all the budding fantasies—no, stories; no, dreams—out of his mind. Somehow.

The first time around, his fingers were still tingling.

The second time around, his legs ached but he knew sleep was still a long way off.

The third time around, his muscles strained and his

breath came as gasps. He would have to rinse himself
well at the basin. Aaron leaned over in the empty street
for a moment, dangling his arms over the cobblestones,
before jogging over to his door. He unlatched the lock
and paused. The hairs on the back of his neck prickled.

Someone was there. Someone or something.

A gust of wind rolled through, blowing his jacket
up, and yet he stood, frozen, waiting. The air stopped
swirling and he remained. He might be out of practice
with his street stealth. But in light of recent events, he'd
better regain it quickly.

He could outlast anyone. The minutes ticked by and
the temperature dropped, but Aaron didn't even pull his
jacket to his body. No, he would not be the first to blink.
He would not.

Scritch.

The small noise rang in the silence like a shot.

Ha. He was not the only one off balance. His lip
curled as he relaxed into character, no longer the
hunted, but a worthy adversary. He turned in the direction from whence the sound came, toward an alley
across the way. "I know you're there," he called. "You
might as well show yourself."

Silence.

"It's practically morning. The shops are going to
open soon," he tried again, making his voice as confident as possible. "Someone will notice you." He
stepped toward the alley.

No response, but another low scratching noise.
Aaron sighed. Probably a cane. Well, he had been
meaning to check on Miriam. After all, he hadn't seen
her for a few days. His body slumped as he fell out of
the role of false tough and back into his own boring self.

"Come on, Miriam. You can stop toying with me. If you have information for me, I'd be grateful. If you need something, let me know. If not, let me sleep, but don't hang around like a ghost." He cupped his mouth to make his words heard in the dark.

And another gust of wind whirled through, blowing bits of debris through the street, almost hard enough to force him backward. Aaron pressed a hand over his face to shield himself, holding steady as the howling breeze calmed enough to reveal the sound of scurrying feet.

"Mr. Ellenberg?" a voice called out, followed by coughing.

He whirled around.

"Miriam?" He glanced back at the alley, his heart now in his throat.

"What are you doing out here?" The woman stepped from the shadows, her ever-present cloak hiding her features as always and—wait. Aaron paused—hadn't the noise come from the other direction . . . ? He squinted. Was he imagining things? Perhaps the lack of sleep was really getting to him.

"I just got back from the Lira house and . . ." He bit his lip, his mind working out how to ask the question without seeming as if he was hearing things. "I beg your pardon, but were you in the alley?"

"The alley? No." Miriam's hood shook. "I came from my house. I do have one of those, you know. I may spy on the streets, but I don't actually live on them." She tapped her cane against the stones. "On the matter you had me look into, I have news. Or at least an opportunity to convey."

Which was good. Except . . . he'd heard something.

Hadn't he? His heart sped again as he gazed around the still-empty street.

Something was off.

Though with the woman there, it was certainly not the time to investigate, only to protect her. Because having her hurt due to her association with him... Aaron shook his head.

Never. He'd never let that happen. He moved around the woman, shielding her body as he indicated his door. "Let's step into my room." He offered his arm, which she refused, but she still moved in the direction he'd pointed. "For some privacy." And some safety.

Aaron swallowed as he gave the ominous space one last glance. Pulling his coat closer to his body, he unlocked the door and followed Miriam down into limited safety.

After lighting the lamps so the windowless room was more cave at dusk than forbidden cavern, Aaron leaned against the door. Miriam sniffed around before sitting on the edge of his rumpled bed.

"If you don't like it, you should tell the Commission of Delegates to get one of those big machers to make a nice donation to the synagogue to improve the furnishings. Or perhaps send someone to do the cleaning and keeping, like I do for the main building," he grumbled before testing the air himself. Oy. He probably should wash the sheets. Though truth be told, he'd barely slept since that first night in Isabelle's garden.

At least he'd been using the basin regularly for his

body. He had some pride, after all. And his garments were new and clean—sort of. Borrowed and clean—ish.

"Perhaps I shall. And perhaps I'll ask for a little aid myself. After all, I'm not the kind of woman who's talented with laundry either." Miriam settled her legs on either side of her cane.

"Fair enough." Aaron rubbed the back of his neck. "I hate to be rude, but what is this news you have for me?" Oy, still rude. Mercy, he was tired and out of sorts.

"I'll answer that shortly." Miriam shifted, and the bed creaked and groaned. "But first, I think you need to tell me some things." She pressed down further on the cane. "What's happening with Miss Lira and Mr. Weiss?"

Weiss? Again?

Why was the banker everyone's favorite topic of conversation now? First Isabelle, then the Berabs, then Pena, and now Miriam. Why did everyone believe he had some great insight? Also, it wasn't Miriam's concern, was it?

"Nothing." Aaron stared at a knot in the floorboards. "Well, not nothing. They're probably getting married." Not probably, almost certainly. He slumped farther down the door before giving Miriam a rueful smile.

"The girl likes him best, does she?" She waved a hand in his direction, and her sleeve slid enough to reveal a ring adorned with precious stones, glinting in the dark, as well as a jeweled bracelet. One that could fetch her much better garments than her ragged cloak. Odd. Was she holding on to it as a token, as a reminder of a past period of her life? He'd never taken Miriam for sentimental, though to each their own.

"Or she doesn't want to credit the Berab brothers for

having any sense regarding what type of choice would benefit the bill?" She sniffed again before straightening her shoulders, her voice cold. "What, you don't think the community's leadership knows what's happening within its bounds?"

And the temperature in the room dropped about ten degrees.

"Beg pardon?" he managed to say.

"I know why you suddenly wanted information on America—the price you will pay if she does not marry a Berab," she stated. "To their suggested concern—while most of the community's leaders don't believe marriage to an aggressive, overly bold Ashkenazi will spoil the bill, if I were you, no matter how good my intentions, I'd be careful not to lurk in libraries with unmarried women. People might make assumptions. Especially important ones, whose opinions are paramount." Miriam's voice held a sharp warning that most certainly sent a shiver through him.

Oy. Very much oy. His cheeks flushed with humiliation even as his mind churned. "Does that mean you or someone connected to the Commission watched and listened to all my..." He swallowed. Humiliation wasn't the half of it.

"No one went into the room with you." Miriam leaned back and the bed creaked once more. "But people have decent imaginations." She tapped the base of her cane on the floor, her tone completely nonchalant, as if they weren't discussing, well...that.

Blast. They were in trouble—well, more her than him. Which wouldn't do. He held up both palms, shaking his head. "We didn't—I can't make any claim on her, or more, no one else could claim that—"

"Let's not embarrass either of you." Miriam sighed. "I have no interest in that."

"Good, because she doesn't deserve it." He glared at the woman. "Nor does her family." No matter how strong and careful and cunning Isabelle was, the world was not kind to elderly widows without a family to prop them up or former valets with no one to serve. "They're doing their best—she's doing her best—to protect and keep what's rightfully hers, and she doesn't need anyone interfering."

"No. She doesn't." Miriam made a circle in the dust with her cane.

Aaron's stomach squeezed at the memory of them together.

"And yes, Weiss is a solid ally and would relish joining her against the Berabs, but she won't be able to control him like she wants." He ground his jaw in frustration. No matter what skills she had. She and Weiss were too much alike and too different in the wrong ways.

"No," Miriam agreed.

"And they'll make each other miserable." He folded his arms tight across his chest as if he could press in the aching feeling. "Or more, he'll make her miserable."

"Unless they're honest with each other and can come to an agreement, give each other a fair chance." The woman waved a dismissive hand. "And learn the rest. Like most couples."

"I suppose." Aaron kicked at the slat floor. Hard.

"It could be a fine marriage." Miriam was nodding, as if saying it aloud could make it true. "He's handsome and clever and, from what I hear, not a bad man, just a bit ruthless." Her voice became wistful. "Not something she'd dislike, nor that doesn't resemble herself. And if the two put their minds together, they could probably solve a lot of problems with the business."

"She deserves better." The words were out of his mouth before he could take them back. But they were true. She did. Yes, Weiss seemed to be at least attracted to her—though who wouldn't be?—but she was still an object to him, still a prize, not a person who deserved all the privileges he'd gain from the union in her own right. "She deserves love from the start."

"What we deserve and what we get are often quite different things." Miriam stroked the handle of her cane.

"I know." His shoulders slumped. Though what precisely did a man like him—someone with no particular brains, nor skill, nor talent, who'd made a thousand mistakes—deserve? Probably what he had. Probably a life sweeping floors.

"The bill will likely fail due to the people's resentment and prejudices, no matter how much the gentry enjoys the flattery—and more, the money—of our wealthy, and thus does not turn on her marriage." She tapped the butt of the instrument on the ground, punctuating each word. "And she will be fine. As will the business."

An image of Isabelle—the determined glint in her eye and the way she tipped her chin when she spoke of her father's legacy—flashed in his mind. Yes, the business would be fine, better than fine. Regardless of what happened in her marriage. She'd make it so, and of that there was no doubt. And even if she couldn't, she'd build something bigger and better without the worthless Berabs.

"She will." He ran a hand through his hair. "But you said you had news about America? For when the Berabs seek their revenge after she, and presumably Mr. Weiss, have frustrated their other designs?" he asked, rubbing his aching neck again. Oy. He really needed some rest.

"Indeed." She slapped a hand against her knee. "Rabbi Raphael himself, from Bevis Marks, has a cousin in New York who is starting a theater company and looking for investors. Especially one who could act as a stagehand on the side." Miriam adjusted her cloak. "Your two hundred pounds and cleaning skills should suit quite well."

Aaron stared at her. They would. Very well.

"I can see the appeal for you, whether or not the Berabs could actually succeed with their threats." The woman's voice was soft beneath the shadows of her hood. "A true chance to start anew, to be any character you desire, has to be rather tempting."

"Yes." Aaron bit his lip. After all, what she said was correct.

He'd be able to make all his dreams come true. Have the family and home and respect he'd longed for. Where he wasn't just a drain on the community he loved. Where he'd finally feel like he truly belonged.

Well... An image of himself in the library, Isabelle's hand in his, flashed in his mind, but he shook it away. That wasn't belonging; that was lust.

And it would expire. At the stroke of midnight at the last festival, when she announced her marriage to Weiss.

He swallowed as a vision of Isabelle threading her fingers through his hair while he bent to kiss her sparked in his mind, followed by Weiss taking her gloved hand. His stomach clenched. Perhaps the change of scenery would be good for him.

"So when would I leave?" Aaron strolled to her side to offer his arm, even if she had too much pride and too much propriety to take it.

"After the last festival. When Miss Isabelle is set to wed." She emphasized the last word as she struggled to her feet, waving Aaron off as usual. "Provided you consent. And there isn't another place you'd rather be."

"It doesn't matter what I want. It's what I need." He stroked his beard. It was close enough to Lag BaOmer that he could justify shaving it before the next festival instead of Friday. After all, this was his last chance to get what he'd wanted from the start. And if it was his only chance to say goodbye, he should aim to look his best.

"Fair." A sharp nod as Miriam hobbled toward the door. "America it is."

"Yes." Aaron strode after her so he could swing the thing open to reveal the night.

"I'll send something special for the festival," she called as she moved through the doorway and onto the cobblestones. "Even you deserve a little amusement once in a while." She waved that hand again as if it could conjure something on her mere whim. "No one should sit in this much gloom."

With that, she moved out into the darkness, leaving Aaron to stare and slink back into his cave to at least wash, if not think, because there was much to consider before the next week.

Chapter Twenty-Two

Isabelle swept the wide ribbons that dangled from the bottom of her new straw bonnet behind her shoulders. A little much. Especially with all the feathers, but something needed to balance out her voluminous upper sleeves.

Careful to avoid a rather large puddle, she slid around the back of the Duke's Place synagogue toward the alley, smoothing her skirts. Purple wasn't her favorite color, but in the sun, it did nice things for her eyes. Made the brown truly pop.

Yes, she had a hundred things to do before the last festival. But somehow, she'd found herself spending extra time on her powder and beeswax that morning, in addition to making sure her loops and curls shone.

Which was silly. Especially as she was supposed to be free from callers. A relief after spending endless hours in her drawing room the last few days, doing the usual dance.

Weiss and several other young men, not to mention all three Berab brothers, under the guise of needing to share "important information," had shown up with gifts and sweets and pointed questions. So much smiling and nodding and trying not to let the world see the panic just below the surface.

But no, today she'd made sure everyone knew she, her grandmother, and Pena were visiting her father's grave. And it wasn't a lie nor inappropriate. After all, it was the anniversary of his death. So in addition to fasting, they'd traveled out past Whitechapel to Bancroft Road and laid a stone at his marker near the hazel tree.

Pena recited Kaddish while she stood and wished for a sign she'd not strayed from the path. But none came.

"You know, he'd want you to be happy," Pena said as their carriage bumped westward, toward home. "That was what made him happiest in the world. Seeing you happy."

"You made him plenty happy too," her grandmother told the other man, reaching out and clutching his hand for a moment. "My son was lucky to have found you. I just hope my granddaughter is looking to your example."

Isabelle shook her head. If only she had that luxury. What her father had achieved with Pena was available only under a very particular set of circumstances, ones that were certainly not present for her.

No matter how much she wanted them to be. Which was why she'd been working so hard not to let her mind go in certain directions and why she was going to need to be extra vigilant from now on. No matter how difficult.

"I will be very happy," she assured them both, breathing in and out of her nose as deeply as possible. "Once I retain the company and our position in the community, continue his legacy. Though..." She bit her lip, not quite certain how to put the odd, unsettled feeling in her gut at ease. "Perhaps hosting three festivals is too much. Not that the idea was wrong, per se. But maybe my execution was not as perfect as it could be. Perhaps the gentiles will truly find us gaudy and gauche."

"Would you like to cancel the last one?" Her grandmother narrowed her eyes. "As I have said from the beginning, this is about you. It's your choice."

"No." Isabelle frowned as she rearranged her hands in her lap. "It's too late. People will assume the business is weak and come for our clients. Or that there is something wrong with us—with me—which will leave no other options regarding marriage, and thus I'll either be forced to live with a Berab brother or watch the Lira half of the company wither and die." The gnawing in her stomach swelled in crescendo, and she pressed a hand against her bodice. "I must go through with the final festival and must marry."

"I believe that things will turn out right for you." Her grandmother leaned close. "Lira women are no one's fool." Her bony hand gripped Isabelle's with firm assurance. "Our line has been marrying well for generations, and the streak will not end with you."

And suddenly, her throat was tight and her voice was thick. Glancing out the window for an exit, she coughed a little. "I, um, think I'll call upon Rebecca. Can you let me out?"

A reasonable request. And one that would do her good. After all, Rebecca was brilliant and loyal, and if there was anyone who could keep her from making a terrible mistake...

"Of course, darling," her grandmother said, a small note of worry in her voice that Isabelle chose to ignore. "Tell her mother I said hello."

The carriage ground to a halt before her friend's house. The coachman ran around and opened the door to help her out.

"You are your father's legacy," Pena whispered as the door closed after her.

She watched them bump into the distance as a new door creaked open.

"I'd invite you in, but I know this is not actually where you want to be." Rebecca's tone was slightly caustic, but her expression was bemused.

"No," she admitted with a slightly sheepish sigh. "But I should be here, and you're supposed to prevent me from—"

"I know what you want me to do." Her friend gave her a small, playful shove. "And if I thought you weren't going to just go there afterward, probably when it is too dark for you to be poking about in these parts alone, I'd take you inside. But given the hour, and the fact my mother and I have work, I'm just going to send you on your way, with this." Reaching behind her, she pulled out a small pouch and shoved it in Isabelle's direction.

"What is this?" she asked, turning it over in her hands in confusion.

"Something you will need, especially if you marry, but it can be used before." Rebecca gave her a long meaningful stare, as if Isabelle didn't get her meaning. As if they hadn't had this conversation in the past.

Mercy. Yes, she was grateful for the sponge, but she'd come for assistance in doing what she was supposed to and not…what she was going to actually do.

"Thank you," she stammered, not quite meeting her friend's eye, as the other woman gave her a quick hug before retreating into her home.

Not daring to look inside the package, Isabelle turned away from Rebecca's door and strode as fast as she could toward the Great Synagogue.

However, now her pace slowed as she made her way around to the back of the building, kicking loose stones into puddles with her new white boots.

Which was ridiculous. And not just because it endangered the pristine state of her garments. But because it was almost as if she was, well, nervous.

And that was ludicrous. Aaron was the least fearsome person she'd ever met. That was why she was so comfortable with him. Not that she needed comfort. She just wanted to say hello, be friendly. That was all. Nothing more.

And yet here she was, stalling.

Which would not do. She was an adult. Clutching her chain purse to her side, she forced up her chin and strode toward his door.

"And the cat asked the ogre to transform into a... Who remembers?" A familiar voice floated around the corner.

"A tiger?" was the high-pitched response of an unseen child.

"A dragon?" another equally young hidden companion suggested as she crept closer along the side of the building, and a small group came into view. An echo of the first time she'd seem him. The first time they'd met.

Before her, right outside the synagogue door, was a circle of small boys sitting cross-legged on the cobblestones. Aaron was at the center, perched on a crate, a calico cat on his lap. No one noticed her, save the creature, who gave a look of distain as the man she sought scratched behind its ears.

Lucky beast.

"No—I know." A small bespectacled boy piped up, raising his hand and drawing her attention back. "A lion."

"That's right." Aaron reached out and gave the boy's head a tousle behind his yarmulke. He turned back to the group, his lip twitching. "And the lion frightens our hero so much he was shaking in his boots."

"Poor, poor cat," another boy said, reaching out and giving the creature on Aaron's lap a gentle pat, which the feline grudgingly accepted.

"And then what happened?" the first boy asked. "How did he escape?"

"Well," Aaron said, glancing from side to side as if he were telling them a secret. "He summoned all his courage and asked the ogre to transform again. Just one more time."

Isabelle's lip twitched. He really was enthralling.

"But why? What would that do? Or more, how could that help him escape the magical ogre?" the spectacled boy asked, his hand raised once more.

Aaron scooted forward on the crate. "Those are good questions. But you're missing a key fact. His plan, you see, turned on the creature he requested. Can anyone guess what it was?" he asked as Isabelle stepped closer, somehow unable to stop her feet from moving toward him.

"A dragon?" a child called out.

"Bah, a dragon won't help. A dragon would light the cat on fire. And don't anyone guess a tiger this time," another boy chimed in before giving him a shove. Soon all were murmuring and arguing over possibilities, probably like they did inside with the rabbis. Though most likely with quite a bit more enthusiasm.

"So no one knows?" Aaron's voice rose through the thrum, clear and confident, but with a hint of mischief that was just magnetic.

"No. Tell us," they cried, drawing up on their knees.

"I think we might have another player in our game." Aaron lifted his chin, his dark eyes meeting hers, and he broke into a smile that could heat a thousand rooms.

Her heart sped as all the little faces turned to stare at her.

"Do you know?" Aaron gave her that crooked grin that did odd things to her knees and made it very hard to breathe.

But breathe she did, as she would not be bested. Especially as she did indeed know the answer.

"A mouse," she told them as she picked her way into the circle, squatting as gracefully as she could so she was on their level, petticoats and skirts be damned. "The cat asked the ogre to transform into a mouse."

Aaron's smile widened, and he gave her a respectful nod that made her feel, well, almost as good as when she handed David Berab a perfectly negotiated and secure contract. "And there you have it, boys. The ogre turned into the mouse, and our hero ate him. A fair and just result. Though you'd never eat a non-murderous ogre mouse, would you, Sir Sleeps-a-Lot?" He snuggled the cat to him, which, well, did rather funny, tingling things to her stomach.

Isabelle wet her lips and rocked forward on her toes, probably creasing her leather shoes, until there was a tug on her sleeve. She turned to find the boy with the spectacles staring at her.

"Are you a princess?" he asked, blinking up at her.

"No," she told him, shaking her head. "I am nothing of the sort."

"Oh." And his little face fell. She glanced up at Aaron, who shrugged, but the cat most certainly gave her a look of disapproval. Which she couldn't let stand.

She turned back to the child. "I'm something better," she told him, sticking her nose in the air. "I'm a Surety Empress."

"What's that?" another child called out.

And in moments, all of them were asking questions at the same time.

"It means she could buy, sell, and assess the risk of all of us," Aaron told them, cupping his hands to speak over the fray. "Which also means she knows as well as I do that it is time for all of you to go back inside and study, before you get scoldings." He indicated the door. They groaned but rose and shuffled toward the building.

"Though, you know, the best way to avoid a scolding is to answer every question with a question. The scolder will get so frustrated and distracted that they will eventually give up and you will win," she called to them as she waved goodbye.

"Really?" one asked.

"Why don't you find out?" Aaron suggested, rising himself.

Rolling their eyes with more grumbles, they each gave him a small salute before disappearing into the synagogue, leaving them alone, save the cat, who, after being released from Aaron's lap, had ambled to the sunniest spot and was now lying on his side.

"That was interesting advice." Hands clasped behind his back, he strolled around to stand in front of her.

"It has always worked for me." She swung her hips a little. "That, and puffing out my lower lip," she added, giving him a rather exaggerated demonstration of the expression that had always worked so well on her father and Pena.

"I can see how that might be effective," he murmured, gazing down at her with an expression that could only be described as hungry.

Which shouldn't thrill her as much as it did.

"So..." He rubbed the back of his neck, his shirt stretching tight across his long, lanky, and for some reason, oh so attractive frame. And her breath caught in her throat once more.

He coughed into his hand. "Look, I know the festival is four days away, but I haven't found you any additional information that might help in your final negotiations and—"

"It's all right." She threaded her hands together. "I mean, I'd welcome help, but today I was just...I was riding past and I thought I'd say hello." And the words were jumbled and fast and nothing like her usual competent, confident, practiced speech.

But he smiled again and stepped closer. "Hello," he whispered. He reached out and she closed her eyes and—a large feline yawn echoed against the walls. And the touch never came.

"So, Sir Sleeps-a-Lot?" she asked, opening her eyes again, a touch disappointed.

"It's an apt description of him. Most of the time." Aaron gave the cat a glare, which made her giggle.

"And you feed him?" she asked, sweeping toward the creature, smoothing her skirts. "Why?"

Aaron joined her stroll, his hands clasped behind

his back once more. "Among other things, it helps keep him away from Lady Dashby and her family."

"Who?" She wrinkled her nose, but he took her by the arm, helping her kneel behind a trough. He indicated a small chamber off to the side. She peeked inside and—

"They're mice," she said as she stared at the squirming creatures on their bed of straw, insulated with bits of fabric and outfitted with thimbles filled with water next to a series of buttons. Aaron gently reached in and put a few crumbs on each as if they were plates.

"That they are. We're neighbors. And neighbors take care of each other, even when we lack the same status." He helped her to her feet and squinted. "What?" he asked.

"Nothing." She shook her head, only able to stare at his beautiful, kind, achingly sincere face. "You're...I don't think I've ever met anyone like you. Certainly not in real life."

Aaron cocked his head. "Is that a good thing?"

Her eyes sparkled. "Most definitely."

And before he could say another word, she reached up and wrapped her arms around his neck. In an instant his hands were at her waist. Bending, he took her mouth, and it was as if the world once again made sense. It was more than tingles. More than want. More than need. It was everything. It was just him and her, a universe of two. If only she could stay there, with him, forever.

But he stopped. And pulled back, squinting down at her, even as he stroked her cheek. "Is Weiss different?" he asked, an odd strain in his voice.

What did he mean by that? She frowned, probably

sprouting those wrinkles her grandmother was always warning her about. "From the Berabs and the men on the matchmaker's list, yes," she said, her heart pounding hard beneath her ribs.

"From everyone else you've ever met?" He narrowed his eyes.

"Very much no." She pressed her lips together. Weiss was just a very motivated version of a specific type.

Which he knew. Weiss was not him. Nor could he ever possibly be. Which he had to know as well. She opened her mouth but paused as he inhaled, his chest rising.

"Isabelle—" he started.

But the door swung open, and a man stepped into the alley, startling them apart. "Aaron, there you are, my—oh, hello," he said, giving her a small bow. "Miss Lira, how lovely to see you."

"And you as well, Rabbi Marcus," she returned, forcing her face into her most congenial, respectful smile, hiding any hint of frustration or disappointment as best she could.

"Tell your grandmother that the festivals were lovely and I'm looking forward to the last one." He put an almost protective arm around Aaron's shoulder.

"We'll be so pleased to see you." She twisted the buttons along her glove.

"As will we. We'll be looking forward to your announcement." The rabbi gave her a rather odd look as he opened the door, motioning to Aaron. "Come along, Mr. Ellenberg," he called, snapping his fingers. And before she could say anything more, the two had disappeared into the synagogue, leaving her alone, a lump in the back of her throat.

Peculiar. Though she had no time to ponder it, or the tightness in her chest or the sting behind her nose. She had too much to do. She was going to be a bride. To the right groom. That was her prize, and her eyes needed to be on only it.

Lifting her chin, she marched back toward Rebecca's house so she could secure transportation home, like any good general, ready to plan the next battle in her war. Which she would win. No matter what. She glanced behind as Sir Sleeps-a-Lot gave her a yawn.

Distractions be damned.

Chapter Twenty-Three

Aaron kicked a loose stone against the gaudy fountain in the Liras' garden. He shouldn't be there, especially following the afternoon in the alley that made him, once again, yearn for things he couldn't even dream of having. Yet somehow, despite all the danger to his heart, there he was. He ran a hand through his newly trimmed coarse hair. A bit uneven, but why should he care? He was still just a custodian, a man whom most people forgot about unless they tripped over his bucket.

He stared at the house. Oy, he was a schlemiel. Bending down, he palmed a pebble, running the smoothness over his rough and scarred palm. Probably a far cry from Weiss, whose touch Isabelle would learn to like better.

Blast. He squeezed the stone harder. He needed to forget about that: stop the dreaming, the wishing, the new scenarios his mind would not stop inventing. Her coming to him, climbing on his lap, grasping his hands in hers, and showing that she wanted him, the same way he wanted her.

Heaving a sigh, he skipped the rock across the fountain with a satisfying splash. Because she didn't actually want him. How could she, a woman who could be matched with the best the community had to offer, even entertain wanting him? No, he was some sort of desperate relief for her nerves before she forced herself into a loveless marriage, not someone worthy of actually being part of her world.

Shoving his hands in his pockets, he spun around and choked as the point of a wide blade thrust out right against his neck. Blinking, he gaped at Isabelle, her hair loose and flowing down her back, standing in the moonlight, this time wearing only a thin night rail, her arms bare, her expression inscrutable except for a small glint of triumph in her dark eyes.

"You shouldn't be in my garden," she said, not lowering her blade—or more sword. In fact, she squeezed the hilt tighter in her hands.

"Why not? I'm still in your employ." His lip tipped up in mild amusement at the vehemence on her face, though he didn't dare move. After all, the blade was near touching his neck and recently sharpened from the looks of it. "And can you put that thing down?" He pulled back a fraction of an inch. "I thought you liked knives, not swords."

"I do. I'm best with a dagger and cloak, especially when I use the one my father gave me, but we practice other things." She closed the gap he'd created, this time allowing the steel to rest right against his flesh so he could no longer swallow.

"'We'?" he asked, his eyes darting around in case she had some sort of army to whom he'd never been introduced. He wouldn't put it past her; she really was like a medieval lord in her thinking, probably would've dug a moat if it were feasible and in fashion.

"Pena and I. Tonight was sword sparring." Her hands

didn't even shake as she held the blade. "Two-hand grip." She indicated her bare, firm hands with her chin. "It's my weakest because of size, but I've come a long way."

"I'm sure..." Nope, not frightening at all. "Though again, I'd prefer it not to be at my neck." However, for some reason it was also alluring, especially as her hair billowed, framing her face, poised and calm yet strong. Oy. And now he was warm. More than warm.

"It's a good thing I had an inkling that you might make an appearance. Cook and I made sure everyone would sleep rather soundly, as your skills in stealth leave something to be desired. Honestly, you splash louder than a gaggle of waterfowl." With a sigh of her own, she obliged, lowering her weapon and sheathing it at her side, the belting now pulling her gown tight against her body. His mouth went dry as a hundred inappropriate thoughts sparked, not the least of which involved her yanking that gown over her head so he could get an even better view.

"I never claimed stealth as a skill." He glanced down at his boots so as not to stare at all the things he shouldn't stare at. "My chief talent—other than scrubbing and sweeping—is storytelling. But only children find me entertaining."

"That's not true. I enjoy listening to you very much. And you have other skills. Including gathering information. Something we have in common. After all, my family has made a fortune gathering information to make predictions of disastrous outcomes and put values on those probabilities." Isabelle twirled a lock of hair around her finger.

"Huh." He cocked his head at her. Interesting. And logical, which seemed quite a good fit for Miss Lira.

His heart squeezed. That one twist of fate. That one small thing. If not for that, her life would be so much easier. Though they'd have never met. And they wouldn't have been in the library together and certainly would not be here now. And while she'd be better off in the other scenario, he couldn't help but be glad for the present.

"At least you're clever enough to understand that you do need a partner, that you cannot lead alone." He waved a dismissive hand as he backed toward the edge of the fountain.

"Yes, even Moses had help." Isabelle shrugged again.

"And you're upgrading—trading Miriam and Aaron for Solomon," he joked, even if it hurt.

"I can only hope this iteration has half the wisdom of the original." She gave him a half smile. "With more fidelity," she added with a sniff worthy of a monarch.

And yet the way she searched his face for a reaction to her dry bravado twisted his innards even tighter.

"I do think Weiss could most certainly make a worthy second for you," he said, hating the words, even if they were objectively true.

"Hopefully. If he'll accept my terms." She tangled the ends of her black waves around her fingers, pulling and tugging and twirling. Aaron worked not to sigh as his foolish mind conjured images of that same hair trailing across his bare chest as she kissed downward. That would not happen. She was not for him. He closed his eyes and instead forced himself to picture the other man smirking at him, ring in his hand.

"He will." Aaron ran his tongue over the back of his teeth. Digging his heels into the back of his boots, he willed himself to look her in the eye. "You are the only one he wants to marry."

"I know." She folded her arms tight. "And I know why. What he wants from it. What it will give him—money for his brother, freedom to chart his own path, not mere access to the community, but near guaranteed leadership." She bit her lip. "But I worry he's too loyal to himself and to his own family and will never be truly loyal to the company. Will never love it. Though if he actually loved sureties, I'd be worried too. I don't believe Weiss is particularly good at sharing. Not that I am either." She shook her head, giving him a rueful smile that didn't reach her eyes. "But I think the business is a means to an end for him, so he should agree to my dominion."

"You should tell him." He sat himself on the edge of the fountain as he'd done before.

"What?" She pursed her lips.

"You should explain all this to Weiss—not just the boundaries of what you want, but the rationale and the stakes and fears. Show him all of who you are. So he can fully know you. And fall in love with you." Because how could anyone not, once they saw the full her?

And she deserved love, even if she refused to see it. Even if it was with Weiss.

"You've been reading too many romantic stories. Or I've grown too cynical." She moved toward him but didn't sit, just stood at the edge of his knees, so close that a light gust of wind would sweep her gown against his trousers. "Or more, perhaps because I can't picture being satisfied with what I was offering if I stood in his shoes. And I'd grow to resent, not love me."

"Resent you? How?" He raised both eyebrows, even as his breath hitched in his throat.

"I don't know." She toyed with another lock of hair. "Perhaps 'resent' is too strong of a word. Still, I believe you were right the other day. As was my grandmother—though if you tell her I said that, I will deny it a hundred times over." She gave him a smile that didn't reach her eyes. "But if we are being truly honest, if my back wasn't to a wall, if I had his flexibility, I'd want more than any of my plans encompass. I'd want to win it all, and my bargain will never offer that." She sniffed, her fingers trailing down her side to her sheath. "I like winning, in case you couldn't tell. Witch, remember? A witch with a sword that I very much know how to use."

"In defense or offense?" Not that he couldn't guess from the confidence in her stance.

"In both." Her chest rose. "And I may be all practice and theoretical knowledge, but would you really want to test my actual mettle in either?"

No, most certainly not. Though, because all his sense apparently left him when he was around the woman, a shivery, shimmery thrill slid down his spine as he gazed at her.

"Is it wrong that I appreciate how Weiss keeps his ambitions on the surface like I do?" She stroked the hilt of her weapon absently. Aaron swallowed but spread his legs apart, welcoming her to step forward despite the danger, despite the fact they were still discussing another man. Yes, there was most certainly something wrong with him when it came to her.

"I don't think so." It was his turn to shrug. "Though, to be fair, you're a bit more subtle in polite society than he is." *Though honest with me.* Which he could not think about, because that would only lead to foolish hope and muddle him, which neither of them needed.

"Very true." She stepped closer, so close that he could easily wrap his hands around her waist and pull her to him once more, even though he shouldn't, even though it would only cause pain. His fingers twitched but remained on his thighs. Because for some reason, with her he didn't play a role, and to believe for even a moment that she wanted him, just Aaron...Impossible.

"Which is probably why my grandmother hesitates with him so much—that, and I suspect a small part of her believes the gentiles' views of our part of the community versus yours, no matter how above that line of thinking she pretends to be. After all, it's hard not to see yourself as superior, nonsense or not." She rolled her dark eyes, breaking him out of his gloomy thoughts. "And it's no secret that she wanted rabbinic lineage. Under all the silks and jewels and practiced manners, she's still a second-rate merchant's daughter yearning for a true learner."

"No matter how much your class of earners has risen in status in the community." He stared up at her, already imagining her hands on his shoulders.

"Correct. We've climbed so high that we are supposed to be able to do only what we were meant to—to only study. To transform ourselves into learners." She gave a harsh half laugh. "At least Weiss has cunning. And clear wants." She cocked her head and refocused on him, tapping a finger against her chin. "What do you want, Mr. Ellenberg?"

Other than for you to touch me? The words soared through his mind even as he fought them. He gazed at Isabelle but she was still staring at him, so he thankfully hadn't said them out loud.

"What?" he managed.

"What do you want? You ask me what I desire in life, talk about what I allegedly deserve, but what about you? What do you wish? What do you dream?" she repeated. She fiddled with the ribbon tying her gown below her neck, and his mouth went dry once more. Oh, for that to be his hand instead of hers...

"Dreams and wishes are too expensive for the likes of me." He shook his head as he worked to focus on a spot above her head, even as the scent of citrus swirled around him, making each sense come alive with not only want, but intoxicating lust. But it wasn't just lust, no matter how much he wanted it to be. "And believe it or not, I really don't mind my job now. At least not most of the time."

"Really?" She rocked her hips closer. His body tightened and he worked not to gasp.

"I benefit the community. And it's the only place where I've felt like I was truly of use, like I could belong." Well, with the exception of his moments with her. Not that he could make that confession. Especially now, as the time he had with her was drawing to a close. He squeezed his eyes shut. "I have no parents, no family of my own. However, the people there and the animals I care for make me feel..." And he couldn't finish the words.

Not now. Not when he was leaving. He swallowed.

He'd be all right. He'd find a new community. This time with the funds and stature to allow him to have that family of his own. To get what he had always wanted.

The cost, it seemed, was just a touch higher than anticipated.

A light breeze rippled through the trees and shiver dimples rose on her bare arms, but she didn't even flinch. She reached up and placed her palms on his shoulders. "Is this all right?" she whispered.

Yes. His body screamed the word even if it was wrong and perilous and dangerous and the last thing either of them needed.

"It shouldn't be." He shook his head.

"Do you want me to let go?" she asked, her fingers tensing on his shoulders.

"No." He leaned into her—he couldn't resist. He wasn't that strong. He wet his lips as every fiber of his being burst into flame with need. "No, I don't."

"What do you want?" Her voice was husky now as her body brushed his, only a few layers of thin material between them.

He should stop this. He should resist. But there was no way. The fire of lust was about to turn him into ash, but he didn't care. All he cared about was this moment and all its promise.

Aaron gazed into her eyes, never surer of anything in his life. "I want you."

Chapter Twenty-Four

Isabelle stared down at Aaron as he wrapped his arms around her waist. Sitting on the edge of the fountain, he pulled her hips toward his, just as she'd imagined.

This was a terrible idea. Not just because she was going to be betrothed to someone else in mere days. No, because she saw him. Saw how he loved and cared for and nurtured everyone and everything. Saw what he wanted. And it wasn't respect or independence, though he'd appreciate those.

No, it was something she could not give him herself but that her money would enable. Something that, if she was a good person, she'd rejoice in him receiving. Except the concept filled her with a whole host of unpleasant emotions that she should not have and did not need.

If she was a better person, she'd pay him now and tell him to run. Far away from her and the garden. She had the power to protect them both. If only she was just a touch stronger.

Except she wasn't. And in the moonlight, right and wrong and good and bad turned so topsy-turvy that she was near lost. She pressed her body against his, already swaying to the delicious friction. "How do you want me?"

"What?" Aaron's brow pinched in confusion.

She swallowed. How to approach this without pressuring him into doing something he'd regret? Perhaps guiding him with action? Isabelle bent down to whisper in his ear but caught his lobe between her teeth, like he had done to her in the library, sucking a little as pleasure shot through her once more. He groaned, dipping his head back.

"What exactly do you want to do with me?" she asked, her body already humming with possibilities.

"I—" His eyes went wide, but apparently not in horror, as his fingers dug into her hips, holding her against him.

"I'm not sure that's an answer," she teased before kissing over his beard, rubbing her lips on the rough bristles along his jaw, and she was rewarded with another groan.

He gazed up at her, his eyes half-open. "You have to understand, I've been dreaming about you since the last time, so my mind is a little foggy sorting out options."

"Have you now?" Her eyes twinkled with pleasure, and the humming was accompanied by tingles, echoing in all the places their last encounter had brought to life.

"Oh yes." He gave her a near wicked grin, which made her yearn for him and only him.

"I've thought about you too," she confessed as she hitched her skirts so she could wrap her legs around his waist and sit, body to body.

"Really?" His voice was reedy but he licked his lips.

Power surged through her, mixing with desire, overwhelming all sense or doubts.

"At night." She rubbed her already aching nipples against him. "Alone in my room."

"Isabelle." He groaned and that only heightened the wicked, wanton thrill that her name on his lips inspired.

"I want you to tell me, Aaron." She dug her fingers into his shoulders, as if she could somehow hold him and this moment forever. "I want the words."

His eyes grew even wider, but as the words settled on her ears, the truth of them shuddered through her. She didn't just want the words. She needed them. She cupped his chin so she could gaze into his eyes. "I want you to make me believe you want me as a person, not as a chess piece—that this is different than the game I'm playing with the rest."

Aaron rocked up so he could take her lips in his. Isabelle closed her eyes, allowing their tongues to mingle, to pleasure each other as the heat built once more, dark and strong and heady. He pulled back and shook his head. "You're no chess piece. No prize to be won. And you are most certainly a person." He licked his lips again, the heat back in his eyes. "A person I very much want to make come."

She laughed.

"Is that too crude?" He wrinkled his nose, an almost worried gaze on his face.

"I like crude." Her voice was a little raspy. "It's real. So little in my world is real. Especially now. And it will only grow more confusing, it seems." She bent to nuzzle his neck. "Please give me real."

"You shall have real." Mischief sparked in his eyes. "If you remove that." He indicated her gown.

Her breath hitched. Wicked wasn't the half of it. They were outside, and while the garden was walled and it was dark and everyone was asleep and they were beneath an ornamental arch, their privacy wasn't guaranteed. The house still had windows. Which shouldn't send a thrill up her spine but somehow did. The danger, the excitement, and more the fact that they were partners in it, doing it together—Isabelle shivered before undoing her sheath and laying it and her sword on the ground. Closing her eyes, she whipped her gown over her head.

Her nudity should make her nervous. But now, when she was there with him and he was gazing at her with something almost like awe, there was only anticipation.

"All right, I did your bidding." She held up her chin. "But you have to remove your garments as well."

"Do I now?" He bit his lip. "But I wanted to have you do that for me."

Fire—that was what was now spreading through her veins. God, she needed him, every moment she could have.

"That can be arranged," she managed, her voice husky. Hands shaking only a little, she pushed off his jacket and undid every single one of his buttons. His chest moved in and out under her fingers. He groaned again.

"Is that part of what you imagined?" she asked.

"There was kissing involved as well." He puffed out his lower lip, which was just... delicious.

She bent down and nipped it with her teeth, already reveling in the sensation of her bare body against his—skin to skin, as they were intended, the coarse hairs of his chest thrilling her senses. "Was there?" she managed to ask.

"Lower." He moved his hands beneath her bottom,

squeezing a little as he lifted her. It was her turn to moan. Liquid heat shot through her lower half as her body readied itself for things she could not have. However, tonight she was prepared to take everything she could, everything he would willingly give.

Isabelle lowered her head and kissed down his chest, stroking her tongue over the different textures, the rough hair and the smooth skin of his nipples, down and down. She scooted back so she could tease the skin right above his trousers, flitting just below. She raised her head to catch his eye. "Like this?"

"Isabelle."

God, the way he said her name like that, as if he was about to lose control, just because of her. Her breath hitched again.

"That good?" she asked before she kissed his stomach once more. She leaned her chin against him. "Now what? Do I go lower?"

"You don't have to." His voice was raspy, and his heart quickened against her flesh.

"That's not what I asked." She pressed another kiss into him as if the action could show him how much she wanted to make their pleasure mutual. How much that would please her. "Do you want me to?"

He fisted his hands in her hair with a garbled grunt.

"You're allowed to say yes." She licked lower and he writhed, digging the heels of his boots into the ground on either side of them. "Actually, I'd prefer you to say something more than just yes. I'd like a little encouragement."

"You want me to beg?" he asked as he gripped her tighter.

"Not beg, per se." She frowned as she worked to

articulate what she needed. "More—no, no, I'd very much like you to beg. I'd like you to want me so much you plead for my lips to touch you. To glide down your body. To wrap my mouth around you and pleasure you with my tongue. Explore every inch of you that you'll permit." As she spoke, the images sparked in her mind, so real and magical that she was already grinding her body against him, the need building. "And more. I, um, I procured a sponge." Her cheeks burned at the confession, even though they shouldn't, because it was the mature and responsible thing to do and—

Aaron swept her hair off her cheek. "Are you sure— I mean..." Even in the dim light, the uncertainty on his face was unmistakable.

"I want it." She pointed to herself, offering a silent plea for him to want it too. "The question is, Do you? Because if you don't, I don't want you to feel obligated." She swallowed, willing all her bravery to push her forward. "However, if you do want to, I'd like you to ask for it."

"All right. Yes. I want to be in you, in your mouth and your quim." He breathed another heavy, rasping sigh before glancing around them. "But, um..."

"Yes?" Her lip tipped up a little at his nervousness.

"Can we..." He inclined his head toward another bench. "That has a back, and I really don't want to fall into the fountain."

She giggled so hard she snorted and had to cover her mouth. Aaron's face broke into a wide grin as he pulled her hand down, bringing his mouth to hers once more. She moaned as he nipped her lip, before opening for him again. God, she could never get enough of this, enough of him. They broke apart, and he pressed his forehead to hers.

"It would ruin some of the pleasure if we fell, wouldn't it?" she asked.

He laughed. "Decidedly so. Especially if we were injured."

"That would be quite embarrassing and difficult to explain. All right." She planted a short kiss on his lips. "Take me to the other bench."

Aaron winked at her, lifting her as she wrapped her legs around him. "Yes, ma'am."

Chapter Twenty-Five

This had to be a dream. Aaron withheld the urge to pinch himself as he moved to the much sturdier seat, Isabelle in his arms, her legs threaded over his hips. He settled down with her on his lap once more, completely nude in the moonlight, her gown forgotten at the edge of the fountain. And yet she didn't shiver, but instead nuzzled him. He strained against his trousers. Never had he experienced want like this. Not for anyone nor anything—money, respect, belonging, nothing.

"Here we go." He adjusted himself, working to hold on to his last sliver of control before he gave himself completely over to her and the night and the passion. "Are you sure you want to do this?"

"Did you like whatever we did the other night is called?" she asked as she ran a soft finger between his eyes, as if she could smooth the worry lines. "When you made me come?"

"Very much." He licked his lip at the memory. God, he needed that again, needed her all over his tongue, bucking beneath him, losing all of that calculation and control for him and only him. As if he was actually important to her, as if she believed he was special despite the fact he was so very not.

And yet when she gazed at him like that, her eyes intent and full of lust, her legs wrapped around him as if he were the only thing in the world, the most important thing in the world, how could he not believe it? And how could he not plead for her to continue?

"Well, I imagine I'm feeling the same way now as you were then." She traced a finger down his chest. "I just need a little guidance and encouragement." She gave him a saucy wink.

"Like begging?" he whispered the question, the idea becoming more and more appealing.

"I like begging." This time she ran the finger down her own neck, tangling it in her hair. She licked her lips. "And again, some direction. Our library is rather extensive, so I have a decent concept of the various acts, but I dare say I'm a bit short on practical experience."

"That's fair." On impulse, he brushed another kiss on her lips, a soft one, as if to give them both courage, before leaning back, his cheeks growing a bit hot. "Well, I suppose we need to remove my trousers and breeches first."

"Yes, that would probably be a good idea." Her tone was dry, though there was an amused glint in her eye.

He gave her a faux sniff. "Are you mocking me?"

"What? Never." She wiggled her hips as she slid off his lap and onto the ground, gazing up at him. "Do you want me to remove them?"

"Please." He gasped the word as he marveled at the view, his body becoming more and more excited.

"With pleasure." And she drew up on her knees to unfasten his trousers, her hands steady. With a swift movement she tugged them off, making quick work of his breeches as well, leaving both to puddle around his boots. He moved his legs as far apart as he could and grabbed himself in his fist.

His heart beat near through his ribs as she swept her long mantle of hair to the side and licked her lips again.

"You're lovely," she whispered, gazing at all of him.

"I'm not sure I've ever heard that be described as 'lovely' before." He laughed a little as he gripped himself tighter, control becoming near impossible.

"I think it is." Her voice was soft, almost shy. "It's part of you and you're lovely." It was her turn to smirk. "Would you care for me to lick it?"

His throat went dry as his need grew. "Please," he managed to say.

"Please what?" Her voice was firm as she straightened herself between his legs, her bearing almost regal despite her position.

Aaron's eyes grew wide. "You're teasing me, aren't you?"

"No, I'm rather serious. I'm not licking anything unless I'm very clearly asked." She ran her tongue over her lips in a slow, careful motion before running her hands over her own body once more, this time dipping between her breasts. "Which is a pity, as I see quite a few things I'd like to run my tongue over at the moment. Or perhaps take in my mouth."

"How are you the one on your knees and yet have all the power?" He clucked his tongue, but he was impressed. More than impressed—he was hard. Harder than he'd ever been.

"Well, first, your trousers are at your ankles, so I think your position might be far more vulnerable than mine." She smiled at him, a full, proud, pleased-with-herself smile that was somehow delightful and seductive and joyous all at the same time. "And second, I'm the prince. Power is who I am."

"Don't you mean the princess?" he asked, sucking in a sharp breath as she laid her arms on his knees.

"No. Princesses are gazed at and act as ornamental objects of desire. Also, I didn't say '*a* prince.' I said '*the* prince.' The type of ruler who is given respect, if they follow Mr. Machiavelli's instructions." Her nostrils flared at the declaration. "And while people believe me the former, I strive to have the trappings of the latter as much as I'm able." Her voice hitched as she scanned his face.

"Fair enough." He inhaled and reached out to stroke her hair. God, he needed this, this gift, this coming together. "Though you do negotiate, don't you?"

"Occasionally." Her lip quirked. "If the terms are reasonable. Or more, advantageous."

"I propose a trade." He moved back to cup her chin. "After you lick me into oblivion, I'd like to return the favor. On my knees. To taste you again, before we put that sponge of yours to good use." He ran his thumb over her jaw. "You're very sweet, Isabelle."

"I'm the opposite of sweet." She threw back her head and gave him a glare. "I had a sword at your neck not more than twenty minutes ago."

"You're very sweet, and for some reason I found you handling a sword rather thrilling." He gave himself a suggestive stroke, and he was rewarded by an eye roll from her, hands on her hips—a rather fetching pose, to be sure. He'd have to make her indignant while she was naked more often.

"So what do you say?" He leaned forward. "Please, Isabelle, let me suck your quim after you suck my shmekle."

"Who said anything about sucking?" Though the gleam was back in her eye, and she twisted her hips a little. "But I'll take it under advisement." She made no movement toward him, just waiting for him. "Especially if I get to feel you inside me as well."

Fuck yes to all of that.

"Please." Aaron leaned forward and reached his hands toward her, imploring her. "Please, Isabelle. I need you." He swallowed as she made him wait, as she drew out the anticipation.

Finally, with a smile, she leaned forward and, closing her eyes, licked the length of his penis from base to tip. He moaned and she repeated the action, again and again.

He dipped his head back, closing his eyes, savoring the movement. "All the way in, love."

She paused, palms on his thighs, raising an eyebrow. His breath hitched in anticipation—would she ask him what he'd meant? Would she acknowledge what stirred between them—and open the door beyond their physical desires?

"All the way in where?" she asked instead.

"All the way in your mouth, please." His voice was thick with need, his desire quickly edging out his disappointment over the unspoken words.

"Better." She kissed along his inner thigh, so close but still so far, before putting her lips around him and pulling him inside her. "Like this?"

"Just like that." He dipped his head back, closing his eyes, savoring the movement. "Yes. Please. More." His hips bucked as she drew him in farther. "That's it, take it all." She hummed a little but paused, her lips in place, teasing him with her tongue but not moving. "Please?" The word was more of a gasp.

She rewarded him by drawing him all the way into her throat. And all the way out again. And in. Her eyes watered a little and he rubbed her jaw.

"Are you all right?" he asked. "You know you can stop or rest or…"

Isabelle shook her head. "Not unless it's too much." She wrapped her tongue around the head and sucked before running her tongue over the ridge, closing her eyes and moaning a little herself.

"So good," he whispered. "So, so good. Yes, please." He leaned back as she resumed. Her ministrations were in no way expert, alternating between hesitant and eager. But her sheer enthusiasm, and the way she gazed at him and the noises she made, as if she really, actually enjoyed it and him, were a treasure. In no time, he was close to the edge. He reached down and tangled his fingers in her hair. "I'm going to—" He cried out in a half grunt, half groan. "Do you want me to pull—"

She shook her head, leaning forward, swirling her tongue faster. His hands fisted in her hair as he sailed through the stars, crying out her name the whole time.

When he was finished, she leaned back, wiping her face and mouth with the back of her hand, and stood up. Even through the hazy afterglow, it was clear she was shaking.

Aaron reached out and pulled her to him, lifting her to his chest so he could hold her as he traveled back to her. She wrapped her arms around his neck and he nuzzled her breasts, reveling in her scent. "God, you're...incredible," he managed to say.

"Incredible in a good or bad way?" she whispered.

"In the best way." He laid his head against her again as his heart returned to normal. As soon as he could breathe, he kissed her again, gentle at first, but soon the passion that could not be quenched flared again. He reached a hand between them.

"Yes." She pressed her forehead into his shoulder. "Yes. Right here, like this." She spread her legs around him as he brushed her curls aside, swirling his thumb above her bud before pressing one finger, then two inside her.

Her hips ground against him. "Like that." She whined the words a little. "Exactly like that. Please."

He continued as she grew impossibly wet against him. For him. She panted and moaned his name before biting into his shoulder as she shuddered around his fingers. And it was the sweetest, most beautiful, most satisfying feeling he'd ever experienced. It was as if nothing in the world mattered but them and they were each exactly where they should be. And for the first time in his life, he was enough.

"That was..." She sighed before kissing the area she'd just bitten. God, was it wrong that he was hoping she'd leave a mark? That he'd have a piece of her to remind him that this was real when he went back to his room?

"Good," he growled, giving her a wicked grin. "For a starter."

"A starter?" She raised both brows, but the corners of her lips twitched in amusement.

He bent down to kiss her nose. "We had an agreement. I'm going to taste you again."

And again. As many times as she'd permit, for as long as they could. Because if he could make time stand still...make the night last...

"Well, I suppose we can't go back on an agreement." With a smile of her own, she wrapped her legs around him, and he lifted her once more before laying her on the bench. So he could have more of her, for as long as she still wanted.

For as long as they would have.

Chapter Twenty-Six

An hour later—a time both far too short but enough to give him memories he'd carry forever—Aaron practically skipped the entire way home to Aldgate. Five miles flew, and not just because he leaped over a few rooftops. Everything inside him sang. He should squash the joy—and worse, the hope—that made his chest near burst. Because anything more with Isabelle than what they'd already stolen was impossible. And yet his heart still leaped, and his toes itched to dance. Even at her final words to him.

Come back to me. At least for these last few days. At least until the end.

Her plea echoed in his head. *Until the end.* Until she had to choose someone who wasn't him. Someone who'd fit the role of her husband, not just her secret, temporary lover. At midnight, when the festivals were over and he had to leave.

Because that would happen—in four days' time. Neither of them had a choice. She had to marry Weiss, and he had to leave before the Berab brothers had him banished.

The price of the lesser of two evils.

One he was happy to pay.

For her.

Even if it hurt.

Aaron exhaled a long stream of air as he rounded a gloomy, dark, dank, empty corner. He paused in an alley and keeled over, panting, as a thought popped into his head. Or more a vision. The most dangerous one yet.

He knew better. He knew how easily dreams turned to wishes—and wishes that could never be only broke your heart. And yet...it was there. Clear as day.

What he wanted. Or more who.

But for it to be accomplished, it would take a miracle, and there hadn't been miracles among their people in a very long time.

Boots pinching his toes, he kicked at the cobblestones. Oy, he was a schlemiel. Shoving his hands in his pockets, he worked to calm his breath so he could keep his wits about him as he traversed the remainder of the dark streets to his lair. To dream of her for as long as he could.

With a sigh, he curved around another corner, head down, his legs pumping once more. He wove around the narrow back lanes, pushing off cellar doors. Finally, he was nearing the synagogue, darting through the last alleys, when a hand reached out and tapped his shoulder. The touch jolted his already keyed-up senses, sending him spinning around. Skidding to a halt, he pitched forward and downward, onto his knees.

"Fancy meeting you here, Mr. Ellenberg," a voice said from above him. A now familiar voice.

Wincing at what would most certainly be cobblestone-patterned bruises, Aaron lifted his head to stare at the man whom Isabelle would marry in mere days, and sighed. "What do you want, Weiss? Besides scaring me half to death. You shouldn't sneak up on people like that. I could've been holding a knife."

"First, I strolled, didn't sneak. Second, if you had one, you'd probably have put your own eye out. And third, I prefer 'Mr. Weiss.'" The other man gave a derisive sniff, hands folded over his well-tailored jacket. "That's what you used last time we spoke, when you wanted information out of me."

Aaron blinked up at the other man.

"Did you truly think that you, a man I don't know, could visit my house three times in less than two weeks and not arouse suspicion?" the other man continued. "Luckily, I have a talent for hunting down information myself."

Oy. Just oy. And fuck. Aaron swore in his head as his mind raced, searching for some way to respond.

Fortunately, Weiss, being not short on words, gave him more time.

"I hear you might have two hundred pounds rather soon." Isabelle's soon-to-be husband eyed him knowingly.

"You know about that?" Aaron asked, finally finding his voice again as he rocked back so he could get up on his knees. He coughed for a moment before staggering to his feet, suddenly settling on complete annoyance as his primary emotion.

"I know many things, including the fact you have a second employer." Weiss's eyes flashed in the darkness. "Though I might need your assistance as well."

"No, you don't, you fucking lucky mamzer." Aaron leaned to the side and spit on the stones, hating himself as well as the other man and the situation.

Weiss didn't flinch. Instead, he stepped forward, cocking his head. "Am I?"

"She's going to marry you." He stuck his hands in his pockets once more, pressing the fabric into the pads of his fingers. "She likes you far better than anyone else."

A snort from his companion. "That's not exactly a compliment. Who exactly is my competition? Roger and Louis Berab? They might have the pedigree of pedigrees, but what else? Boring. And old. Both of them." Weiss gave him a half smile through the gloom at his own joke.

"They aren't bad to look at, though." Aaron toed the ground, eyes downward to hide his own smile.

"Compared to who? I'd take my brother and I in that bet any day." A full grin from the other man that wasn't at all obnoxiously charming. "Though I'm not sure that's something particularly important to Isabelle Lira." The other man gave him a hard stare, the charm and put-on comradery gone. "At least not for more than a few minutes of pleasure in a library, or in a, say, garden."

Blast. Panic rocked through Aaron. He swallowed, stepping back, raising his hands as if in surrender. "I don't know what you believe you know..."

"Oh, save your breath, Ellenberg." Weiss scoffed, waving a dismissive hand at him. "Half the community knows you've been shtupping her or are close to shtupping her. You're all just lucky it's the good part— the part with the sense to look the other way instead of scolding, lest the gentiles find out and use it against her. Or, considering how important she is, us." He glanced up, scanning the skyline as if there was actually someone there and as if he could see them.

And an outline of a man appeared against the sky. Aaron squinted for a moment before it winked away.

A million curses released in his head. He stared at Weiss as a breeze blew between them, ripping through the puddles on the ground, spraying droplets over each of their boots.

"We took precautions against pregnancy," he finally blurted.

"I—I don't need to know that." Weiss closed his eyes and pinched the bridge of his nose.

"Why not? It should matter to you if you want her." Aaron spread his arms wide in frustration as righteous indignation beat below his ribs. "You do still want her?"

"Yes. Obviously. I have the same information that I had when I found you." Weiss breathed and clasped his hands together. "What happened between the two of you is immaterial to what she and I could be if we married. As I said, she's perfect. She's a clever woman, charming, ambitious, and knowledgeable about the way of the world. Beautiful too. She's an ideal wife for me."

Naturally. Aaron crunched down on his back teeth. "And what of her? Are you ideal for her?" Could he make her happy? Would he even care if she wasn't?

"I would give her all she could want. I'd build the life that we're both supposed to have." The other man laid his palms flat before wagging a finger at Aaron. "And if you think about it, you know I'm correct."

Aaron stared at the cobblestones so he'd not have to acknowledge the truth in the words.

"I can join with her and accomplish all our goals." Weiss widened his stance. "No one would work harder to make her business more successful. No one else would support any efforts she might have regarding society and politics. My family may not have communal prominence, but we are positioned for it, and I am ready to take up any mantle she desires."

The confidence, the certainty rolled off the man as he wove the tale. "We'd make fine, clever, enviable children together." Aaron closed his eyes as if that could block the images that so easily came into his mind from Weiss's words. "Given the chance, I could give her everything she could possibly dream of."

"Well, good for both of you." He kicked the ground once more and hugged his body tight.

"Right." The other man shook his head almost in disgust, as if Aaron had somehow offended him by not bowing to his arrogant will.

Aaron blew out a sharp breath. "What do you want from me? You've already won. There's nothing else I can offer you. Nothing else I can do to help you."

"You could leave." Weiss stuck his nose in the air a little.

"I am leaving." Aaron ran a hand through his hair.

"I know. The Berabs gave you no choice. Or at least that's what my information tells me." He took another step forward, hands clenched in fists. "The trouble is, you've changed the game. You need to leave now. Miss the last festival."

What? Who did he think he was? This was Aaron's last and only chance to, well, be with the community. To say goodbye. To it. And her. And maybe, just maybe, Isabelle would look at him and . . . He shook his head.

Miracles didn't happen. Isabelle wanted what she wanted. No matter how she felt about him.

It was as if the wind were knocked out of him once more. He ground his jaw and spun around to go and find some way to drown the swirl of pressure behind his eyes.

"Your presence is a threat." The other man rushed over and scooted around him, blocking his path out of the alley. "Not to me, but to her."

"I'd never hurt her." Aaron slammed a hand on his thigh. Never. He'd rather be dashed against the stones headfirst.

"Then what are you doing?" Weiss leaned against the wall, a smug expression twisting his handsome mouth. "Think about it. Like I said, the cleverer part of the community knows what's happening. If the Berab brothers wise up…do you not think that they wouldn't use that information against her? They could make her do anything they wanted, marry who they want. Or steal the business. You know how the gentiles see our women. If they found out she shtupped a man she had no intention of marrying and didn't marry, do you think they'd associate with her in any way?"

Aaron stumbled backward as if he'd been punched.

"You're not the only one researching angles." The other man raised his chin in pride. "I'm not a fool. I knew there had to be a reason the Lira family needed a groom so fast. I know about the Shavuos deadline."

The world spun and Aaron began to shake.

"If you stay, it will happen. Mark my words. How can you not have predicted this? After they threatened you?" He shot to his feet and gave Aaron a glare of disgust before clenching his fists as if to calm himself. He shook his head. "Blast, Ellenberg, what were you thinking, practically serving them extortion material?"

His mind stuttered and spun. What had he been thinking? His shoulders slumped.

"We were careful," he mumbled.

"You were outside." Weiss near spit. "And even if, by some miracle, they haven't been watching the house, the amount of time the two of you spent alone in the library..."

Aaron opened his mouth, stepping forward. "We were just talk—"

"You're a terrible liar." The other man cocked his head, a knowing smirk on his face.

Aaron turned to the wall and gave it a hard kick. "Shut your trap, Weiss." Though he should probably take his own advice.

"You need to leave. Immediately. We protect our own, but the company at the festivals is mixed. All they need to do is catch you one time, with witnesses, and the entire gentile community will know. And she'll pay for it. For the rest of her life." Weiss wrinkled his nose. "For goodness' sake, you're a custodian. Think of her humiliation." The other man moved closer again, his breath hot as he whispered the taunting words. He raised his fist as if he was ready to strike.

Mercy. Aaron widened his stance, readying his own hands, pushing Miriam's scolding from his mind. He inhaled a deep breath through his nostrils. This was foolish, on both their parts, but apparently unavoidable and—dark fabric flapping in the wind brushed Aaron as a new party entered the fray, sliding between them like a ghost.

Back to him, the cloaked figure set upon Weiss. Isabelle's soon-to-be husband stumbled on the same stone that had felled Aaron earlier, with similar results. A flash of silver glinted in the moonlight as a dagger rose into the air before plunging downward.

"No," he cried, regaining his bearings and rushing forward. Weiss was an arse, as the gentiles said, but not evil. The stranger paused, dagger point at the other man's throat.

Before he could think of a better plan, Aaron leaped on the man's back, shoving him forward so they both flipped through the air, landing with two distinct thuds.

Groaning, Aaron stared up blearily at the dark sky as pain radiated through his body.

"Aaron," Weiss breathed from the ground next to him. "Look out."

Biting down nausea, Aaron rolled just quick enough to dodge the rising cloaked villain. A gloved hand reached for the knife that lay just to the north.

Crawling on his elbows as fast as he could, Aaron reached for the hilt of the dagger. Before he could grasp it, a fist collided with the back of his head. He cried out in pain but threw himself toward the weapon, even as more blows rained down on his back and his neck.

A heaviness pressed on his back as the other man positioned himself on top of Aaron's body, holding him to the pavement.

Fuck. He was going to die there. Him and Weiss. And Isabelle was going to be at the mercy of the Berabs, all because they both couldn't help sniping at each other instead of watching their surroundings.

Elbows now bleeding, he pulled himself further to at least cover part of the knife with his chest. Pain nearly blinding him, he held his ground until, all of a sudden, a whop rang through the air, and the weight was off his back.

Shouts rang out as the attacker grappled with a wildly swinging Weiss, who was making up for what he lacked in aim with shear enthusiasm.

"Get the knife," Weiss ordered him. Quick as he could, Aaron obeyed, palming the thing and swinging around Weiss—whom their attacker was now holding by the lapels—so he could press the weapon to their attacker's temple. Or at least where he believed the man's temple was, as the thick hood remained over his head, shadowing his features.

Aaron reached for the material, but before he could make contact, the attacker shot to his feet, rushing out of the alley, though not before giving Aaron one sharp, stinging crack to his jaw.

And for a moment, everything went dark. When he came to, the blinking stars yielded to Weiss standing over him, staring down.

"Are you...," he asked, reaching his hand out to Aaron.

"I'm...fine." Accepting Weiss's arm, he struggled to his feet. "A bit bruised, no doubt, but it could've been worse." With a groan, Aaron managed to lean against the rough wooden frame of the nearest building. Wincing, he stepped forward as pain radiated from his side. Oy, he was going to be sore in the morning.

"I'll say." Weiss gave him a once-over as he brushed his own rumpled garments. "I will also say, that was...impressive."

"Impressive?" Aaron wrinkled his nose, not quite sure if the other man was sincere.

"Yes, I mean, I had heard you were tough, but you really..." Weiss let out a low whistle. "You saved us both."

"I had some hel—" Aaron started just as the other man collapsed on the ground.

Aaron rushed to Weiss's side and kneeled on the stones. A flash of lightning illuminated the sky above as the fallen man clutched his knee. Aaron reached out a finger and poked the area, which was already so swollen it was straining within Weiss's trousers.

"It's nothing," the other man said through slightly gritted teeth. "Before I got here, I took a tumble down a cellar, and this just aggravated it a touch." He rubbed the joint.

Oy. Weiss was in no shape to walk. And limping down these streets alone in the middle of the night? Not a good idea if you wanted to remain alive. Especially if you were wearing rather shiny buttons sure to draw the eye of every thief worth their salt.

Aaron closed his eyes for a moment and inhaled before wrapping Weiss's arm over his shoulders and hoisting him a little. "Come along," he said to the other man. "Let's get you home."

Quickly. With hopefully a little help at some point.

"Thank you," the other man whispered as he leaned on Aaron.

Grunting, Aaron pushed toward the mouth of the alley and the road, a nagging thought at the back of his brain.

This was his fault. Somehow, someway. No, he couldn't quite make out the particulars of it, but it had to be something he'd done along the way. Some task he'd mucked up with his schlemiel ways.

He glanced at the other man. "I think you might be right," he said, though he hated to admit it.

"Of course. I'm always right," Weiss said, grinning,

before wincing and clutching his knee again. "About what?" he asked.

Aaron closed his eyes. "I think it might be better for everyone involved and the community if I leave, sooner rather than later."

Weiss didn't say anything, for once, and instead nodded as both of their steps grew firmer and the first light of dawn struck the horizon, heralding a new day and bringing them another step closer to everything being settled, once and for all.

Chapter Twenty-Seven

Three days after the glorious night in the garden, Isabelle was once again pacing her sitting room, marble fireplace to window seat to chamber door and back, over and over, Baron at her heels. She'd not seen Aaron since that magical night they'd shared, and they were running out of time. Or she was. The final festival was almost upon her. And she was going to have to officially choose a husband, have to marry someone. Whether she wanted to or not.

Weiss was the correct decision, the best way to save the business and protect her family and the community and her place in it. Even Aaron himself had said so. Which meant it should be settled. She should tell her grandmother and Pena today so they could begin the negotiations with the older brother. However... She bit her lip.

She couldn't push Aaron from her mind. Why hadn't he come to her again? Yes, he had another job and had found her all the information there was to get, but... She bit her lip again. She had to see him before it was all over—one last time. Had to. It was a need, not a want. Because if she could see him, she could sort out the muddle in her head and somehow make things come out right.

Which meant if he wasn't coming to her, she'd just have to go to him.

Quick as she could, she rang for Judith to assist her in changing into a simple paisley light wool gown and a bonnet. After calling for a carriage, she dashed into the parlor to inform her grandmother she was going to see Rebecca.

"See if you can convince her to style her hair less severely tomorrow night," her grandmother instructed, barely glancing up from her correspondence, Pena at her side, a frown on his face.

Isabelle paused. "What is it?"

"Nothing," they both said a bit too quickly.

"Not nothing." She frowned, hands on her hips, staring as the two sat in grim silence. Not good—which meant one of two things. "Is it me or the business?" Her blood pumped faster in her veins as she offered a silent prayer that the entire community had found out what had occurred in the garden. Because she could survive that damage better than another blow to her father's legacy.

The pair exchanged guilty expressions, and a lump grew in the pit of her stomach.

Isabelle closed her eyes. "It's the latter, isn't it? Or the latter combined with the former." She stalked over, snatched the letter they were fretting over before either could stop her, and scanned the contents. Her mouth dropped open as panic spread through her body. She pointed at the words. "You weren't going to tell me? This is a threat."

"It's not a threat," her grandmother muttered. "It's more of a reminder. Of things you already know."

"One that you weren't going to share with me." Isabelle slammed a hand on the table.

Pena ducked his head. She closed her eyes. That was the only answer she needed. "They've already sent the documents, haven't they?" she whispered. "The ones they referenced—the division of assets, a ketubah, crafted without our input, with a space to write in the groom, the spellings of each of their names."

"We didn't want to worry you." Her grandmother took Isabelle's hand in hers and squeezed, the scratchy lace of her sleeve rubbing against Isabelle's skin. "The terms of the ketubah are at least fair. I don't think we would have negotiated anything substantially different with any potential husband for you. And you have so much pressure on you already. You didn't need another thing to fret about."

"But I do need to fret about it. Fair or not." Isabelle pulled back her hand. "They've moved up the deadline from Shavuot if I choose to marry someone else. They're demanding a meeting with my betrothed the day after the final festival to negotiate whether the business goes forward or dissolves, with his contributions being the deciding factor. They've gathered a group of gentile clients demanding to know who they will be dealing with before they continue their association, already weakening any independent company I might form." She shook her head, marveling at how fast this had all come, how organized and lined up against her. How fast the life she knew was ending. "The final battle is upon us."

She was going to really, truly need to marry Weiss. Not that she hadn't known, but somewhere, a small part of her had believed there might be an exit strategy, another way. That David Berab would actually be reasonable for once. But clearly, that was not going to happen.

"Which we shall win." Her grandmother smoothed her skirts, not meeting Isabelle's eye. "I know you are leaning towards Mr. Weiss, and he is a fine choice. His family has quite a few plum gentile connections. There will be no reason for anyone to leave, and we will have enough power based on your husband's attributes to retain our control. Your plan is playing out as expected. Everything will remain as close to what it was when your father was alive as it possibly could."

"It will. Especially as everything your grand-mother recounted is still accurate, isn't it?" It was Pena who spoke, raising a suspicious eyebrow as he placed his hands on her grandmother's shoulders. His eyes searched Isabelle's face and narrowed.

"Yes." Isabelle's cheeks heated, but she managed to keep her chin up. "Don't worry—I will marry the right person and we will win." With a lift of her skirts, she rushed over and gave them each a kiss on the cheek.

"I'll be back shortly." Before either could question her further, Isabelle slipped out of the room and down the stairs, her heart pounding with guilt in all possible directions.

After wrapping herself in a loose cloak, she climbed into the carriage. "To the Great Synagogue," she told the driver. Closing her eyes, she leaned back as the vehicle bumped over the stones, cutting through the bustle of the shipyards that carried up from the south. The sun shimmered through the curtains but provided no warmth as she shivered with nerves. Unease stirred in her stomach the entire ride.

Finally, the carriage halted, and the driver assisted her onto the ground. "Thank you so much. I'll return in a moment," she told him before pretending to enter the building and instead ducking around the side. She rapped on Aaron's door.

No answer. Isabelle frowned. It was between services. He should be resting at this point. She repeated the action, louder and more insistent.

"Aaron," she called. After rapping harder, the door swung open to reveal the man himself, wearing nothing but trousers and an unbuttoned shirt, and what appeared to be fading bruises. However, before she could inquire as to their origin, his gaze met hers and his entire face lit with a broad smile. Though his eyes held a darker note. Almost like fear. Or worry.

"What are you doing here?" He pulled her into the room, yanking the door shut behind her. "You're going to get yourself in trouble. There are people about who will most certainly tell your grandmother. And Weiss." He cocked his head. "Isabelle? What's wrong?"

"Nothing." She waved the clear concern in his eyes away before grasping his bare hands in her gloved ones. "I just wanted to see you." *Even if I shouldn't. Even if I can't have you. Even if it's wrong to keep you about.* And liquid swam in her eyes.

"It isn't nothing." He squeezed her wrists together before guiding her to sit upon a wooden chair. "You're shaking."

Her heart was in her throat. This was a mistake, wasn't it? Coming here? It was selfish and awful and—

"It's just..."

"Just what?" He leaned forward, lips almost brushing hers. She stroked his hair, probably for the last time, before taking a breath and letting go of him. Like she had to.

"It's the Berab brothers." She inhaled. "I thought I had handled them—well, I was handling them." She drew her hands back so she could grip the edges of the chair for support.

"I—I don't understand." Aaron rose, wrinkles marring his brow.

She pressed her fingers to her temple. It had all seemed so reasonable in the beginning. But what did the gentiles say? The road to hell was paved with good intentions? Or something like that. "They've moved up the deadline, and they're better organized than previously believed. If I'm to marry someone other than Louis or Roger, they want a meeting after the announcement to negotiate new terms or dissolve the partnership. A group of gentile clients has decided to hold their renewals until they meet my husband and approve him." She drew in another breath. "Which means I have no choice but to marry as planned."

Aaron didn't say anything, just stared at her.

"Marry someone with the assets and connections to make sure it's in their best interest to not dissolve the partnership and to keep the terms as they were when my father was alive." And the tears were in the back of her throat, stealing almost all her control. "Who the clients will find above reproach."

He blinked. "Ah" was all he said.

"I'm not enough myself." Which meant she had to go through with the plan. It was her only option, her only choice. He had to understand that.

"Ah," he repeated with no emotion whatsoever.

"If I don't save the business—my father loved the company." She stood, her voice rising as if the volume could make him see and, more, absolve her. "He worked even when he was sick, probably making himself sicker, and if I let the business fall..."

"You kill his legacy. You've said this already." Aaron folded his arms across his probably bruised ribs. "You're fighting for the life he built. The life you enjoyed with him. Your place in it. You've explained this all before." He gave an exasperated shake of his head, as if this was all somehow her fault, not the circumstances'.

It was Isabelle's turn to cross her arms. "And you don't approve."

He waved a hand at her. "What I do or do not approve of doesn't matter, does it?"

It did. More than anything. Or more than almost anything. Which was why she was being torn asunder. Stepping back, she raised her finger to argue, or more explain, make him see that if she chose a different path, chose what she wanted—what she didn't deserve but truly desired—her father would die again. Because of her. Because she let him. "No, but—"

"What do you want?" He straightened himself and locked eyes with her.

She stared at him for a moment, but the words, all of them, the ones just at the tip of her tongue, would not come.

"I want to win," she said finally. Because it was still true. She had to win. For her grandmother, for Pena, for her father, and for herself. She could not let them down.

"Well, you're doing a poor job of it." He shoved his hands in his pockets.

"I beg your pardon?" Frustrated rage rose in her breast. Could he not understand how difficult this was

for her? How painful? How if she could just somehow
be more, things would be different, *could* be different,
and they might be having another conversation?

"You're playing not to lose." He squeezed his palm
into a fist, pressing it against his lips, eyes flashing in
the dim light. "Because if you were playing to win…"

"What?" She slapped her hands on her skirts. "If I
was playing to win, what?"

Aaron stared at her, his voice clear and firm. "You
know what. You know what you would do."

And everything inside Isabelle crumbled. Because
he was right, but she didn't have it in her. She wasn't
brave enough or strong enough or good enough. "I—"
she started, the words dying in her throat.

He shook his head in disgust. "And you can't, can
you?"

No, but every fiber inside her wanted it, wanted
to scream that she wanted him. That if she had her
choice, it would be him, a thousand times over. And he
deserved it. Well, he deserved more than the likes of
her. So much more.

But she couldn't even give him the words. Because if
she said the words, well, she would break and never be
whole again. Because she would have lost. Utterly and
completely.

"I'm not going to be the one to say it." His voice was
still low and calm, but with a furious, beautiful dignity
behind it. He rolled back his shoulders. "I may not have
much to offer—may not be much. I'm not learned or
wealthy or clever or special. I'm about as ordinary as
they come. But even so, I do have value. And my own
dreams and wants—and they are important too. I'm not
going to waste them on someone who—" Shaking his

head again, he turned from her, deliberately giving her his back, which she deserved, and moved to his desk. "I really am just an errand boy to you, aren't I?"

Why was he doing this to her? He knew she didn't see him like that. He knew he was more. That they were more.

"No, I—I believe you are more—" And it was as if the gears in her brain could no longer move. The words stuck in her throat. "But I mean, yes, I hired you for information. Only the rest was separate." She was shaking now. "But yes, I'm paying you—"

"I haven't been paid." He didn't turn around and instead began shuffling papers.

She blinked at him and his stiff back. Would that somehow make this right? Everything in Isabelle longed to run to him, but her feet would not move. It was as if she were in a dream, as if someone else were speaking, because all her mind could do was scream *No*, to no avail.

"I was waiting until after the festival, but fine." She reached into the pocket in her sleeve and held out all its contents. "Here." She shook it in his direction. "I've paid you." Her stomach roiled, but she pressed on, hating herself and every word. "We're even." *And now can we talk about the rest? Somehow?* But those words stuck in her throat too.

He pushed it—pushed her—away without even turning around. "I don't want your money."

Why not? Because that was what she could give. Easily and freely. What was the point in having it if it couldn't make everything right? Why, the one time she needed it to be enough, was it not? She placed the money on the dresser. It was his, whether he wanted it or not.

"If you don't care about your wages, what do you want from me?" She slapped her hands against her skirts, frustration seeping out as she squinted through the dim light. "Because I don't understand." Except that was a lie. She did, very much, but she couldn't permit herself to follow that line of thought, not if she was going to do what she needed to do.

"I want—I need you to go away. To leave me be." He'd turned to face the bare stone wall. Staring at the cracks instead of looking her in the eye. As if to do so was somehow beneath him. His shoulders rose and fell as if he was taking a deep breath. "I'm going to America, Isabelle."

"America." Her knees buckled as she whispered the word—the name—the land a world away.

"I leave the day after the festival." His voice was resigned.

"Why?" Why hadn't he told her? Why had he behaved as if he cared about her, as if he was being honest with her, when he was hiding this? Her lower lip quivered. She pressed down with her teeth to hold it in place, to keep control, even as another wave of hurt rippled through her.

"Rabbi Raphael has a cousin who has a theater company, which needs a stagehand." He straightened, pressing his hands against his lower back. "It would be an opportunity to start anew in that community, make new friends, meet new people, be regarded highly without the burden of my past." He waved a dismissive hand, still not turning around. "There's nothing for me here anyway."

Nothing. She was nothing to him. Not that she was supposed to be.

And he was everything to her. She wanted to scream it, but again her tongue held fast to the roof of her mouth. The pressure welled between her eyes as she struggled to contain the painful emotions swirling within her, to keep them in, keep her dignity. She sucked in a shaking breath.

"I suppose not," she managed, the statement surprisingly clear. She exhaled, slow and steady, like she was supposed to. As if she was all right. "But why so soon?"

Aaron turned around slowly, a haunted look in his eyes. "I'm more of a liability than an asset to you. Because while you might not think very much of me, I still hold you in high regard. In the highest regard." His voice shook a touch, yet he kept his chin level, leaned back against his table, his body closed to her. "But under the circumstances, I think it best if we say goodbye now."

"You aren't coming to the last festival?" Dash it all, her voice cracked. She glanced at the large crevice in the plaster above his head, following its tributaries, focusing on the here and now and the real to force herself to remain steadfast and calm, to not lose her dignity.

He wasn't worth it.

And a lump choked off her air at the lie. He was—a hundred times over—but he couldn't be. She had to force him not to be.

"You no longer need me." He tilted his chin, his voice firm. "Besides, it's better this way. We've both made our choices, and this is the only option."

"Yes, you should be rested for your journey." The words were strangled at the end, and she moved her gaze from the ceiling to a spiderweb in a corner, following the fragile strands that somehow held together to create something beautiful in the darkness.

"You should focus on your upcoming marriage." His entire body slumped this time. "Weiss will make a good husband." His jaw tightened but the words were sincere, and she hated them—hated him, at least in that moment. "He wants to do right by you, and his goals are your goals." Aaron ran a hand through his thatch of black hair, like she had in the garden, but with no pleasure on his face. "You will be happy with him."

"Will I?" Because right now happiness was so...far-fetched.

"Yes. If you let yourself be." He waved a hand toward the door. "Which means you need to go." He moved now, brushing past her to the exit.

"But what about us?" she followed him, her voice bordering on a pleading whine.

"There is no 'us.' You've said as much already. I might not be brilliant, but I do listen to you. I've seen the writing on the wall. I'm not going to continue to hurt—" He spun around, frustration marring his features. "We had what, a few kisses? A few conversations? That isn't an 'us.' That was a desperate attempt by you to sabotage your goals because you're afraid. Because you've realized that whomever you marry will be a person, not an object you can manipulate. Someone with their own wants and needs and feelings, that you can't control any more than you can control your own. You want to use what happened between us as an excuse to ignore that. To put everyone back into the little boxes you've crafted: whether they're a witch or wolf or prince or villain. Including yourself. I'm not going to be part of that, watching you craft a story that best fits your version of events."

And every word was a wound, like a dagger in her.

"It was more than that. It is more than that." And now the tears were brimming, threatening to fall. She squeezed her fists to keep them at bay. She would not, could not be weak. Not now. Not when she could least afford it.

"Then why can't you say the words?" He shook his head, his jaw clenched beneath his beard. "I'd give up my life to make sure you aren't hurt, but why won't you live for me? For us?"

She stared at him. She needed to speak but her throat closed tight.

He shook his head in disgust. "Leave. Go back to your world, play heir to the throne, save your father's legacy. Perhaps then you can learn to get over your fear so you can love Weiss. Or at least try to. Because like I said before, no matter what I think of him, he's a person too. Not a chess piece on a board or what have you. You'd be better off if you allowed yourself to treat him as such, and him to do the same. No matter how frightening. Fear doesn't become you, Isabelle."

Fear? She blinked. She wasn't afraid. She was doing the bravest thing she could, sacrificing desires for duty.

"But as of now, I—I can't speak to you anymore. And if you care about me even a little, you will let me be." He pressed a finger into his chest. "Leave, Isabelle."

She stepped forward. "Aaron—"

"Now." He indicated the door before swinging it open, filling the space with sunlight and cold. "You're the one who has to stop the bleeding."

Her heart twisted beneath her rib cage. That was

what it was like, wasn't it? An oozing, festering wound that would not stop? Unless they made it—unless she made it. Unless she was the strong one. Unless she was the one who freed them both.

"All right." The words were soft, but she managed to make them clear. She lifted her chin with as much dignity as she could as she moved to the doorframe, staring him straight in the eye even as everything inside her ached. "Goodbye, Aaron." She grasped the frame and paused for a moment, biting her lip, wishing it could be different. "I'm—I wish—I—if you ever—" She shook her head as he stood there unmoved. Ducking her head, she slipped out onto the street.

"Goodbye, Isabelle," he called as he closed the door behind her.

Chapter Twenty-Eight

Isabelle pressed her fingers against her temples before signing yet another document. Another contract term analysis demanded by the Berab brothers. She glanced at the early-morning sun peeking cheerfully through the window—mocking her. In a few hours it would set to the noise of arriving guests. The last festival. The last midnight. The time when all her plans would come to a head and her fate would be sealed. When she would agree to marry Solomon Weiss, with whom she could preserve her family's influence over the company and their place in the community. Take back her role—force David Berab to give her a fair chance to prove herself.

Keep her father's name on the door. Keep him alive, even if he wasn't.

Leaning forward to keep the pressure off her stays, she inhaled as deeply as she could, permitting the spring air to swirl through her lungs. She could do this. She could. She would tell her grandmother she was going to marry Weiss, and they'd come to an agreement with his brother and announce it at midnight, like she'd planned from the beginning.

Simple. And necessary. And practical. And what everyone wanted.

She fingered her dagger beneath the folds of her day dress, her thumb rubbing the etched "L." *It's who we are—who we both are.* Her father's voice from so long ago whispered in her mind. She was strong enough to bear it all. The community would advance, her family would be secure, and Aaron would...find happiness someplace else with someone better. Someone who could actually give him what he deserved.

Sighing once more, she stared at her personal ledger. Two hundred pounds. Gone. Well, not gone. Where it belonged. Where it would do good. She straightened the corner with her thumb, making it neat and tidy once more. Like her life would be once she completed the plan she'd launched less than a month ago. Her first solo success.

"Are you ready for tonight?" Pena's voice from across the room nearly made her jump from her skin.

"I won't be if I accidentally gouge out my eye." She laid down her pen before rising to walk over and give the man a kiss on the cheek. "It's customary to knock before entering someone's quarters, you know." She smoothed her skirts before pushing the door shut again.

"Attackers do not follow protocol," he told her as he moved through the threshold. "Don't tell me you've forgotten all of our lessons? Or is it that you have a great deal on your mind?" His voice was gentle, and for some reason that made pressure sting behind her eyes.

"I always have a great deal on my mind because I have a great deal of responsibility. That's part of adulthood." She puffed her sleeves.

"Part of adulthood is knowing what responsibilities are yours alone and what are best shared." Pena's dark eyes searched hers.

"I'll meet with grandmother today so we can finalize arrangements," she told him. "Take on another member of the household to whom there can be some delegation." It was time. She had forestalled long enough.

"So your choice is truly resolved?" Pena raised a single eyebrow as he moved farther into the room, standing before the fireplace. The flames, like the bright sun outside, barely affected the chill that spread through her bones.

"I'm sure we'll all grow to enjoy the Weiss family." She kept her chin steady through the entire statement, even as that damned lump came back.

"We'll do our best." He leaned against the mantel, crossing his legs, his eyes boring into her. "Including you, apparently."

"He's the most reasonable choice. And the right one."

"Is he?" Both graying eyebrows arched, and somehow that near broke her.

She threw her fingers over her eyes and pressed for a long moment. She'd readjust her soot later.

"What do you want me to say?" She stared at the black lines marring the tips of her gloves. "There are more things afoot than my own happiness."

"Yes, the business, your father's seat on the Commission of Delegates, a bill—all demanding a certain type of man at your side, I know. All of which are important and worthwhile." Pena raised a finger. "But I can tell you that your own happiness, as you call it, still has value too."

"I'll be happy enough." She sucked in a breath as Aaron's face flashed before her eyes. And the tears were right below the surface, but she was almost beyond caring. Mr. Machiavelli would tell her this was a mistake and that she was being weak, but then perhaps she truly was weak. Or didn't deserve the things she'd been given. She gripped the back of a carved mahogany chair, grounding herself in the firm, stalwart wood.

"The world does not allow—the plan is the only way to keep the life he created for me." She stared into the fire, the lump solidifying so it took everything in her to push the words through. "The life I want." She forced a calm, dignified nod. "I'll learn to love Solomon Weiss as best as I can. Because you can love more than one person." Her lungs pressed against her ribs as she studied the man she'd known for so long. "My father did, didn't he?"

Pena's swallow was visible as he shook his head, and she hated herself a little for forcing the question on him, but she had to know, had to have the reassurance.

"I never met your mother, but based on everything he said, yes, he loved her very much." He stared at the ground, and she hated herself more than a little for the pain she'd brought.

"And he loved you as well. Very much." Her voice was choked. "So it is possible."

"It's possible." Pena nodded before moving forward. He took her chin in his hands. "I just—you deserve better than what you're choosing."

She stared up at him as her eyes grew moist to match his. "There's no real choice, though, is there? At least not for me."

"There's always a choice." Pena shook his head again. "Your father could've remarried, could've given you siblings..."

"Yes, but I don't resent him for that. He deserved to

be happy. You deserved to be happy. And to be happy again, if the opportunity arises." She closed her eyes again.

"As do you." Pena's thumb stroked over her jaw. "Though sometimes I wonder if that isn't what you're afraid of."

"What?" Isabelle blinked at him. "Afraid of happiness? That's ridiculous. No one is afraid of happiness."

"Are you sure?" He cocked his head. "What are you doing? None of us need the money. And you are your father's daughter—if they push you out, crush your part of the company, you'd build something else. Something bigger and better."

"But it wouldn't be like it was when he was—" And she couldn't quite say the word and instead pulled away from him, staring at the floor.

"No, but it would be yours." He pulled a handkerchief from his pocket and handed it to her. "Just like your memories of him and the life we all shared." He rubbed her arm. "Building something new after something wonderful ends doesn't cheapen the value of either."

He was right, of course, but why did it have to be so hard? Why did the dulling of the pain still feel like a loss? And more, if she was honest, make her into a coward? Like Aaron said. Defending the broken bits of what was instead of building what she actually wanted.

Isabelle swallowed. "I know," she whispered as she blotted her eyes. "I just—I don't know which hurts more now: allowing it all to change or realizing that I ruined—"

Pena thankfully didn't force her to say the words and

instead wrapped his arms around her and held her for a long moment as the tears flooded her defenses.

"I just want him back," she sobbed. "I want him back so badly."

"I know you do," Pena whispered, kissing the top of her head. "I know."

She clutched the older man's coat. "We're going to be the only ones who remember him, aren't we?" she whispered.

"Perhaps. But I think we're enough." Pena's voice was hoarse as he stroked her hair. "I think this is a situation where the quality matters more than the quantity, both in years and those who remain behind. Which is how it probably should be."

And the two fell into silence as the tears continued.

"Do you think he'd be disappointed in me?" she asked as she blotted her eyes again.

"Never," Pena assured her. "Win or lose, he would see what I see—how magnificent you are."

Except she didn't feel particularly magnificent. No, she felt like, well, a cad, as the gentiles said. Or something worse. She was going to lose it all, wasn't she? Unless... She ran the handkerchief between her fingers, rubbing it as a spark, an idea, popped into her head. And the contours of a plan began to form.

It wouldn't get her the ending her heart now acknowledged it wanted nor, as Pena said, bring her father and the life they all had shared back. That was gone. What the future held, however, depended on her. Whether she would be someone whose memory someone would want to hold. Time would tell on that front.

However, now she had the opportunity, if she tried,

to help someone else. Someone who was, as a wise man had pointed out, a person too.

"Isabelle?" Pena cocked his head, his expression suddenly worried.

"I have to find someone." She reached up on her toes and gave the man a kiss on the cheek. "Thank you, Pena." Before he could say another word, she darted from the room.

It took her the better part of an hour to arrive at the Weiss house, unannounced. A rather confused butler showed her to a small study far removed from the grand parlor with its towering, if not slightly eerie, collection of mirrors near the entry to wait for the "younger Mr. Weiss." A touch dark for her taste, with almost no windows. Frowning, she rubbed her gloved thumb over a faded damask curtain.

"Hello, Miss Lira." A familiar male voice boomed through the dimness.

"Oh, you startled me," she told him as she whirled around.

"You surprised me," he said, indicating one of two chairs before the large desk.

She sat as gracefully as she could while he remained standing across from her, curiosity etched on his handsome features.

"To what do I owe this pleasure?" Weiss smoothed a stack of papers before lining up three pens parallel with each other. Glancing up at her, he inhaled. "Though I'm glad you're here. There is something you need to know, Isabelle—may I call you that?"

Asking permission after already taking the liberty—how very much like him. Her lip twitched. Something to watch for in the future. She leaned back in the chair. "Yes, I suppose. We've had intimate discussions before—"

"I have it on some good authority that the Berab brothers are so determined to marry you that they are willing to go to extreme lengths to get their way," he interrupted. "This is more than business to them—it's personal."

Personal? Isabelle wrinkled her nose. How could it possibly be personal? She had almost no relationship with Roger and Louis. She hardly knew anything about them. There were a dozen heiresses that would suit either of them. Her appeal was the business and only the business.

She opened her mouth to remark the same to Weiss and then closed it as a notion popped into her head. *David*. His brothers had offered marriage only at his suggestion. His idea, in truth. Could this be personal to David?

Isabelle thought of all their conversations—and the expression on his face during—beginning with the one that occurred the third day of Shiva, for her father spirited into the forefront of her mind. She'd been, well, upset, and implied—not intentionally, but out of her own grief—that her father had been the true brains behind the business, instead of David, who had been by their side for every step of his illness, who probably longed for the before times as well, for his friend. And while she'd meant to apologize...She grimaced as another memory rose.

She'd been in the offices. There was an important

contract that needed to be renegotiated. One of her father's first clients. The one he used as an example to teach her. She'd commandeered most of the staff to help her. She bit her lip. Without even asking David.

He'd come in later, red-faced, after he was left unprepared for a meeting that day. And she'd been, well, rather on edge, having just come from sorting through some of her father's personal items, searching for his notes on business. She'd given him a shrug and a not particularly sincere apology.

True, there had been times such as when he'd merely shrugged off her hurt at not being invited to a staff meeting. *You had other commitments.* A remark she'd taken as an insult when he'd then enquired as to a social call she'd paid, but perhaps, he'd been attempting to be considerate as she was in the first month of sheloshim...

After too many moments like that from them both... well, it had never been the same.

Weiss was right, wasn't he? Very right.

Yes, David Berab had given as good as he'd got, but she'd been thoughtless and self-centered, and when he reacted, even if it was an overreaction, she'd not soothed the situation, only escalated. Until they were at war.

Blinking a little, she turned back to Weiss. "The idea that this is personal to the brothers, namely to David, well, that's rather intriguing and most likely the correct analysis. Though I'm not sure it's personal in the way you are imagining. I think certain statements and actions on both our parts might have led David Berab to believe that I do not respect or value him, leading us both down this path where more than a business has been fractured. And while I'm not sure that there is a way to ever mend the chasm we created, not after the threats—no matter my earlier role—I do appreciate the new perspective on the situation. You're very astute, Mr. Weiss."

"I try to be. And thank you for the compliment." His lips tipped in a soft smile as he too leaned back. "But in addition to the motivation, there is still—"

"Can it wait for a moment? I think there is something you can do to assist me with what we were already discussing, which was, coincidentally, the purpose of my visit." Isabelle gripped the arm of the chair to give her strength. "I came to speak with you regarding the future—our shared future."

"Shared, did you say?" He clasped his hands in front of him, his eyes wide with excitement. "Is this the conversation I expected to have later tonight?"

"No, but I think you will, in time, prefer it." She folded her hands in her lap.

"I don't like the sound of that." He frowned.

Her chest rose and fell with the enormity of what she was doing, but she filled her lungs and pressed forward. "I'm sorry, but I can't marry you."

His eyes grew wide, and he stepped back as if he'd been struck. "You're marrying one of the Berabs?"

"What?" She wrinkled her nose. As if she'd do that. "No. Never. David Berab would hate me more in the end. Trust me."

"Then who? Is it that Ellenberg fellow?" Weiss's expression turned worried, and he lowered his voice. "Isabelle, I know he's a kind and generous person—I mean, I owe him my life."

She blinked at him.

"He stopped a ruffian from robbing me the other

day," Weiss explained. "Though I heard he'd do the same for anyone in the community. He's truly good, but he's, well, what I wanted to talk to you about. The Berab brothers will skewer him. And you through him." He glanced from side to side uneasily. "They'll see it as an insult and escalate further."

"Possibly. Though that says more about them and their values than anything else, does it not?" She gave him a half smile before shaking her head. "But no, I'm not marrying Aaron Ellenberg. He's all but left for America, keeping him safe from any potential skewering, as I—I made quite a hash of, well, many things." Her voice cracked a little at the end. She squeezed her hands together. Foolish emotion.

"I think any hash in this case was caused by the actions of more than one person." Weiss rubbed the back of his neck, his expression sheepish. "But I am sorry."

"Why?" She smoothed her skirts.

Weiss stepped forward and laid his hand over hers. "I'm not an ogre, and though I want to win, and honestly need to win, need to have this match for the sake of my own family, I did—do—did see the way you two looked at each other. As I alluded to priorly, or I at least was attempting to, I know of what transpired in the garden."

"You what?" Fire shot through her cheeks. This man had seen her...nude.

He bit his lip, his own cheeks turning redder than her gown. "I might have been doing some research...right before I almost got robbed—twice, actually—once with Mr. Ellenberg, and once just before, when I initially hurt my knee. It was a very long night, and—"

"You're joking." Oh, she could die, melt into the floor and die, which might be better, as she'd not have to deal with any of the rest. Though... She heaved another sigh. She was an adult and she had responsibilities, but mercy, it was so, so, so humiliating.

"I'm not the only one." He held up a palm, as if that was a decent excuse. "That's the rest of what I've been trying to tell you. Do you really think your family doesn't have you watched? You're lucky they hire people who are circumspect. Or despise David Berab and his 'my family was invited by Cromwell and the goyim believe my lack of accent means I'm directly descended from Christ's favorite uncle so I'm better than everyone else' attitude enough to have kept him in the dark. One or the other." He gave her another abashed expression, glancing down at the rug. "It might have been prudent to spend more time indoors together."

And "humiliating" wasn't even the word to describe it. Mortifying. How many people exactly had seen them? And she'd have to find a way to look them all in the eye... She bit back a groan. Leader, she was a leader, and leaders could do such things, head held high. And she would. After potentially murdering them all herself.

"Noted. And I will need to find a way to guard against—" She raised her chin, her voice steady again, her strength beginning to return despite or maybe because of the ridiculousness. "But regarding him, none of that matters now." She dug her heels into her shoes, grounding herself.

"No, and I'm sorry for that, because the two of you really did seem to..." He toed the fringe on the edge of the floor covering before lifting his gaze, perplexity in his eyes. "But if you can't marry him, why not marry me? I would be advantageous for you. Just let me at the company. I could help it, secure it, and protect your interest in it. And I can and will handle the Berab brothers. I'm very observant. And resourceful. And I do not give up easily."

"I've definitely noticed." She stepped toward him. "Which is why I have another sort of proposal for you."

"Pardon?" He squinted at her, his entire face scrunching.

"How would you like to assist me in running the Lira portion of the company?" she asked.

"As..." Weiss shook his head, confusion in his tone.

"As an employee at first, but with a chance to be a partner, gain an ownership interest from our share, provided we acted as a team and voted as a block, in most circumstances." She clasped her hands together, already outlining the details in her mind, the details that would allow her to continue to rule without a husband. "Though obviously, I'd be giving up some control and taking a calculated risk. Trust someone I wouldn't dominate and hope for the best in the future."

"That's quite the sacrifice on your part." He cocked his head. "So what would remain for your children would be both what your father built and something new?"

"If there are any children." She shrugged, though she couldn't imagine it, not without Aaron. She raised a finger. "If not, for whoever comes along and can use it best, for good. Regardless, it would be something new. Three families. With you acting not only as my protection, but as peacemaker. Managing the relationship with the Berabs, perhaps mending it or, ideally, making it into something new, something better for the present in which we find ourselves. Moving forward, so we reflect the full community—invited by Cromwell or not. Remembering that while we might want rights, we don't want to gain them by denigrating each other. A good leader is mindful of the past but reaches for a better future, even if they might not get to see it." They were a new generation, with their own challenges to meet and vision to create. "You'll be free to use the funds and the position to help your brother. If you need my assistance with that, I will always be there to help. As a friend."

Weiss opened his mouth and closed it and opened it again. "You'd offer me that?"

"I don't see why not." After all, it truly was the best of all possible worlds. "As we've clearly established, I could use a fresh perspective in the surety company and in general. You're rather intelligent, and if we can align our interests, write a proper contract, we could each accomplish what we wanted without joining ourselves in other ways." They could win—as partners.

He tapped two fingers to his lips. "I don't know if I should be grateful or insulted."

"You're a handsome man. I'm sure you'll make someone happy." Truly.

"Just not you?" His eyes were a bit sad as he gazed over at her.

"Just not me." She pursed her lips, swallowing that pesky lump, because it could not and would not ruin this moment, this taking charge of their futures. She threw back her shoulders. "But as I said, I'd like to be your partner. And possibly your friend." Isabelle offered him her gloved palm. "What do you say?"

With a broad smile, Weiss grasped it and shook. "I say, Miss Lira, you have a deal."

"Excellent." She clapped her hands together before glancing at the door. "We should go speak to my grandmother and Pena and our legal counsel and formalize this, back at our offices." She paced toward the exit, Weiss in tow.

"What are you going to do about the announcement tonight?" he asked as she turned the knob.

"If only I knew." She grimaced. Not something she was looking forward to, but she could survive. A touch of embarrassment wasn't the worst thing now and then. Kept you humble. The heartache, though...

"Well...you know..." Weiss's voice broke her thoughts. He clasped his hands together, shifting from foot to foot.

"What's wrong?" she asked, her heart beginning to speed a touch. He wasn't having second thoughts, was he? Just when she had found a solution that should be correct as well.

He glanced from side to side before coughing into his hand. "Seeing as now we are to be friends, and friends are honest with each other..."

She closed her eyes. What was it now? Or more, what faux pas had he noticed that she'd somehow overlooked in her quest for power? "What is it?"

"About Mr. Ellenberg." His swallow was visible despite his neatly tied cravat. "I know it is not my place to say, but in the event he has not yet departed for America, there's still an opportunity for you to perhaps say things you have not, things you might regret leaving unsaid."

And the pressure was back behind her eyes. Because there were things. So many things.

"I—I can't." She shook her head. "It wouldn't be right or fair, not after I had the chance and failed." She gazed at Weiss. "I hurt him. Very, very badly, and I had the opportunity to do better, and hurt him once more. I don't deserve the chance to say those things."

"Perhaps." Her new partner nodded and threaded his arm through hers, leading her toward the front of the house. "But doesn't he deserve to hear them? Or are you not brave enough?"

"I'm not sure I am," she told him as the lump squeezed her throat shut with the enormity of what she'd done to the person who had done nothing but listen to her, care for her, and love her. The person who wanted only the same in return. And she'd denied him that—withheld it. Because she'd been too afraid to do what was right. "And I—that's a battle I don't even know how to begin to fight."

"I certainly wouldn't rely on your usual weapons." Weiss indicated the folds of her dress covering her sheath before throwing back his head and laughing. "You really do need me, don't you?" he said more than asked. "Come along—we'll take my carriage and go to the Great Synagogue, and I can tell you why you're wrong the entire way there."

Chapter Twenty-Nine

Isabelle bumped along through Aldgate toward Duke's Place, gripping the seat of the Weiss carriage. The vehicle was ornate, the inside draped in gilded fabric accented with small silver mirrored jewels. Surprising, given the family's only newly resecured financial position, though perhaps the two went hand in hand. Something she should probably discuss with her partner at some point, but not that day.

No, all she could do, all she could think of, was Aaron and how she needed to speak with him one last time. To at least apologize and let him know that what she'd done, how she'd treated him, was abominable and that he deserved so much better, so much more, and that she hoped he would find it. She closed her eyes. Because that was the right thing to tell him. The unselfish thing. And she could be unselfish.

Or at least she could try. Provided she arrived on time. She turned to Weiss, who was lounging across from her, legs stretched out, humming, as if he didn't have a care in the world.

"Can we go any faster?" she asked through gritted teeth.

"We're being pulled by mere horses, not Pegasus,"

he said, folding back the thick, tasseled curtains to peer out the window. "Also, there are people in the street. I thought you were in the risk business."

A fair point—not that she would acknowledge it. She was still his boss and needed her dignity.

"But this is important." She pouted, folding her arms. "This is—" And the carriage skittered to a halt just past Bevis Marks, causing her to bump her head against the seat, probably crinkling the back of her bonnet and wilting her feathers. Not that such things mattered at the moment, though if she was going to see Aaron one last time, she might as well highlight all the good qualities she did possess.

"What was that?" she asked her companion as she restyled herself.

"I don't know, but it looks as if another carriage just stopped short and is blocking our path." He frowned as he rose. "I'll see what is happening."

Before Isabelle could say anything, Weiss slid out the door, leaving her alone, tapping her toe. She folded her arms as her pulse began to speed. What was the matter? Aaron was waiting. Well, not waiting, but with limited time before he left for America and—the door swung back open and Weiss stuck his head inside.

"We have company. Or more, you do." He slid inside, settling next to her, as all three Berab brothers entered and took the seat across.

The five of them sat in an uncomfortable silence for a long moment.

"To what do I owe this honor?" she finally asked, working not to squirm nor appear disengaged, even if her entire being longed to bolt from the carriage and run, not walk, to Aaron. Because that would only make things worse. Especially if she'd truly insulted them, as Weiss had suggested. Even if the chasm was rooted in a misconstruction, she needed to try to put it right.

"I apologize for any inconvenience, but we were finishing with the morning service and I saw you through the window of Mr. Weiss's carriage and decided that we needed to speak. Needed to have this out and set a plan into motion to best protect our clients. Before tonight." It was David who spoke. "Before our most likely final meeting."

"I suppose we do." Isabelle took a deep breath, working to choose her words as carefully as she could. "I—I believe we might misunderstand each other."

The older man paused, cocking his head. "Do we?" He narrowed his eyes, his thick, graying brows knitting.

"Yes." She nodded before swallowing. Mercy, this was so difficult, but if she was to be a true leader, she was going to need to learn when to set her pride aside for the good of the whole. If only Aaron was here to squeeze her hand while she did it.

But he wasn't. And that was her own fault, so she was just going to have to go it alone. She cleared her throat. "I, um, I would like to apologize if I ever made you believe that I do not respect you and all you do for the company." Grimacing, she tried again. "More so, for not properly acknowledging and showing respect for what you do for the company. What you did for my father. You were such good friends—for so many years."

"I considered him a brother." David's voice was soft.

"I know he felt the same." She leaned forward and pressed a gloved hand to her collar. "And I would never, ever want to imply that I seek to dislodge you, or know more than you do, or that he knew more—I respect you and your judgment too much. I don't want to lead the company—I want to be a partner to you. Not in the same way my father was—I know I will never be him—but in a new way, based on a new relationship that we build together. Where I listen to and learn from you, if you will permit it."

Not that she'd ever articulated it that way completely, not to herself, but that was the full plan, the goal, the hope.

He blinked at her for a moment. "Truly? Then why, the moment he died, did you burst in and try to run me out?"

Run him out? Isabelle stared at him. Was that how he saw what she had been doing? Were his purposes the same as hers?

Isabelle wet her lips as she again sought the correct phrasing. After all, while what they'd done to her wasn't exactly forgivable, sometimes, when emotion was involved and everyone was hurting, someone needed to de-escalate, whether they were in the wrong or not.

"I apologize. The last thing I wanted was to run you out. I was grieving and wanted to feel close to him again, and I was disrespectful to you and the business. I was rude and pushy and arrogant, and I'm sorry."

There was a moment of silence. Louis glared at her, while Roger cocked his head pensively. However, David just stared, eyes wide.

"Yes, but you're twenty-three," he finally said before hanging his head, shoulders slumping. "I'm almost twice your age. I should have reacted better. Not gone to war. Not treated you as an enemy when you are practically family."

"Yes. Not to mention try to force her into marriage," Weiss said mildly.

"She's twenty-three and would have been thinking about marriage anyway. My brothers are available and suitable." David waved a dismissive hand. "I just thought you were determined to wrest control of the company. Which would have been foolish, given your experience, and harmful to the business." He turned to Isabelle. "I'm not an ogre. I presumed—wrongly—that if working together was truly important to you, enlisting one of my brothers as a buffer was the best way to keep us both at peace and worms out of my coat pockets."

"Pardon?" Weiss gasped, turning to her.

Apparently, they were going to be airing all the dirty laundry now.

"No one can prove they didn't crawl in there on their own." Isabelle gave a slightly guilty shrug. "That occurred the same day I discovered he'd hidden multiple files from me," she added.

"After you opened personal correspondence of mine and left it strewn about the office," David responded, his face reddening.

"I was looking for papers which belonged to my father," she explained, folding her arms.

"I hope you two don't do this to the staff," Weiss interrupted, with more than a bit of nervousness in his expression.

"Of course not," David snapped. "Neither of us would ever mistreat or be discourteous to someone over whom we have power."

"Never," Isabelle agreed. "We are only interested in fair fights, so to speak."

"We're very kind to most people," David added. "As there are very few people who are our equals." And, wonder of wonders, he gave her a small wink—like he used to when she was small and he'd let her have sips of his coffee when no one was looking, even though her grandmother told her it would stunt her growth—making something unclench inside Isabelle.

She smiled at him. "No," she agreed. "Very few."

"Well." Weiss slapped his hands on his thighs. "It seems that you two agree about quite a few things, including that you are equals. Perhaps it won't be so bad working with you."

"Working with us?" It was Louis who asked the question. "What do you mean, Mr. Weiss?"

Right. She hadn't explained that yet. Well, no time like the present.

She glanced at the three. Louis's hands were tightly closed, but Roger's expression was thoughtful, and David certainly had her full attention. She threaded her fingers together. "I've considered the matter and think that even though I've been trained by my father, I lack experience in the business. Moreover, as you've said, I'm a woman and rather young, so making contacts is challenging for me, especially in gentile society. Expansion is important, and I came to the conclusion that adding an outsider, with different personal connections than our families, might strengthen my contribution to the company. Help us all."

"Truly?" David's eyes narrowed as he turned toward Weiss. "And, I take it, marrying Mr. Weiss will accomplish that?"

"No." She shook her head. "But he will provide the assistance I spoke of." She gave the man a soft smile before turning back to the brothers. "I will pay him a salary out of my own profits, not out of the business's funds, and both of us can work together, with the understanding that one day, provided you all approve, I might transfer him some of my stake. As a friend and partner, not as a husband."

Isabelle gazed at David again, willing him to accept the proposal. To allow them both to save face and begin not anew, but differently. Better. Looking to the future, instead of holding on to the past.

It was Roger, however, who spoke. "That seems rather reasonable. Not that I should truly have much say. After all, it isn't as if either of us pull our fair weight." His lip quirked as he pointed to himself and Louis before releasing a long, slow breath. "And while you're a lovely woman, and it would be an honor to marry you, I don't believe we would suit. Or at least I'm not ready to find out, so this choice benefits me."

"But you're still going to continue with the festival tonight?" It was David who asked the question, his eyes once again sharp.

"I am." She gave a nod. "The community is expecting it. As are the gentiles. And we can't afford to insult or disappoint either. Especially with the bill. Even if it turns on the people, not the gentry, I don't want to be an excuse for them not to give us our due." Her stomach flipped a little. "But I'd very much like you to be there with me, as part of the family. Like my father would have wanted."

David didn't respond, but he gave a nod of assent.

"What are you going to announce?" It was Roger who asked the question.

At that she had to laugh. With everything going on, it had been the least of her concerns.

"I haven't the foggiest idea," she confessed. "The truth is, while there is someone I'd like to marry, I, um—I don't think he is interested in the union." She glanced down at her lap as her throat tightened. Not just at the loss, but because she most likely wouldn't be able to tell him about any of what had just transpired. And Aaron would've loved the story, including the part where she had to admit that Weiss, of all people, had been right. And that Aaron had been as well.

She swallowed, forcing herself to focus on the present task and company. "Though you don't need to worry about him. He has no interest in the business either."

David gave a grunt. "Sounds like a fool."

"Some people have more-valuable things to offer than business acumen," she told him, gritting her teeth. "Things like kindness and care and an ability to listen and to love. Things I wish I could do half as well." And the lump in her throat nearly choked her as the pressure grew behind her eyes.

Aaron wasn't the fool. She was. A thousand times over, and if she could do it all again...

"Still a fool," David proclaimed, folding his arms tight. "If he doesn't want to marry you."

And now her eyes were wet. Dash it all.

"You don't know what I did to him," she whispered.

"I'm sure you'll make it right," David said with a confidence she certainly did not feel. "It takes a very brave person to do what you did here, so you should have no trouble with this man. And if he is indeed a fool, we will stand by you."

"If the man is Aaron Ellenberg, he most certainly is a fool." It was Louis who spoke, gritting his teeth audibly. He lifted his gaze and frowned at her. "And he's already gone."

"What?" Isabelle gasped, his words stabbing her heart. "When?" she managed to ask. And why? Well, she knew why, but this wasn't right. He wasn't supposed to have left yet. She was supposed to have more time. She squeezed her fists—she deserved more time, damn it.

"He left for New York this morning." Louis dusted his lapels as he confirmed her fears. "I was at my tailor's. One of his rabbis uses the same man and told me himself. Already gone. With a new set of fancy garments. Apparently, he came into some money."

And now the lump was choking off all her air. Though she supposed it was good and right. He'd earned that money, and he deserved its benefits and probably looked so handsome. Not that he didn't always look handsome. Very handsome. Her eyes misted.

"I'm very sorry, Miss Lira. I—I think that this might be our—" Roger started, his tone achingly gentle. Pitying.

Which she could not have. Despite their renewed relationship. She forced air into her lungs, forced herself to lift her gaze.

"It's all right. It's fitting that things end like this," she told him, squeezing her hands together so tightly the seams of her gloves dug into her flesh. "Like they should. Like they would have if I had been better at communicating with you three from the start."

"We're still sorry," David said. "But as we said before, we will stand by you tonight, and in the future. Like we should have after your father died." He rose, adjusting the etched silver buttons of his neatly pressed jacket. "However, I suppose we should exit, allow you to ready yourself for tonight. I'm sure you will be lovely and end your festivities with a grace that the entire city will applaud."

"Besides, there's much for us to do. We have some clients to contact." Roger gave David a sharp nudge.

"Yes." The man coughed into his hand. "I'm sure they will be disappointed that the meeting tomorrow is canceled, though I will send around a few small gifts for their time. And we most certainly do look forward to seeing you tonight. I am sure you will shine."

"Thank you for saying that," she told him, working to hold his gaze as a swirl of gratitude rushed through her veins. She'd won. And the future would be bright, like she'd wanted. She swallowed. "I know, with you three and my grandmother, tonight will be wonderful. The start of a beautiful beginning." The one she had wished for, even if that wish had changed. But wishes were for children, and she was no longer one. And this was a victory. In many ways, better than she'd originally conceived.

Weiss slipped her his handkerchief before squeezing her gloved hand and whispering in her ear. "It will be. Even if I too am a bit disappointed you won't be making a certain announcement. He'd be good to have around. Astoundingly determined in a fight," he murmured before turning to the Berabs. "We'll see you tonight," he said in full voice.

"We're looking forward to it." David gave them one last nod and, with a tip of his hat, slipped out of the carriage, his brothers in tow, shutting the door behind him.

Chapter Thirty

The sky turned from gray to inky navy as Aaron laid his broom against the wall inside the door of the synagogue for the last time. After the latch clicked behind him, he made his way back to what would soon no longer be his room. His belongings were already packed—he was all set to leave for America from Dover at first light.

He had made sure he fed the mouse family and placed a few worms in the sparrows' nest on the eave outside his door. He'd sneaked one last bowl of milk for Sir Sleeps-a-Lot and the other alley cats and would leave them another in the morning. He'd given instructions to some of the regular minyan attendees, and they'd made him promises, but he had his concerns.

However, despite the worry, tomorrow he would be gone. On a ship. In a private cabin, with the fine new clothing he'd been measured for earlier that week, already sent ahead.

Rabbi Marcus's idea. Upon hearing the whole tale— well, the whole tale except the library and the garden parts—he and the morning minyan crowd had forced Aaron not to send back Isabelle's money that he'd discovered on his dresser several hours after she'd left.

"You earned that for services rendered. It's yours." Mr. Sinzheim had clapped Aaron on the back. "It does no good being gifted back to her. Besides, she has enough people advocating for her and her interests—it's time you took care of your own instead of worrying about everyone else's."

The rabbi himself insisted on accompanying Aaron to the tailor's shop after morning prayers and had even taken it upon himself to advise him about various types of wool.

"I think you'll be very happy in New York," the man had said. "The community there is growing and bustling and ready to welcome newcomers into its leadership. We'll certainly miss you. You were an asset to the community."

He'd snorted a little bit at that. "I think you will get by."

"We will. Though not as well." The rabbi had shaken a finger at him. "You, however, I just—I hope this brings you joy. You deserve joy. However, while we would fight to make sure you could stay—no matter what anyone else says—it has become clear that you might require different circumstances to do so. Not so many stumbling blocks, eh?"

Aaron had clutched his broom to his chest. Anything had to be easier than being there. Even if he wasn't banished, he'd know she was just a few short miles away. Know that he would always love her, but she could not bring herself to return those feelings.

Not that she wasn't capable of them. He would just never be enough to inspire them in her. Which was why there was no choice. He had to leave. Had to find some way to forget Isabelle. Had to—

A rapping rattled the rusty hinges of his door.

"Coming," he called as he rocked to a standing position and lumbered out of bed. He swung the thing open to find Miriam leaning on her cane.

"Fancy seeing you here." The hood of her cloak swayed as she moved her head from side to side.

"Are you here to say farewell?" He cracked his back. "After all, my bag is packed and I'm indeed ready to go."

"I can see that." Miriam stumbled past Aaron into the room, her hood dipping lower so even her chin was hidden. "You don't plan to attend the festival tonight?" She squatted on the bed.

"It's already evening. It's starting in less than two hours. And it's for the best this way." He gritted his teeth at the memory of the encounter the prior night. "My job is finished. I've already been paid. There's no reason for me to be there." His chest tightened at the half-truth.

"No, I suppose there's not." She kicked out her heels, bending to rub her calves over her woolen skirts.

"May I?" he asked, indicating to her pained movements. After all, there was no need to make her work alone, not with him lazing about.

Miriam made a huffing noise but finally nodded her assent. "It's a shame."

"What is?" Aaron bent over and took over the woman's actions, kneading Miriam's stiff muscles.

"You not seeing the festival, not getting to truly participate with everyone else instead of serving on the sidelines." Miriam stretched her legs farther. "Even more unfortunate, there's a theatrical performance tonight. You love theater." She leaned back a little as

Aaron worked. "And stories. You're very good at sharing them, after all."

"I'll have enough of that in New York." Aaron pushed down harder on a knot. "Besides, I threw away my invitation."

"True." She grunted. "Though there are extras lying around, if anyone cares to look." Miriam reached around and pulled a black half mask followed by a white envelope from some hidden pocket in her voluminous garment. She could give Isabelle a run for her money when it came to useful clothing.

"That doesn't take care of my garments. What I have is not appropriate, and I'm not actually invisible," he mumbled.

"Thank you." She tapped Aaron on the shoulder with her cane, indicating she'd had enough of the leg work, and Aaron stood again.

"Perhaps it's time you were less invisible." Miriam readjusted her skirts. "Besides, with the right attire, you'll shine so brightly that no one will see the synagogue custodian or failed apprentice or orphan."

"Bah." Aaron sniffed. Most certainly stubborn. Or perhaps the woman had fallen and hit her head. She needed to let him be. It was over. He strolled over to his meager baggage to thumb through it, hoping Miriam would take the hint and leave.

"Haven't you ever wanted to glitter with your own light? Make people see you? Feel like you're not only tolerated, but welcomed? That you belong?" she called, lingering on the last word.

"The only person I want to see me already has. And I wasn't enough." He folded his arms. "To her I don't shine and I'm certainly not special. I'm just a man who cleans messes and once in a while gets asked for a touch of information. Not worthy of time or attention and certainly not the type to dazzle. Not her nor anyone here. Perhaps in New York..."

"I don't know—I've heard rumor that you gave quite a performance with almost no lines in the Lira garden the other night."

"Stop." He raised a palm, working to keep his voice as respectful as possible despite the fury ripping through his veins. "I don't know what you heard, but—well—don't repeat it. Not for my sake—for hers. She doesn't deserve that sort of gossip ruining her chances for respect. Or the Berab brothers using it against her, thwarting her when she's sacrificed so much to preserve her father's legacy. What happened between the two of us is no one's business but our own, and if anyone needs payment to ensure that it stays that way, well, they can have it."

"Oh, stop, I don't want money from you. However, the synagogue might care for a parting donation." A sniff from Miriam. Though he'd never seen her full face, he could certainly picture the wry expression on it. "I will say nevertheless, that was quite the diatribe in defense of her honor, especially considering her overtures towards Mr. Weiss. She most certainly does not deserve you." She poked him with her cane. "No one is mocking anyone, Mr. Ellenberg."

Right. As if he could truly believe any of that, especially about Isabelle not deserving him. Aaron released something that was suspiciously like a growl, but Miriam shrugged.

"But back to my prior point." She shook a long finger at him. "Or more yours. You don't believe you glitter, you don't believe you can walk into a ball as you truly are and woo the host so she has eyes for no one else."

"I believe that is the plot to a Rossini opera." The first he ever saw, when he'd sneaked backstage, hungry and half frozen to death. His favorite. Which the woman probably knew somehow. Which was both charming and irritating. Aaron leaned against the table, still scowling.

"The one that is being performed tonight, in fact." Miriam was definitely mocking him behind the cloak. "Such an interesting variation on the story, different than both the Perrault and the Grimm brothers—disguises and no glass slippers."

"Yes, but it's the prince who hides his identity. Something that's not occurring here, as everyone knows who Miss Lira is and she likes it that way." Aaron toed a hole in the floorboards with his boot. "And in the story, Angelina flees but she asks the prince to follow, find out who she really is." Which would never happen in real life. Isabelle would never chase him.

"So you can take liberties with the plot." She leaned further on her cane. "Though I'd argue Angelina was always who she was, as was the prince, and the beauty in the story was them being able to see each other."

The way Isabelle allowed him to see her when they were alone. And the way she seemed to see him in those moments, better than he was, as he wanted to be, as he could never—

"Don't you want to show yourself once more to the woman you love, as you really, fully are, in front of everyone? Let not only you, but the truth shine?" Miriam added.

"I don't love her," he lied even as the scene she

painted stirred every longing, every secret wish buried deep in his chest. Wishes that would never come true. "Or more, she doesn't love me. At least not enough."

"No?" Miriam readjusted her cloak, wrapping it around her body. "Interesting. I'll have to tell some hired guards that they've lost a few bets."

"Let them lose all they like. Gambling is always a waste." He kicked at the hole this time, stubbing his toe through his boot, the pain somehow welcome.

"Is it now?" The bed creaked as the woman rose and edged toward him.

"What do you want, Miriam?" He shoved his hands in his pockets.

Miriam pointed that damned finger once more. "It isn't what I want—it's what you want."

Despite the impossibility of anything and everything he wanted, a shiver ran down Aaron's spine. "I can't have what I want," he whispered, almost to himself.

"Says who?" Miriam leaned against the wall.

"Says Isabelle, and her opinion is the only opinion that matters." Aaron slammed his fist down on the table in frustration. It was over, in the past, and he was leaving. It didn't matter anymore. "I'm not enough."

"Did she say that?" Miriam asked.

What kind of question was that? Aaron glared at the woman. "She didn't deny it." He kicked at the ground. "She had every opportunity to tell me that she—" He swallowed. "Why couldn't she give me the words?" Why couldn't she say it out loud? Give him the words so they could figure it out together? Why was he not enough to merit that?

"Isabelle Lira is a frightened girl." She rocked a little

as she moved toward him once again. "I'm not saying what she did was right, far from it, but—"

"Let's not rehash this, please." He tugged at his beard, which was getting bushier by the minute. "She made her choice."

"Did she? Or did she merely stumble, miss a cue?" Miriam snapped, now so close she was practically on top of him. "Have a temporary lapse in judgment which there's still time to correct?"

"I don't know. I'm not even sure it was a mistake. I have nothing to offer her. Even if I stayed, even if the Berab brothers didn't seek revenge, I've no status nor money. I'm not learned or clever. I can't lead the community or help the business. I have no trade, no talent. I have nothing to recommend me. I'm the last person anyone would want as a husband."

"Yes, because that's what Isabelle Lira needs—a man who is first in line for a title when they finally realize allowing some of us the illusion of power will keep us even further in check, or one who can write commentary or speak twelve languages." Miriam placed a hand on her hip.

"Are you mocking me?" He clenched his fist.

"No, I'm making an observation. I think the bigger question is why Isabelle Lira needs a husband who is any of those things." Miriam grunted as he stared at her, his mind spinning. "Think about that while you inspect what I brought for you. And remember, my hands might be old but are still quite skilled at tying a cravat, if you need them. Though I heard Rabbi Marcus isn't so bad himself." She indicated a satchel lying on the bed.

How had he not noticed it before? Aaron squinted,

but the item was still present. He must really be out of sorts. "Why?" he managed to ask, blinking at the woman. What did he matter? What was Isabelle to her? After all, the community was her primary concern, and if she truly cared about that, she'd be pushing the Berabs harder. As that union would at least have political benefits.

"If the bill fails over a twenty-three-year-old heiress's choice in husband, it would never have succeeded in the first place." Miriam inhaled a deep breath, seemingly reading his mind once more. "The bill is important, but not a panacea. If Sussex and his consortium are true friends, the match will have no effect on their opinions. Rights aren't rights if they are contingent on us yielding to each and every gentile whim." She squeezed the head of her cane. "We are people. If they'll only permit us rights if they like everything we do or say, then they'll never be full rights. We'll never be equal, and always be at their mercy."

Aaron stared at her, his jaw going slack.

"There's always something," she continued. "One of us will commit some sort of crime, or they'll find one of our practices or beliefs repulsive, and all those feelings they have now, the ones just under the surface, will rise once more. They'll use this or that as a pretext to justify not only the hatred they still harbor but taking away anything we receive."

"I don't understand." Aaron shook his head. What did any of this have to do with him?

Miriam reached out a shaking hand and gave him a pat on the arm. "That means you can't use the bill as an excuse. Just as the business is not an excuse." She moved back toward the bed. "Now, I can't guarantee anything magical will happen if you come to the festival tonight, but I do believe you'll regret not attending, not giving her that second chance you're itching to give her, whether she deserves it or not." Grunting, she reached for the satchel, straining as she bent.

Which wouldn't do. Aaron moved to her and retrieved the item, clutching it against his chest. "Impossible," he murmured, even as his mind was already brimming with curiosity about what exactly it contained.

"Only if you make it, only if you let your own doubts and someone else's fears and foolishness cover you in muck, cover that hope that you manage to keep alive. People do see you, Mr. Ellenberg, more people than you think. More than you do yourself." The woman gave him a nudge. "Go on, peek inside."

Against his better judgment and with a grunt of his own, as well as a few choice words under his breath, Aaron complied and gasped. Even in the dim candlelight the fineness of the fabric glistened.

"It will be perfect on you." Miriam gave him a jab to the ribs. Why all the touches all of a sudden? Not that it mattered, but the night was getting odder and odder.

"And it's right here in front of you," she added, "with no one wearing it. And truly, someone should be wearing it."

"I won't be wearing it for very long," he grumbled, running his hand over the velvet of the cravat. He turned to Miriam. "My ship departs tomorrow, from Dover. I need to leave tonight to arrive on time."

"You should stay at least until midnight. That's when Miss Isabelle will be making her announcement." Her hood dipped to the side, as if she was cocking her head behind it.

Was Miriam joking? She wanted him to stay for that? Already, he was terrified that he'd shatter the moment he saw Isabelle again, and hearing her announce...

Miriam was wrong about him and her—he wasn't enough. And staying and watching her choose Weiss, knowing everything he knew—no thank you. A terrible idea.

Even going at all was a terrible idea.

And yet here he was, already tugging the jacket out from the bag, ready to slip it over his shoulders. Because he had to see her one last time. Even if only for a moment, if only until midnight.

"I will certainly not be staying until midnight." Aaron closed his eyes. "But I believe I'm going to a ball."

Chapter Thirty-One

Aaron stood at the top of the stairs, behind a merchant and his two sons, waiting to enter the ballroom from the front door for once. He yanked at the bottom of his waistcoat—a bit tight, but the starched white fabric gleamed with respectability in the chandelier light, especially against the ridiculous deep ruby cravat Miriam had given him. Rabbi Marcus had smoothed and futzed with it as well before assisting him with his Lag BaOmer shave and shear. Coupled with the tighter-fitting trousers and smooth stockings loaned by other congregants, he probably did appear to belong.

With his still-rough fingers—one of the few things the surprisingly resourceful woman couldn't polish and disguise—he rubbed the back of his newly trimmed hair and adjusted the black mask over his eyes. There was a fluttering in his stomach, but not the butterflies that performers talked about. No, these were giant creatures, beating to the rhythm of Isabelle's name. Despite everything.

"Sir?" A shorter man in a dark coat tugged at his arm as the group in front of him traveled down the stairs into the gold-hued fairyland that was the Lira ballroom, this night glittering with crystals and beads dripping from the ceiling.

Aaron blinked at him. "Pardon?"

The man cleared his throat. "Your name, so you can be announced."

"Oh, right." Aaron tugged at his cravat. He wanted to be a big macher, so he'd better learn to play the part. "Um, I'm...Aaron Ellenberg."

"Very good," the man said. "Mr. Aaron Ellenberg," he called out into the air, and the crowd fell silent for a moment, all heads turning toward him.

And they were...nodding. And bending in respect as he started down the staircase.

"Aaron." The voice—her voice—crisp and clear, echoed through the ballroom, over the heads of the milling guests. Even the actors making their ways to their positions on the stage that had somehow been built overnight paused their work to stare.

Well, Miriam was right. Apparently, he could truly make an entrance. Murmurs swelled as the sea of well-dressed bodies parted, clearing a path to her. And all of a sudden, his feet would not move—and not due to the too-tight velvet-covered shoes. Well, not just due to them. He really should've worn his own, but the consensus among his helpers had been beauty over practicality. Something he was beginning to regret.

The chandelier above her acted as a spotlight. Dressed in deep red, a perfect contrast to her shimmery black hair, her cheeks flushed below her jeweled half mask, she was something out of a fairy story. Bold and bright and beautiful and commanding, ready to do and be anything. Breathtaking.

We need to talk. She mouthed the words before biting her lip. *Please?* she added, her eyes nearly pleading.

It took everything in him not to run to her and fall to his knees and beg her to—well, just let him be with her, to love him. Because he couldn't. They'd said all they had to say already. Miriam was wrong, no matter how much he wanted her to be right.

He wasn't enough for Isabelle. His love wasn't enough. Not to make her love him in return.

But the way she stared back at him, even from behind the mask, the way her chest rose and fell, that was everything. The way that one word cut into him. *Please.* He would carry it and the tiny bit of hope it sparked inside him, the hope that should rightly be dead, forever.

With as much grace and dignity as he could, he nodded to her before moving over the golden runner to the edge of the ballroom, head held high, as if he belonged. And it appeared he did, because the moment he stepped down, whatever spell had taken the other guests' tongues broke.

The chatter began once more, and a throng approached him with more bows and curtsies and introductions. A flurry of words rushed at him—from compliments regarding how he looked and carried himself to thank-yous for small things he'd done in the past that he'd believed no one noticed. Returning Mr. Feld's lost tallis bag in the snow, slipping the Herzogs an extra parcel of matzahs the Passover the creditors had been calling but they'd been too embarrassed to say, adding an extra cushion to Mr. Millstein's seat when it rained and his hip was acting up. Normally he'd have flushed with pleasure. And while an odd aching filled his gut, his mind was completely directed elsewhere. Toward her and only her.

Aaron craned his neck, as he had to get to her, but the obstacles continued. Oy. What was he to do? This was beyond—no. No, it wasn't. He'd wanted this—this moment—and now was his time. Besides, these were the people, the community he'd longed for, and though he was leaving, he wanted to be with them again too, just a little bit, one last time. Smiling, with as much dignity as possible, he acknowledged every well-wisher personally as he wove through the crowds, still focused on his goal—to get to her a final time.

Though that was a trifle difficult, as the guests kept coming, until someone else cut through the crowd with long, firm steps—not Isabelle, but a man. A man in a mask, with a rather familiar gait and set of the shoulders, though he couldn't quite place him.

"Mr. Ellenberg." The man clapped him on the back.

"Yes?" He squinted in an attempt to decipher the features through the mask. His hair was dark, though graying at the temples, suggesting he was a few years older, so not a former fellow apprentice or orphan. Perhaps someone from the synagogue?

"I work for the Lira family," the man explained in a voice so familiar, but just out of reach in his memory. "Miss Isabelle would like to have a word with you before the performance starts."

"Yes, I would like to speak with her as well." Because he would. Even if he shouldn't.

He craned his neck over the throng, working to catch a glimpse of anything red, anything that might be a part of her. He glanced at the other man. Maybe he could be of assistance. "In private, if possible," he added, lowering his voice, though working to keep his tone still respectful.

The man's lips turned up in a half smile. "Naturally. And it is not only possible, but preferred." He placed a hand on Aaron's arm, his grip rather tight. "Come this way," he said, tugging him toward a hall he'd never used.

"Where are we going?" He worked to keep up with the servant's quick pace as they moved through an empty, narrow corridor, a touch darker and less well decorated than the one leading to the library, where Isabelle usually went to breathe. Which, come to think of it, would have been perfect. He opened his mouth to suggest that location, but the other man hushed him.

"We're going to the garden," he told Aaron as they hurried down a winding staircase.

"Oh, I know a different way." He glanced over his shoulder, an unease beginning to spread outward from the pit of his stomach.

"This is a more secluded entrance," the man returned, though he finally released his grip. They reached the bottom stair and creaked open a small door, lengths of ivy waving like a curtain to reveal the night sky. A soft, cool breeze ruffled through his borrowed garments.

"Follow me, please," the servant added, pointing toward what Aaron could now make out as the fountain and the statue where he and Isabelle had sat and talked and, well, done quite a bit more.

He reached down and ran his fingers through the water. "Interesting, I didn't know we could exit—" An object crashed against his skull, causing him to lurch forward, striking his temple on the stone. The action was so fast he didn't have time to even cry out. Instead, there was a flash of pain, and darkness took him.

Isabelle rushed and pushed through the crowds of well-wishers in the ballroom. Aaron, she had to get to Aaron. She rocked up on her toes, craning her neck. Why was she so short? And why were skirts so voluminous this season? However, when she reached the bottom of the grand staircase, he was nowhere to be found. She glanced around at the nearest guests and approached a woman in lavender.

"Thank you so much for coming," she told her, working to be gracious even though she was desperate to speak to one and only one person. "You look lovely."

"Thank you." The woman fluffed her skirts. "The gown is new. From Paris."

"Stunning." Isabelle bit her lip. "It truly is. I—I hope you don't mind, but I have a question. Have you—did you perchance see a man wearing a black mask and a red cravat recently?" A cravat she would know anywhere, as it had belonged to her grandfather.

How Aaron had obtained it, she had no idea, though the way he looked in it... She wet her lower lip despite herself and the situation.

"A moment ago," another guest said, fluttering a plum-colored fan. "He was just..." She glanced around and shrugged her puffed silk sleeves.

"Yes, he was speaking with a gentleman," her companion added, leaning into their conversation. "The two of them walked that way." He pointed toward the small servants' corridor nearly hidden by a potted fig. "They appeared to be headed toward the gardens."

The gardens. Isabelle inhaled. That made sense. That was where they'd met so many times and was a perfect place to talk.

"Thank you," she told the couple as she hitched her skirts and started toward the hall, darting around an ornate vase. "Please enjoy the production—it will begin shortly," she called over her shoulder.

Something that, if she could find him and properly apologize, would be lovely to watch with Aaron by her side. Because there was hope now, was there not? He'd come. So provided she could get the words right...She shook her head as she scurried.

Her current activity was truly thematically fitting. After all, in a few hours, onstage, Angelina would tell Prince Ramiro that if he really cared for her, he'd find her. Well, she would find Aaron. And prove the same.

"Miss Lira." Her name halted her as she reached the entrance of the passage.

She whirled around to find Roger Berab, mask in hand, biting his lip as he approached her.

"What is it, Mr. Berab?" she asked as she indicated behind her. "I'm—"

"Searching for Mr. Ellenberg?" He cocked his head, though there was something odd, almost nervous in his posture.

"Yes." She frowned as she studied him. "How did you—"

Roger's swallow was visible. "My brother—Louis— he was speaking to him, and the two of them left together."

Isabelle wrinkled her nose. "Louis? Why were he

and Aaron speaking?" And what did that have to do
with anything?

"I don't know, but—we should hurry." Roger swept
past her into the servants' hall and beckoned her to follow. "May, I, uh, be frank with you?"

"Naturally," she said as they moved downward to the
lower stairs, taking them two at a time. "I meant what I
said in the carriage—I see you three as more than partners, as family."

"That's good to hear, as I do hope you are understanding with your family members." He glanced back
at her through the dim light as they descended. "My
brother has—he hasn't been himself for some time,
and after our prior discussion...I believe he lied to
you about Mr. Ellenberg leaving, perhaps in the foolish hope that you would turn your attentions to him if
you believed that situation hopeless. It was a plausible
lie, as we might have, um..." Roger glanced down for
a moment. "Oh dash it, we threatened Mr. Ellenberg."

"What?" she nearly screamed, turning on him.

He held up both palms. "Not after we came to an
understanding," he said rather hastily as rage spiked
through her body. "Before. After the first festival. Told
him to get you to marry one of us or we'd make sure he
was banished from the community."

"My God." She gawked at him. This was just...

"Yes. I'm sorry. Truly sorry. And just so you know,
David was never part of this," he added before grimacing. "Not that it matters, but while he merely wanted
you managed, Louis might have actually desired to
marry you. He's resented the fact that both of us married and he'd never been matched. Felt it reflected
poorly on him. And the idea of you preferring someone

else, especially Mr. Ellenberg...And now, when Mr. Ellenberg appeared at the ball...I'm concerned. Very concerned. Especially as they went off alone."

And it took a moment for all the implications of the man's words to fully settle in her mind. A cold horror crept through Isabelle. Because if what he said was true...

"My God," she repeated, reaching out and gripping the railing for a moment, steadying herself, before they reached the bottom. Rushing past Roger, she pushed open the side door and burst into the night. "Where is he?" she demanded as she gazed around the empty lower terrace, trotting through the plantings toward the fountain.

An object in the grass caught her attention. Bending down, she grasped it and held it up to the moonlight. A handkerchief embroidered with the letter "L" in cherry-colored thread, designed to match a particular cravat. The one Aaron had been wearing.

Blood marred the delicate white fabric, and everything in the world froze. There was a pounding in her ears, and before she could think, her dagger was unsheathed, her hand wrapped around its familiar, cool, firm handle.

"Miss Lira." Roger raised his palms as if to shield himself and backed away as she moved on him.

"Tell me where he is," she nearly growled, pointing her weapon. "Now. Because if he's hurt in any way, I will—"

"What are you doing to my brother?" Another voice boomed from her left as David Berab approached, her grandmother, Pena, and Weiss all trailing behind him down the terrace steps.

"Louis has Mr. Ellenberg," Roger called to his brother, hands still raised, though he was no longer backing away. "As in, he has taken him either by force or trickery, though for everyone's sake, hopefully the latter." He glanced at Isabelle and grimaced.

"What?" David gaped at his relation. Pulling down his mask, he stalked toward the other man. "That's ridiculous. Why would he do such a thing? We'd resolved our conflict. Miss Lira decided not—"

"To marry anyone other than Aaron Ellenberg," Roger finished. The two brothers stared at each other for a long moment before the elder hung his head.

"My God," he whispered, shoulders slumping.

"Would your brother... hurt Mr. Ellenberg?" It was Weiss who spoke, moving between her weapon and Roger Berab, glancing back and forth between the two.

"Normally, I'd say no, but Louis has been so peculiar as of late, and I thought the information he gave and his demeanor in the carriage earlier were... a touch off." It was David who spoke, drawing closer, his voice strained. "I apologize, Miss Lira. I should have said something or done something or—paid more attention."

"Apparently, yes. As you seem to have no idea what your own brothers want or even believe." She frowned and lowered the dagger a little despite herself.

"Clearly." The man raked a hand through his graying hair. "I thought he and I were on the same page. But I had been so stuck in my own anger, I didn't see that he'd lost a bit of his grasp on anything but his own flights of fancy." His shoulders sagged, and he appeared much older now than his forty-five years.

There was a noise that sounded suspiciously like a

snicker from Roger. "More than a bit," he said, coming
to his brother's side.

David pinched the bridge of his nose. "Fine. More
than a bit. My brother, he's . . . he's never been good with
change."

"Nor losing," Roger added.

A sigh from the eldest Berab and a nod. "That too,
and—"

"But where are they?" she asked, gripping her skirts
with her free hand. Because this was all well and good
and possibly—probably—the correct analysis, but
Aaron was out there, alone, with a very angry Louis
Berab, who was doing God only knew what to him.

"Where would he have taken him?" Her voice
cracked, and her grandmother was at her side, arm over
her shoulders, as she worked to stay strong, to not burst
into tears even though everything was falling apart.

If only she had been brave. If only she'd told Aaron
the truth, showed him how much she loved and appreciated him and always wanted him at her side, perhaps he
would've been better protected instead of . . .

The brothers exchanged glances. David tapped his
fingers to his lips. "I'm not sure. I—"

"The ship." Roger gasped the word. He turned to her,
hands clasped, imploring. "Louis won't hurt Aaron, not
truly. I promise. But he would make sure that he is definitely on his way to America without the ability to easily return."

"I've got to get to the ship." Sheathing her dagger,
she whirled around, dashing in the direction of the
street and the waiting coaches and horses.

"You can take our carriage. You'll get out easier."
David was already racing beside her.

"Unless he's already taken it. Then you'll take mine," Weiss added, jogging along at her right. "Though be careful of the seats—my brother is particular." He swung open the gate for the group. "What about the festival?" he asked as they poured out over the cobblestones, rushing toward the golden Weiss monstrosity.

Isabelle glanced back at him as the coachman stretched out an arm to help her inside, while the Berab brothers assisted her grandmother on the other end. "As my partner, after the opera is over, at midnight, can you...?"

"Make an announcement?" Weiss cocked his head and nodded. "Certainly." He moved to the window as the door shut behind her, reaching in and patting her sleeve. "And you don't have to fret. I will protect the company and all your names."

"Thank you, Mr. Weiss. I look forward to working with you." It was David Berab who gave their new employee a small salute, climbing in as well, Roger and Pena behind him as the driver retook his post.

"Come on," she called to the coachman when he'd slid onto his seat, sticking her head out the window. "We have to hurry."

And with a bump they were off, into the night, hopefully fleet enough to catch Aaron before it was too late.

Chapter Thirty-Two

Aaron woke lying on his stomach, a throbbing in his temples and his arms bound rather tightly behind his back. His stomach lurched as the ground—no, wood floor—beneath him rumbled forward. Rolling onto his side, he forced his eyes open and saw a pair of shiny black boots.

"Where am I?" he asked, craning his neck to stare at the man who had dragged him into the garden and—what had he done? Aaron's mind spun as he strained against whatever was binding him.

What was going on?

"We're in my family's carriage." The man removed his half mask to wipe his brow. A flash of moonlight illuminated his familiar features. Aaron gaped at him as he worked to place his face.

"You're one of the Berab brothers. The middle one." He managed to get the words out as memories of the first festival, the way his captor and his brothers had pushed and crowded Isabelle, rushed to the front of his mind. As well as all the information she and Weiss had given him about the group afterward.

"Louis. My name is Louis. My God, you really are brainless. We've met on multiple occasions." The man gritted his teeth, a vein popping up on his forehead. "But you will remember my name now, I suppose. As the man Isabelle Lira will marry, once you abandon her for America, leaving her heartbroken."

Oy. Not very likely, considering she'd created an entire series of festivals to avoid marrying him or his brother. Not that he could tell that to this clearly rather dangerous and disturbed man.

"What about Solomon Weiss?" Aaron asked as he rocked backward, rubbing his hands against the seat, searching for anything that could break whatever was holding him.

Berab wrinkled his nose. "What about him?" he asked before his lips curled into a rather cruel smile. "Oh. You don't know? No one told you? They aren't marrying. She hired the man and plans to make him a partner in his own right instead. Imagine that—after all those years, giving a portion of the company away to a stranger who won't even be family? It's too bad murder is forbidden, or neither of you would have made it out of that alley."

Wait. What did he say? Aaron halted his struggles and stared at the man for a moment. Did that mean he had attacked them? To do what? Panic roared through Aaron's head. He needed to get out. Now. If not for his own sake, for Isabelle's. Who knew what would happen if this man got back to her?

"The woman is a menace. And needs to be taught a lesson. Several. Someone needs to knock some sense into her arrogant, spoiled head, as she wants to marry *you.*" The words were bitter, though he now had Aaron's full attention. "A complete nobody," Berab continued. "Without any business acumen or scholarly pedigree.

A penniless orphan who cleans floors, from the wrong part of the community."

The toe of his boot collided with Aaron's cheek.

Ow. He clenched his jaw and swiveled his wrists in an attempt to stretch what appeared to be some sort of fabric that was binding him. Perhaps he could wriggle loose and have some sort of chance at escape. Or at least to fight back.

"Why would a woman want a man like you when she could have a man like me?" Berab practically spit the words before giving him another kick, this time in the gut, stealing his breath as pain burst through his muscles. "You have no family. You're not learned. You're not skilled in trade. You're not bright in the slightest. You have the flimsiest sort of charm. You're not even that handsome. And your hair is thick and always a mess, as is your beard. The Omer doesn't require us to look frightful, you know."

"I—" Aaron managed to gasp, working to stay conscious.

"Worse, she was spouting nonsense about 'kindness' and 'caring' and 'listening.'" Berab gave a derisive sniff. "It was enough to make you heave."

"She said all that?" Aaron whispered despite himself, a warm tingling spreading through his bound and rather bruised limbs. "Truly?"

"That and more." Berab gave him another kick with his foot, sending Aaron back so far his head smacked the seat.

But it didn't matter. Or at least not that much.

"She wanted to find you earlier, speak with you, tell you some ridiculousness about kindness or such rot. Told her you had already left. But you couldn't stay away, could you?" Berab near spit the words. "Though the one thing I can't figure out—where in the world did you get that ridiculous, out-of-date costume?"

"I—" Aaron managed to swivel his hips just in the nick of time so the blasted boot didn't get him someplace really uncomfortable. He clenched his jaw. That was enough. Completely and utterly enough. The hitting, the threats to Isabelle, the threats to him, and the insults lobbed at the garments that had been given to him with love. By good people. People who cared. Hands behind his back or not, he was getting out of here and thanking Miriam and Rabbi Marcus and the rest once more, one way or another.

And he would find Isabelle and tell her he loved her. Because even if he was the only one brave enough to say it, he was not going to waste another moment without her knowing it. Without her hearing it. She was everything to him, and he couldn't leave. Not now, not ever.

"It doesn't matter, because I won't have to see it or you anymore soon." And Louis was still yapping between blows. Did the man ever shut up? Though when his mouth was moving, he wasn't kicking, which had to be a good thing.

"You're going to be on that ship," his captor sputtered. "Locked in your cabin until you're in the middle of the ocean. I will make sure of it. And you will never return. Never—"

"Like hell." And as hard as he could, Aaron rocked up on his shoulders, slamming both feet into the man's chest. After all, at this point it was self-defense, and he'd had quite enough.

With a great cry, Berab fell backward, his body

thudding against the back of the carriage so loudly that the horses squealed. With a horrible groan, the vehicle lurched to its side. There was a snapping sound, and Aaron curled his body into itself, bracing for impact. His only thought as the crash came was that he needed to crawl upward if he was going to have a chance of ever seeing Isabelle again.

Dagger in hand, face pressed against the window, Isabelle shifted in her seat as the Weiss family carriage bumped along past tightly packed houses southward, until the paths became wider and the space between the buildings larger and the night air quieter.

"Come on, come on," she whispered as they sped onward toward Dover. Pena reached out and took her hand, pulling her fingers off the dagger.

"You're going to put your eye out," he told her, with a pointed glare.

"I will not." She squeezed the metal harder.

"You're also making people nervous," Pena murmured as he set about removing her fingers from the dagger again. She should've taken off her gloves. She'd have had a much better grip.

Her grandmother leaned forward to address the two other men, their expressions a touch perturbed. "She won't harm your brother. I promise." She tapped David Berab on the knee.

"Well, I don't promise," Isabelle snapped, even as she permitted Pena to pull back her last finger and slip the dagger into his own sheath. She folded her arms.

"So those sentiments you enjoy parroting about

how intercommunity violence puts us all in danger are merely for you to speak and not hear?" Pena arched an eyebrow at her.

"I—this is—" Isabelle started, her cheeks heating a little.

"Don't fret. Besides, you'll be much more concerned with someone else when we find them." Her grandmother gave her shoulder a warm squeeze. "Trust me."

Isabelle glared at both traitors, despite the fact they were indeed correct and she would probably only want to hold him in her arms—if he'd permit her. Someone still needed to be taught a good lesson. After all, how dare he?

"Allowing Pena to hold onto your dagger would be a gesture of goodwill," her grandmother added, giving her a strategic elbow to the ribs. How did she manage to always slip through the whalebone? Her and Pena really didn't play fair and had no idea what poor Aaron was going through. But her grandmother cleared her throat and indicated both nonviolent Berab brothers, who were still her partners and had come along to help, not hurt Aaron.

Heaving a large sigh, she acquiesced with a nod.

"Don't worry, Miss Lira, my brother David here will do more damage than any of your..." Roger started and gasped as Pena readjusted his own defenses. "Rather impressive array of weapons," he murmured. "Your family really doesn't leave anything to chance."

"Thank you," her grandmother whispered as the older man smiled a little. She, however, could not return the gesture; her chest was too tight and her brain too full of horrible possibilities, no matter what comforting words and expressions the others gave her.

This was all her fault. Why had she been such a coward? Why could she not have just told him that she loved him? Loved every part of him and who he was. She should have proclaimed it from the rooftops, and now he was out there, possibly injured, alone, with a stranger bent on—

"I can't believe it. I just can't believe it." David Berab muttered the words as he shook his head and wrung his hands. He lifted his chin, meeting her gaze, and the bewildered horror in his expression made her heart squeeze just a touch.

"A thousand apologies, Miss Lira," he said. "This is—to do this to you and Mr. Ellenberg and the community. I'm just so, well, embarrassed and upset and outraged. At my brother, but also at myself."

"Just remember this feeling when Isabelle irritates you by overstepping her bounds. Or wants you to teach her about a product, or for you to introduce her to a client, or continue working with a client's widowed cousin who is now in charge of her deceased husband's business," her grandmother said, sniffing a little. "Or maybe that woman who runs that gentile gentlemen's club." This time, she gave Isabelle a wink.

She gasped in return. "Grandmother. How can you think of business at a time like this? Aaron could be hurt." And saying the words out loud brought everything to the surface once more, pressure building up behind her eyes. "I never even told him that I loved him," she whispered, staring out the window again, praying that the horses could go just a little faster, that they'd not be too late.

Her grandmother gave her another sympathetic squeeze. "You will, darling. You will. I promise you—"

But she was cut off as the carriage came to a quick stop, causing the entire group to thump against their seats. For a moment, they all merely gazed about, rubbing their heads, stunned.

Isabelle, however, was the first to move once more, dragging her gown onto the seat as she rocked up on her knees and threw her head out the window. "What is that?" she cried, pointing to a large dark object thwarting their path.

Pena pushed open a door on the opposite side and stood, peering over the carriage roof. "There's an overturned carriage blocking the road," he shouted, indicating straight ahead.

"That's our carriage." Roger Berab had joined him and was shielding his eyes, squinting. "And is that—"

She gaped as the form of a man rose from the upturned door. A familiar man. With a shape and build that she'd know anywhere. Through the moonlight, it was clear that his jacket was ripped, his cravat undone, his hair mussed, and he had some sort of torn cloth dangling from his hand. But he was alive. Very alive.

"Aaron," she screamed as she threw open her door and leaped from the Weisses' still-swaying coach. "Aaron."

Running with all her might, she leaped into his outstretched arms, vowing to never let go.

Chapter Thirty-Three

His name on Isabelle's lips was the most wonderful sound Aaron had ever heard in his life. Despite the pain in his head and gut, he scooped her up—skirts and all—and held her to his chest. The soft weight of her body was so right in his arms and exactly what he needed.

"Isabelle," he whispered as she buried her face in his neck. Sniffing a little, she raised her chin, and her dark eyes were rimmed in red.

"I thought I would never see you again." She reached up and brushed his cheek. "And I just—I love you. I love you very much. I'm sorry I didn't say it before. I'm an awful coward and you deserve so much better. You were going to leave the community you loved to protect me. You didn't even consider pushing me towards the Berabs, even if it was going to cost you so much. We barely knew each other, and yet you thought only of my protection, not of yourself. Without hesitation. You're incredible. Breathtaking. Twenty times better than I could ever be."

A single tear rolled down her smooth cheek, nearly breaking his heart.

Oy, she was going to kill him, finish whatever the

errant Berab brother was attempting. As gently as he could, he stroked the drop of liquid away with his thumb, shaking his head, his throat thick. "Don't say that, Isabelle."

"But it's true." She hiccuped before shaking her head. "If I deserved you, I would never have—I've wanted you since the beginning, since I first saw you, even if I couldn't admit it to myself, because I was so stuck in my head, fretting over things that don't actually matter, while you care for and protect us all."

"Your father matters, as does his legacy, as does your own career." Shifting a little, he placed her on the ground. Shrugging his formerly fine but now tattered jacket off, he wrapped it around her shoulders, pulling her against his body once more. "You're brilliant," he told her. "You deserve the chance to be able to show the world—"

She placed a finger against his lips, hushing him. "I can't bring him back, no matter how much I want to. Someone very wise once told me that I'm his legacy, and living well would be the best way to honor him and the memories he gave me. As for the rest, if I'm as clever as you believe, I'll find a way, no matter what." She gave a sharp, firm nod, leaving no room for doubt that this would occur, before brushing a loose curl off her forehead. "Actually, Mr. Weiss is going to help me with that. I'm not marrying him—he's going to be an employee and maybe a partner. He had some wonderful suggestions about how to handle the Berab brothers." She grimaced. "All except one."

Aaron gazed over at the carriage that had now been righted, shading the groaning but now thoroughly guarded man being assisted with his injuries next to it.

"Don't worry—we shall handle him," Roger Berab said, strolling over to them, his oldest brother in tow. "He won't be bothering either of you anymore. We promise."

Isabelle's eyes grew wide. "What are you going to—"

The eldest Berab brother's lip tipped up, though his eyes remained serious. "I believe my brother will be making a journey to America tomorrow. To perhaps find something he can call his own." He swallowed before turning to Isabelle. "I am—I'm very sorry, Miss Lira, both for how I treated you and for my part in what my brother did. I promise, when we return, after Shabbat, you and I and Mr. Weiss will meet and figure out a plan of action on how to move forward. I hope you can find a way to trust me."

Aaron glanced at Isabelle, ready for her to tell the man to, well, do something impolite, but instead she gave him a gracious, serious nod.

"I know I can," she told him, reaching out to give his sleeve a gentle tug. "We're family, after all. We might argue, but we are stronger together."

"You're truly a marvel," the man said before tipping his hat and returning to his task, Roger right behind him.

Aaron gaped at them before returning to Isabelle. "What was that?" He shook his head, still in disbelief at the scene. "A great deal happened since we last spoke, it seems."

And for that he was rewarded with a small smile. "Yes, quite a bit." She pursed her lips. "I did quite a few things I should have done months ago."

"I wish I could have seen you," he murmured as he tugged her closer, not caring how many people were milling about, probably staring at them, as he was not letting her go.

"I wish you could have as well. That was something I realized—that anything good is better if I get to share it with you." She reached up and stroked his most certainly dirty and now wet hair. "I was coming to see you, though, to grovel, as they call it, in a much more eloquent and clear and concise and organized fashion than I am now."

At that he had to smile. She was just so, well, adorable. "Is that what you call this?"

She wrinkled her nose. "It's an attempt." She bit her lip. "I had wanted to do it earlier, but I was told that you were already on the ship."

"By whom?" he started before rolling his eyes. "Oh, let me guess." He indicated the prone man who was now being loaded into the Berabs' coach, his brothers sliding in after.

"Yes, and I'm sorry. So sorry." She shook her head before glancing around at the remaining coachman, her grandmother, and Pena, who had all averted their gazes in different directions, very clearly working not to make eye contact but listening to every word. "I would have done this so much better and without an audience if I'd had the chance," she said through clenched teeth.

"They're at least pretending not to spy," he said with a smile, stroking her cheek again. Because it truly didn't matter to him, not when she was looking at him that way, which made him feel a hundred feet tall. "Though, while I'm not going to enter the who-deserves-whom debate, I will say that the two of us do, at least at some point, deserve privacy, for once."

"Perhaps we can have it," she whispered, reaching

up and wrapping her arms around his neck. "Quite a bit. Every day."

He stared at her, his heart beginning to pound. "I'm listening," he managed to say, still holding her close as a flurry of emotion fluttered through his organs.

She chewed her lip. "Now, I don't want to make you feel obligated, and as I said, you deserve better, but I was wondering, as I am not marrying Mr. Weiss..."

And Aaron's heart was so full he near burst into song. It took everything in him to stop himself from lifting her once more and twirling her around. Instead, he ran a hand through her hair, smiling with the satisfaction of it all. "I thought you weren't so keen on marriage, especially the potential power a husband might wield against you?" he teased.

"Not if it's a husband I trust." She took his hand and squeezed. "And I trust you, Aaron. With all I am."

"Don't you want someone useful?" he pressed, just checking, just making sure, because this was truly exactly what he had longed for, wished for, dreamed of, but had never dared to articulate. "Someone who can help in the business or politically or who is smart or skilled or talented or, well, something?"

She rolled her eyes. "First, I'm all of those things, and I don't deserve you, so, ergo..." She wagged a finger at him. "Second, you aren't just something—you're someone. Someone who is everything to me. Everything that is important. You're kind and good and caring, and there is no one else I'd rather talk with or spend time with. I wake up wanting to see you and listen to your thoughts and tell you mine. I want to fall asleep in your arms." Her beautiful lips spread into a smile. "And do other things in your arms. All the time. Every day."

She reached up and stroked his jaw. "And every day I can be with you would be a gift."

"Are you sure you aren't just asking me because your midnight announcement is approaching?" he teased.

"Midnight can hang," she told him. "I don't want you to save my face."

He blinked again, still staring as her words washed over him.

"It's a very lovely face, though," he couldn't help but add.

"I just want you," she said, her eyes and voice serious. She took an audible breath. "And if you want time to consider it, you can take as much as you require. I don't need an answer today or tomorrow or the next. I'll wait however long. Just please know I love you and I just want to make you happy."

And his heart near burst. It was so full and so complete.

"Who knew I had so much in common with a Surety Princess, because I want the same things. So very much." He clutched her to him. "Yes, Isabelle, I'll marry you. There's nothing I want more in the world. Even when I thought you were marrying Weiss, I couldn't stay away, couldn't not want to see you, make sure you were all right, because I love you so much. There would be no greater honor than being your husband, even if I don't contrib—"

"None of that." She shook her head. "First, it's 'Surety Empress.' And second, and more importantly, you are everything I want and need. And if I have to spend every day of the rest of our lives convincing you that it's true, I will. I will spend every waking hour—"

He bent down and took her mouth in his, and the kiss

was everything. Sweet and tart and all her. Just beautiful. And soon to be his, as he was already, and would always be, hers. He drank her in, stroking her, and they burned together, despite the chill of the night and the sprinkling rain that had started to roll in through the skies. He could stay there forever, just with her.

But she slipped a little in the growing mud, and when he caught her, a flash of lightning streaked across the sky and she gasped, staring at his face.

"Oh, Aaron, you're hurt." She reached up and brushed the area near his eye. "I am—I should have noticed. My God—"

"Am I?" He frowned. Well, he was, but he could barely feel the bumps or bruises anymore, not with her. "On my face?" he asked, reaching up and touching the area. A little tender, but compared to the rest...

"Are you injured elsewhere?" she asked, unfortunately moving away from him so she could inspect his body, and not in the way he was longing for.

"Um...," he managed to mumble as he debated with himself over how much honesty she needed, especially if she would nurse instead of kiss, because he wanted kissing, damn it. He was still not convinced he should have her, but after this night, he did deserve at least a bit more kissing, right?

He glanced over her shoulder and caught Pena's gaze and grimaced. So perhaps no more kissing. At least not until they were married and it was a commandment, so no one in the community could scold them.

"I need to see." Isabelle's voice, in addition to her fingers on his buttons, brought him out of his thoughts and back to the now cold and wet situation.

"It's really nothing. Just some bumps and bruises,"

he managed to say as she opened his shirt, her eyes growing wide.

"Aaron," she cried. "What did he do to you?" Eyes flashing, she turned to where the other carriage had been. The Berab brothers were quite lucky they'd left when they did.

"He kicked me a few times when I was tied up," he admitted. "But I gave as good as I got." He pointed to his feet. "These might be uncomfortable and don't fit at all, but that was probably a good thing, as it kept them on my feet despite the scuffles and kidnapping. They have nice hard soles, which make for excellent self-defense."

"The slippers hurt?" She knelt down, her gown billowing in what was most certainly mud. They were going to be quite a sight when they returned to the ball. "We need to get these off. Now." She started on the laces.

"Pardon us," a male voice called. "Would you two—are you in need of some assistance?"

"Pena," Isabelle called, not bothering to look up from her work. "Aaron's injured, and grandfather's shoes are bothering his feet."

Wait—what did she say? He stared down at her. "Grandfather's?" he asked as Pena guided Isabelle's grandmother over to where they were standing.

"Yes. Your garments—well, a good portion of them—belonged to the late Mr. Lira." Pena glanced at Isabelle's grandmother. "The elder one." He gave Aaron a long, lingering once-over. "They've seen better days."

"That's hardly his fault," Mrs. Lira said, leaning forward with the assistance of a gold-topped cane. "And you looked lovely in them before all of this." She waved a bejeweled hand at him, and his mouth fell open.

He knew that bracelet. He'd quite recently stared at it and pondered its origin.

Aaron gaped at her. "Miriam?"

Isabelle wrinkled her nose. "Yes, my grandmother's name is Miriam. How did you—"

"Mr. Ellenberg and I are old friends," Mrs. Lira—Miriam said as Isabelle rose to her feet, holding the slippers, so his stocking feet were now in the mud. More comfortable, but muddy. Not that it mattered. Not with, well, everything, including . . . He shook his head at the older woman, barely believing what he was seeing.

"How?" Isabelle glanced between the two of them and folded her arms. As if Miriam's deception was equally both of their faults.

"You truly don't think all I do with myself is visit with orphans and have teas?" Her grandmother gave her cheek a pinch, winking at Aaron. "I'm much too clever and good at gathering information."

Aaron could only stare back before returning to Isabelle. "She works with the Commission of Delegates," he explained. "She was the one who helped get me out of trouble and back into the community and . . ."

"I made sure he was taken care of, like we'd do with any member of the community who needed our help. Not that Mr. Ellenberg didn't contribute himself. He's hard not to like, after all," Miriam told them. She leaned down and whispered in his ear, "But I did a good job with my part, did I not?"

He gazed at Isabelle, who had started toward the carriage with Pena. Turning around in her muddy skirts, she smiled at him with such, well, love, it was as if they were being blasted with sunshine instead of pelted with rain. "The best job," he told her. "Thank you."

"Come on," Isabelle called, running over to him. "It's storming, and we're going to need some time to look, well…not frightful, especially if we want to be there before midnight." She bit her lip. "If you still want…"

"I wouldn't want to be anywhere else," he told her, squeezing her hand in his as he helped Pena guide Miriam toward the carriage with his other. Because they were going to have to go quickly if they wanted to make it by midnight, and he wouldn't miss whatever Isabelle was planning for the world.

Chapter Thirty-Four

They'd made it back to the festival with almost an hour to spare, giving Isabelle necessary time to change. Into a lesser gown, to be sure—cerulean was pretty but inferior to red. Judith had been almost apoplectic about her hair, grumbling and fretting the entire time, but they'd managed to reset a significant number of curls and style the rest with enough ribbons and jewels that no one could possibly notice any lingering mud or rain.

Weiss had been a touch miffed that he'd not been able to make a full speech, though she'd assured him that there would be plenty of opportunities in the future, given his new role. Instead, at the conclusion of the opera, after the prince and his Cenerentola took their final bows, she took the stage to make the announcement herself.

She told the assembled crowd that she would indeed be getting married, as soon as possible, Lag BaOmer crowds of couples be damned—she'd already made enough of a spectacle. She would be marrying Aaron Ellenberg, the most wonderful, kind, caring, and lovely man in all of London. She would even make more appearances at the Great Synagogue, if he wanted.

Oh, and that they should visit her, David Berab, and Solomon Weiss at Lira & Berab for all their surety needs. Because there was no better gift than the gift of peace of mind. The statement had been met with appreciative laughter as well as properly raucous applause for the betrothal announcement.

And best, Aaron was inundated with well-wishers and congratulations and much-deserved attention afterward. By the time everyone had left an hour later and the staff was cleaning, he was weary but still beaming with such clear pleasure that her heart near burst.

However, she'd not been able to steal him away like she craved, as they were both quickly whisked off for secondary baths—mud and all—and placed into separate bedchambers with warm milk.

Except she had no desire to sleep. Even if her complexion would be a mess. She'd not wait another day if she didn't have to.

Besides, the Berabs had already procured a ketubah her grandmother deemed fair. With their connections, procuring the other documents and making the arrangements for the small ceremony was now her grandmother's job. Isabelle was just going to show up in a pretty gown. Perhaps the silver.

The image of Aaron's appreciative face the first time she wore it soared in her mind.

Definitely the silver. Which meant she had plenty of time to do what she wanted. Rising and not bothering with a shawl, Isabelle strolled down the hall and knocked on the door of the guest room Aaron had been given.

"What are you doing here?" he asked, yawning in

the doorframe. Her heart skipped. His shirt was off and his feet were bare and his hair a disaster, and he'd never been more handsome.

"I came to check on you. Make sure your injuries were healing," she told him, moving into the room and sitting down on the unmade bed.

"My injuries are bumps and bruises." He patted his chest before gazing at her and folding his arms. "You're not wearing any clothes," he accused, though his eyes twinkled, sparking every desire and ounce of mischief in her.

Any residual touch of tiredness was definitely gone.

"Chemise." Smoothing her sleeves, she rocked up on her knees and crawled to the foot of the bed. "Do you want me to wear more clothes?" she asked, deliberately running her tongue over her lower lip.

He rolled his eyes at her. "No. Well, not in the abstract. But..." He indicated the now closed and hopefully locked door. "If your grandmother and Pena—"

"They won't." She gave him a grin. "They will sleep well tonight. Like everyone else in the house." Sitting up, she patted the section of the bed next to her.

Shaking his head, Aaron obliged and climbed up next to her before pulling her onto his lap.

"You and your cook really need to stop. Someone's going to get hurt," he said as he allowed her to push him onto his back so she could straddle him.

"Soon." She gasped a little as he lifted the skirts of her chemise. "Once we're married and you won't be scolded if I'm found here." She moaned as he stroked her thighs.

Mercy. Though two could play at that game. She

bent forward and planted a soft kiss on his chest. And another. And another.

Aaron groaned. "Won't you be scolded too?"

"Possibly." She ran the tips of her fingers down the same area. "It'll depend on how effective my powers of misdirection are." She flipped her night braid over her shoulder. "Though either way, you'll feel guilty, while I'm too tough and shameless for guilt."

"So that display earlier?" He reached up and stroked her cheek. "The tears over you not telling me you loved me right away . . . ?" He cocked his head.

"An aberration. At least if you tell anyone about it," she teased. "I don't want to let my reputation slip." She gasped once more as he sneaked a hand beneath her skirts again. She shifted, allowing him to move higher like she craved.

"Perish the thought," he murmured. "So why are you here?"

"Why do you think?" She moaned the words as he moved his rather clever fingers to stroke exactly the spot she wanted. She rocked her hips forward, begging him for more.

"We're getting married the day after tomorrow," he protested. "Can't you wait?"

"No." She shook her head. "I love you too much. And lust for you."

"You're incorrigible and very hard to say no to—do you know that?" he told her as he shifted her forward so he could thankfully kick off the rest of his garments.

"You love it," she said, settling back on his lap after he was finally gloriously naked and all hers.

"Yes, I do," he whispered. "Very much." He pulled

her down to him, taking her lips, and very soon, she could barely remember her own name, let alone what time it was.

Yes, if this was what forever could be, it was a risk worth taking.

Acknowledgments

As always, writing a book might seem like a solitary activity, but it not only takes a ton of hardworking professionals, but is always better with a community.

Thank you to my incredible agent, Becca Podos, who not only believed in this book and championed it but dealt with anxious, perfectionist, type A me and my very nerdy jokes the entire way, which is not easy. Thank you to my extremely brilliant, thoughtful, fun, and absolutely incredible editor, Sam Brody, for being the best and absolutely making the spirit of this book truly shine. Thank you to production editor Luria Rittenberg and copyeditor extraordinaire Janice Lee for your patience, wisdom, and care. Thank you to Dana Cuadrado for working so hard to make sure this book got into the hands of readers who (hopefully) enjoyed it. Thank you to Estelle Hallick and Junessa Viloria for all the extra-special assistance and to Daniela Medina and Shirley Green for making the cover amazing.

Thank you to all the wonderful writers and beta readers from all the communities I am so lucky to be included in, especially RChat and Romance Shmooze.

Thank you to Eva Leigh, Lauren Accardo, Luna Joya, KD Casey, Elsie Marrone, Meka James, Michelle

McCraw, R. R. Taylor, Liana De la Rosa, Jessica Lepe, Noreen Mughees, Helena Greer, Rosie Danan, and Kelly Preeper—all of you are wonderful, and your support and friendship mean everything to me.

Thank you to Lisa Lin—I'm so lucky to be your friend. You made everything about this book's journey better and just made life better in general.

Thank you to A. R. Vishny, Julie Block, and S. A. Simon—you make me smarter and better and are fun and fabulous doing it. I love you all so much.

Thank you to Ella Stainton. Nothing I write is any good without you. You are brilliant and fabulous, and I will love and adore you forever and always, no matter what.

When I set out to draft this book, not only was I in an odd place in my writing career, but my father had recently passed away from a brief but devastating illness. I didn't really have a direction, but the incomparable Stacey Agdern told me to write my "fluffy blanket book" and held my hand all the way through it. Without her, this book would not exist, and I would have also had a much tougher time during my eleven months.

Finally, thank you to my family. Dan, kiddos, I love you all more than anything in the world and hope I make you just a little bit proud. Mom and Marni, you are the best mother and sister anyone could have, and I'm lucky you are mine. Thank you to Susan for not being "Lady Tremaine." Figaro, you are very cute.

And, Dad, I wish you were still here, every day, especially for the good and the fun, because you knew how to appreciate the good and the fun. And while I know you wanted more time so badly, I'm so glad that you were able to live during the time you had. As you always quoted, "life's a banquet, and some poor suckers are starving to death." You most certainly "live, live, live[d]," and I'm so thankful for every moment of it.

Author's Note

Marry Me by Midnight is a work of fiction, and it should never be taken as literal history. While there are no magical interventions, it is based on a fairy tale in all its glory.

That said, when writing the book, I did try to portray the real challenges and triumphs of London's 1830s Jewish community in an authentic way. I also worked to center the Jewish position and experience of the time and place, because when the history of most countries and periods is recounted, the Jewish experience often goes unaddressed, treated as a niche digression rather than part of the main story.

While Jews have been considered a race, a religion, a nationality, and various combinations of all three at different times and in different places, the labels are usually assigned not based on accuracy or for our benefit, but for the benefit of the dominant gentile community—based on their own needs and their own frameworks. Moreover, not only are such labels often either inaccurate or lacking, but the labeling is almost always done as a way to minimize, marginalize, and control a Jewish population to the benefit of the larger gentile whole.

Writer Dara Horn has called us a "counterculture," especially as there is a history of Jews being considered "from" places but not "of" them. My mother used to simply say, "We are a people." In the end, in periods and places we are not actively being killed, and thus basic day-to-day survival is not our sole focus, I think of us as a community that merely wants to be both ourselves—without fear of death and/or expulsion—and, at the same time, part of the greater whole. Something that historically, even in the best of times, has not been particularly easy.

With that context in mind, it is also important to understand that the modern British Jewish community was built, similar to the American Jewish community, from people with keen expulsion fears and trauma left over from the expulsions in Spain and Portugal. While many of those original Jews assimilated into the larger gentile communities and were replaced with a different, poorer group of Jewish refugees fleeing active genocides in the east, those original Jews formed the roots of the culture, political strategy, and direction, as well as the foundational legacy institutions, of both Jewish populations.

Further, in the 1830s, Britain's Jewish community was a young one, though British attitudes toward them were very old. The prior population of Jews, who came to England in 1066 with William the Conqueror, were expelled from England by Edward I in 1290, forced back to France, from which they were then expelled a century later, and forced farther and farther east through a series of subsequent expulsions. Thus, for centuries, though Jews were villains in cultural milieu, they were not part of the population. Not until Oliver Cromwell, in the mid-seventeenth century, were Jews legally permitted in England once more. However, they were not truly "welcomed" until the reign of William III and Mary II at the end of that century. As previously alluded to, the core population of Jews was initially from the Netherlands, mainly descended from Jews expelled from Spain and Portugal in the late fifteenth and sixteenth centuries who found refuge there.

Those Jews were joined, especially during the second half of the eighteenth century, by Jews from France and the German states, especially given the unrest in both regions at the time, which often turned antisemitic. Additionally, they were joined by Jews from the Italian states, which also saw political turmoil and change during this period.

Thus, it should be noted that in the 1830s, a high percentage of British Jews were the children or grandchildren of immigrants. And, in turn, Jews with longer histories in the country, especially Jews of Sephardi descent, were heralded as more "civilized" by the gentile contingent. This often took on a nineteenth-century race "science" flavor, with the popular assumption that the more Western European-seeming Sephardi Jews were "purer" and descended directly from the Jews of Jesus's time while the Ashkenazi Jews were "mixed" with non-white, non-Western European non-Jews and were thus "lesser" or even not "true" Jews, justifying hatred and discrimination while preserving love and admiration for Jesus.

The idea that Ashkenazi Jews, especially those who

had been forcibly relocated to the former Pale of Settlement by the Russian Empire, are "lesser" Jews in some way (often coupled with the idea that they are less "authentic" than other Jews due to a perceived "mixing" with various non-Jewish populations—usually populations which the particular gentiles in question also perceive as "threatening" or less "innocent") or are the "wrong" kind of Jews is still a feature of modern antisemitism, though the language shifts depending on the perceived idea of "goodness," or "innocence," of the particular type of gentile gaze.

The same is also often part of internalized antisemitism among Jews and Jewish communities. The internalized antisemitism aspect is a tragedy as one of Judaism's earliest features was subversion of hierarchical structures based on birthright. It can be found in almost every Torah story and in how we define ourselves, not by the purity of our blood, but by our participation in our communities. However, reality and practice often diverge, especially when living as a minority within a larger society where identity and opportunity are intimately connected to the opposite.

As such, due to both this perception and longevity in England, Sephardi Jews often held roles of more prominence in the Jewish community than their more Germanic counterparts. These Jews generally set the cultural backbone of the community because of their political favor with the gentiles as discussed above. And due to that favor, it was believed that assimilation into the Western form of Jewish culture they'd created was the key to eventually gaining full rights and citizenship for all Jews, regardless of background, as well as guarding against expulsion. While these Jews might have viewed people like Aaron and Weiss with unfair disdain, they still cared for and about them, and wanted them to ultimately thrive and survive.

Thus, while the Jewish community was made of different populations and quite a few synagogues, including the Great Synagogue of London (the oldest Ashkenazi synagogue in England, which was destroyed in the Blitz, like so much of the East End), it worked hard to politically and socially speak with one voice.

To this end, the Board of Deputies of British Jews was established in the Sephardi community in the middle of the eighteenth century. There was an Ashkenazi organization established slightly later called the Secret Committee for Public Affairs. Both sought to protect the Jewish community as a whole, politically, socially, and culturally. The organizations combined in the early nineteenth century to form the London Committee of Deputies of British Jews. It is currently called the Board of Deputies of British Jews.

The London Commission of Delegates in *Marry Me by Midnight* is inspired by this organization, in spirit and purpose—however, it and its activities are still purely fictional.

Nevertheless, the intercommunity struggles and concerns portrayed were very real, as was the lack of true rights and the precariousness of the Jewish position. The Jew Bill, a real bill supported by the real Duke of Sussex, the future Queen Victoria's uncle, who was indeed the head of the Royal Society at the time, did fail during this time period.

As a result, Jewish men weren't given full rights in England until the second half of the nineteenth century. This was earlier than in the countries controlled by the Russian Empire, but later than in much of Western and Central Europe, where Jewish men were given rights in the late eighteenth and early nineteenth centuries. This was also a bit later than in the United States, where Jewish men were given full political rights in all states by the early 1830s.

The danger to and the limits on even the wealthiest Jews in England given their identity were very real and are still something materially present in Europe and everywhere European nations colonized. There was (and still is) immense pressure on Jews to cease being Jews in exchange for safety and political rights in all these societies, with the ultimate goal, even if it is not conscious or explicit, of Jews no longer existing. This takes many forms, some of which may be hard to recognize but are still present, and were certainly real, large, and notable in Isabelle and Aaron's world, affecting their families' and communities' behavior and experiences.

And yet they and their real counterparts still managed to thrive, still found joy, and still could create happily-ever-afters. This work is obviously also influenced by quite a few versions of the Cinderella story: obviously the Grimm brothers and Perrault, but also Rossini and Ferretti's *La Cenerentola*, Rodgers and Hammerstein's *Cinderella*, Sondheim and Lapine's *Into the Woods* (probably the most Jewish version, even if it isn't explicit), and Disney's 1950 film (less the film itself and more the stated intent of blacklisted and uncredited Jewish writer Maurice Rapf, who really wanted to talk about class). I know I'm standing on their shoulders and hope I can make them and the community just a smidge proud.

Thank you so much for reading!

XOXO,
Felicia

After an attempt on his life, Solomon Weiss
is forced into hiding, with only a mysterious,
albeit lovely thief, and several rather
odd women, for help…

Don't miss his story in the next
Once Upon the East End romance!

AVAILABLE SPRING 2024

About the Author

Felicia Grossman is an author of historical romance usually featuring Jewish protagonists and lots of food references. Originally from Delaware, she now lives in the Rust Belt with her family and Scottish terrier. When not writing romance, she enjoys éclairs, cannoli, and Sondheim musicals.

You can learn more at:
FeliciaGrossmanAuthor.com
Twitter @HFelicaG
Facebook.com/Felicia-Grossman-Author
Instagram @FeliciaGrossmanAuthor

Get swept off your feet by charming dukes,
sharp-witted ladies, and scandalous balls in
Forever's historical romances!

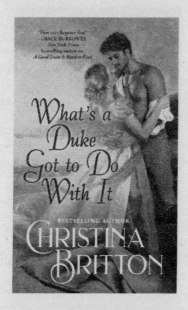

WHAT'S A DUKE GOT TO DO WITH IT
by Christina Britton

The last thing Miss Katrina Denby needs is another scandal. So when
one lands in her garden and the rumors start affecting her friends, she
will do anything to regain respectability and protect those for whom she
cares. But her plans to marry one of the few men who will still have
her are thrown into turmoil with the arrival of the Duke of Ramsleigh:
the only man Katrina ever loved…and a man who is about to become
engaged to another.

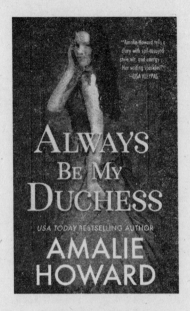

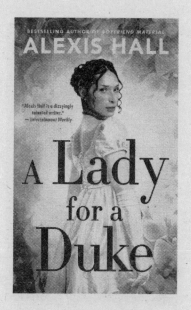

A LADY FOR A DUKE
by Alexis Hall

After Viola Carroll was presumed dead at Waterloo, she took the opportunity to live as herself. But Viola paid for her freedom with the loss of her wealth, title, and closest companion, Justin de Vere, the Duke of Gracewood. Only when their families reconnect years later does Viola learn how lost in grief Gracewood has become. But as Viola strives to bring Gracewood back to himself, fresh desires give new names to old feelings. They are feelings Viola cannot deny…even if they cost her everything, again.

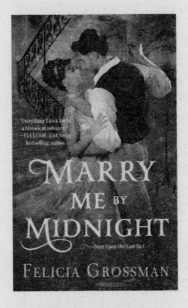

MARRY ME BY MIDNIGHT
by Felicia Grossman

Isabelle Lira may be in distress, but she's no damsel. To save her late father's business from a hostile takeover, she must marry a powerful stranger—and *soon*. So she'll host a series of festivals, inviting every eligible Jewish man. Except that Aaron Ellenberg, the synagogue custodian, provides unexpected temptation when Isabelle hires him to spy on her favored suitors. But a future for them both is impossible...unless Isabelle can find the courage to trust her heart.